BLOOD AND FATE

ANTONIA KANE

Published by Carashan Press

www.antoniakane.com

Cover Illustration by Selkkie Designs

ISBN: 979-8-9890994-1-2 (Paperback)

Printed in the United States of America

To my kiddos.
I love you.
Bunches and bunches.
Oodles and oodles.
Always and forever.
With all my heart.

CHAPTER ONE

SATORI

"Your Highness."

Satori didn't need to turn around to know who had addressed her. Henrik's smooth voice sliced through her like a blade of ice, making her skin crawl. And that was just his voice. When he touched her. . . The thought sent a slight shudder through her, and she shook it off. She would not let him ruin this evening.

She squared her shoulders, plastered a polite smile on her face for the sake of their guests, and turned to face him, speaking through clenched teeth. "Lord Henrik, how are you this evening?"

"I am well, and you look breathtaking, Satori." He bowed slightly at the waist as he spoke, his pale blue coat brushing his thighs. She didn't miss how his eyes dipped to her chest.

She resisted the desire to take a deep, calming breath. *Satori.* Yes, it was her name, but she was also the Princess and his superior. Advisor to the king or not—Duke or not—he ought to use her proper title. Though he certainly didn't see her as his superior, did he?

"Thank you." Maybe her clipped tone would be enough hint for him to leave her alone.

He held a hand out to her, the full white sleeves of his shirt peeking from the arm of his jacket and brushing his knuckles. "May I beg a dance?"

A shiver rushed over her. Henrik was not one to miss any reason to touch her. Though it wasn't like he ever acted as though he needed a reason. She glanced around at the swirling couples creating undulating rainbows on the dance floor, the busy waiters carrying trays of savory hors d'oeuvres, and the orchestra with its strings and lively soaring melodies. There had to be some excuse somewhere. Then she saw the mass of red curls, Tessa, on the balcony waving at her. *Thank Shala.*

"Apologies, Lord Henrik. I was just going to meet Tessa. Maybe later." She said nothing further, but she didn't miss the slight narrowing of his ice-blue eyes or the side glance he shot Tessa.

Satori would no doubt pay for that later, but at least here, in public, she could pretend she was the one in charge. With her chin raised, she brushed by, leaving him standing with his hand still outstretched. Smiling to herself, she lifted the hem of her skirts, the shining rose gold material reflecting the glow of the candles, and climbed the grey marble stairs to the balcony.

She met a servant at the top of the stairs bearing a tray of tall, thin champagne glasses. Carefully she plucked one up.

"Thank you," she said before lifting it to her lips and drinking half of it in one pull.

"You'd better be careful with that. Your head will be all bubbles when our *guests* arrive." Tessa's giggle was sweet and musical and caused her mass of red curls to bounce around her head.

Satori rolled her eyes again. It probably wasn't the best habit for a Princess, but she just couldn't find it in her to care. Instead, she raised the glass, and with a pointed glance at her friend, she drank another quarter measure.

Tessa laughed. "Maybe they'll surprise us all."

"First, I'm insulted, and my father should be too. If two countries are to form an alliance of this magnitude, no matter how small they are, the rulers should meet." She took another sip of her drink. "It should be the king and his heir arriving tonight. Instead, we get a contingent of soldiers? Barbarians, most likely. They'll probably be half naked, carrying clubs."

Tessa's brow rose. "Wouldn't that be interesting?"

Satori ignored her. "How can either party know how an alliance will go under these circumstances? This is a truce for the holiday. Everyone knows that when this party is over, their country will return to stealing our resources, attacking our outlying cities, and trying to gain the upper hand."

She drained her glass.

"What do you really think they're like?" Tessa asked, sending the subject in a slightly different direction.

Satori waved her glass in dismissal. "As I said, barbarians, the lot. They don't deserve all this—" She waved a hand at the green garlands, the tables at the far side of the room piled with food, and the Covington roses that decorated the space. "That's for sure."

Tessa leaned over the balcony rail, stretching on her tiptoes to accommodate her shorter stature. "It's all so grand."

She smiled and waved at someone below.

Indeed, the Great Hall of Satori's home was decorated to the fullest extent of the word. Torches and candles lit every corner, and garlands of deep green branches hung along the wall and from every balcony. Large bouquets of their country's unique, autumn-blooming, cyan roses broke up the monotony at regular intervals. Satori inhaled deeply, the scent of flowers permeating the air. The orchestra played lively tunes, and people crowded the dance floor. The annual Rose Festival had been one of Satori's favorite holidays since she was a child. Twenty-three years later, it still held magic for her. No other place had the beautiful blue roses that Covington did. Indeed, few other places had any roses at all that bloomed so late in the season.

Satori watched the swirl of people. She longed to join them, but it would not be on the arm of Henrik. Of course, hiding on the balcony, it might not be on the arm of anyone else, either. She shivered at the thought of the Duke. He had everyone fooled. Every one of them, including her father. Even Tessa could only see his charm and wit and good looks. Satori had kept everything that he'd done to herself. She could never tell them what occurred in the dark; would never mention that he visited her rooms. And even if she wanted to say something, Henrik had subtly hinted more than once that it might be *harmful* to those around her should she tell anyone. And she had no doubt he would follow through with those threats. She could never tell anyone.

"There's Dimitri." Tessa waved again down toward the swirling crowd below.

Satori looked to where Tessa was waving, grateful for the distraction from her thoughts. Indeed, Dimitri stood below, a broad grin on his face.

"He likes you."

Tessa shot Satori a look out of the corner of her eye that said, *yeah, sure.* "He's literally royalty."

"Distant cousin." Satori tried to sip from her glass and remembered she'd finished it. She needed a refill. "Besides, you might as well be royalty. I know you're a lady's maid, but I love you like my sister." She rested her arm around Tessa's shoulder.

Dimitri waved an arm, beckoning them down.

Satori sighed and turned her back toward the throng. This really was a ridiculous, pointless affair. It would have been fine just to have it with their people, but no, they had to invite the enemy. Why? What good would it do?

She was scanning for another servant with more champagne when she felt it. A shift in the air. No, that wasn't right; it was more akin to the sensation of someone breathing on her neck. The tiny hairs on the back of her neck and her arms stood on end, and she looked to find her skin prickled with goosebumps.

She straightened, glancing side to side. "Did you feel that?"

"There they are," Tessa spoke at the same time as Satori, and her inquiry was lost in the exchange.

A hush had fallen over the room, even the orchestra had stopped playing, and Satori turned as the large wooden doors at the front of the room opened fully.

Tessa leaned slightly over the balcony rail, "Is that the leader?"

"What?"

"Satori, what's wrong with you?" Tessa stole a glance at her but quickly returned her attention to the group of men who had just entered the hall. "I said they're here. Is that the leader?"

The Princess looked at the men—large men—who had entered the room. There were fewer than she expected, fifteen, maybe. They were well-dressed, with clean black pants and tunics, shining boots, and large swords that seemed to be more ornamental than combative. They all wore deep blue sashes across their chests with what appeared to be an insignia pin at their shoulders.

She scanned the men, trying to figure out which one Tessa was referring to, then she saw *him*. The force of his presence hit her like a sack of grain, and she reached out to steady herself on the railing. The air left her, and she scowled at the strange sensations that danced through her stomach. She tried to pull a breath in, but it was as though no air would flow. She swore under her breath. Was she getting ill? Now was a terrible time for sickness.

The man stopped, his dark waves of hair swinging against his forehead. The blonde man behind him bumped into him, though the dark-haired one didn't even seem to notice. Instead, his eyes ran over the room, sweeping from side to side as though he were searching for someone. And somehow, the Princess just knew who he was looking for.

When his eyes reached the balcony, Satori finally found the ability to move again; spinning, she ducked behind the pillar beside her, making certain she was out of sight.

Tessa turned a slightly amused gaze on her. "Are you alright?"

Satori stared at the space where he had been standing.

"Satori?"

Her eyes snapped to her lady's maid. "What?"

Tessa turned toward the Princess, her amused expression shifting to concern. "What's wrong?"

"I . . . I . . ." Words, where were her words? "I don't feel well. I think I need some air."

"Now? They just got here."

"I know, I'm sorry." She reached out and squeezed Tessa's hand. "I won't be long, I promise. I just need to catch my breath."

She was already turning to leave, not waiting for Tessa's reply. Satori could barely keep her stride measured as she found the stairs and descended, leaving the balcony behind. As soon as she hit the ground floor, she picked up her pace, though not enough to draw attention to herself.

The tingling sensation at the back of her neck remained, and she didn't dare turn to see what was happening behind her. Her stomach did another flip, and she laid a hand on it, covering her mouth with the other. She needed to get outside.

She slipped behind a pillar and found the servant's entrance from the kitchen to the Great Hall. The passage was full of people carrying trays, both full and empty, back and forth from the kitchen. The temptation to reach out and snatch another glass of champagne was strong, but with the way she felt, she was afraid she wouldn't be able to keep it down. What in Shala's name was happening to her?

The passage emerged into the kitchen, and she skirted the edges of the hot room until she found the door that led to the courtyard. A blast of cool night air hit her as she pulled open the door. She inhaled deeply, gulping it down as though she had been drowning. What in Helias was wrong with her? She had never felt anything like this before, and it had only started when those men had entered the castle. Maybe Shala was trying to tell her something, to warn her?

She had never been one to give much stock to the stories of the old gods, but right now, she might entertain anything.

She couldn't stay away all night, that much was certain; she was the Princess, and someone would no doubt notice her absence. But she wasn't ready to go back in so soon. Instead, she chose to take a long walk around the castle. She would enter again through the front door. She was only about a quarter of the way around, just long enough of a walk to clear her head but not so long that she would be worn out or gone too long.

She folded her arms across her chest, wishing she would have thought to bring a shawl. The sleeves of her fluffy gown were barely there, and her cleavage was also slightly more on display than usual. Not to mention the feeling of hyper-awareness still followed her.

When she finally reached the front door, she paused, still not ready. Instead, she slipped into an alcove near a side entrance. It was unnaturally quiet outside the castle. Everyone was inside at the dinner, dancing and waiting to see what would happen now that their guests had arrived.

Satori peered into the sunroom that the entrance led to. It was blissfully empty, thank Shala. She could enter here and reenter the Great Hall, and maybe no one would notice she'd been gone.

She closed her eyes and pulled in a deep, cleansing breath, but her calm was shattered as a shiver shot up her spine. The sensation was so sudden and strong that she startled, and it left behind a feeling of unease as her throat began to close again.

Her attention was drawn to a sound at her feet, and she glanced down just in time to see a small stone go skittering past her. Then the cold was replaced with a feeling of warmth that started at her head. She spun to find herself face-to-face with the tall man from the Great Hall. Up close, she could appreciate his deeply sun-tanned skin and the waves of dark hair that curled softly at his forehead.

Face-to-face was, of course, not entirely correct. The man was so tall she was actually staring at his breastbone. The feeling she'd had when she was inside was back, but here, standing so close to him, it was a hundred times amplified. Goosebumps rose on her arms at the same time that the warmth seemed to seep over her. She took a step back away from him, then another, uncomfortable with the reactions he elicited from her.

The only move he made was to tilt his head to the side as he observed her through slightly narrowed eyes. When he spoke, his voice was low with a pleasing accent, indicative of Evandor.

"Do you feel that?"

She couldn't have answered him even if she had wanted to. Words would not come; there was no air in her lungs. All she could do was shake her head in a quick lie of denial and hope he would go away. She glanced around, over his shoulder and then over her own, looking for anyone who might be near, for any indication that she was not alone with the enemy.

He didn't move save for his eyes as he scanned the area along with her. "I do believe we are alone, Princess."

Her heart skipped. *Princess.* He knew who she was. Bad, this was very bad.

He moved half a step toward her, and she jumped again. "You don't need to be afraid. I asked, 'Do you feel that?'"

Yes. No. Maybe? Didn't need to be afraid?

Words finally formed. "I don't know what you mean," she lied. "If you'll excuse me, I must get back, or someone will miss me."

She tried to emphasize the last part, hoping to dissuade him from any unseemly idea he might be forming.

She stepped forward, and his arm shot out so quickly she could barely track it. His large hand slapped into the stone beside him, level with her neck, easily blocking her way.

She gasped, barely containing the yelp that pushed its way up her throat.

He inclined his head toward her. "You must know what I mean."

She turned, looking up to meet his gaze. His dark brown eyes bored into her own. She could feel her body begin to tremble, and she cursed her limbs, and these men who made her feel powerless, to Helias. She swallowed and was sure the gulping sound was audible, along with her erratic heartbeat.

His head tilted, his brow furrowing.

"There's no need for you to fear me," he repeated the words he'd said earlier, but it was of no comfort to Satori.

She dredged up every bit of defiance she could and forced her words not to shake, "I am not afraid of you."

He pursed his lips. "You are a beautiful liar."

Satori broke eye contact, focusing instead on the arm across her vision. It unnerved her that he knew how she was feeling. A lucky guess, no doubt, but still correct on both counts. She *was* afraid, and *did* feel something between the two of them. Something was there, like a knot in her stomach and a thread stretching between them. It was terrifying.

She pulled a slow breath through her nose and blew it out through barely opened lips. "If you will please excuse me, I need to return to the ball before I'm missed. Please?"

She could feel his scrutiny on her, could *feel it* like a breath on her cheeks. Slowly he removed his arm. She tried not to show her relief, but still, a shudder coursed through her body. She didn't look at him again, she simply left as fast as she could without actually running.

"Where have you been?" Tessa hissed the words into her ear, momentarily drowning out the music.

Satori jumped and cursed herself silently. Why was she so jumpy tonight?

"Satori?"

"I just needed some air, that's all." It wasn't a total lie; she had needed air. She simply omitted the part about the man she had met. "I went for a walk."

"Your father's been looking for you."

Satori glanced at Tessa and then scanned the room. There was no sign of the man from outside. She didn't even know his name, although that was fine with her; she had no need of his name. She took a quick breath and moved to the raised dais at the front of the room to join her father, snatching a glass of champagne off a tray as she went.

"You should not drink so much, my darling," her father chided through grinning teeth as she took her place beside him.

She took another sip.

"I do not drink *so much*, Father; this is only my second glass," she assured him through her own smile.

"Mmm," was her father's reply. "Have you seen our guests? Handsome group of brutes." His eyes moved over the room. "I seem to have lost track of them."

Satori looked up at him, a golden circlet resting on his greying hairs, the look in his eyes the same as she'd become used to recently. He'd started to seem off to her in the past few months, as though he was always slightly confused, a faraway look glazing his eyes. It had begun to worry her, especially since he'd seemed to be relying more and more on Henrik's advice. She'd mentioned it to Tessa, but the lady's maid didn't spend enough time with the King to notice. She even brought it up with Henrik, much to her discomfort. He also dismissed her concerns, assuring her that he would take care of everything, including the King and herself.

"No, I have not seen them." She sipped again, her eyes wandering the room.

Was it too much to hope they'd all left?

"Ah, here he is."

A flush passed over Satori. All the tiny hairs on her arms and neck stood on end as she turned.

The large man stepped in front of her father, flanked by another large blonde man. He offered the barest of bows.

Her father made a sound, hesitated, and then faltered into a cough. Clearly he had forgotten the man's name. Satori realized then that she hadn't learned it, either.

"Kais, your Majesty," the man answered, with a glance toward her.

She looked away, but not before realizing the flush that she had felt was the same strange warm feeling from earlier once again seeping over her. It unnerved her.

"Yes, yes, General Kais," her father repeated. "Have you met my daughter, Princess Satori?"

Kais turned toward her and offered a slightly deeper bow than he had given her father. "Princess."

She wanted to roll her eyes and look away, but that wasn't exactly the reaction a Princess should have in a diplomatic situation. So she squared her shoulders and stood tall like a Princess would be expected to. What she really wanted was to run away.

"Actually, your Majesty," Kais continued, "I was wondering if I might beg a dance of the Princess?"

No, no. Surely her father wouldn't just pass her off to an enemy? She shot the King a pleading gaze, not even having the presence of mind to hope no one else noticed. But he wasn't even looking at her.

"Of course." Her father's hand extended toward her, taking the champagne glass. "The Princess loves to dance and is quite good at it." He leaned very close, whispering in her ear, "Don't worry, darling, he wouldn't try anything here."

Kais turned to her, his smile growing wide, accentuating his darkly handsome features. He extended a waiting palm toward her. "I shall endeavor to keep up."

Satori didn't school her glare as he stepped aside, unfurling the fingers of his other hand toward the already full dance floor. "May I, Princess?"

Her father placed a hand of encouragement on the small of her back. "Go on, my dear, don't be shy. Show him how we dance here in Dunleigh."

Satori looked toward her father, hoping he was right about them not trying anything.

She forced her features to smooth out, pulled in a breath, and lifted her chin. "Yes, Father."

She stepped off the dais and descended the few stairs, though she made sure to offer Kais a withering stare as she walked past, ignoring his outstretched palm.

His response was a knowing sort of smile, and the hairs on her arm returned to their standing positions. Why did he look at her like he could see inside her? Arrogant idiot.

The crowd seemed to part for them, and Satori wished the people would just go on dancing. Instead, every eye was focused on her and Kais. When he reached the center of the floor he stopped and turned, waiting for her. She stopped in front of him, craning her neck up to properly glare at him. So what if others noticed? He wasn't exactly their closest ally. It should be expected that she would be wary of him.

"Relax, my Princess." The half smile turned up his mouth again. It was attractive, and it annoyed her. "I can dance. I promise not to embarrass you."

He extended his hand. She glanced at the waiting palm and then back up to his face. Her neck was beginning to ache from looking up. Helias, the man was tall. She relaxed her neck, looking straight forward instead, pinning her gaze to his chest. The longer she put it off, the longer it would be before it was over. She lifted her hand and placed it into his.

The sensation was immediate. A jolt that, at first, reminded her of touching something far too hot. She snatched her hand away. Her alarmed gaze shot to his, even as she realized it hadn't actually hurt.

His eyes widened the slightest bit, his mouth in a line. But it was the only indication that he had noticed anything.

"What was that?" she hissed through her teeth in an alarmed whisper.

He dipped his head toward her, his voice loud enough for only her to hear, "I don't know. Though, I expect it was something to do with whatever the connection between us is."

This again? She gritted her teeth. "We have no *connection.*"

"No?" His expression almost looked amused. "Then by all means—" He moved his still outstretched hand closer to her, waiting. "People are beginning to notice, my Princess."

"I am not *your* Princess," she hissed again and shoved her hand into his.

The sensation was still there, though not as sharp as their initial contact had been. Heat radiated into her palm from where their hands touched. It spread up her arm and across her whole body, and she had the sudden irrational thought that if she looked down she would find herself glowing.

What was happening to her? She stiffened, ready to pull away again, but he must have sensed her desire to bolt because he pulled her closer. The heat grew and grew until she thought she might perspire, though she didn't.

Kais dipped his head, and his breath coasted over her ear. "How can you feel this and deny a connection?"

"Feel what?"

She cursed herself as her voice shook. Thankfully she was too close to be able to look him in the eyes. She didn't think she could handle that at the moment.

She felt his huffed laugh in his chest, nearly pressed to her ear. "Indeed."

He spun her expertly around the dance floor, and she met him step for step. Her father had not been overly generous when he had said she was proficient. Dancing was one of her favorite things about being a royal. Though, she was having difficulty enjoying the dance due to the roiling feeling in her chest, like a wave crescendoing and cresting again and again but never crashing. And the idea of it crashing—whatever *it* was—in front of so many people made her heart beat even more wildly.

She was about to flee when Kais stopped instead. She looked up and immediately saw why. Henrik. Tension poured into her limbs.

Her father's advisor stood behind Kais, waiting. It took her a moment to realize he was trying to cut in.

"May I?" Henrik's smile was just on the side of slimy.

Kais looked at him and then glanced down at her, his eyes narrowing. When he returned his attention to the other man, Kais' eyes swept over him in dismissal. "No, I don't think so."

Henrik's eyes widened. "No?"

"You'll forgive me, I'm sure." Kais' fingers tensed on her back. "This is my first dance with the lovely Princess. I would like to see it through to its conclusion."

For a moment, Henrik stared, his eyes moving between Kais and Satori, but then he nodded slightly and backed away, tugging at his tan waistcoat, his cheeks taking on a bit of color.

"That was rude," she bit out at Kais when Henrik had gone and they had resumed their dance.

Kais glanced down at her for just a moment. "If you would like, I can call him back and release you into his, no doubt, more than capable hands."

Her body seized for only a moment; she couldn't help it, couldn't stop it. In all truth, she was glad he had refused Henrik. She'd heard that the devil you know is better than the devil you don't, but at that moment, she wasn't sure she believed it. So far, Kais, as arrogant as he seemed, had been above reproach. It was far more than she could say about Henrik.

His thumb slid across her back where his hand pressed. "That's what I thought."

There was something wrong with her. Her emotions and sensations were going mad, and just then, she was taking comfort in the fact that she was in the arms of a potential enemy and not in those of her father's advisor. *Helias.*

She couldn't, not anymore. She needed space—room to breathe.

She stopped and placed a hand on Kais' chest, stepping back and away from the heat. She bowed her head slightly, only for a brief moment. "Thank you for the dance."

Kais' brows knit together as she turned to move away, off the dance floor and through the doors that led outside into the cool night air.

Her palms slapped against the stone railing that ran along the veranda outside the Hall. She bent over it slightly, putting her weight on it as she closed her eyes and pulled in as much air as possible. She was so warm. Her insides seemed to be writhing with some pent-up force; her skin was tingling, everything felt more and extra and too much. She wanted to rip her dress off and let the air soothe her skin.

A throat cleared behind her, and she spun around, her breath hitching. It was not whom she had expected.

"Who is he?" Kais' eyes on her held no emotion. It was simply a matter-of-fact inquiry, as though he was asking if she liked dogs.

"Who?" she asked, though she knew who he meant.

He inclined his head back toward the hall where the music seeped outside. "The one who tried to cut in. Who is he?"

"Lord Henrik, my father's advisor."

Even speaking his name left a bad taste in her mouth.

Kais' brow rose. "Advisor?" His eyes moved to the side, considering, and then back to her. "Why are you afraid of him?"

How he could know of her fear was more unnerving than the question. She squared her shoulders. Why wouldn't he just leave her alone?

"I am not afraid of him."

After another moment of scrutinizing her, during which she tried not to flinch, he spoke again, "Of course. My mistake."

Why was he following her? She just needed space, room to relax for a moment, and she couldn't do that with him there. Something about his presence caused her body to react in ways she couldn't control. She nearly rolled her eyes at herself. Of course, it wasn't him. How could he possibly have any impact at all on her physically?

Was she afraid of Kais? She would be a fool not to be. Evandor's reputation as a country was severe. Not to mention Kais himself was much bigger than she was; she would be at his mercy should he decide to act unseemly. It wasn't as though the Princess was taught how to defend herself. She had guards for that.

She swiveled her head around. Guards. There were no guards with her. No one was around.

She felt his gaze still on her. She glanced at him and found him scrutinizing her, head tilted to the side, eyes narrowed.

"Now you're afraid of me," he pointed out as though analyzing her.

Lucky guess. Again, why wouldn't she be?

She swallowed and hoped it wasn't visible. "Excuse me, please."

She moved around him and back toward the Hall.

CHAPTER TWO

KAIS

Kais watched the Princess leave. *Flee* was a more accurate description. When he was alone, he finally released a breath and the tension he'd been holding in his shoulders. What in Helias was that? He knew beyond a doubt that she was afraid. But of course, she would be frightened of him—he was the enemy. No doubt stories had been told about them, true or not. But he knew she was afraid of that advisor, too, though it was a different feeling than when she was around Kais.

Which was worse, fear of the unknown or fear of the known? For her, it had been fear of the known.

He let out a frustrated sound, feeling like he could punch the wall. A good question was: why did he care? A better question was: how did he know? How did he know she was afraid? What made this girl special? A thought poked at the back of his mind, a story from his youth. He pushed it away, burying it. He would have to be mad to entertain *that* possibility.

"Sir?"

He'd heard Teague approach, though he didn't look at the other man, only turned his head slightly in his direction.

"We weren't sure where you'd gone, Sir. It's nearly time for the meal."

He was expected to go back in there and eat with those people. Not for the first time, he wished he had declined the invitation. Holiday or not, they were a questionable crowd to be associated with. Some of his men had told him as much, pressing to know why he had come.

Why had he come? Curiosity. He wanted to see for himself. To see these people who were taxing the land to the brink of collapse and hoarding provisions until their people starved. People who sat in their comfortable castle and threw parties while other people died. He wondered if that precious, frightened Princess knew what her father was really like. The King put on quite an act of cluelessness. But Kais and his people knew better. They had ridden through the land and had seen the people starving and barely surviving. Outside of Covington, the quality of life rapidly diminished the farther from the castle one r ode.

When the time came, Kais would have no problem working to overthrow the land. It would benefit the people greatly, whether they understood that or not.

He turned his head fully to Teague. "What do you think of all this?"

Teague's chin lowered slightly, and though his expression didn't change, Kais knew him well enough to see the shadow there.

"They live in excess while their land goes to Helias. I have many thoughts."

Kais lifted his eyes to scan the dark stone walls of the castle. He also had many thoughts. He returned his gaze to Teague.

"Come, let us *feast*."

The words tasted sour on his tongue.

CHAPTER THREE

SATORI

Adjoined to the Great Hall was another room, the twin of the one in which everyone danced. Rows of tables lined the room with enough seats to accommodate every guest. Instead of being set at the front of the room, the head table was set in the middle.

Her father was seated at the head of the table, and she was seated in the first position, to his right on the long side. Across from her, General Kais would be seated. She was so tense waiting for his arrival that her shoulders ached. It unnerved her tremendously that this man knew so much about her. It unnerved her more the reaction her body seemed to have around him.

She closed her eyes and drew in a few quiet, cleansing breaths. Nerves. It was only nerves. Her body was having no actual reaction to him, only the sight of him set her on edge.

As she was explaining this to herself, eyes closed, she felt it. Her eyes shot open at the oddly warm sensation that poured over her. She only had to glance to her right to see him making his way along the table to where he would sit opposite her. She would have no choice but to stare at him throughout the meal.

His eyes were already on hers, and she quickly glanced down at her hands in her lap, pretending to adjust the napkin that already lay perfectly.

"Satori."

Her head shot up. She had been so focused on ignoring their guests that she had missed Henrik's approach. He stopped beside her chair, reaching out to pull a few strands of her hair off her neck and back over her shoulder.

Just before she jerked away, she remembered all the eyes in the hall. Instead, she dropped her shoulder just enough that his skin no longer touched hers. Henrik did not stop what he was doing. In fact, he made a point of moving his hand so it, once again, brushed her skin. Her stomach turned, but still she schooled her features. Henrick was careful when in public, keeping his touch to her hair or a brush along the small of her back.

He removed his hand and pulled out the chair next to her. *Helias*. She should have assumed he would be seated beside her. She pulled her eyes from her lap, lifting her chin. She would not appear weak. Not in front of Henrik and certainly not in front of their *guests*.

Her eyes met Kais'. She had forgotten about him completely when Henrik had approached. Now he stood, eyes narrowed, observing her. *Breathe, Satori.* She felt like she was going to crawl out of her own skin. She reached for the water goblet in front of her and downed the entire contents in two long pulls.

Trumpets blew, and she jumped at the sound. She placed her goblet back on the table as all around her people stood. Henrik pulled her chair out and she rose to her feet along with everyone else.

"His Majesty, the King!"

Her father appeared, and two servants pulled out his chair as he sat. He lifted his hands. "Please, sit."

Chairs scraped and rattled as they slid along the stone floor, the buzz of voices filling the room once more as everyone took their seats and resumed their conversations.

Despair poured into Satori. She was trapped there with Kais across from her and Henrik beside her and no means of escape. Through six courses she would have to sit and stomach Henrik's hands beneath the table and Kais' unnerving attention above. She tried to take a breath but only the slightest bit of air would come. She would not flee the room. She would stay. She would perform the duty that was required of her as the Princess. She pulled in a slow, deep, deep breath, letting it out in a long drawn-out exhale. She would not be afraid.

She met Kais' eyes again, and the hairs on her neck stood. She *would* be afraid. But she would not show it.

"Did you see the one who was always with the leader— what's his name again? Kais? The leader, I mean, not the other one." Tessa had Satori's hair ribbons in her hand and was twirling around the room as though dancing with them. "His eyes were like a jet stone. I've never seen eyes so dark. And the other one, the one I was talking about, tall and blonde."

Satori's head was pounding. She wanted nothing more than for Tessa to finish her hovering and leave her alone. But Tessa was far too engrossed in gushing about their guests to realize that.

Finally, Tessa spun to a halt, her skirts swishing about her ankle with the momentum. "Where did you go?"

Satori lifted her eyes to look at Tessa in the large mirror on the dressing table in front of her. She raised a brow.

"You disappeared twice." Tessa turned to hang the ribbons in the cabinet that hung on the wall beside the other various hair accessories. "And you were terribly quiet at dinner."

"There were so many people, I just needed some air. And I wasn't feeling very well."

It wasn't a lie, not exactly. She certainly hadn't been feeling well.

When their guests had left, Kais had taken her hand in his, sending a white-hot wave through her, even as Henrik rested a hand on the small of her back, causing her breath to seize further. It was too much. She had barely remained standing, and the moment Kais' party had left, she fled to her rooms.

Tessa turned back to her, concern wrinkling her forehead. "Are you feeling okay now?"

"Better, yes."

Tessa moved back toward her and picked up the brush from the dressing table, beginning to drag it through Satori's long golden blonde locks. "Their leader, or whatever he was, seemed to be paying extra attention to you."

Satori's eyes met Tessa's in the mirror again. "Oh?"

Had everyone noticed their *connection*, as Kais had called it?

"You didn't notice?" Tessa's hands stalled. "After you danced he couldn't take his eyes off of you."

Satori didn't trust her voice, she only gave a small shake of her head and dropped her eyes to the table in front of her. The room was closing in on her again. She shifted in her seat even as she counted the strokes of the brush through her hair. Tessa was a second-generation lady's maid, and she had been taught that the way to keep a royal's hair shining was one hundred strokes every night. Usually Satori didn't mind, even found it relaxing, but tonight she needed to be up, away, and out.

Ninety-eight... ninety-nine... one hundred.

As soon as Tessa set the brush down beside her, Satori stood, her knee knocking into the dressing table. She barely noticed as she turned and moved toward the large set of doors that opened onto her own private balcony. Pushing aside the curtains, she grasped both handles and wrenched the doors open. She was met by a chilly evening breeze that sent her night dress billowing out behind her, plastering the front to her legs.

Wordlessly, Tessa handed Satori her dressing gown. She paused for a moment. "Are you sure you're alright?"

Satori pulled the gown tight around her. "I'm fine, Tessa. Really. You can go."

"Alright." Tessa dipped into a slight curtsey. "Goodnight, Your Highness."

"Goodnight," Satori said as she stepped up to the balcony rail.

Her rooms were many floors up, giving her a lovely view of the castle grounds. Though at this hour, with only a sliver of moon, she had to rely on her memory to see below.

The balcony was long, running the length of her suite of rooms, and it was one of her favorite places.

"Good evening, Satori."

She nearly jumped out of her skin, her head whipping toward the silken voice on the other end of her *private* balcony. Henrik was still a way off, but he was coming toward her. The light from the moon glinted off the bright gold thread running through his pale blue coat. Panic filled her as she backed away, clutching her very thin dressing gown tightly around her. *Not tonight, not tonight.*

She cleared her throat. "You're not supposed to be here."

Her voice shook, and she tried to steady it, but it was a response he had elicited from her since she was young.

He had visited her on her balcony before, but it had been quite a while. Recently he had favored her rooms. She had finally started to feel safe here again. Her heart thundered in her chest, and her vision was beginning to swim. *Don't pass out, don't pass out. Pull yourself together, Satori.*

He was still advancing on her, slowly, the long fingers of his left hand trailing idly along the stone of the balcony rail. Henrik was forty years old and still staggeringly attractive, and she hated him all the more for it. Courtiers would come to visit and Satori would have to sit in rooms and listen to them gossip about the King's advisor and how blue his eyes were, and how they would love to run their fingers through his wavy, sandy brown locks. How his hands were a work of art, and what it must feel like to be caressed by them.

Vile. It felt vile.

"It's cold out here tonight."

Her eyes snapped from his hands to his face. He was tall, his height always making her feel small. Her breath hitched as he drew closer still, nearly in front of her. If only Tessa would return. He stopped inches in front of her.

"You are not supposed to be here," she repeated her earlier words, but they held no volume and less threat.

He reached out and trailed one finger down her cheek, along her jaw, and over the collar of her dressing gown. She looked away, silently willing him to leave.

Powerless is how he made her feel. When she was younger, partly due to Henrik, she had begged her father to allow her to train with the captain of their guard. Nothing too involved, simply basic concepts to defend herself. Her father had not allowed it, saying that as the Princess she would have guards with her at all times. All times except when she was alone in her room. She suspected Henrik had some say in her father's choices.

She stepped back, out of his reach, fully aware of the end of the balcony behind her. If he advanced on her, there would be nowhere to go. Nowhere but down. She allowed herself a glance at the railing. Maybe down would be preferable.

Henrik, hand still hovering in the air, noticed. He glanced over the balcony and then back to her. Another step. She was caged in.

"Surely my company is preferable to death?"

She dropped her head, the fight gone. She was exhausted from the evening. Too many people, too many emotions, too many mysterious men who could read her mind.

"I'm tired, Henrik. Please, please go?" She absolutely hated the quiver, the fear, the pleading in her voice.

He lifted her chin. "I could make you forget your exhaustion."

A tear slipped from her eye. "Please."

He swiped slowly at it with his thumb, considering her. "Very well."

She let out a breath of relief before she could catch herself. It was no use, anyway. Henrik knew exactly the effect he had on her. It was part of why he delighted in keeping company with her.

"But first..."

He tilted her chin up further, his other hand slipping behind her back, low. Her thin dressing gown provided barely any barrier to his touch. He pulled her close until she was pressed against him and dipped his head, placing a kiss on her mouth.

No fight—she had none left. She allowed him to kiss her. He ran his tongue over the seam of her lips, parting them, deepening the kiss. She squeezed her eyes shut until it was over.

He released her, stepping away. "Goodnight, Satori."

She sensed his retreat but didn't open her eyes for a long time, waiting until she knew he was gone. When she did open them and found herself alone, her stomach rolled. She raced inside, barely making it to the chamber pot before being sick.

CHAPTER FOUR

KAIS

He sat, elbow resting on the desk, index finger sliding back and forth across his bottom lip with his eyes fixed on a spot on the floor across his tent. Pages of documents lay spread across his desk, forms on rationing provisions, others on the predicted weather patterns for the coming winter. When you were in charge of an army of men, their lives were in your hands. Somehow Kais had to get all his men through to the other side, alive, warm, and with full stomachs.

That was what he should have been doing. Instead he sat, his mind far away in a castle with a brown eyed, golden haired Princess. If there was a worse person for his mind to fixate on, he didn't know. What he did know was that there was something clearly different about her.

Kais was no stranger to women. He was a thirty year old soldier—he'd been around. But never, in all his years, had he experienced what he did when he walked into that Hall. An immediate sense of being dipped into light. He huffed and rolled his eyes at the comparison, but there was no other way that he could put it. He had felt her eyes on him. *Felt them*. Like a brush of fingers against skin.

And then, when he had discovered the source, and followed her outside . . . His mind boggled. He knew what that woman was feeling, just as real as he knew his own emotions. Anger, unease, mistrust, fear, all of it, as though it was written across her forehead. And as she had walked away, it was as though some invisible cord had snapped out and caught her, tethering her to him. He had known as soon as she had come back inside because the cord had gone taut.

"Sir?"

Kais' eyes snapped to Teague. From the way the other man had spoken, it was clear that it hadn't been the first time.

"What?"

"The men are restless. They want to leave at dawn. They don't trust the king."

Kais stood. "No, neither do I. Tell them to start packing what they can tonight. We'll finish in the morning and clear out by first light."

Teague nodded. Then his body relaxed, switching effortlessly from soldier to friend and counselor. "How do you think it went?"

Kais began unbuckling the leather gauntlet from his wrist and forearm. "I think it was a waste of time. I think all they wanted was to see us, to gauge our men and numbers." He dropped a brace on the desk in front of him and moved to the other arm. "Did anyone show up while we were gone?"

Teague made himself at home, moving to the small liquor table Kais had just inside the door.

"Yeah," he spoke as he held up a bottle, a question in his eyes.

Kais nodded as he dropped the other brace on the desk and moved around in front of it.

Teague continued, "Levin said some soldiers were sneaking around the perimeter. No one said or did anything threatening. He was pretty sure they were just counting."

Kais took the glass that Teague offered him and sipped, savoring the burn of the liquid down his throat.

"Good thing we left so many behind." Teague sipped his own glass.

Kais' eyes flicked to him before returning to the glass in his hand. "Yeah."

"Hey, are you alright? You seem a little distracted."

Kais lifted the glass and swirled the amber liquid, studying it as it slid around the inside of the cup.

"That Princess..." He pursed his lips.

"What about her?"

Kais looked back at his friend. He'd been told when he was younger that the leader of an army did not get to have close friends. Did not get a confidant. But the damage had already been done. Teague and Kais had grown up together, inseparable, and Kais was continually grateful for the other man. Teague knew when to be a soldier and call him "sir" and when to be a friend and share a drink.

Kais opened his mouth to answer, but could not find any words that would make sense and not make him sound mad. He shook his head and shrugged.

"Got under your skin, did she?" Teague smirked, moving to sit in a chair in front of Kais' desk.

Kais moved his arm behind his back and placed his glass on the desk. His brain tried to put together sentences that wouldn't leave Teague looking at him like he'd lost his mind. Behind him, Teague sat quietly, waiting, most likely having learned long ago to give Kais room to form his thoughts.

Kais turned back to him, using his thumb to pop open the snap that secured his whip to his hip. He pulled the coiled length of leather off and laid it carefully on his desk.

"It was more than getting under my skin."

Teague gave him a smirk, raising his brows.

"Not like that."

At least, he didn't *think* it was like that. He pulled his bottom lip between his teeth, pushing it out again. His next words were going to make him sound insane, but it was Teague, so he spoke them anyway.

"Do you remember the old tales of Shala and Miram?"

Teague leaned back, the chair creaking. "The stories we've been told all our lives? Our valiant warrior gods? A love for the ages?" he teased. "Yeah, I remember."

"The stories of—" Kais paused, and pulled in a long breath. He wouldn't dare speak his next words to anyone but Teague. "Blood mates?"

Teague's brow pinched and his lips moved as though he might speak, but then his mouth closed again. Kais waited as his friend processed the words.

He gave one small shake of his head. "It's a myth."

Kais nodded, but his voice was quiet when he spoke, "I know." He swallowed. "But what if it's not?"

"Kay, are you saying that—"

"I don't know," Kais interrupted Teague before he could go on. "All I know is that I've never experienced anything like this before."

"And you're not just infatuated?" Teague waved a hand toward the door. "Like you go, have a roll around, and get over it?"

"It's not even that I wanted that. I mean, sure, she's beautiful; that was there too, but..." He paused, well aware of how crazy he sounded. "It was like I could feel her thoughts. Or, more her emotions." He shook his head. "I don't know. I need to talk to someone."

Teague studied him for a moment. "You could go see Kezia while we're here."

Kais turned toward him. "Kezia."

He'd meant to make it a point to go see his old friend while he was in the area, but the Princess had driven everything from his mind.

Teague shrugged. "If anyone would know anything, she would."

Kais nodded, he knew better than anyone the validity of Kezia's words. "I was going to try to see her anyway."

He would go in the morning as they packed up and left.

CHAPTER FIVE

SATORI

"Good morning, Your Highness!"

Satori groaned as she pulled the pillow from beneath her and slammed it down on top of her head. Morning came far too early, especially when she had been up half the night trying to calm her panic.

"Go away."

"I'm afraid I can't." Tessa threw open another curtain, allowing more of the offensive sunshine into the room. "Your father is asking for you."

Satori groaned again. Her father wanted to discuss suitors. Again. She did not want to discuss suitors, especially not after the previous night. Would *he* be there? Watching her as her father planned her future? Or worse, had he already been there and convinced her father that *he* would be the best choice for her? Her stomach turned as something attempted to crawl up her throat. She pulled in a long breath, swallowing it, pressing the panic down along with it. She absolutely hated how Henrik made her feel. How helpless he made her seem to herself.

"Satori?"

"Yes." She threw the pillow onto the bed and sat up.

Might as well get it over with. It would happen eventually, whether she was late or not. She stood and heaved a sigh.

"Blue or yellow?" Tessa stood in front of her, a dress draped over each arm.

Which dress did she want to wear when her father told her she had to marry Henrik?

"Don't you have a black option?"

Tessa's shoulders dropped, and her head tilted to the side. "No."

Satori reached out and snatched the blue dress, tossing it on the bed before she pulled her nightgown over her head. She slipped the dress on and allowed Tessa to help lace a light brown corset over top of it.

"Don't I get breakfast?" Satori glanced at the small table that sat empty in her room.

"Your father said he'll have fruit while you speak." Tessa tied off the last of the laces. "And after, if you're interested, some of us are going riding."

A few hours outside, enjoying nature, far from the castle walls and those who inhabited them? Sounded like bliss.

She met Tessa's eyes. "Don't leave without me or I'll have you flogged."

Tessa's mouth broke into a grin. "I wouldn't dream of it, Your Highness."

Satori's lip curled. "Let's get this over with."

She stopped outside her father's door, hand outstretched toward the latch. Was Henrik in there? Her stomach churned at the possibility, and she hated him for it. Hated him with everything in her for making her feel this way.

She couldn't stand there all day. She took the latch in her hand and pulled the door open. She did a quick scan of the room and found only her father standing behind his desk, studying some parchment strewn across its wooden surface.

"Good morning, Father."

The King looked up. "Ah, Satori. Good morning, dear." He gestured toward the seat on the opposite side of the desk. "Sit, sit. I ordered fruit."

Relieved to be alone with him, she moved to a chair in front of the desk and sat. "Is everything alright? Tessa said you were looking for me."

Her father lowered himself into the large chair behind him and waved a hand toward the parchment. "It's another offer of marriage."

She straightened, casting her eyes anywhere but at that cursed letter.

"Oh, Satori, why don't you just accept one of them? Or, better still, just marry Henrik." Alarm filled her as her gaze shot to his, and in his eyes was a concerned confusion. "He's here, he's willing, you know him."

Which is exactly the problem. She shook her head slowly at first, and then harder. "I can't."

"Satori," her father chided her as though she'd stolen the last cookie, not as though she was refusing a man's—a monster's, really— hand in marriage.

She looked again at the letter on the desktop before she reached across the surface and snatched it up. "Give me the rest. I'll make a decision."

For a moment he just watched her, and then he moved back behind his desk, locating the other letters from suitors. He handed them to her, and she nearly ripped them from his grasp.

"Henrik, Satori. Marry Henrik. Marry someone you know."

No, she would never marry him *because* she knew him. Not ever. Not under any circumstances. She would have to be dead. She couldn't be in the room any longer, the walls were beginning to close in, and the longer she sat there the more chances there were for Henrik to walk in. She stood.

"If that's all, Father." She worked a smile onto her face. "One of the kitchen servants told me that there are kittens downstairs, and I would so love to see them."

It was a lie. Well, there *were* kittens, but she wasn't going to see them. Tessa's offer to join their ride was at the forefront of her mind, but she wasn't sure her father would approve of her spending the day with the servants.

He released a soft sigh, leaning back in his chair. "Go see your kittens."

"Thank you, Father."

She had made it all the way to the door and had it open before he called out, "Satori?"

She turned to look over her shoulder at him.

"Please reconsider Henrik."

Just his name alone made her skin crawl.

"Have a good day, Father." She swept from the room, pulling the door closed behind her.

She started toward her room to change but paused, glancing down at her dress. The skirts were thin and extra full. She would have no problem riding a horse and saw no need to change. Instead, she turned and headed toward the kitchens and the servant's entrance.

Smiling servants greeted her as she passed by them. Many people had left after the ball the previous night, but a number had stayed and would still be staying for some time, so the kitchens were far busier than normal.

With no desire to be in the way, she swiftly found the exit, pausing to snatch some sugar cubes from a large ceramic canister. She pushed open the door and was greeted with bright sunshine, blue sky, and a warm breeze. The scent of chrysanthemums hung in the air, emanating from the various multicolored bushes that grew around the castle. Even well into the autumn the flowers still bloomed in gorgeous rainbows around the grounds along with some of the roses from Covington. It was one of her favorite things about her home. She closed her eyes and turned her face toward the sunshine, pulling in a deep breath.

Loud laughter came from the direction of the stables. Immediately she could pick out Tessa's musical laugh and Dimitri's answering voice. Satori smiled. A few hours with no worries, only the company of those around her age who knew when to address her as the Princess and when to allow her to be one of them. She picked up her pace, eager to reach the stables.

"Satori!" Tessa called out when she saw her. "We have your horse ready. Though, Dimitri thinks it's having a bad day."

Satori came to a stop beside them, addressing Dimitri. "How can you tell if a horse is having a bad day?"

"That sounds like the start of a joke." Clinton, another servant, approached, leading Satori's horse.

Pepper was a dappled grey mare who lived for sugar cubes. She could be moody, but if you had treats, she warmed to you immediately.

Satori held out her hand, and the horse dug in greedily. "She looks to be in a fine mood to me."

"Well, of course." Dimitri waved a hand toward her. "You have sugar. I'm telling you, she tried to eat my head."

Satori pressed her face against the horse's soft cheek. "She would never."

As if in agreement, the horse gave a soft whinny.

Dimitri stepped up to the horse, a look of betrayal playing on his features. "Are you calling me a liar?"

Satori glanced at Tessa who was giggling again in her musical way. She took the reins from Clinton who disappeared back into the stables to collect his own horse. He emerged with two other female servants behind him.

"Ready?"

Satori mounted Pepper, her full skirt flowing up and over the horse easily with plenty of room to spare. "I am."

They had only barely begun to move when the sound of hooves greeted them, and a huge, impeccably groomed white horse came galloping into the yard.

Satori's stomach rolled over, her throat growing tight with anxiety.

Henrik pulled on the reins of his beast, causing the horse to rear up as he sat confidently in the saddle, his short dark cape brushing across the back of the horse. "Good day to you all. I heard something about a ride and wondered if I might join?"

Behind her, two of the servant girls giggled and whispered as Satori fought the urge to cry. No one would tell him no, even though that's what she wished. They would all find themselves *privileged* to share a ride with the Duke.

"Please, your Grace." Clinton lifted an arm, inviting Henrik to join them. "We would be honored."

Satori said nothing as she ran a thumb over her palm again and again. How could she enjoy any part of this ride now? How could she concentrate on anything besides his presence? And the chittering of the servant girls was sure to make her even more ill.

Henrik pulled his horse up to hers, so close that their legs brushed. He reached over, laying a hand over where her thumb circled over her palm. Shivers chased up and down her spine.

"I look forward to our ride, Your Highness."

His touch brought awareness back. Servants surrounded them.

She pulled in a long, steadying breath, lifted her chin, and turned her head to face him. "Of course, your Grace."

He responded with a half smile, a smug smile, and she had visions of knocking him off his stupid horse and watching it trample him.

"Let's go, then!" Dimitri shouted, kicking his horse into action.

There was no slow start for their group as they immediately urged their horses into gallops, flying from the stable yard and eventually the castle grounds.

Satori may not have been able to hold her own in any sort of physical situation, but she could ride a horse like any knight. She relished the feel of the powerful beast's muscles churning beneath her and the wind whipping through her blonde hair.

"We should race to Covington," Dimitri called out. "In teams!"

"Yes!" Tessa shouted loud enough to be heard over the pounding of the horses' hooves. "Let's go see the roses!"

"Come on then, Tess!" Dimitri pointed his chin at Tessa and then jerked it away.

Tess let out a loud laugh as she encouraged her horse to follow

"Servants against the Princess and the Duke!" Clinton called, racing past her, followed by Shiri and Mallory, the last two servant girls.

They rode by, casting undisguised longing looks in Henrik's direction. Clearly, they would have preferred to be on his team. Satori wished they were, as well.

She slowed Pepper and then stopped completely even as the others were disappearing down the tree-lined road leading from the castle. The trees had begun to change and the red, yellow, and orange leaves covered the path in a gorgeous canopy. Satori barely noticed. Henrik reined in his horse and turned, walking back toward her. He circled behind her before coming even with her and stopping.

"You wouldn't leave me alone to lose, now would you?"

"I find I've lost my desire for riding." She glared at him. "Good luck without me, your Grace."

She lifted the reins to turn her horse, but Henrik's hand shot out, snatching them from her grasp.

"You will not humiliate me, Satori." The edge in his voice was deadly, and that fear that she hated, that made her feel weak, lodged in her chest. "Come." The edge was gone, replaced by lightness, as though they were simply good friends out for fun.

He tossed the reins at her and she caught them.

"Hold on."

It was the only warning he gave her before he leaned over and slapped Pepper hard on the flank. The horse took off beneath her, leaving her grasping for dear life until she got her bearings.

Pepper raced on and Satori considered for a few moments trying to shake Henrik, but his horse was faster, and he kept pace well with her. She couldn't fathom any other option than to see it through to the end of the race and meet up with the others in Covington.

She kicked lightly at Pepper, encouraging the horse to move faster, but Henrik and his pale devil of a beast kept up easily.

She stopped pushing her horse, allowing it to slow. She wouldn't evade Henrik, and they wouldn't beat the others who'd had a head start, so she decided to allow her horse a bit of relief.

"Finally surrendering, my dear?" Henrik had slowed his horse as well to walk alongside her.

Emboldened by the fact that they both sat astride moving horses and he couldn't simply reach out and grab her, she turned to him. "Never to you."

His only reply was a cold smile, and she was glad he couldn't see the chill that ran over her.

She refocused her attention on the road. Before them an enclosed cart was stopped in the way, beside it two men seemed to be arguing, gesturing toward the wheel.

"What's this?" Henrik mused, moving his horse slightly in front of hers.

She nearly laughed at his ridiculous show of chivalry, as if he were noble. As if he cared about her safety.

He held an arm out behind him in her direction. "Stay back, Satori."

"You are not my keeper," she snapped.

His head whipped around, and he pinned her in place with an angry look. "Stay. Back." Before she could respond, he returned his attention to the men in the road who were now directly in front of them. "Do you need assistance, sirs?"

The men ceased their arguments, turning to face Henrik. In unison, both sets of eyes drifted behind Henrik to Satori, leering, and then back to Henrik.

"We, uh, seem to have a problem with our wagon wheel," one of the men said. Curly orange hair covered his head, and a long scar ran across his jaw from below his ear to his chin.

Henrik lifted his chin, craning his neck to inspect the wagon wheel from his position atop his horse. "What sort of problem?"

"Well, it won't turn, now will it?" The second man's features were completely opposite to the first. His head was shaved completely, his nose crooked as though it had been broken and never set properly.

Henrik looked between the men and the wagon wheel before he turned again to Satori. "Stay."

It irritated her that he felt he could command her, that he just assumed she would simply obey his whims. So when he dismounted and moved toward the men and the wagon, she took the opportunity to move her horse closer, as well. Not too close, just enough where she could see what was happening.

Henrik leaned in. "There's a large branch jammed in the wheel."

The men exchanged looks like Henrik was an idiot. "By Shala, we are so thankful you stopped to tell us this. We never would have known otherwise."

Henrik shot an annoyed glance at the red-haired man who had spoken, and Satori couldn't help smiling at the joke made at his expense. He wasn't often teased. No one dared. She relished his annoyance.

"We know what the problem is, just can't pull it out on our own." The man glanced at Satori as he spoke. The look pressed on her and she wanted to go home and scrub it off her skin.

Henrik's shoulders rose. It was a calming breath, she'd seen it before, usually when she was being obstinate in his presence. "If you grasp that end, I will endeavor to aid you."

He bent, taking hold of one end of the limb.

"Duff." The orange-haired man jerked his chin at the bald one, presumably ordering him to grab an end of the stick jammed into the wheel.

But instead of moving toward the stick, Duff stepped toward Pepper. Satori barely had time to register his movements when the orange-haired man pulled what looked like a club from some hidden place beneath the wagon and brought it down hard on Henrik's back. Henrik let out a grunt as he fell forward, smacking his head off the wagon wheel. He was still awake though, and turned toward the man, a growl emanating from him. But he stood no chance as the man brought the club down again, silencing him as he fell back into the dirt, unconscious.

Satori had been so shocked by what was happening that it hadn't registered that Duff had grabbed her horse's reins, holding her in place. Then the orange-haired man was moving toward her, his grin causing her blood to run cold.

He reached up, grabbing her, and hauling her from the horse. She screamed and kicked, flailing her arms, but it was no use. He was bigger than she was, and she had no defense training whatsoever. She was easily overpowered. The man locked her arms behind her, and she had no hope of fighting free.

"Come on, then. Let's go." The orange-haired man's breath coasted past her ear as he issued the order.

Duff released Pepper's reins and slapped the horse hard on the flank. She let out a loud whine in protest and took off like a flash, back the way they had come. He moved to Henrik's still form, grasping him under the arms and hauling him off the road and back into the tree line. Satori had no idea if he was dead or alive, nor did she know which she wished for him to be. Duff slapped Henrik's horse as well, and the massive white beast followed Pepper.

The orange-haired man, who had a hold of her, pressed the side of his face into her head, turning enough to drag his tongue along her cheek. "We're going to have a good time, *Princess.*"

Her blood ran cold, and she fought down the bile that rose into her throat. *Princess.* He knew who she was. She had no idea what he would do with her, but it would clearly not be good.

Duff yanked the large stick that had been "stuck" in the wagon wheel free with little effort. "Alright. Come on. Throw her in the back." He pulled open the back door to the wooden box that was their wagon.

"Time for a ride, Princess," the man who held her said, pushing her toward the wagon. "Gonna need you to be quiet, though."

Fear raced through her, but she had no more time to process his words before his hand came around her face, a cloth in his grasp. He pressed the stinking rag against her mouth and nose. The wagon spun, blurred, and went black.

47

CHAPTER SIX

KAIS

Covington was bustling as Kais made his way along the streets. He wore a long cloak and pulled the hood further over his head as he moved. It was unlikely he would be recognized, but with so many people in town for the roses, he didn't want to take chances.

It didn't take him long to locate the place he was looking for. The building was a row of shops and doors, but the one he sought was painted a deep blue. Above it hung a charcoal sign with the words *Herbal Apothecary* etched in dark gold paint. Three starbursts floated above the words.

He looked around and then felt silly for doing so. He twisted the handle and ducked into the shop. A tiny bell chimed, announcing his presence. The room was blanketed in shadows, lit only by a few candles placed strategically around. The scent of sage hung heavy in the air.

"We're closed," a heavily accented female voice called from somewhere behind a curtain on the opposite side of the counter.

"Even to old friends?" he called back.

Through the curtain, a woman appeared. Her dark hair was curled into a mass of ringlets and piled on top of her head, a bright green and gold scarf wrapped around the style, bits and strands hanging from all over. Instead of looking messy, she made it look elegant and mysterious. The woman's dark skin blended into the shadows of the room, and her eyes were winged in a dark gold liner. Eyes which were wide on him, her mouth open in a small "O" as well.

"Kais?"

He lowered his hood, flashing her a grin. "I've missed you, Kezia."

"Kais!" She rounded the counter, rushing toward him.

She stopped just in time to clasp his face in both hands, kissing one cheek and then the other before planting a lingering kiss on his lips.

He laced his fingers at the small of her back and smiled down at her when she broke the kiss. Kezia was his most uninhibited, platonic friend. She had lived in Evandor but had moved years prior. Now their meetings were far too infrequent.

"I woke up thinking about you." Her palm rested on his face. "This must be why." She grasped his hand, pulling him behind the counter and through the curtain she'd emerged from. "What brings you to my abode?"

Kais opened his mouth to answer, but she held up a hand, stopping him. Her head tilted to the side as she studied his face. "She is special."

He closed his mouth, pressing it into a line and raising a brow. Kezia certainly hadn't lost her touch.

She turned his hand over, lightly brushing her fingers over his arm and palm. Her eyes met his. "Do you even know how special?"

A lump lodged in his chest.

"Kezia." It was a plea, her name; a plea for her to tell him more, to explain, to show him something. What was special about her?

"You sit." Kezia's finger speared toward a pile of cushions arranged around a low table. "I'll make tea. Then we'll talk."

He let out a sigh. He didn't want tea. He wanted answers. But he said nothing, lowering himself, legs crossed, onto the pile of cushions.

It wasn't long before she returned with a steaming pot and two mugs. Silently she poured the drinks while he watched, waiting. His insides buzzed, impatience threatening to make him leap to his feet if only to pace around the room. To move. To let out the pent-up anxiety flitting inside him.

Finally, Kezia was finished pouring the tea, and she took a spot on the cushions opposite Kais. For a long time, she only looked at him, studying every bit of him, her eyes running from the top of his head to the tips of his fingers.

"I can see her on you. Sense her as though her scent lingers in your veins."

Kezia spoke in the strangest sentences, but she always managed to get to her point, so he said nothing, waiting.

"How long have you known her?"

At this, he let out a laugh. "I only saw her for the first time last night."

Kezia waved a finger at him. "But you knew. You *know*. Why are you here? You don't need me. All your questions have answers in your blood."

The word *blood* struck him like a nearly physical blow. It was as though Kezia had known what he'd been thinking the previous night.

"It's not possible. It's a myth."

"Myths are grounded in fact, sweet Kais. Don't you know that?" She offered a sympathetic tilt of her head. "Rare. So very rare. I haven't seen it ever in my lifetime. I'm honored to know you during this time."

During this time? What time? His mental breakdown?

He threw his shoulders into a helpless shrug. "What am I going to do? That woman hates me."

"Yes."

He blinked at the bluntness of Kezia's response. "Well, then, you know."

"She does hate you. But she feels the pull as well. Nothing like this could go unnoticed." Kezia reached across the table and placed a hand on Kais'. "She cannot be ignorant of this."

He heard her words, but believing them was another thing entirely.

Then, without warning or preamble, Kezia's fingers closed around his hand, her grip like a vise, her fingers surprisingly strong, crushing the bones in his hand. Her eyes snapped open wide, staring at him, or through him, or into him. She was looking at him, but it didn't feel like she was seeing him.

"Kezia? Kezia, are you alright?"

"She will come to you. She will need you. She will fear you. You will strike terror into her core until she is sick. You will bleed, and she will bleed."

Kais' heart kicked up as he stared wide-eyed at Kezia. The words she spoke struck fear directly into his chest, as though they were carved into the edge of a blade.

Kezia continued her blind statements, "She will know you. She will see you. She will love you. She will rest in your arms and be safe. You will die."

Kais blinked at the final statement, pulling his hand from the painful grip of the seer.

She blinked, pulling in a stuttering breath, puffing out the air with shock. "Kais."

He stood, backing away from where she still sat. "What was that?"

Kezia climbed to her feet. "I'm sorry, sometimes I can't control what I see." She moved swiftly to his side and he flinched when she grasped his hand again. "Kais, the future can be changed. It doesn't have to be set. Don't give it that ground. Let the girl get to know you. Let her love you and end the prophecy there. Don't allow it to complete."

"How in Helias am I supposed to do that?" he said, angrily snatching his hand back.

Her face fell. "I don't know. I only know what I see. But, Kais, you can't allow it to come to fruition. Petition Shala, petition Miram. They know. The gods, they have the bond. They have given it to you."

Kais shook his head and ran a hand through his hair, resisting the urge to roll his eyes. Shala and Miram. Right. Wasn't it their stupid, *unique* bond that landed him in this place?

"I have to go."

He didn't wait for Kezia to say anything further as he turned and all but fled from the building, the door crashing closed behind him. He was in such a hurry to put her and her visions behind him he, didn't even bother with the hood.

He pushed his horse to meet up with his men. They had packed up the camp and left before dawn, quite some time before he had gone to see Kezia.

CHAPTER SEVEN

SATORI

Satori woke to darkness and a throbbing head. She groaned and nearly choked. Something was shoved in her mouth and she couldn't spit it out or dislodge it. She tried to lift her arm to rip the material from between her teeth but she met resistance. Then she realized something else: her eyes were open, yet it was still dark. Had she gone blind?

She twisted her head from side to side, noticing the soft material of the blindfold shift with her movements. Panic seized her. She was gagged, blindfolded, and chained to the chair in which she sat. She pulled at the metal clamped around her wrist, sending pain shooting up her arm. She paused. Where was she?

She stilled further, listening. Her ears registered a creaking sound just as another jostle hit, and she realized she was still in the wagon.

How long had she been out? Had they traveled far? Only a few minutes? She turned her head from side to side, trying to pick up on any other sounds, but there was nothing beyond the wagon.

Her chest began to tighten. She had never been one to panic, never one to shrink away from things that others found frightening, but she was chained to a chair, being taken to points unknown, and she could only imagine what would happen when she arrived.

The men who took her had called her *Princess*. They knew who she was. Would she be held for ransom? Tortured for secrets? She almost laughed at that. She knew next to nothing thanks to Henrik convincing her father that she needn't *concern* herself with such things. So why did they want her?

The wagon wheels creaked to a stop and she looked up again, trying to hear anything that would tell her where they were. The wagon rocked from side to side as she assumed the two men who had taken her were climbing down from the driver's seat.

"Who are you and what do you want?" a male voice barked. The unmistakable sound of blades sliding from sheaths accompanied the question.

Sweat prickled along her back, it was hot in the wagon, but this had nothing to do with temperature.

"We are not here to fight," a voice answered from beside the wagon. One of the men that had taken her and attacked Henrik.

Henrik, was he still alive? Did she care? Not really.

"We want to speak to Kais."

Kais. She sucked in a breath, her stomach bottoming out. Of course.

"How do you know I'm not Kais?" said another voice coming from farther away.

A low chuckle emerged from her captor's throat. "We have heard of the man. We know what he looks like and he does not look like you."

In the wagon, through the slat board walls and who knew how many yards between them, she felt him. The hairs on her arm stood straight up, and she felt the blanket of heat as it started from the crown of her head and made its way over her, all the way to her feet. It was such a strange sensation, like being under a warm waterfall of honey. The reaction her body had to his presence unnerved her, like she was no longer in control. Loss of control made her panic, and her heart reacted accordingly.

But then another sensation started, like a wire or cord had been attached to her chest, and someone was tugging on it. Helias, what was wrong with her? And then, an erratic thumping began to beat, like a drum being played quietly. Was she hearing it? Feeling it? Could anyone else hear it? It was like the thumping of a heart but wild and erratic and getting stronger, wholly different from her own pounding heart. She shifted in her seat as though she could get out from underneath the pressure of it, but no matter how she moved it was there, pressing on her.

"What's this?"

She'd barely met him once, but she recognized his voice immediately. His accent was distinct, but it was more than that. His words seemed to crawl under her skin in a way she'd never felt before. She was losing her mind.

"Ah, the famed Kais." Her captor's voice was pleased. "I have something that might be of interest to you."

"Indeed?" His smooth tone sounded bored, like he would rather be anywhere else.

Still, all the while, she felt that erratic tapping, and now, with him so close, she knew he was the source.

Something struck the side of the wagon, and she would have jumped out of the seat had she not been chained in place.

Her captor spoke, "In this wagon, I have the Crown Princess of Dunleigh."

He sounded as though he was selling something and her heart dropped. He *was* selling something—her.

"I will give her to you for a fair price. No doubt the King will pay well for her return. Or you can do with her what you want, I care not."

Silence followed for a few more erratic beats before Kais spoke again, his voice steady, commanding, "Show me."

"You do not trust me?" There was a sort of offense to her captor's words.

"I do not know you," Kais' voice held amusement as he mimicked the other man's tone. "I have no reason to trust you. Show me the girl."

"Very well." The amusement was gone, replaced by annoyance.

The heavy lock knocked against the door, followed by the clinking of a key, and then the door was pulled open. Daylight flooded in, lighting the space beyond the blindfold.

"She is here, and she is well."

There was a long breath, and the erratic tapping slowed to something steadier.

She could feel eyes on her before Kais spoke, "What do you want?"

"We do not ask for much. Supplies, that is all."

"What kind of supplies?" Kais' voice was closer, moving toward her and not toward her captor.

"Blankets for me and my man, and our horse. It's growing cold," her captor answered. "And enough food for three weeks."

The last part of his request seemed to end on a hesitantly hopeful tone, as though he didn't expect Kais to give in. It wasn't hard to understand. Three weeks worth of food was a lot, especially for people who were camped in the woods in a land closing in on winter.

If Kais refused, would she be taken and traded off to someone more willing to share? Would they just keep her? Where would she be better off—with these men or with Kais and his men? Her heart began to drum quicker, and she shifted in her seat, anxiety pressing in.

"Done."

Done? He was agreeing? Just like that? Still, was that a good thing or a bad thing? She'd heard stories about the soldiers from Evandor. Maybe she was safer with the two men who took her from Henrik.

Kais continued speaking, "Doran, get these men what they need and see that they resume their journey. Bring the girl to my tent."

Her next breath stuttered at his words, and she stiffened, desperately wishing she could see what was happening. Whatever he thought he was going to get in that tent, he would need to think again. She might not be a fighter, but she would do her best. He wouldn't leave unscathed, that was for certain.

The wagon jostled as someone climbed inside, and hands were on her, unlocking her clamps. But then her hands were tied again in front of her. She was helped to her feet and lifted from the wagon, the blindfold and gag still in place. The hand on her arm was firm but gentle in a way she hadn't expected.

They had only taken two steps when Kais' voice stopped them. "Doran, when you get there, you can remove the blindfold, but the gag and bonds stay."

If only they'd removed the gag so she could spit on his boots. A very un-princess-like action, to be sure, but she didn't care.

Her boots scuffed over the ground, sinking into dirt, crunching on fallen leaves. She tripped once on something, a rock or root, but the hand on her arm kept her upright. They slowed, a heavy tent flap was pushed aside, and she was ushered inside and seated on a cushioned chair.

Her hands were untied briefly only to be rebound to the wooden slats that made up the back of the chair. She flinched as Doran removed the blindfold with a swift tug that took a few strands of her golden hair with it. He said nothing and barely spared her a glance as she glared at him. And then, pausing to let her know a guard was stationed outside, the heavy tent flap fell back into place and he was gone, leaving her in silence.

As if she needed a guard. Where would she go, anyway? She surveyed the space. It was large for a tent but not excessive. Though, she supposed, as the leader of a group this size, Kais warranted some luxuries. She turned her head to the right and found a large cot. A dark blue blanket trimmed in gold thread covered the bed.

Poles held the tent up on either side and slightly in front of where she sat. To her left, a table held a basin, a pitcher, and a few towels. She couldn't see behind her very well, though when she turned her head from side to side, it looked like there might be a desk and chair.

A chill ran over her as that same feeling of seeping hot honey returned. She was starting to resent it.

"You can go." Kais' voice outside the tent flap made her heart skip and she scowled. Her body's reactions to this man annoyed her. It certainly wasn't attraction, so what was it?

The flap parted, and Kais ducked inside, placing a bow and quiver of arrows just inside the tent wall while simultaneously unhooking a long coiled whip from his belt. He moved behind her, where she could no longer see him, and she heard him set something, presumably the whip, on the desk.

"You're expensive."

People said they could feel when someone was watching them, but she could truly *feel* it. Could feel the heat of his gaze as it spread across her back, as her hair lifted at the root. She tried to straighten in her seat, but the ropes around her wrist prohibited much movement.

He moved closer, the air growing stifling as she tried to take a breath. He stepped beside her enough so she could see him.

"I'm going to remove this gag. Don't scream."

She rolled her eyes at him. What did he think she was, some hysterical maiden? She certainly was not. She was afraid, being alone with him in his camp, in his tent. But she was no stranger to fear and she certainly would do her best not to show it.

He stepped behind her again, and his fingers began to work the knot at the base of her skull, though he never once touched her. Soon the gag was loosened, and he pulled it carefully from her mouth.

She opened her mouth wide, stretching and flexing her cheeks. No doubt the material had left angry red marks. He had stepped back to her side, and she looked up, meeting his gaze, glaring.

"Go to Helias."

His jaw fell open. "I just saved you. I could have left you with that mongrel and his friend. And by the way they were looking at you, the companion especially, I think he would have rather had *you* than all the extra food and blankets I gave up."

She hid the shiver that coursed through her. Were there no kind men in the world? "And I'm to believe that I'm so much better off here with you?"

"Believe what you want, Princess." He sounded annoyed. "But you know I'm right. Now, I'll untie you, if you promise not to try to kill me."

She narrowed her gaze on him. "I won't *try*," she said, emphasizing the last word to get her point across.

The corner of his mouth quirked up. "It'll be hard to kill me without a weapon."

She slid her eyes from him to the bow across the tent. He followed her gaze before returning his amused expression back to her.

"*If* you were to get to it, you certainly wouldn't have time to kill me at this range with a bow."

She lifted her brows. "I bet the arrows would work fine."

A small amused laugh puffed from him. "Fair enough. Well then, it's your call, Princess. What'll it be? Freedom or murder?"

Freedom, indeed. As if just because he untied her it would mean she was free. But her wrists ached as well as her shoulders.

She met his gaze. "Untie me. I promise not to kill you... *yet.*"

His shoulders shook with a chuckle as his head swayed from side to side. He moved behind her, still not touching her, as he cut the ropes. The fibers snapped and the pain in her arms was immediate as they protested the new direction she was trying to make them move.

Kais backed away and sat on the bed behind him, resting a forearm on one black clad leg and a palm on the other. "Take it easy. It's going to be a minute before that doesn't hurt."

She ignored him as she stretched her arms, working through the pain. "Now what?"

He studied her for a moment before leaning back. "Now it seems as though I've had a hostage delivered to me on a silver platter."

The rhythm of her heart picked up its pace as they held each other's gaze. Of course he would use her as a hostage. She was wildly valuable. But what would he do to her in the meantime? Fear crawled up her spine and she fought desperately to keep her expression controlled.

Kais' eyes scanned her face, her whole body, his brow taking on a crease. He lowered his chin, as though to level their gazes.

"Fear not, Princess. That's not who I am. Now," he repeated. "I'm going to take you back to your father and his precious advisor."

Her head snapped to him. He wasn't going to keep her as a hostage? He would deliver her home? Then a rogue thought pushed its way in: maybe she didn't have to go back. Maybe, if he truly was going to take her home, she could convince him to take her somewhere else. The thought was momentary and fleeting. She had to go back; she was the Princess, the heir to the throne. And anyway, did she really believe Kais? Did she really expect that he was just going to return her? No ransom demand or anything? She narrowed her eyes at him.

"But," Kais continued, as though he hadn't seen her skeptical look, "I do need to make a stop first. I'm already behind, and taking you back now would take too long."

Was she in a hurry to get home or did she want more time away? But would *away* with Kais and his men be worse than being home with Henrik? Henrik was only one person.

"And how long will that take?"

He moved his hands, threading his fingers together between his thighs. "A week or two."

She released a breath, the conflict of emotions in her mind muddling her thoughts. "Two weeks?"

Would they use her until she was dead and dump a corpse on her father's step? Or nearly dead? Would her father send men to find her? Would Henrik come? The thought brought a lump to her throat and she swallowed it down.

Kais didn't speak, only studied her and she wondered at what sort of things were playing across her face.

"I've had a tent prepared for you."

Her mouth opened. Alone in a tent in the middle of a camp of enemy men?

"You'll be safe, you have no need to fear."

Sure, no need to fear anyone but him. If he gave the order to keep their hands off, his men might obey, but that didn't mean he would do the same. He had seemed eager to touch her when he had been at the castle.

She did her best to steady her voice, hoping it wouldn't shake. "And where is this tent, then? Next door to yours?"

The look he gave her might have been comical if it hadn't come across so serious. He muttered something about never getting any sleep below his breath, and a chill ran over her. He didn't think he could control himself? Great.

"No." He stood. "It's on the other side of the camp."

Unfurling his hands toward the door, he invited her to go ahead of him.

Slowly she stood, reminded once again of how much bigger he was than her. Not just taller, but broader. A nervous breath puffed out of her. She would stand no chance in a fight against him.

He moved to the heavy tent flap and pushed it open, allowing her to exit in front of him. "Teague."

A group of soldiers stood around a fire and one of them turned when Kais called, he wore a long dark coat that swung just above his ankles. He looked familiar, and Satori wondered if he had been at the castle.

"Please show our guest to her tent."

Teague dipped his head. "Of course, Sir. This way, Your Highness."

Satori glanced from Kais to Teague, surprised she was being passed off, though it was preferable to spending the night in Kais' tent. She stepped toward Teague, following him when he began walking.

"Goodnight." Kais' voice behind her was soft. "Princess."

She glanced at him from the corner of her eye, but didn't acknowledge him. She was grateful for every step. The farther she moved from him the more the hot honey feeling receded. She had almost grown used to it in his tent, and now that it was gone, she felt the chill.

CHAPTER EIGHT

SATORI

Satori followed Teague through the camp, aware she was being scrutinized by everyone they passed. Soldiers whispered to each other as their eyes followed her. Apprehension crawled over her but instead of shrinking into herself like she wanted, she straightened, lifting her chin into the air. She may be weak but she had no desire to put that weakness on display.

Finally, Teague stopped just outside a small tent. He held a hand out toward it, as though welcoming her in. "Your Highness."

Your Highness. She turned an unamused look on him. "Are you making fun of me because I'm your prisoner?"

He looked genuinely surprised at her question as his brows dipped together to form a V in his lightly tanned forehead. He shook his head slightly, sending his blonde hair waving. "I wasn't aware you were our prisoner."

"No?" He had to be joking, playing with her.

"No." From his tone he sounded sincere, and his eyes met hers in a way that seemed as though he was willing her to understand. "Kais will return you home, and you will be safe here until that time."

She wrapped her arms around herself and looked away from him, feeling anything but safe.

"Your Highness... Princess?"

She blinked back at him when his voice softened on her title.

He met her eyes. "By Shala, you will be safe here and if anyone touches you they will answer to me. Do you understand?"

She nodded once, glancing toward the tent entrance, wishing she was already inside.

Teague's eyes followed her gaze and he stepped up to the tent, grasping the flap and pulling it open.

"Your Highness." He gestured with his free hand for her to enter.

She moved past him, ducking inside.

When she turned he still held the flap open. "Goodnight, Your Highness."

"Goodnight."

The entrance fell back into place with a dull slap and she turned to examine the small space. The floor was covered with a woven cloth reaching to the edges of the walls. To her right sat a small cot, and to her left a table with a pitcher and bowl and a few cloths. When she stepped closer she could see water already in the pitcher. Beside the cot and along the back of the tent sat an oil lamp, a box of matches resting on the table beside it.

Now what? She moved to the cot and sat, blowing out a long breath. A twig snapped somewhere outside followed by laughter and she jumped nearly off the bed. Teague had promised she was safe, but how could he possibly guarantee that? She pressed her eyes closed and pulled in a fortifying breath. This was nothing new. She was just as safe here as she was at home. Thanks to Henrik. She hoped he was dead in that ditch he'd been knocked into. Though she didn't expect it. He hadn't looked dead, and she wasn't that lucky.

A wave of exhaustion washed over her. She'd awoken that morning in her bed and now she was in a tent in the enemy's camp, surrounded by soldiers, with no idea what sort of morals any of her captors had. But she was so tired.

She lay down on her side, head on the pillow, feet still hanging off the bed and, in spite of her situations and surroundings, slept.

Hands. One holding her down, the other pawing at the laces of her dressing gown. A mouth moved over hers, preventing her from screaming. Her heart thudded and her breath would not come as she wrestled to be free of the weight of the man on top of her. She freed one of her arms and brought her curled fingers up, digging her nails into his face.

His head snapped to the side but his gaze quickly returned to hers, his look glaring at first and then morphing into something more sinister as he repinned her arms above her head.

He leaned in, his lips brushing her cheek as he snarled into her ear, "When will you learn that you can't fight me?"

His hand moved below her line of sight, resting on her hip, pinching the skin there until it hurt.

"Get off me!" she cried, fighting and flailing, but he only laughed. She screamed again. "Get off me!"

Nothing. He didn't budge and he didn't stop. She whipped her head from side to side, trying to move her arms, her legs—anything.

"Get off! Get off! Get off!"

And then the words were lost in a scream.

CHPTER NINE

KAIS

Hands pulled at his clothes. Eyes glared. A female voice screamed, "Get off me!"

Kais' eyes snapped open, already half sitting up before he realized he'd been dreaming. Had the voice that had woken him been real? He inclined his head, holding his breath, listening. No sounds greeted him.

Something in his chest squeezed, cutting off his air for a moment before he could pull it back and refill his lungs. *Satori.* He threw the blanket off, and, grabbing his pants from the chair, dove into them. He snatched his whip from the desk and flew from the tent, not bothering with a shirt.

He raced through the camp, the few men still awake or keeping watch looking on, alarm filling their eyes. He didn't pause to explain. Again his chest seized with panic as fear hit him. Was it his fear? Hers? He skidded to a stop outside her tent. Quiet. All was quiet. What in Helias?

"Kais?" Teague jumped to his feet from where he had been lounging just outside the entrance to the tent.

He was guarding her. Kais hadn't told him to do that. He gave a quick shake of his head; he would think about that later. "Where is she?"

Teague's eyes were wide, swirling with confusion. "The Princess?" He glanced from the tent flap to Kais. "Sleeping."

No. Kais' breaths heaved. She couldn't be alone, there was too much panic. As if to punctuate his thoughts, a pained moan filled the silence, followed by a piercing shriek.

Kais' eyes went wide as he dove into the small tent and skidded to a stop. Asleep. She was asleep and clearly having a nightmare. He stepped closer, and before he realized what he was doing, he had laid his hand on her shoulder. That same jolting spark from when they'd danced together shot up his arm, and he froze, waiting, but instead of waking, she stilled.

He lowered himself to his knees, studying her face. Her brow was pinched, and pieces of her golden blonde hair were pasted to her forehead with perspiration. Her heart thudded, and it took him a moment to realize how he knew that. He felt it. The thudding of her heart reverberated in his own chest. His forehead creased. What was she doing to him? How was this even possible? And what had caused her so much anxiety? What did a Princess have to fear as she s lept?

As he watched, studying her, trying to understand, her pinched brow smoothed, and her breathing, which had been erratic and labored when he'd entered the tent, returned to normal.

He stood, finally removing his hand from her shoulder. A shudder or a shiver worked its way through her. He lifted her feet onto the cot and carefully shook out the blanket folded at the bottom of the bed to cover her.

There was no way to ignore the strange connection they had. It was most definitely not his imagination. It was real and odd and unexplainable, at least by him.

He rose and turned to find Teague standing at the open flap, a confused, questioning look on his face. "How did you know?"

Kais met his friend's gaze. With a slight shake of his head, keeping his voice lowered, he said, "It woke me up."

"What did?"

Kais pulled his lip between his teeth before releasing it. "I think I was having the same dream she was."

He pointed his chin toward the entrance, and Teague stepped through. Kais followed, allowing the flap to fall closed heavily behind him.

"The same dream?" Teague's eyes roved around to see if they were being overheard.

Kais ran a hand over the back of his neck. "I don't— I don't know. It wasn't a situation I've ever been in. It felt like her, and then I heard her scream."

"She didn't scream." Teague shook his head. "I was right here. I didn't hear anything."

"In the dream, I said. It was strange. In her dream she screamed. Someone was..." He couldn't bring himself to finish the sentence.

Just the thought of the few seconds he had seen burned in his chest. Was that a fear she had being in his camp, or had that actually happened to her? Was she reliving a memory? His stomach rolled at the same time an odd sort of protectiveness rose inside him. He found he wanted to injure anyone who would do that to her. But, of course, he would deal with any man who treated any woman that way. This protective feeling wasn't localized to Satori. But then, why did it feel different?

"When we make camp again, put her tent next to mine."

Teague nodded. "You should get back to bed. We have a lot of work tomorrow."

Teague was right. They would pack the camp tomorrow and continue their journey. He glanced again at the tent, the scene in the dream replaying. He found he didn't want to leave her. "I think I'm going to stay here for a bit."

"I can stay here."

Kais swallowed, allowing himself this vulnerable moment. If it were anyone but Teague, he wouldn't, but Teague knew him. "I have to stay. I can't explain."

Teague eyed him for a moment before nodding. "Of course. I'll be in my tent if you need me."

"Thank you."

"Kay?"

Kais looked up in time to catch Teague's long coat as he threw it at him.

"So you don't freeze. Goodnight."

Kais barely registered Teague leaving as he pulled on the coat and lowered himself to the log in front of the tent, resting his forearms on his thighs. What was going on?

CHAPTER TEN

SATORI

Muted light filtered through the fabric of the tent as Satori blinked her eyes open. Tent? She sat up, looking around, and it all came rushing back. She let out a long breath as her feet made contact with the ground. She wanted nothing more, at that moment, than to stay in the tent and avoid everything, but the sounds from outside told her that wouldn't be an option.

She reached up, feeling the wayward strands of hair. She must look horrific. She pulled her hair down, combing through it with her fingers before she rebound it in a simple braid down her back.

"Princess?"

Satori stood and crossed to the tent's entrance. She wrapped her fingers around the fabric, inhaled deeply, and pulled the flap aside. Teague stood on the opposite side, his own blonde hair tied at his neck.

"We're packing up, Your Highness." He indicated the movement behind him with a nod of his head. "We'll need to get your tent taken care of as well. If you would like to follow me, I can show you where you can get some breakfast."

She nodded once, almost turning around to check that she had everything when she remembered she had nothing. She'd been kidnapped and then traded away. A sinking feeling struck her chest, but Teague was still watching her, and she refused to let him see what she was feeling. She lifted her chin, met his gaze, and stepped through the flap into the bustling camp.

"If you'll walk with me?" Teague held a hand out as they began to walk into the heart of the collapsing camp. "We don't have much, but there's some fruit and bread and a bit of cheese."

"Thank you," she responded softly, not knowing what else to say.

She was famished; she wasn't even sure the last time she'd eaten. The previous morning? It must have been before she left on the ride with the servants. Were they looking for her? Did Henrik make it back, or had their attackers killed him? If he were dead, she would not mourn.

" . . . right here."

Satori looked up when she realized Teague had stopped. She turned to face him. He had an arm extended toward a small pathway that led off into the trees. She'd been so wrapped up in her own thoughts she had no idea what he was saying. Did he want her to go that way?

"I'm sorry?"

"I said, if you need to attend to personal needs, you may do so this way before I show you to the food."

She felt her cheeks heat. Personal needs. "Oh, I'm sorry. I was distracted. Yes, thank you."

She was grateful for this stop, but she had also never taken care of her *personal needs* in the woods before. Satori rolled her eyes at herself. *Don't be such a princess.* She moved down the path, and with some difficulty, though it was easier than she had expected, she took care of her needs and rejoined Teague.

They resumed walking, and she studied the men breaking down their tents, talking and joking familiarly as they worked. None of them wore a uniform, instead they were all dressed in normal daily attire. Boots, dark britches, comfotable shirts. Some wore jackets, others had their sleeves pushed to their elbows. All of them looked at ease. "Where are we going?"

Teague turned his head toward her as they wove in and out of the melee. "We will be returning you home, we just have a stop to make first."

There was genuine sincerity in Teague's deep, smooth voice.

"Yes, I know." She lifted her skirt, stepping over a small stream of something spilled. "That's what the General said, but where?"

"Our next big stop is Whitehall to replenish supplies. Of course, we'll need to stop before we get there; that's just the next destination on the trip."

"And the final destination?" she asked.

He had gone back to watching where he walked and the bustle around them, but at her question he turned to look at her, his eyes sweeping over her face. "That's not for me to share. If Kais wants you to know, he'll have to be the one to tell you."

So shady. Where were they heading? Why was it such a secret? The thought flew from her mind as Teague stopped by a small table spread with food. No one was seated there eating, but she noticed that as people passed by they would snatch bits from the selection. One man pulled a large green grape from a bunch, his eyes met hers, and he shot her a wink and a smile as he tossed the grape into the air and caught it in his mouth.

Teague nodded toward a small stack of dishes. "Grab a plate and some food. I need to check on some things. Kais wants to get on the road as soon as possible so we can make a decent dent in our trek. Is there anything else you need?"

Her head spun with the movement of the camp being broken down. "No. No, thank you, I'm fine."

Teague dipped his head and left without another word, leaving her standing at the table of food. She already felt like she stood out, and she had no desire to draw further attention to herself. She snatched a bunch of grapes and a chunk of cheese off the table, foregoing the plate, and moved out of the center of the bustle, looking for a place to sit and eat.

She found a large tree out of the way and lowered herself to the cold ground, leaning against it, facing away from the camp. She bit off some cheese, listening to the working and occasional playful jests the men threw at each other. Kais had been true to his word; she had been safe, at least, through the night. But that was only the first night. How many of the men could even have known she was there? What would tonight hold? Or the next?

Two weeks. She had two weeks of traveling with these people before she could return home. *If* Kais continued to keep his word.

The cheese turned in her stomach. Home. She should be glad to return, but she wasn't eager to meet what awaited her. Of course, she missed Tessa, but Tessa was a very small part of what Satori would face at her return.

Marriage. Either to a random royal she'd never met, from a country she'd never been to, or to Henrik. The idea brought tears to her eyes, and she blinked them away, tossing the cheese into the bushes in front of her. What kind of life would that be?

No. She wouldn't marry Henrik. Not ever. She would marry the prince three times her age before that ever happened. But she knew Henrik. No doubt he was already plotting for a way to do away with the princely prospects, leaving himself the only option.

Again, she found herself hoping he was dead on the side of the road. Maybe the birds were eating him, plucking at his eyeballs. No doubt he turned their stomachs, as well.

She couldn't eat anything else, but she didn't want to waste the grapes, so she tucked them carefully into a pocket on her skirt. Now, what should she do? She wasn't left to wonder for long as a sensation that was becoming far too familiar overtook her. The warmth rested on her head, flowing over her. It wouldn't be an unpleasant experience if it weren't for the cause of it. Though, she had no idea *why* he caused it.

She waited for him to speak, but there was only silence. She could feel him there. Not only the syrupy feeling, but also his stare. She knew he was watching her, could feel his gaze on her shoulder.

"You ignore it so well."

His deep, accented voice always took her by surprise. It was like she knew what he sounded like, but her mind couldn't create an accurate replica of the sound.

A soft chuckle followed. "See?"

He stepped around in front of her, his black boots, worn and dusty, were all she could see from where she sat.

She raised her chin, allowing her eyes to take in the entire length of his body. Brown pants, belt, from which hung a rather large knife and a coiled braid of leather, black shirt, laces loose at his neck. She continued to tilt her head up to meet his gaze. "See what?"

He ignored her question, instead posing one of his own. "How did you sleep?"

Her hold on his gaze faltered for just a moment, her pride struck by the fact that she had slept well even in the camp of her enemy. "Fine."

His brow creased momentarily as though her answer confused him. What had she said that could possibly trip him up? She'd slept fine. Was he waiting for a 'thank you'?

Then, just as quickly, it smoothed out. "I'm glad to hear it. I see you've eaten as well."

If you could call it that. She'd become too queasy to eat as she considered the possibilities of her future.

"There's a horse waiting for you. Do you know how to ride?"

Really? She climbed to her feet with a huff, brushing at the dirt and leaves clinging to her dress. "Of course I can ride. What kind of question is that?"

He dipped his head slightly. "Forgive me, Princess. I'm unaware of what is taught to royalty."

She planted her hands on her hips. "Well, we are taught to ride."

She thought for a moment she saw the corner of his mouth twitch up, but she blinked and his face was serious once again.

"If you'll follow me," he unfurled his hand in the direction he had come, "we can get on our way."

She stepped toward him and he began walking. She followed, watching him. His shoulders were so broad. He was built like a tree. He made Henrik look like a piece of straw. The sleeves of his tunic were rolled up past his elbow and the veins in his forearms stood out along his deeply tanned skin. She eyed the whip, coiled at his hip. Satori had never seen anyone use a whip like the one Kais carried. It seemed far too long to be of any use. His dark britches hugged the curve of his backside so well that she could see the muscles shifting as he walked. Warmth bloomed in her chest and rose to her cheeks.

"See something you like, Princess?"

Her eyes snapped away from his backside and up to his head, but he hadn't turned to look at her; he couldn't see her at all. How had he had any idea what she was looking at? She had no intention of giving him the satisfaction of catching her staring.

"If you mean the trees, I'm not overly fond of them."

His shoulders shook as he laughed, but still, he didn't turn around. "I didn't mean the trees. You and I both know you weren't studying the foliage a moment ago."

The heat in her cheeks burned hotter, and she bit back a curse. Ladies, especially Princesses, shouldn't use the words that were perched on the tip of her tongue. She chose instead to glare, silently begging Shala or Miram—whichever deity would listen—to take away the burn before Kais turned around.

She was so caught up in her thoughts that she didn't notice when he stopped. She barely registered his still form in front of her before she ran into him. He didn't even budge, turning a surprised look on her.

Her cheeks burned, but at least this burn covered the last. "Apologies."

The corner of his mouth tipped up in a smirk. "Forgiven."

He reached out, accepting a set of reins from Teague who was already seated atop a beautiful fawn-colored horse, his long coat fanning out behind him, the split in the back allowing him to ride comfortably.

"This is Luna. She's gentle and doesn't mind new riders."

Satori had never been so grateful that she had been taught how to ride. The last thing she wanted was to look like a helpless, novice Princess in front of these men. She accepted the reins and moved to the side of the brown horse, giving it a friendly pat before expertly swinging up into the saddle, glad as well that she was wearing a full skirt.

She didn't miss when the men shared a look. "I told you I could ride."

Kais gave her an appraising nod. "But can you keep up?"

With a nod of his head to Teague, he gave his horse a soft encouraging kick, and the black and white paint took off like a flash.

Teague's horse moved beside hers as he leaned over slightly. "I think he wanted you to follow."

Satori glanced at Teague and then in the direction Kais had disappeared in. Not likely. That would leave her alone in the woods with him. Of course, she was alone with Teague now, but there were plenty of people not far back. She knew all too well what could happen when she was alone with a man.

She voiced none of her thoughts to Teague. Instead, she looked at him. "Do I look like the sort of woman to chase after a man?"

A smile broke across his face, lighting his blue eyes, and a small laugh issued from his lips. "No, Princess, you don't." Then he nudged his horse into a walk.

Satori, having no idea where they were headed, encouraged her horse to follow.

CHAPTER ELEVEN

KAIS

They'd been riding for hours and had already stopped once, but Kais remained far away from Satori, still trying to sort out his thoughts. Thunder sounded in the distance, and the feel of impending rain hung heavy in the air. He would have liked to have made it farther, but he also had no desire to ride in a storm. And the terrain farther on was more hilly and difficult than what they had just come through, which would slow them down. He knew where the next place large enough to camp was, they wouldn't make it there before the rain. He pulled his horse to a stop, surveying the area around him. A small stream ran off to his left, and there was a large enough clearing to stop for the nigh t.

Even if he hadn't heard the horses approaching, he would have known she was nearby.

Blood mates. He turned his horse, waiting. Teague crested the small hill first, followed closely by Satori. She hadn't been lying when she'd said she knew how to ride. She sat on the horse perfectly as it slowed to a canter. Her blonde hair had escaped from its braid and hung all around her head, giving her a slightly disheveled look. His next breath barely reached his lungs. She was beautiful.

The words pushed in again. *Blood mates.* Did he even believe in blood mates? He'd never met anyone in his life who'd been mated like that. Plenty of people who'd fallen in love and married, but none of them were divinely destined.

"Water?" Teague shouted.

Kais lifted his chin in the affirmative as he indicated behind him with a point of his thumb.

Teague slowed his horse further, Satori doing the same. He leaned over and said something to Satori, who nodded.

Kais' entire body grew warmer, though not uncomfortably, as she drew closer. Could a feeling be both unsettling and comforting? If the way he currently felt was any indication, the answer was *yes*. She didn't look at him, not at first. She really did ignore it so well.

Another thought struck him. Maybe she wasn't ignoring it; maybe she really didn't feel anything. Maybe he was the only one drowning in unexplainable sensations when she was around. But the thought was fleeting as a memory entered his mind.

Taking her hand on that dance floor in her home, she'd jumped, recoiled from the shock of his touch. And then there was the nightmare. She had visibly calmed when he'd touched her. She'd also told him she'd slept fine. Had she been lying, or did she have no memory of the dream? He hoped it was the latter. He didn't know what she'd been dreaming of, but she'd been in such distress he hoped she had forgotten, that she didn't have to relive it when she thought of it

She looked up, meeting his eyes for a moment, before darting her gaze away as though she was afraid to be caught staring. Kais didn't suffer the same sort of modesty. He watched, fascinated by the woman who provoked such an intense and odd reaction in him.

A throat cleared beside him, and he turned toward Teague. The look on the other man's face told Kais that he may have called his name once or twice already.

"What?"

An amused expression played across Teague's features, but he didn't address it. He gestured to the ground beneath them. "Camp here?"

Kais surveyed the large clearing again, allowing his roving eyes to rest a beat or two on Satori. "It's big enough." Another rumble of thunder vibrated in the distance. "Better get it set up fast." He focused his attention fully on Satori. "Princess, if you have business, I suggest you take care of it quickly. A storm is stirring, and it doesn't look like it will be a light one."

Satori's gaze ran over the sky above them, her eyes widening at the dark clouds churning low in the air. Without a word, she turned her horse and walked it just inside the tree line before dismounting.

Kais swung off his horse as another man collected the reins from his grasp. "Pitch her tent first, next to mine."

If he was going to have to attend to nightmares again, he had no intention of running across the camp in the rain to do so.

He shoved at his sleeves as he began to pull packs from horses, opening them and laying out poles and canvas for tents.

The men worked double time, and the rain still arrived before the final tents were erected.

CHAPTER TWELVE

SATORI

Satori huddled close to the horse, trying to stay under the thickest leaf cover and remain as dry as possible. The men, including Kais, worked erecting tents. She could admit she was a little impressed that he chose to be in the storm, helping his men, and not in his own tent which had been built first. Henrik would have been hiding to escape the rain and allowing everyone else to do the work for him.

"Princess."

She turned to find Teague, head bowed, eyes squinted against the rain and the collar of his coat turned up, standing in front of her.

"Your tent is ready. You can follow me."

She took half a step and then froze. "What about Luna?"

"The horse will be fine, I assure you." Teague lifted his head, surveying the men nearly finished building the camp. "Clarke!" One of the men looked up at the sound of his name, and Teague gestured for him to come over. "Take care of this horse, please."

Clarke nodded once. "Of course." He took the reins and led the horse away.

Teague glanced at her, his expression asking if she was satisfied. She gave him a nod.

He took her in. "Would you like my coat, Your Highness?"

The offer took her off guard, and as though her body remembered it was raining and cold, she shivered. She should accept, but for some reason she couldn't form the words as she held his gaze. Finally, she shook her head no.

"Very well," Teague said, and he began leading her toward the camp.

They didn't walk far before Teague stopped and turned toward her. "Here, Your Highness."

She recognized the worn grey canvas of the tent she had slept in the night before, but it was in the wrong location. Turning her head slightly to the right was all she needed to do to tell her that much. Kais' much larger tent sat directly beside the one she had been granted use of.

She blinked away some of the rain dripping into her eyes. "I don't think this is correct."

Teague glanced from her tent to Kais' beside it and then back to her. "This is where they were told to put it."

Apprehension filled her at the proximity to the leader's tent. It must have shown on her face because Teague spoke up again, "Your Highness—" He paused, waiting for her to look at him. "You're safe here. You won't be harmed, certainly not by Kais, and being this close to his tent, I would wager *if* any of the other men had designs on your honor previously, this will certainly dissuade them."

The sincerity in Teague's eyes and voice disarmed her. When he used her title, it wasn't in a disrespectful way or mocking. He genuinely paid her honor.

She hadn't interacted with many of the men in the camp—very few of them, actually—but none of them seemed to have ill intentions toward her. What she saw warred in her head with what she knew.

These men were from Evandor. There had been rumblings and rumors for ages that they intended to attempt to overthrow her father and take over. They had her in the palm of their hands, so why weren't they using her? Why would Kais simply return her? She was spectacular leverage. The only child of the reigning King of Dunleigh; she was gold. And yet he said he would return her. Was he lying? Trying to put her at ease? Was this all an elaborate scheme to make her feel comfortable before turning on her? Perhaps Kais hired the kidnappers in the first place? Maybe taking her back was a way for him to get close to her father without all the fanfare of that first ball.

Satori ran a thumb across her palm as her stomach rolled over with all the possibilities, and she found she needed to sit. She swallowed hard at the lump that had formed in her throat and thanked Teague before moving quickly toward the heavy tent flap and ducking inside.

Her breaths came quickly as she sat on the small cot, squeezing her eyes closed, continuing to rub her palm. The more she thought about her current situation the more she believed that Kais was behind it all. She was simply a pawn until the time was right, and then he could kill her and her father. The only thing that comforted her was knowing that Henrik would probably be there as well if he were still alive, and Kais would kill him too.

One thing she knew, she was not safe in this camp among these men. Voices from outside reminded her how thin the barrier between herself and the rest of the camp was. A flimsy cover of canvas. She would give half her kingdom for a door and a lock.

Outside, somewhere behind her tent, a loud crash rang out followed by shouts and curses from several men. The aggressive voices were soon replaced with laughs and loud teasing, but Satori's heart raced again. There were so many of them. Would she even make it home to be killed alongside her father, or would it happen here, in her tent?

She pressed her palms into her face, begging her heart to slow. Losing her wits wouldn't help her at all.

The flap to her tent suddenly flew open, and she yelped. Jumping from her seat on the cot, she recoiled back, tripping over the bed and nearly crashing to the ground.

Kais stood half in, half out of her tent, the large, vicious-looking knife that had been on his hip earlier, held tightly in his fist. His eyes darted wildly around the small space before resting on her. "Are you alright?"

She wrapped her arms around her torso, holding tightly to herself. She couldn't tear her eyes from the blade in his hand.

"Princess!"

The word, like a dog barking, snapped her eyes from the knife to his face. His dark brow was knit tightly over his eyes, his dripping wet hair curled against his forehead.

"Are you alright?" he repeated.

"No!" she screeched the word. "I'm not alright. What are you doing in here?"

Kais seemed to take another look around the space and then his gaze came to rest on her for a moment, then two.

"Apologies, Princess." He seemed to consider his next words before he said, "I thought I heard something. I won't bother you again." The giant knife hissed quietly as he slid it back into the sheath on his belt. He pushed the tent flap to the side, but turned back to her with one foot out the door. "You're safe here."

She pressed her lips together to keep them from quivering. His words did nothing to tamp down her panic. Lies. She was anything but safe.

"Someone will be outside at all times." He paused. "Goodnight, Princess."

He disappeared through the flap, straightening it so it lay perfectly closed.

The breath Satori had been holding stuttered out through her lips as she dropped onto the cot once again. She had to get away. Could she run? She was being guarded. Would she even make it anywhere? She had no skills, nothing to save her from whatever she met in the woods. She wasn't even sure where she was or which way to go. But would taking her chances outside be better than certain, eventual death with these men?

Kais had said someone would be outside at all times. Was that to keep others out or to keep her in? Were his words meant to soothe or threaten?

CHAPTER THIRTEEN

KAIS

Kais ran a thumb slowly, absently, over his bottom lip. His eyes studied the surface of his desk, analyzing a dark knot in the wood, its edges coming to a point. The tent flap opened and closed again, but he ignored whoever had entered.

She'd been alone. He had felt the panic rise, felt it as though it were his own. The feeling of being cornered with nowhere to go, danger imminent. He was sure someone had been in there. But when he had burst in, knife drawn, he'd found her alone, and his presence had not had a reassuring effect.

"I know that look." Teague strolled across the tent to the drink cart and helped himself.

He filled two small glasses with dark liquid, bringing them to Kais' desk and setting one in front of him. The heavy glass thunking onto the wood drew his attention first to the drink and then to Teague who stood, swirling his drink and looking at Kais with a question in his gaze.

"What?"

Teague shrugged, taking a small sip. "You aren't usually this distracted."

Kais acknowledged the other man with a quick lift of his brow. It was the truth. Distraction wasn't really his thing. He was focused. He had to be. He was responsible for a lot of men and a lot of people in general, and he couldn't afford distractions. So what was going on with this girl?

If she was just some pretty female, he could ignore it. Or do something about it and then ignore it. But Satori.... she was different. There was something almost supernatural about the effect her presence had on him. Even now, as he sat in his tent, he could *feel* her, yards away, still scared. Of him.

She had nothing to be afraid of with him. He wished he could make her believe that, if only to give her some peace while she was in the camp, to let her know she was safe. And why couldn't she tell? Why could he feel her emotions as though they were his own, and she couldn't seem to feel anything about him? She only seemed to panic when he was around. If she could feel his sincerity, it would help them both. Of course, charging into her tent with a drawn weapon probably hadn't helped. Maybe her panic drowned out all other senses?

The term *"blood mates"* pushed its way into his consciousness again, and he physically shook his head, trying to rid the idea. Blood mates was a myth, or at least something reserved only for Shala and Miram and maybe one or two other ancient couples. He hadn't heard of the phenomenon in his lifetime or the lifetime of his recent ancestors. And again, it wouldn't be only one-sided. It had to be some sort of cruel punishment from Shala for something he had done. What else could it be?

"Kay?"

His eyes snapped back to Teague, and he realized he'd been lost in his thoughts for far too long. He rolled his eyes at the other man and lifted the glass to his lips, downing the contents. He would need another one of those.

Maybe changing the subject would help. "Everyone settled?"

Teague gave him a look that said he knew that wasn't anywhere close to what was actually on his mind, but he answered anyway. "They are." He set his glass on the edge of the desk, pulled off his coat, and slid into the small chair on the opposite side of Kais. "Some of them are curious about our destination... If we're detouring to take the Princess home or if we're going on."

"We're going on."

That was one thing Kais knew for sure. He would take Satori back to her father and her castle, but not before he finished the task at hand.

Teague nodded once, then appeared to be considering his next words. He pulled in a breath, squinting slightly around another sip of his drink. "And what route will we be taking?"

Kais had known this question was coming; he was surprised it hadn't come sooner. Obviously, the presence of the Princess in their camp had been a distraction to more than just himself. He moved his glass to take another drink and remembered it was empty. He could really use a refill.

As though he read Kais' mind, Teague stood without a sound. Instead of taking Kais' glass to refill it, he opted to retrieve the bottle of alcohol and bring it back to the desk. He filled Kais' glass and topped off his own before retaking his seat, eyes on Kais expectantly.

Kais swirled the drink and met Teague's gaze. The other man's blue eyes bored into his own. He would have preferred not to answer while looking him in the eye, but that seemed cowardly.

"We're taking the crossing."

To his credit, Teague's reaction was nonexistent. He simply stared back for a moment before he spoke, "It's not going to sit well with some of the men."

Some of the men. Kais knew very well it would be more than some of the men who would take issue with his choice. It was a dangerous game to play, pitting men against the river. But it was necessary.

"Taking the crossing will shave days, a week or more, off our journey. The faster we get to Burnell, the faster we can get the Princess back to her home."

And he needed to get the Princess back. He needed her away, out of his camp, and not having nervous breakdowns next door to his tent that kept him awake at night.

Teague placed his glass on the desk and slid it away from the edge. "At the expense of lives?"

"It doesn't have to be at the expense of lives. People cross all the time without dying." The words tasted bitter even as he spoke them.

It was dangerous, extremely dangerous. But there were people who needed him and he had no intention of letting them down. If he chose to take the Princess home first, he might not have the opportunity to get to Burnell before the weather turned.

Teague's head fell back slightly as his eyebrows climbed up his forehead. He opened his mouth as though he were about to speak.

Kais raised a hand, halting the other man's speech. "Look, spread the word. Anyone who has a problem with it and would like to voice their opinion you can bring by in the morning. I'm tired, and I don't want to do this tonight anymore."

Teague's eyes ran over Kais where he sat. He could only imagine what he must look like, slouched back into his seat, cradling his second glass of liquor. He could only hope he looked better than he felt, because he felt like he was coming apart at the seams.

He still had men whom he was responsible for. He still had a task ahead of him and the responsibility to keep his people alive in the interim. And he still had *her*. Next door.

He could still feel her, was still aware of her presence. There was a warmth around him that wasn't cast by the fire. But there was also an elevated heart rate and the feeling of being wound up and wound up until you were sure you were just about to snap. And on top of all that, there was his desire to help her. When he looked at her, he wanted nothing more than to convince her she truly was safe. He wanted her to believe him when he said he had no intention to harm her, that he would never hurt her, and she had nothing to be afraid of. He was a person in chaos.

"Try to get some rest," Teague said, rising from his seat, concern evident in his eyes and voice. "I'll make sure someone watches her."

Kais only nodded his thanks. He didn't move from his spot for at least ten minutes after Teague had left. He was tired and easily could have dropped into bed and passed out, but he was waiting.

Another five or so minutes passed before someone slapped the outside of his tent flap, "General?"

Finally.

Kais sat up straighter. "Come in."

The man stepped through the flap, a paper-wrapped package tied with twine in his hands.

"Sir, I got everything you asked." He placed the bundle on the desk in front of Kais. "I appreciated the assignment as well, sir."

Kais pulled his gaze from the parcel to look at the other man. "Why's that, Sawyer?"

A half smile curved Sawyer's lips. "Well, sir, I was off shopping for you and missed the opportunity to set up camp in the rain."

Kais laughed once. "I suppose shopping is certainly preferable to that."

"Yes, sir." Sawyer shifted on his feet. "If there's nothing else, sir? I'd like to find a meal before I turn in if I can."

"Of course." Kais stood, straightening his shirt. "Thank you for this. If you would do one more thing, and then you're free for the evening."

"Of course, sir." Sawyer clasped his hands behind his back, standing a bit straighter. "What can I do for you, sir?"

Kais nodded toward the package. "Take that next door and leave it with the Princess, please."

Kais would have taken it himself if his last meeting with her hadn't gone so poorly. He didn't expect she wanted to see him again anytime soon.

"Of course, sir," Sawyer said with a nod as he stepped up and reclaimed the parcel. "I'll leave it there right now. Is there anything you'd like me to tell her?"

He gave a slight shake of his head. "Only that we thought she might like a change of clothes."

"Certainly, sir."

"Thank you, Sawyer. Have a good night, you're dismissed."

"Thank you, sir." Sawyer stepped toward the door. "Good night, sir."

And then he was gone, leaving Kais alone and finally able to crawl into his bed. Sleep, unlike he expected, did not come. Instead, he lay, staring at the canvas, kept awake by the flutter of what felt like a second heartbeat inside him.

CHAPTER FOURTEEN

SATORI

Voices, nickering horses, clanging dishes, a loud, boisterous laugh followed by a chorus of amused groans. Satori pulled the pillow up around her ears, scrunching her eyes and face. How did anyone get any sleep in a camp full of soldiers? It was constantly noisy. It was morning, but it was so early. She had never been one to sleep in late, but she also wasn't awake at the crack of the dawn's light. It seemed the entire camp was up before dawn, and felt it was their duty to make enough noise to wake the sun itself.

She blew out a huffed breath and opened her eyes, letting the pillow relax back into the cot. She sat up and almost immediately the feeling of dread and danger from the previous night settled back on her. She closed her eyes and drew in a slow stream of air, but when she let it out, it stuttered from her lips. She swallowed deeply. This was ridiculous. She couldn't exist in this camp full of her enemies if she was going to be on the edge of a breakdown at all times. They wouldn't hurt her until they delivered her back to her father. She was almost sure of that. Certainly, they wouldn't kill her. She felt that if they harmed her, her father wouldn't trust them to grant them an audience. No, it would be far wiser for them to keep her safe and deliver her unharmed. Then the king would see them as saviors and welcome them into his home, where he would be more vu lnerable.

Satori shook her head again, attempting to rid her mind of the intrusive thoughts. Today. She needed to get through today. Then she would worry about tomorrow. When she looked up, her eyes fell on a paper-wrapped parcel, tied with twine. Unease flooded her again as her eyes ran around the small space. There was, of course, nowhere for anyone to hide; it was only the thought that someone had been in her tent while she'd slept and she hadn't known.

She stood and moved slowly to the package, hesitant to touch it. Finally, she stopped, rolling her eyes at herself. This package wasn't going to bite her. She reached out, hooking her finger through the twine, and carried it back to her cot. She sat and pulled at the ends until the bow unraveled and the strings slackened. Tearing the paper, the package fell open to reveal its contents.

Her brow creased. Clothes? A light olive green shirt, and she lifted the heavier brown material—a pair of pants, clearly tailored for a woman. They matched her corset perfectly and the size looked right. Where had they come from? Was there a woman her size in the camp they had swiped these from? They didn't look worn or damaged. In fact, they almost looked new.

It took Satori less than thirty seconds to decide she would wear the items. She didn't particularly want to accept gifts from her current captors, but the dress she was in had seen a lot of trouble in the past couple of days and was currently sporting several rips and tears.

She pulled the dress over her head and stepped into the pants. They did indeed fit her, and fit her well. The material was soft on her skin, and she ran a hand lightly over where it fit to her thigh. She pulled the light green shirt over her head and laced her corset over top of it. She was amazed how well the trousers matched the corset. She didn't allow herself to dwell on that fact for too long—someone had brought these into her tent.

A shiver ran down her spine. One of them had been in her tent while she was sleeping. From now on, for as long as she was stuck in this camp, she intended to put something in front of the flap. At least if someone came in while she slept, she would know it when they tripped.

She surveyed the small area, looking for something, anything, she could place at the door to alert her of an intruder. Her eyes fell upon the pitcher of water, and she moved to pick it up when raised voices caught her attention. This was more than joking between comrades, more than just a spirited conversation. She stopped moving and turned her ear toward the voices. They were coming from the direction of Kais' tent.

"Mason!" Teague's voice barked out the name in a reprimand. "Remember who you're speaking to."

"No, no, that's why we're here. I invited them to voice their concerns." Kais' unmistakable, deep accented voice raised the hairs on her arms. A stupid reaction she hated.

"What good is voicing our opinion if it's going to be ignored?" This was another voice that she didn't recognize.

What were they arguing about? She assumed it was important to make Kais' men feel justified in raising their voices to their leader. The voices grew softer, but her curiosity did not ebb with them. She moved to the tent flap, pushing it aside slightly to peek out. She saw no one. She slipped out of the tent.

She was greeted by a surprising chill, one her tent had managed to keep out, and a light frost coating the ground. She wrapped her arms around herself as she moved on quiet feet in the direction of the voices.

CHAPTER FIFTEEN

KAIS

Kais' hands rested on his hips as he listened to a few of his men sharing their thoughts. But it was beginning to get carried away now. Yes, he wanted opinions, but he was ultimately still in charge, and it was his choice. "We are—"

The hairs on the back of his neck rose, every bit of his skin tingling, at the same time the warmth that was becoming so familiar slid over him.

He held up a hand and all voices around him ceased. "Forgive me, gentlemen, we'll have to resume this at a later time. "He stepped around the edge of the tent, knowing exactly what he would find. "Princess?"

She froze mid-step, looking like a deer caught in the path of an arrow. Her eyes, dark amber rimmed in dark lashes, were wide. But it was her clothes that he noticed. She wore them. He actually hadn't expected her to.

"The clothes fit, I see." They more than fit. They hugged her curves like they were tailor-made for her, and Kais inhaled deeply.

If she noticed his extra concentration, she didn't show it, she only blinked rapidly a few times and then glanced down at her outfit. "Yes. They were in my tent. Did you—"

"No," he cut her off.

He wanted to be perfectly clear, wanted her to understand that he had not been in her tent without her knowledge. Sawyer had delivered the clothes and, apparently, she had been asleep when he had left them.

"One of the other men did. I apologize, I didn't realize you hadn't been awake."

She glanced away before asking, "Did you get them from someone in the camp?"

He laughed. "Not in my camp."

There were very few women in his camp, and none that came even close to sharing the dimensions of the one before him.

"Where did they come from?"

"They were purchased for you."

Couldn't she tell that they were new? He could see from where he stood that they were fresh clothes, not worn through by the day-to-day life in the camp.

"Purchased?" She looked down at herself and back to him. "For me?"

He nodded once.

"Why?"

"Well, your dress looked a bit worse for wear and we still have some traveling to do yet. I thought this," he gestured toward her, "might be a bit more appropriate."

Her eyes fell to her clothes and then ran across the ground at her feet. Frustration burned through him, and he knew it was hers.

Finally, she looked back at him. "Thank you."

That was it? She'd been fighting through her frustration until she could work up the words, "thank you"?

He laughed once. "You're welcome, Princess."

Her frustrated expression quickly turned to annoyance. Clearly she didn't enjoy being laughed at, even though he wasn't strictly laughing at her.

She turned a glare on him. "Why are your men mad at you?"

The smile on Kais' face evaporated. He knew she'd been listening. He'd felt her attention, her presence, as though she had been beside him. He bit down on his bottom lip, slowly pushing it back out through his teeth as he studied her.

"They're mad because we're taking the crossing. They think we should take Carter's Pass."

"I've heard of the crossing." Her face slackened. "It's large and rather dangerous, is it not?"

He didn't answer her right away. Not as her words and the reality of their situation settled further still onto his shoulders. He would be taking not only his men through the crossing, but Satori as well. It wasn't fair to her. She'd been kidnapped and forced from one danger to another, and now he was taking her to the next.

He opened his mouth and closed it again, blowing all his air out through his nose before he tried again. "It's faster."

"Why are you in such a hurry?"

"I'm delivering something." Never mind that half of his cargo had been traded off for her.

"Something?" Satori said, as though she were waiting for him to elaborate. He didn't. "Weapons?"

Did she really believe a man of his position spent his days crossing massive, dangerous bodies of water to smuggle weapons?

"You think I'm delivering weapons? I'm not a smuggler, Princess."

She raised a hand slightly, waving him off. "Pardon? It was only a question."

He took half a second to compose himself. Had she really thought that, or was she just trying to provoke him? And why did he care what she thought? Time to change the subject.

"Breakfast?"

She gave him a wary look, and the feeling of mistrust smacked him.

"It's only breakfast, Princess. There are no nefarious schemes at work."

Her brows dipped toward her nose, suspicion clouding her gaze. How was it that he could sense her emotions so easily, and she couldn't seem to feel his?

"Sausage, oatmeal..."

Her brow smoothed out, and she nodded. He held out a hand in invitation for her to join him, and they began walking toward the food tent.

"How old are you?" Satori asked.

He looked down at her, surprised by her question. But she didn't look at him. He was met with the sight of the top of her golden-blonde hair.

"I'm thirty. Dare I ask how old you are, Princess?"

"I'm twenty-three."

It was nearly unheard of for a Princess to reach that age and still remain single. Other countries were selling their daughters off at the age of sixteen or younger in order to form alliances.

"Don't take this the wrong way, but aren't you a bit old to still be unwed? No one's caught your eye, Princess?"

His chest tightened with the thought. His mother used to tell him not to ask questions that he didn't truly want to know the answers to. But why wouldn't he want to know the answer to this one? She was nothing to him, only a nuisance at this point. That's what he told himself, and then he glanced down at the top of her head, and his chest tightened further. He needed to get his head on straight. Teague was right, he was too distracted.

"My eye has nothing to do with it." A scoff edged Satori's words. "I have no say in the matter. I'm a bargaining chip. I'm currently on the table for two separate countries."

An unmistakable and sudden spike of anger hit him and he physically coughed when Satori's head shot up, her eyes meeting his with a confused look. She must have felt that one.

Thankfully they had arrived at the tent with the food. Kais raised a hand, holding two fingers up. Jed, their cook, was quick to grab and fill two plates.

Kais gestured to a small table set with two chairs. "You're welcome to join me here. Or, if you'd like, I'll carry your plate back to your tent for you."

She pulled in a deep breath as her eyes moved between him and the table. "I'll eat here, no need to carry it back. Thank you."

Kais held the back of the chair as she seated herself before he took the opposite seat. In moments, Jed delivered two plates.

"Thank you, Jed."

"Thank you," Satori echoed.

Jed only nodded before leaving them alone again.

"What do you mean you're on the table for two countries?" Kais speared a bite of sausage with more force than he intended, and his fork scraped across the plate with an unpleasant sound.

She flinched slightly before she looked up at him. Their eyes met, and a spark seemed to spring between them. Satori's eyes widened slightly for a moment as though she felt it as well. She lowered her gaze to her plate and spooned a bit of oatmeal in her mouth, taking her time swallowing.

"Deshan's ruler is a grey-haired, bearded man with a wrinkled face and hands. He is sixty-seven years old and has been petitioning my father for my hand for three months now."

Kais' stomach turned, immediate visions of those wrinkled hands pawing at Satori's skin dancing in his mind.

"The other is Apolonia. Their ruler is a twelve-year-old boy who is run by his advisors. They've been advising him to take a wife. Apparently, there are no prospects of his age, only me." With those words, she looked up. "And if I refuse them, my only other option is . . ."

She paused and swallowed thickly, and Kais was struck with a sudden fear. Was it hers? His?

When he spoke, the word was choked, and he had to clear his throat and repeat it. "What?"

"My father seems to think it would be best if I chose Henrik, his advisor, to marry."

"And which is your choice?"

Her gaze snapped to his. "None of them. I would rather remain unwed than marry any of them. Especially . . ."

Again, her words halted, and the fear hit Kais' chest. It was hers, not his. He remembered the night they had met and danced. That advisor had tried to cut in, but she had tensed, and Kais refused. And when he gave her the option of going back to him she chose instead to dance with Kais, her perceived enemy, rather than move into that man's arms.

Without thinking, Kais spoke, his gaze narrowed, his words slow and clear, "What did he do?"

CHAPTER SIXTEEN

SATORI

Her stomach turned. She had taken one bite of sausage and it was now threatening to reappear. Why would Kais think Henrik had *done* anything? She had to get her features and self under control.

She pulled herself together and looked him in the eye, ignoring the jolt his gaze sent through her. "What are you talking about?"

Kais' jaw clenched as irritation and anger seemed to roll off of him. She felt them so strongly, like they were her own emotions.

"This advisor, will you choose him?"

Satori pressed her lips together, though she felt the color drain from her face. She would never, never choose Henrik. She would die first.

"I haven't decided. I have options, as you know."

She needed to change the subject. Whatever was rolling off of Kais was disconcerting, to say the least. Mildly frightening, to say more.

"So, you're taking the crossing. Why is it that you're in so much of a hurry as to ignore your men's warnings?"

Kais sat slowly back in his chair, placing his fork neatly on the edge of his plate. Clearly he wasn't eager to revisit the subject, but she had to stop thinking about Henrik. A shudder passed through her and he leaned forward slightly, his eyes sharpening.

Please, please, she silently begged. *Please, I need to talk about something else.*

Kais relaxed back into his seat again. "I already told you, I have something to deliver."

His voice had lost its edge and regained a conversational tone, but she thought she still felt a tension in him. Whether in his words or his posture, she couldn't tell, but it was there.

"When?"

"We'll stay one more night here and then pack up in the morning." He took a sip of the water that the cook, Jed, had delivered. "Tomorrow we'll stop for the night but without tents."

No tents? She looked up to see if she'd heard him correctly.

He answered her unspoken question, "It's only one night and not worth the trouble. We sleep on the ground."

The prospect was certainly not appealing to her. She didn't even like the tents.

"Apologies. We don't usually have a Princess along with us."

"Clearly." She took a moment to breathe, resigning herself to sleeping *on the ground.* "So, what are you delivering? You never told me."

"Supplies." He swirled his glass but didn't drink. "There's a village up above the Vardan. Winter arrives earlier there and fiercer. I'm taking them some extra things to see them through."

Winter supplies. He'd traded winter supplies for her on the road. "The supplies that you traded to those men, for me, they were for this village."

His chin dipped slightly, his gaze leveling on her. "They were."

Guilt hit her. She was rescued at the expense of someone's protection for the winter.

"There's still plenty for the village," Kais assured her, once again seemingly reading her thoughts. "As long as I can get them there before the weather hits."

"And that's why you're taking the crossing."

"Yes."

She took a moment to study him. His features were dark, his frame lean but muscular. But in his eyes sat a weight. It could just be the responsibility of all these men, but there could be more. Was there someone special in this village? Was it *his* village? No doubt there were a number of towns along the way where he could dump off goods and supplies and appease his conscience.

Finally, after the silence had stretched on for a beat too long, Kais spoke, "Well, Princess, forgive me, but I must go." He stood, taking a final drink of the water and placing the glass back on the table. "There are things to see to."

He paused as he appeared to be having a silent conversation with himself. His head dipped and his tongue ran over his teeth. Finally, he looked back up at her, seeming to have come to a decision.

He cleared his throat slightly. "Teague and I are going into the small town close by. If you're interested in getting away from the camp, you're welcome to join us. I promise you'll be safe."

His sincerity washed over her, at odds with her own mistrust of the man. Though, for some reason, she did trust Teague, and the thought of being alone in the camp without him there made her uneasy.

"Thank you."

Kais' eyes widened slightly at her words, but he quickly schooled his features. If it weren't for the fact that she could feel his surprise, she might have thought she had imagined it.

"Feel free to take your time." He indicated to her plate, though she was almost finished.

Satori scooped the last bite of oatmeal from the bowl and picked up the final sausage link. "I'm through."

The look Kais gave her was mildly amused, and she offered him a slight shrug as she stood. "Why are you going into town?"

She didn't mean to pry, but he was giving her the strangest look and she wanted to divert the attention.

Kais began walking and Satori followed. "We're trading some of our older horses for fresh ones, also picking up a few extra supplies. I would offer to let you take Luna but I've seen you ride. I have no doubt you can handle an unfamiliar horse or two."

The comment gave her a warm feeling in her chest. It was nice to be praised for something she did well, but she schooled her features, refusing to let it show. Though, as she held Kais' gaze and his eyes flitted over her face, before his features softened, she was fairly certain he already knew the effect his words had. *Blast this connection to Helias.*

Kais let out a laugh and tried to cover it with a cough, but because Satori was desperate for the moment to pass, she did not call him out.

"Saddle another horse." Kais' shouted words startled Satori out of her thoughts and she looked up to find they were approaching Teague. She noticed right away the absence of his long coat.

Teague looked up from where he stood with a group of horses. "Princess, will you be joining us?"

"I suppose I am." She stepped up to one of the horses, rubbing its face softly. The horse responded with a soft whinny.

"I guess you can ride that one." Kais smiled. "Just don't get too attached."

Satori looked around, Kais had disappeared somewhere. "Why does he do this himself? Surely he has men who could do this task."

Teague tossed a blanket on the horse's back and then lifted the saddle on top of it. "He likes to go into the towns and see things for himself when he gets the chance." She didn't miss the surreptitious look Teague stole in her direction as he buckled the saddles. "The taxes hit some towns harder than others."

Taxes? This town must be very poor indeed to have a problem with the taxes. Last she'd known, her father's taxes were more than fair. Though she had to admit, she didn't actually know much about the fiscal state of the country. She suspected Henrik had something to do with that. She voiced none of her thoughts, though, choosing instead to see for herself.

Warmth flowed over her and she turned to find Kais approaching with what looked like a blanket flung over his arm.

"I found a cloak for you. It'll keep you warm and you can wear the hood if you'd like. I would hate for someone to recognize you and kidnap you again," Kais spoke as Teague stepped up beside him and took one of the cloaks from his arm so that Kais could hold the other one out for Satori.

Unease brushed through her again. Was he trying to keep her safe or keep her to himself should any of her father's men be around?

Kais' brow dipped slightly as he stood, holding out the cloak and waiting. Something like sadness hit her before he spoke again, "You're safe here, Princess. Teague will be there as well."

Did Kais know she felt the most secure with Teague? If he could feel things the same as she did, he was most likely aware of that fact. She pulled in a breath and stepped toward him, turning so he could rest the cloak over her shoulders. She reached up and pulled it close, securing the clasp.

Teague handed the other cloak back to Kais and he flung the dark fabric around and over his own shoulders, fastening it at his collar. The cloak replaced the coat he normally wore.

He moved to his horse, patting it gently on the shoulder. "Ready when you are."

Teague handed a set of reins to Satori and waited as she mounted the horse before he climbed onto his own. Kais seated himself atop his and they began moving. A few of the men called out to them as they passed, five more riderless horses following along behind them.

They rode in silence for much of the journey, horses' hooves crunching on fallen leaves the only sound. Then Satori started to see what looked like little rugged huts set up haphazardly among the trees.

"There are more than last time." Teague's quiet observation drew her attention.

"It's worse." Kais' answer was laced with anger that Satori thought she would have picked up even if she couldn't feel it dripping off him.

"What's worse?"

She was now noticing people around. They were thin and dirty, some eyeing their small group with unease, others with clear expectation. Some even came to the side of the road, little children by their sides with their hands outstretched.

Teague reached into a pouch and drew out some coins, tossing them at the people who scrambled to scoop up the scattered funds. Kais did something similar, although he tossed small pouches of what looked like dried meats and nuts.

They were begging.

She nudged her horse until she was nearly even with Teague and Kais. "Why do they live out here and starve when the town is right there?"

Kais glanced at her before exchanging a look with Teague.

"They don't have money to purchase food," Teague answered.

"Couldn't they find work to support their families? To find homes that aren't scraps of fabric?" The scene around her made her heart ache. No one, especially not children, should live like this.

"Many of them have jobs," Kais spoke up, though he didn't look at her. "But they're taxed so heavily there's little left to feed their families. Even in the towns, the conditions aren't much better. Often they have homes only because they're inherited, or multiple families share the rent, which is also exorbitant."

"Taxes?"

They hadn't crossed into the neighboring country. These were her father's people. Her people. She had no idea her father was asking so much of them. Why would he overtax the people? She felt sick to her stomach at the sight. An irrational desire to hide her face hit her. Even though these people didn't know who she was, she was still ashamed that this was happening with her father's approval. She would speak with him as soon as she made it home. She would make this right.

A throat cleared in front of her, and she looked up to find both men watching her, waiting expectantly. She nudged her horse to follow them, and they continued on.

Inside the town limits, things were not much better. Some people still begged for food along the streets, and at one point, she saw a group of about five children passing a small loaf of bread between them, tearing off the smallest bites. Emotion clogged her throat at the sight.

She followed Kais and Teague to what looked like a stable and dismounted when they did. Teague came around and took the reins of her horse from her hands.

He glanced around once before he spoke quietly, "We're going to be here for a bit. Feel free to look around, Princess. There are small stands with wares just down this road." He indicated with his chin.

She had no money but didn't mind having a look around. She pulled her cloak further around her and moved along the street in the direction that Teague had suggested. Homes still looked rough, people standing in front of carts full of wares looked desperate. She wished she had coins to purchase things. There were scarves, mittens, and blankets at one cart. Another held jarred foods of all kinds. Yet another cart was laden with small carved animals and dishes. It was all lovely, really.

She made her way along the lines of carts, inspecting the wares. She was nearly at the end of the line, next to what looked like an inn or a pub with seating inside and out, when she overheard the conversation.

"How are we supposed to find this Princess if we don't even know what she looks like?" The man dropped into a chair, bringing his large tankard down heavily on the table in front of him.

Satori's heart skipped and sped at the man's words. *Princess.* She continued her perusal of the wares at the small stand in front of her but she no longer saw anything, her entire focus now on the conversation happening behind her.

"We have a description." Another man seated himself across the table from the first.

The first man made an unimpressed huffing sound. "Blonde, thin, short, and beautiful? The description fits half of the women we see. Could be that one, or that one, or that one."

Satori didn't dare turn to see who the man had indicated, though she did pull her hood a bit closer around her face. Then another thought hit her. Were these men soldiers sent by her father? Should she make herself known to them? She could be that much closer to home. As carefully as she could, she turned her head just enough to get a glance at the men behind her. Not soldiers. They wore no uniform nor any identifying markers of any kind. Why would her father send these men when he had guards to do this work?

"It could be anyone but I don't want to chance taking the wrong girl back to that Duke. He seemed the type to get upset at those kinds of mistakes."

Duke. Henrik. Satori worked to swallow the lump that had formed in her throat and nearly choked on it. Her hands began to shake, and she clasped them together. Henrik had sent these men to find her, not her father.

"I don't know about that. I mean, I know he wants the Princess, but he also seems the type not to turn away any pretty piece of flesh." The man followed his comment with a laugh, making Satori's skin crawl.

"Or we could just bypass him and take her to the King. He's bound to pay better than a Duke." The man's tankard clanked back onto the table.

"Now, wait a minute. Don't get any ideas," the second man said. "He made it perfectly clear that if we found her, we were to deliver her to no one but him." A pause as the man took a drink and added the next thought quietly, "And Miram save her when he gets his hands on her."

A sob threatened to punch out of her throat, and she choked it back down. She had to get away from them before they recognized her. She was about to turn when a hand caught hold of the back of her hood and yanked, pulling it from her head and taking a few of her hairs with it.

"Look at this, Simon." It was one of the men whose conversation she had heard. "Blonde, thin, short, and beautiful."

"Get your hands off me." Satori tried to pull out of his grasp, but his grip tightened as he pulled her closer, wrapping his free hand around her arm. She pulled again. "Let go of me!"

"I'm afraid not, you see, we're looking for someone who looks just like you." A sneer appeared on Simon's face.

Further panic took hold in Satori's chest. She wanted to be back with her father, but these men had said they would take her to Henrik. She couldn't go to him.

"Excuse me. I respectfully request you remove your hands from my wife."

The blade of a sword accompanied the voice behind her as it appeared out of the corner of her field of vision, pointed directly at the man who held her. Her eyes widened as relief poured through her.

CHAPTER SEVENTEEN

KAIS

"Wife?" One of the men stepped back, hands raised, away from the reach of the sword's blade. "Apologies sir, we thought she was someone else. Rafe, let her go."

The man with his hands on Satori released her, and she fled his grasp directly into Teague's waiting arms.

Kais let out the breath he had been holding. Relief poured through him, his own as well as Satori's. The men backed off and Teague wrapped both arms around Satori as she buried her face in his tunic.

Kais swallowed the bitter taste in the back of his throat. It was ridiculous to feel any sort of jealousy at Teague for saving her, especially when Kais had been the one to send him to do it.

He and Teague had been bargaining for horses when he'd felt her sudden spike of fear. He'd barely had time to shout for Teague, and by the time they found her, that man was already reaching out to take her. Panic hit Kais—his own—and he barely held himself from flying to her side. But she still didn't trust him. She was afraid of the strange men, but was she still afraid of him, too? He had only to motion to Teague, and the other man was moving.

Kais approached Teague, who was still holding Satori. Even from his place, he could see that she was trembling. He could feel the thunder of her heart.

"They're gone, Satori," Teague soothed, running a palm over her back. "You're safe."

Satori turned her head in Teague's arms and met Kais' eyes. Her voice was so quiet when she spoke, "They weren't taking me back to my father."

Kais had assumed as much. Even if they had told her they were taking her home, she was intelligent enough to know men lie.

"They're not taking you anywhere, but we will. I promise we'll get you home. Safely."

He wished there was some way he could infuse his words with sincerity. She didn't trust him, and that didn't surprise him. Not really. What *did* surprise him was that if she could sense him the way he sensed her, why didn't she believe him?

Teague looked at him with a question in his eyes.

She was safe. Kais allowed himself one full, deep breath before he spoke, "Alright then. We should get back to the horses so we can get back to camp."

Satori nodded, fully disentangling herself from Teague's hold and looking him in the eye. "Thank you."

"Kais is the one who knew you were in trouble. I told you, you're safe with us."

She nodded again at Teague's words as confusion pooled inside her.

Teague extended an arm toward her and a small mischievous smile, unique to Teague, turned up the corner of his mouth. "Wife?"

She laughed, and the sound danced straight into Kais' chest. Her face lit up as she threaded her arm into Teague's, and they began to walk back toward the horses. Kais let out a sigh. What was this woman doing to him?

CHAPTER EIGHTEEN

SATORI

They had returned to the camp, and with nothing else to do, Satori wandered through the collection of tents, taking in the bustle of lives. The men were occupied with various tasks, sharpening swords, washing horses and saddles, and repairing clothes, tents, or shoes. Some sparred with each other, practicing their skills with blades and even fists.

She came across a group who seemed to be taking inventory of several wagons and paused when she heard their conversation. She ducked behind a wagon to listen without being seen.

"He gave up a lot for that Princess, blankets especially. But there's still a decent amount here. It should be helpful," one man said, marking some numbers onto a piece of paper.

"For sure. He gave them far more than I expected he would," another answered. "Princess, indeed. Think he's hoping for some *gratitude?*"

The way the man said the word made Satori's skin crawl.

"From the King or the girl?" the other man asked.

"I don't think Kais' predilection runs in favor of kings."

Both men laughed, and Satori moved away, not wanting to hear any more of their vulgar discussions. Did they really believe Kais had saved her just to get a chance to sleep with her? If he had, he was sorely mistaken. He could just be one more suitor on the list of men that were horrible for her.

She weaved around a few more tents, growing bored.

What now? Perhaps she could find Teague and see if there was a book available somewhere she could read? She stopped when she spotted some berries off to the side of where she walked. They were small, deep red berries with a black smoky sort of design running through the flesh. Her mouth watered. She didn't know whether they were safe to eat but decided to pick some, just in case. She could ask someone.

She had gathered a handful when the sound of metal dishes clattering to the dirt, and a short groan, stalled her movements.

Afraid someone might be injured, she rushed in the direction of the sound. There, on his knees, an older man gathered a tin cup and saucer from where they had fallen. His skin was tanned and wrinkled, and he appeared much older than the rest of the men she had seen around the camp.

She moved to where the cup had fallen and retrieved it, handing it back to him. He looked up and offered her a warm smile that wrinkled the corners of his eyes.

"Thank you, Princess." His movements were shaky as he climbed to his feet, and when he stood he was still hunched over a bit. "I was just getting some water so I can get back to these tents before I lose the light." His eyes found the pile of berries that she had dropped in her haste to help him. "Best not eat those. Helian Currant."

That sounded ominous. "Helian?"

The man brushed off the knees of his pants. "We call them compulsion berries. You eat those, you'll do whatever I tell you. With a smile. Wicked little things. Legend says once they only grew in Helias, but now they're here."

Satori shuddered, glad she hadn't tasted them. The idea of losing that control to another person made her blood run cold. She glanced at the pile of fabric the man had indicated.

"What are you doing with the tents?" Satori asked.

"Mending tears. These saw a storm and were damaged. Some of the men are bunking together, and I know they'd like their own spaces back. So, for the men that are busy with other things, I mend their tents. Gives me something to do."

He moved to a fallen log that it seemed he had turned into a makeshift sewing area. Beside it sat a basket of supplies, and on the opposite side, masses of canvas lay piled up.

"That looks like a lot of work," Satori said, gesturing to the tent canvas. "Would you like some help?"

The man's head shot up, eyes wide. "Oh, no, Princess. No, thank you. I can manage."

Satori smiled. "Please, sir, I may not be well equipped to hunt and fight, but if there's one thing I can do, it's sew. Please allow me to help, it will give *me* something to do. And anyway, I owe you for saving me from the berries."

"Very well, Princess."

The man slid down so she could sit next to him. He picked up the basket of supplies at his feet, chose a large needle, larger than any Satori had ever seen, and deftly guided the sturdy thread through the eye. He handed the needle to her and pulled one of the large pieces of canvas from the pile. Turning it over and over until he found the hole, he handed that to her as well.

"Any special stitches I should know?" she asked as she positioned the fabric on her lap.

"We're not picky here, Princess. Just close the hole." He threaded his own needle and lifted another portion of canvas into his lap.

There was silence for a bit while they both worked before Satori decided to ask some questions. "How long have you been here?"

"I've been around since Kais was small. Before he ever thought about leading these men." The man stabbed the needle through the fabric, pulling the thick thread through.

Satori was careful not to look at the man when she asked the next question. "Do you enjoy working for Kais?"

The older man paused his work to look Satori in the eye. "There are a lot of stories around about Kais and these men. But I'll tell you the truth now, and my words are sincere. I've known many men in my life, few of them, if any, are of a better breed than Kais. He's a natural leader, and he loves the men, and he loves his people. If you make a friend of that man, he will be loyal to the very last breath."

His words were certainly in opposition to what she'd heard about the *barbarians* living in Evandor. Though, what she'd seen since she'd met him, even at the castle, was also in opposition to what she'd heard. But was that real, or was that what her body, and whatever reaction he caused, wanted her to see?

"Are you concerned about his decision to take the crossing?"

She was careful to keep her tone neutral. She wanted to know this man's sincere opinion, not what he thought she needed to hear.

"The crossing is the only way to get to Burnell before winter sets in. He has good reason to get there, and if he believes we can do it, we can do it." He reached over and patted Satori on her hand. "Don't fear, Princess."

"What's your name?"

The man picked up his needle again. "They call me Bram, Princess."

She smiled at him. "It's a pleasure to meet you, Bram. Please call me Satori."

Bram was fun and full of information that he wasn't shy to share. By the end of the work day, they had repaired four out of five tents, and Satori had learned a wealth of information about Kais and his men.

Somewhere in the camp a gong rang out, signaling dinner was ready, and Satori was grateful to see Bram lay down his work and begin to pack up the supplies.

She stood and stretched. "Thank you for allowing me to help you with this."

Bram stood. "Thank you, Princess, for stopping to help an old man."

She smiled. "Satori, please. And it was my pleasure."

Bram returned her smile and held out his arm so Satori hooked hers into the crook of his elbow, and together they walked to the food tent. When they arrived, there was already a line, but the men immediately parted for Bram, their respect for him clear.

"See how they move to allow a Princess to the front?" Bram tightened his grip on her arm for emphasis.

"I'm sure these men are moving for you, not me."

She eyed the gathered men, no doubt in her mind that she was correct. Especially considering the looks she sometimes caught them sending her direction, mistrust and sometimes dislike clear in their eyes.

Then he was there. She straightened, looking up, but didn't see him. Bram gave her a quizzical glance which she ignored. He must have been behind her, but he was there, she was certain. Warmth dripped over her, and after the dampness of the log, it wasn't entirely unwelcome.

"Princess." The deep baritone of his voice penetrated into her, and the hair along her arms and neck stood on end. "Bram."

"General." Bram turned, causing Satori to turn as well as he responded with the slightest tip of his chin. "The Princess and I repaired four of those tents today."

Kais' eyes drifted over Satori before returning to Bram. "I'm sure the men will be pleased to hear that. I've heard nothing but complaining from Asher and Hunter for days now. They're no use to me like that."

Bram laughed, and Satori couldn't help but smile at the sound. When her eyes moved to Kais, she found him watching her, studying her face like he was working out a dilemma, though the look was soft and not harsh. She blinked and looked away, unwilling to hold his deep brown gaze.

"Princess, you had a hand in this work as well?"

Before Satori could say anything, Bram spoke up, "She's quite handy with a needle, this one. Her stitches were better than mine. Though that may be due to her young hands."

Kais looked at her hands, and even more heat seemed to radiate from him. She fought the urge to clasp her fingers behind her back.

"You sew, Princess?"

"I may not have knowledge of swords or," she nodded at the whip coiled at Kais' waist, "whatever *that* is. But I was certainly taught to sew. Apparently, it is a necessity for young ladies."

Kais watched her for a moment before dropping a hand to his waist and popping the snap that secured his whip to his belt. "This is a whip."

He held the coil out to her, and she disentangled herself from Bram's arm to accept the braided leather. It was heavier than she expected, and she held it closer to examine it. It was just a long strip of braided leather. How was this efficient at any sort of self-defense or offense?

"It can be quite handy," Kais answered the thoughts that must have been apparent on her face.

She handed it back to him. "It doesn't look very useful."

Bram laughed again. "You should have him show you. It's quite amazing. I've never seen anyone wield a whip the way the General does. I think he could remove a hand in one move and rescue a kitten in the next."

Kais chuckled deeply as he reattached the whip to his hip, and the sound rushed around inside Satori. "I'm not sure that's accurate, but I could show you if you really are curious."

Bram shook his head and leaned in toward Satori. "Don't let him act modest; he is proficient."

Sensing her turn to speak but not knowing what to say, she finally settled on, "Maybe one day I'll get to see how it works."

With those words, an entirely unwelcome thought pushed into her mind. She hoped she wouldn't witness the merits of the whip firsthand as it took her father's life and then her own. Her heart stuttered at the image that had invaded, her father hanging from the end of Kais' whip, and she blinked quickly, trying to clear the scene.

Kais, who hadn't taken his eyes from her, now scrunched his brow, his head tilting to the side. "I assure you, if I show you how it works, you will be safe."

She swallowed thickly and met his dark eyes. How was he doing that?

His expression didn't change. "Are you well?"

She nodded once. "I'm just hungry."

Bram, who had been watching their interaction carefully, placed a hand on the small of her back and pressed gently, ushering her toward the man serving the meal. "Well, then, let's get you some food."

An enormous cauldron-like pot sat in front of the man, and he ladled out a large scoop of the stew inside. Chunks of meat, carrots, and potatoes swam in the brown liquid, and fragrant steam billowed from the bowl as he handed it to Satori. She waited until Bram received his bowl and then found a seat.

"May I, Princess?" Bram gestured at the chair across from her.

She smiled. "Satori. And you may, please."

"Satori." He spoke her name so softly as though it made him uncomfortable. "Thank you."

CHAPTER NINETEEN

KAIS

Bram seated himself with her like it was expected. Like he was an old friend. A pang of jealousy hit Kais, and he turned away. That was twice that day he had found himself jealous of another man where Satori was concerned. He moved toward where Teague and Sawyer sat. The men were still unhappy with him about the crossing, but he felt he would be more welcome with them than if he tried to seat himself with Satori and Bram.

She was still afraid of him. He had thought for a moment it had been unease about the whip, but he realized it was him. She was afraid of *him*. What had he done to give her cause to fear him? Neither he nor any of his men, that he was aware of, had made one threatening move against her. On the contrary, he had given up supplies for her, prepared a tent for her, set a guard for her, bought clothes for her, and ensured she was fed. What could it be that still caused her to mistrust him?

"General? Kais?"

He looked up, the sound of his name pulling him from his thoughts.

A frown line creased Teague's brow. "Are you alright?"

Not at all. "I'm just fine."

Teague looked like he didn't believe him for a moment. He turned to Sawyer. "Would you excuse us, please?" Then Teague stood, grabbing his coat from where it was hung over the chair. "Sir, may I have a word, please? Outside?"

Irritation sparked in Kais' chest. *Now what?*

He stood. "Of course."

Kais followed Teague as he weaved through a number of tables where men sat, eating. They exited the tent, into the chill air, and moved far enough away so their voices wouldn't be overheard.

"Kais, I wasn't going to say anything, but I'm concerned. Are you alright?" Teague's brow was drawn together and a deep crease sat above the bridge of his nose.

Kais looked left and right, making sure they weren't overheard. "Come with me."

They walked silently for a few moments while Kais sorted out his thoughts, trying to figure out how he would put them into words.

"I didn't tell you everything."

He could feel Teague's gaze heavy on him. "What does that mean?"

"I asked if you believed in blood mates." Kais halted his steps so he could look Teague in the eyes. "I didn't tell you that I'm sure—*sure*, Teague—that that woman is my blood mate."

The words felt odd leaving his lips. Teague must have thought he had lost his mind.

Teague's mouth opened and then closed again, a breath issuing heavily from his nose. "It's a myth, Kay."

Kais shook his head just slightly. "It's not a myth. I don't know how to explain it, but I can feel what she feels." His hand curled into a claw like he was holding an invisible ball, and he pressed his fingers into his chest. "It's how I knew she was having a nightmare the other night. It woke me up! It's how I knew she was in trouble today."

The expression on Teague's face clearly showed that the man was unconvinced. "Kais—"

"Kezia knows too," Kais cut him off. His stomach lurched as he spoke her name. Every time he thought of her and her words, he felt ill.

At the mention of Kezia Teague's chin tipped up, his eyes becoming more alert. Even Teague knew that Kezia's words were not to be questioned. She had told them what would happen with Silas, that he would die. None of them had wanted to believe it. And he'd forgotten about her words until after it was all over. But she had told them, and they had written her off.

Ever since then, even Teague, with his logical beliefs, didn't question her.

Teague's voice was quiet when he spoke, nearly a whisper, "What did she say?"

Kais blew out a breath, looking around for a place to sit. They had stopped walking outside of a tent where a number of stumps had been pulled around the fire. He seated himself, and Teague took the stump across from him, flinging his coat out behind him. Teague's forearms rested on his thighs as he leaned forward toward Kais, waiting.

"She told me what I already knew." Kais shook his head. "She was right, I'd known immediately. But like you, I thought it was a myth. Like my better judgment and wisdom didn't want to believe it, but still I'd known." Kais ran a palm over his face. "We talked, and when she touched me . . ."

Kais' mind drifted back to the look on Kezia's face—the absent void of nothingness in her eyes as she spouted off sentence after sentence about his future.

"Kay?"

Kais' eyes snapped back to Teague. "She said Satori would come to me and would need me, but she would fear me." He waved a hand toward where Satori ate with Bram and the other men. "She's here; she came to me, though not of her own free will. And she *is* afraid of me."

"You haven't done anything to her." Teague's tone implied he was trying to dismiss the idea of Satori's fear.

Kais shook his head. "No. She fears me. I don't know why. It's why I sent you to her in town today. And tonight, when we were discussing my whip, she was looking at it and then it was like a bolt of fear hit her. I thought maybe it was because someone said I could show her how to use it. Maybe she was afraid of injury. But it was more than that. She looked at me, and even if I hadn't been able to feel it, I would have seen it in her eyes. Terror."

Teague shook his head dismissively. "Okay, but that makes sense, doesn't it? She's been told you're the enemy; that we're the enemy."

"She's not afraid of you." Kais examined the darkening sky. The men would be finishing dinner soon and returning to their tents. "Come to my tent."

Kais eyed Satori's tent as he passed it. He'd tried to tell them where to put it so he wasn't constantly inundated with her emotions, but it hadn't been far enough. He pushed through his own tent flaps, unsnapping the whip and tossing it onto the cot.

"Drink?" He didn't wait for Teague to answer as he made his way to the cart.

"Sure," Teague answered, coming up behind Kais.

Kais poured two drinks and handed one to Teague before moving to his desk and sitting. He drank deeply, a sort of fortification for the things he was about to say.

Teague placed his glass on the desk to remove his coat. Then he sat, waiting. Where to begin?

"Kezia said she would fear me. She also said she would love me."

Teague's brows rose at that.

"Then she said I would die."

He hadn't spoken the words aloud, not ever. He'd only mulled them over at times endlessly, in his mind. Speaking them aloud seemed to give them life. The irony.

Teague's brows crashed together as he leaned forward suddenly. "What?"

"That's not all." Kais reached up and rubbed at the tension in the back of his neck. "She said we would bleed."

"Bleed?"

"Satori would bleed, I would bleed. She said Satori would find rest and safety in my arms, and then I would die."

Slowly he looked up and met Teague's gaze. For a long moment, the other man didn't speak. They only held each other's stares. Then, slowly at first, Teague began to shake his head. It started with a subtle movement but soon morphed into full, exaggerated denial.

"The future can be changed. Nothing about the future is set. What if it's her? What if she's the reason you end up dead? The whole thing, everything Kezia said, it was all centered around Satori." Teague was standing now, gesturing as he spoke. Then he stopped. He turned to Kais and laid his hands on his hips. "Get rid of her."

"What?" Surely Teague wasn't suggesting . . .

"Kais! For Shala's sake, I don't mean kill her." He threw a hand in the direction of Satori's tent. "I mean, *get rid of her*. Get her out of here, out of our camp, away from us. Pay someone in the next town to take her home and get her away from you. I like her, I do, she's sweet. But if she's not here to start anything, she can't be the cause of your death."

"I didn't say she was the cause of my death, did I?"

"You didn't say that, no." Teague shrugged a helpless gesture. "But how could they not be connected? Everything else started with her."

"You expect me to just dump her off in the closest town and hope she gets home okay?"

"Why not? I mean, obviously, make sure she's safe and a letter is dispatched to her home. But why not?"

"You were there today, Teague! We would be leaving her at the mercy of men like the ones who had her." Kais' voice rose as he spoke, "She would never see her father again, and if she did . . . what would she be going home to?" He took a drink. "A father trying to barter her off to the highest bidder? An advisor that—" His words stalled.

He didn't know, not really, what had happened. Even if anything had happened. He only knew what he felt from her when the man was brought up.

"That what?" Teague asked, his tone growing quieter.

Kais ran a palm over his mouth. "I don't know. She didn't tell me. I just know, whatever he's doing, it makes her extremely uncomfortable."

Teague blew out a heavy sigh. "She's not your responsibility, Kay."

She's not your responsibility. The words rang in his head, and his stomach rolled.

He looked up at Teague. "Isn't she?"

Disbelief crossed Teague's features. "No. Kay, you didn't even know this girl less than two weeks ago. Take her home and move on. She's—"

Kais held up a hand, halting Teague's words as warmth rushed over him. It was such an odd feeling, but at the same time, it was so welcome, like being wrapped in comfort. He gave a shake of his head.

He lowered his voice when he spoke, knowing she was in her tent. He placed a hand on his chest. "She's in here. It's too late. Whether she hates me or fears me or loves me. It doesn't matter because she's in here. I couldn't leave her like I couldn't leave you."

"What happens when you have to leave her?" Teague sat again, his voice also growing quieter. "When you take her home to her father like you promised?"

"Will I even be alive to see it?"

"Shut up," Teague said. "Respectfully, sir. If I have anything to say about it, you will definitely be alive."

"In that case, we'll have to see what comes of it all."

He relaxed back into his chair, closing his eyes and allowing the warmth of Satori's presence to rest on him. Did he care about her, or was it just the strange bond? Or was that part of the bond? Real, genuine feelings? He didn't know the answer, but he knew he couldn't just dump Satori in the next town and forget about her.

"Is she here?"

Kais didn't open his eyes, only nodded once with a soft, "Mmmhmm."

Silence sat for a moment. Kais could feel Teague's attention pressing on him.

"What does it feel like?"

"What?" Kais asked, still not opening his eyes.

A small laugh breathed out of Teague. "I don't know. Whatever it is you're feeling. However it was you knew she was walking by. You look . . . I don't know. Peaceful."

Kais smiled at Teague's description. He hadn't realized it, but that was how he was feeling. Peaceful. He still had the cares and issues, but they all seemed to quiet in her presence. Did she feel the same with him? Based on what he felt from her, she did not feel peaceful around him. On the contrary, she felt fear.

But hadn't Kezia said that, as well? That Satori would fear him? Of course, the thought of Kezia's words coming to pass was, ultimately, not a comforting one.

"Kay?"

Kais realized he hadn't answered Teague's question. He opened his eyes and looked at the other man.

"It's like . . ." How to articulate this feeling? "It's like you're chilled, and someone brings a warm blanket. Not just a blanket, but one that's been baking by the fire so it will be extra warm, and drapes it across your shoulders. It's warmth and comfort; you want to relax into it, pull it tighter, and just be. That's what it's like when she's near me. But when she touches me . . ."

Teague's eyes widened at the inference.

"Not like that." Kais laughed. "Nothing like that. She's still afraid of what I might do. It's just been an accidental brush of fingers, or when we danced. There's something like a spark that passes between us. Everything inside me seems to buzz. Like the sound of a beehive, but in my veins." He smiled and shook his head. "I know I'm sitting here trying to explain it but I'm not really doing it justice. I wish I could show you what it's like. It's unlike anything I've ever experienced before. It's ridiculous to say this, but I think I know why it's ca lled *blood mate*. It's because when she touches me it's like my blood is singing."

Teague had remained quiet, but at those words, he smiled. "I don't know what's going on or what the future holds, no matter what Kezia might say. But I changed my mind."

"How's that?"

"Don't get rid of her. Keep her. I've never seen you like this. Not ever. I wish you all the best with this girl." Teague rose from his seat, downed the last of his drink, placed the glass back down with a thunk, and planted both hands on Kais' desk, leaning in toward the other man. "I won't let death take you so easily, my friend. You deserve to be happy." He picked up his coat. "And now, I'm going t o bed."

Kais laughed. "Goodnight. Thank you."

The next morning Kais did his best to ignore Satori. Not because he didn't want to see her, or talk to her, or be around her; he stayed away to give her some space. He hated the fear he felt from her sometimes when she looked at him. He would do what he could to avoid that. And if that meant staying out of her vicinity, he would do it.

Of course, he could still feel her around, especially in her tent. She slept fitfully but didn't have any real nightmares. Kais slept very little, distracted by her array of emotions. He'd lain on his cot, staring at the fabric of his tent ceiling, wishing he could do something for her. But his presence only seemed to make it worse. Well, his presence when she was *aware* of it. There had been the night she'd had the nightmare that woke him. When he had stepped into the tent and touched her, her body had stilled, her breathing evening out.

Kais' chest tightened at the memory. What was it that a young, sheltered Princess had to cause those kinds of terrors as she slept? He thought he knew. That man, that advisor who had tried to cut in on their dance. He'd felt something from Satori then, but it was such a new sensation to him that he hadn't known what to make of it. Now, looking back, he thought it might have been fear.

His body tensed as anger rose inside him. A sweeping wave of territorial protectiveness washed over him at the thought of that man laying a hand on Satori. Kais had been with women; he expected she'd been with men. It wasn't jealousy that bothered him. It was the idea that that man had touched her in a way that caused her fear and nightmares.

Kais' stomach turned over as thoughts and images crowded his mind. Surely what he imagined was worse than what actually happened. He swallowed hard and sent a prayer to Shala and Miram that his imaginings were worse than truth.

After a quick breakfast, they packed up the camp. They traveled all day, only stopping when necessary for the horses and men, or for a quick lunch and were back on the road. Kais had a point in mind that he wanted to get to. They'd camped there before. It was close to the water with enough space for everyone without tents. Then the next day, they would arrive at the crossing.

Kais turned his attention to Satori, where she rode beside Bram. She was far enough in front of him that her presence wasn't overwhelming physically. It didn't matter, though; he was still painfully aware of her. As he watched, someone around her must have said something funny. She threw her head back, her long blonde braid that had been slung over her shoulder fell down her back, and she laughed.

He'd never heard her laugh before, not a real, genuine laugh. The sound stole his breath away, knocking it completely from his lungs. She turned to look at the man on the horse behind her, and her smile lit her entire face, transforming it from the fear and mistrust Kais was used to into pure delight.

Jealousy hit him. Again. Helias, he'd never been the jealous type. Yet he was jealous of Sawyer, who had made her laugh, and he was jealous that her bright smile was only for him. Guilt followed quickly. He was jealous of Sawyer because Satori smiled at him? He nearly growled in frustration.

He swallowed hard and, with great effort, tore his gaze away from her, focusing instead on the back of the man that rode in front of him.

"I've never heard her laugh."

Go away. Kais thought as Teague guided his horse alongside him.

"She's beautiful," Teague continued. "I never really looked before."

"Why are you looking now?" Kais shot, twisting his neck toward Teague.

Teague raised both hands in front of him. He looked like he was trying to hide a smile. That annoyed Kais more. Ugh, why was he having this reaction?

"I'm sorry," Kais said quickly, ashamed at the way he'd snapped at his friend. "I don't know what's wrong with me."

Didn't he know?

"I just meant," Teague continued, though it appeared he was choosing his words a bit more carefully, "that after our conversation, I'm paying closer attention to her. If she's special to you, I want to know her too. And I want to make sure she stays safe."

Kais' annoyance quickly morphed into gratitude as he looked at Teague. "Thank you."

"So, tell me," Teague began, looking from Kais to Satori and back, "why are you here if she's there?"

Kais let out a small sigh, glancing sideways at Teague. "You know why."

"Because she's afraid of you." Teague's blue eyes flashed with his smile. "She'll always be afraid of you if you don't do something to change her mind."

Kais chuckled. "Yesterday, you wanted me to drop her at the next town and never think of her again."

Teague's smile softened into a more serious, contemplative expression. "I was wrong. You give and give, and you deserve happiness." He leaned in conspiratorially. "If you want, I'll go talk you up."

Kais laughed again. He almost wanted to allow Teague to *talk him up*. But he could handle it himself. With a nod at Teague, he nudged his horse forward and moved beside her.

He saw the moment she felt his presence, her back stiffened, her chin raising just a bit.

She turned to look at him. "General."

A half smile curved his mouth, but it felt sad. "Kais."

"Kais."

If you could hear the sound of an eye roll, that was how she said his name. But she had said it, and it was like music. He was already waiting for the next time he would hear it.

He tilted his head slightly. "May I ask you a question, Princess?"

The other men riding nearby seemed to sense something from Kais and drifted away to give them some privacy. When Satori noticed, unease flitted through her, but it seemed she refocused on him, doing her best to ignore it.

"What is that?"

Kais pulled his lip between his teeth, pushing it out slowly as he took a moment to consider his words. "Sometimes I think you're afraid of me. But I can't think of anything I've done to merit that. Please tell me what it is so I can remedy it. I don't want you to be so uncomfortable around me."

She watched him for a moment, and he waited as different emotions washed through her. Surprise, discomfort, uncertainty, confusion.

"I— I'm not afraid of you."

He smiled softly, repeating a phrase he'd spoken to her when they had met, "You are a beautiful liar."

She glanced away from him, her cheeks taking on a pink hue.

Kais slowed his horse so he could offer as much eye contact as possible. "I need you to understand."

He didn't miss the way her throat bobbed as she swallowed.

"I give you my word. By Shala and Miram, I will never do anything to purposefully bring harm to you. I just want you to know that." He paused. "If ever you feel unsafe, you can come to me."

Mistrust drifted through her again, and then the fear.

"Wait, tell me what you're thinking," he pleaded. "Just then."

Her eyes grew wide at his question.

"Princess, please. It's not a surprise that I can feel the fear when it spikes through you like that. I know you feel it too when I'm near. Please tell me why."

Resignation. "Very well."

He turned further toward her, desperate to catch every word she spoke.

"I've only known that you are the enemy. It is difficult to suddenly trust you, as you ask. My logic tells me you're waiting to return me to my father, gain an audience, and kill us all."

His face fell at the same time his heart dropped. Bile churned in his stomach.

He shook his head. "Never. I would never. I truly do intend to return you to your father and your home."

Something he couldn't quite catch raced through her. Some unpleasant emotion at the mention of returning her home, but then it was gone.

He added his next words, just in case. "Unless you don't wish to go home. Then I'll take you wherever you desire."

She laughed bitterly. "As if I could go anywhere else. He would hunt me down."

The feeling that accompanied her last sentence told him she wasn't speaking of her father.

He reiterated his earlier promise, "Princess, if you *ever* need protection, find me." He shook his head in wonder. "Call out to me. I may hear you."

For a long time, she watched him, looking as though she were working up the courage for her next words. She opened her mouth, slowly wetting her lips. The sight did things to him that he chose to ignore. If she felt anything from him, she ignored it as well.

"Why?"

He blinked, pulling his attention back to what they were speaking of. "Why what? Why will I protect you?"

"Why do you hear me?" Her eyes glistened as though she might be on the verge of tears. "Why can you know when I'm afraid? How? How can I know when you're near me without seeing you? What is this?"

Surprise hit him as she admitted that he affected her as well. He'd already known it, but to hear her say it was different. Something that had been knotted inside him loosened. But what answer could he give her? The truth? Should he tell her what he assumed—what he knew? Would that frighten her as well? Or did she already know, as he had known before he ever even spoke to Kezia? At least she was admitting that *something* was there. It was hard to deny it, but she could do just that if that's what she wished. She could deny anything existed between them forever if she so chose. The thought caused a slight tightening in his chest. He would think about that later.

Satori deserved to know, to understand what was going on between them. He studied her for another long moment before he raised a hand into the air.

"Take a break!" he shouted to the men.

He turned back to Satori, inclining his head before he led his horse away from the group and didn't look back. If she truly wanted answers, she would follow.

CHAPTER TWENTY

SATORI

She watched him as he steered his horse away from the group. The decision warred within her. Follow. Don't follow. Trust him. Don't trust him. But if he had even a theory as to what was happening, she needed to know. She needed some kind of answers—any kind.

She pulled on Luna's reins and nudged her to follow Kais. He hadn't gone far, just off the path inside the treeline. He dismounted and turned toward her. When she was close enough, he took her horse's bridle, holding it while she climbed down.

He gestured to the ground around them. "I'm sorry, I have no seat to offer you."

She surveyed the area until she found a bit of ground covered in leaves and pine needles. She moved to the place and lowered herself to the ground, waiting.

A half smile curled up the corner of his mouth, and he joined her in the leaves. He studied her for a moment. "You surprise me, Princess."

"Because I sat in the dirt?"

"Because you sat in the dirt." He glanced back toward where the voices of the men could be heard. "Because you followed me at all."

"I'm curious." She gave her head a shake, she had to know what he thought. "What's happening?"

Kais scrubbed a hand over his face, glancing around as though he didn't know where to look. "I want to say that this is just my theory, and I can't be sure, but . . ."

She hadn't missed the way he'd said the word *want.*

"But you are sure." Chills ran over her arms at his sincerity. Just because he was sure of what he was about to say didn't make it a fact. Sometimes people were wrong. "Tell me," she pleaded.

He cleared his throat, appearing to be fortifying himself. "Do you know the old stories of Shala and Miram?"

The gods? What did they have to do with anything? There were many, many stories she'd been told growing up of Shala and Miram. Their meeting, their destiny, their judgments, their ruling.

"Which stories?"

"Their relationship."

She straightened at the word *relationship* in the context of discussing the connection between her and Kais.

"They were mates." As soon as she spoke the word, she realized what he was implying. Defensiveness kicked in immediately. "You're not suggesting . . ."

She couldn't even finish the sentence; it was too far-fetched.

"I'm not suggesting anything."

He held her gaze. He wasn't *suggesting*. He was certain. Her legs began to tingle and she could no longer sit still. She pushed to her feet and spun around to her left, to her right. There was no room to move. She needed to move. She couldn't be still. His words—mates? Ridiculous. She wrapped her arms around h erself.

Slowly Kais climbed to his feet as well, keeping his distance. His gaze was heavy on her, tracking her as she moved aimlessly, just needing to move.

She spun to face him again, her mouth going dry. "It's impossible. It's a myth. They're *gods!* Do you believe in sea monsters too?"

He pressed his lips into a line and nodded. Though he ignored the last part of her statement as he answered. "They are. But it's not a myth. Can you really not feel it?"

Feel it? She could admit she felt something, but *mates*? She couldn't help it; she laughed out loud.

Kais' brow pinched together, but he said nothing.

"Mates." She said through her laughter. "That's absurd."

Kais' eyes drifted to the ground and then back up to her. "A few nights ago you had a nightmare."

She stopped laughing. She didn't recall a nightmare, though she had them often. She didn't speak, waiting for him to continue.

"This was before your tent was moved. You were on the other side of the camp. It woke me. I thought someone was attacking you. But when I got there, you were only dreaming." He bit down on his lip, slowly pushing it out, his eyes taking on a distant look as though lost in a memory. "But not just dreaming. You were distressed. I stepped closer to you, and I touched you."

He had touched her? What? Her eyes grew wide at his admission.

Kais raised a hand to stop her line of thought. "I only placed a hand on your shoulder. Your restless movements stilled. Your labored breathing came easier. But you never woke. I waited the next day to see if you'd say anything, but you didn't. I didn't think you remembered."

Indeed she had not remembered any of what he said. Could he be making it up?

Kais took the slightest step toward her, his hand still stretched out slightly in front of him. "And now you're unsure if I'm telling you the truth."

He was right, of course, but how did he do that?

Kais continued, "Two nights ago, do you remember? I burst into your tent with a knife."

"Of course I remember that."

"You were scared. I felt it so strongly. I thought someone had you cornered, that someone was in there with you. But you were alone then, as well. What were you so scared of?"

He didn't ask her if she had been scared. He knew she was. He asked *what* it was that had her scared. She remembered. It was him. She had been thinking of him, killing her father and then her. Thinking about how unsafe she was in his camp.

When she answered, her voice was soft. "You."

His face fell. She nearly felt bad for the admission, such was the look on his countenance. It would have been the same if she had stepped up to him and struck him. Then his shoulders slumped.

"I'm so sorry. I don't know what I've done that makes you think you need to fear me. You don't. There's nothing you need to fear from me. On my life, Princess. Satori. I promise it."

Satori. She sucked in a breath as he spoke her name. His voice seemed to reach inside her chest and take hold of something. She could find no words, form no sounds. She simply nodded once, looking away from him.

She believed him. She could *feel* it. She wanted to deny that fact, but it was there, inside her, and there was no way she could explain it away. She could deny it to him, to people around her, but she couldn't deny it to herself.

Satori rallied all the strength and fortitude she could at that moment and met his gaze once more. She intended to speak louder, but when the word emerged, it was a whisper that even she could barely register. "Mates?"

He nodded. "Blood mates."

Her throat ached, and she fought the tears that stung her eyes.

"Blood mates. What does that even mean? Why me? Why you? I don't even trust you." She could see the words stung him, but they were the truth. "Why would this happen to you and me? I'm a Princess, spoken for by at least three different men. What will you do when I go home and am married off?"

He remained quiet. She had no idea what his intentions were. Maybe he would kidnap her and keep her for his own. The air seemed to become scarce as she fought to fill her lungs.

Kais interrupted her thoughts, repeating his earlier words, "Princess, don't be afraid of me. When it's time for you to leave, you will be free to go. No one will stop you."

"Thank you." She didn't know what else to say.

"But let me ask you this," he began, bringing his eyes to hers, the connection further frustrating her breathing. "Is that what you want? Not the going home part, of course; you want to go home. The part where you're promised to three different men. Is there one among them you desire? One you wish to spend your life with?"

As if it were up to her. As if she could choose her own path. The sixty-year-old? The twelve-year-old? She had no prayer for a normal life or even as normal as a Princess could hope for. And Henrik. Her breath hitched at the very thought of his name, the sound of it curling around her throat and squeezing.

"Satori?"

A shudder ran through her as she looked up.

His expression had turned hard, serious. "I don't know what you're thinking right now, but I could guess. So, allow me to offer you this as well. I've already told you that I'll deliver you home safely. But, if you don't wish to go back—"

She opened her mouth to defend herself, but he held up a hand, halting her words.

"If you do not wish to go back for *any* reason, you may remain here. Or, I'll take you wherever you wish to go. Wherever you feel you'll be safe."

The sincerity in his words cracked her chest, and tears pricked her eyes, but she blinked them back.

"General!" Teague's voice pierced the quiet that had settled between them.

"Yeah!" Kais called back, though his focus remained on her.

"Ready when you are, sir."

"Ready, Princess?"

She nodded.

"Mount up!" Kais yelled back. Then he extended a hand, gesturing for her to go ahead.

They exited the woods, reseating their horses. The men had already started riding out, and Satori and Kais joined them. They rode in silence for a long time, for which Satori was grateful. It gave her time to process everything Kais had said to her.

CHAPTER TWENTY-ONE

KAIS

Kais nudged his horse, picking up pace and riding out in front of the men. Partly to distance himself from Satori, partly so he could hear better. Even Teague stayed back, keeping anyone from following him.

He slowed his horse to a walk, tuning his ears to the sounds around him. The breeze rustled through the treetops, sending a cascade of dead leaves drifting to the ground. Several birds called to each other, their whistles answered by others farther along the path. But no other sounds greeted him.

He encouraged his horse to move a bit faster until the quiet was replaced by the unmistakable rushing of water. The Vardan River was the largest in two countries. Safe places to cross existed, but they were much farther downstream. It was too far out of the way when his destination was barely half a day's ride on the opposite bank.

He glanced behind him but heard no sound of his approaching men. He'd ridden far enough ahead of them that he had some time. He squeezed his horse's flanks, encouraging the animal toward the sound of the water. He rode through the area where they would spend the night and through more woods until the treeline gave way to the wide banks of the Vardan.

He reined in his horse and pulled in a breath that tasted of wet earth as he took in the sight before him. He knew what to expect, and yet, for some reason, it always took his breath away. The water rushed downstream, a roar filling the air, the surface frothing white as it crashed against rocks and in on itself. He walked the horse only a bit farther up the stream until he saw it.

The bridge was just as he remembered it, mostly destroyed. He lifted his eyes to the opposite bank. The rope still hung, suspended above the river's flow. It stretched from one bank to the other, passing through a small island with a massive tree just off-center in the river.

The idea was to tie yourself to the rope and take your chances on the bridge. But you had to stop at the island and change ropes to continue to the opposite side. Depending on the weather, the island could be mostly dry or mostly underwater. Today the water flowed in a thin stream over its surface. Not too bad. It also looked like someone had tried to add to the bridge by dropping some tree trunks on or beside it. Would that help or hinder? They would find out soon enough. With a last look, he turned his horse and headed back to his men.

"How's it look?" Teague asked when Kais met back up with the group.

Kais shrugged. "Like the crossing. The island's wet but not flooded. Fallen trees on the bridge. I think they're there on purpose. The rope looks intact."

"And the water?"

Kais nodded, looking around at the men. "Flowing."

"It rained." Teague's response sounded matter-of-fact, but Kais recognized the undercurrent of apprehension.

"It did, but it's no worse than other times we've crossed." Kais raised his voice. "Stop here. Relax, get some rest. We cross in the morning."

He finally looked around to find Satori. She was still with Bram, having made friends with the older man. Kais looked at Teague, but his eyes soon found Satori again.

"Check on her, please? Let me know if she needs anything."

"And you're not asking her... why?"

Kais bit his lip as he watched her. She looked up, and he looked back at Teague. Why look away? It wasn't like it was a secret he was drawn to her.

"I told her."

Teague's eyes found Satori and he smiled at her, giving her a quick nod. "Told her what?"

"Everything I told you."

Teague's attention snapped back to him. "The blood thing? The bond?"

"That's the one."

Teague's eyes darted between Satori and Kais. "And how did that go?"

Kais raised his brow. "Better than I expected, actually. But I think she already knew. I knew. I knew before I ever talked to Kezia. It's just there, inside. I think she wanted to deny it, but it's just there."

There was no big meal that night. They pulled out their packs and ate dried meat, hard cheese, and crusty bread. The men still chatted and talked among themselves, but there was something different in the atmosphere of the camp. A seriousness rested on them all. The knowledge that while they hoped everything would go well in the morning, there was no guarantee they would all make it across the river.

Kais made his way from group to group, greeting the men and chatting with them. While he interacted with many of them daily, some were just quieter and he didn't often hold conversations with them. That evening, he made it a point to speak to every one of his men.

Finally, he made it to where Bram, Satori, Sawyer and Teague sat around a small fire. Bram was telling a story about crossing the river as a boy. A bridge stood then, and getting from one side to the other had been much easier. Satori's back straightened as he approached, and he knew she was feeling him—that same feeling, or similar, at least, to what he felt. It was a comforting feeling to him. Was it the same for her? Judging by how her back went rigid and her shoulders squared, it still made her uneasy. Would that ever change? She didn't turn around to face him, and he took the opportunity just to watch her.

Her blonde hair was braided in one long, thick plait down her back with shorter waves free and falling to frame her face. In her delicate hands she held a length of yarn that Bram was teaching her how to crochet with. Her fingers worked the long hook easily, like she'd known how to do it all along.

The voices became quieter as he approached.

Teague moved to make room for him, a grin on his face and the fire reflected in his blue eyes, making them glow. "Kais, sit. Bram is teaching us to knit."

"Crochet," Sawyer corrected.

Then Kais noticed they all had hooks and yarn, and a quiet laugh escaped him. He seated himself between Sawyer and Teague, across from Satori. "It doesn't look too hard."

"No? No offense, sir, but if you think that, maybe you should try it yourself," Sawyer said, and then as if to punctuate the words, a frustrated groan issued from his mouth.

Satori glanced over, and an exasperated smile curved her pink lips. "That's because you're doing it wrong. I told you, like *this*."

She leaned over and touched his hand, her fingers moving his hook and rewrapping the yarn.

Kais watched her skin glide over Sawyer's and was amazed that the other man didn't even seem to notice the touch, too caught up in his project. Kais would have lost all concentration if those hands had touched his. Was that jealousy or longing he was feeling? Or both?

Satori must have sensed the sudden rise of emotion in him; her head snapped up to his, their eyes meeting. Her eyes burned in the light of the fire, the red and orange flames making her brown eyes appear almost red. The sight stole his breath. *Mine.*

He quickly looked away with a shake of his head, slightly ashamed at the sudden possessive thought. She was not his. They were subject to some ancient bond, but that didn't mean anything would come of it.

When he looked up again, she was no longer looking at him, but a blush seemed to redden her cheeks.

Teague's elbow bumped into his arm, drawing his attention. "Kay, have you ever *crocheted* before?"

He put extra emphasis on the word, shooting a pointed look at Sawyer. Though the other man was far too lost in his work to notice.

Kais took the opportunity to slip into the group and into the conversation. "I have. Let me see that."

He held out his hands, and Teague eagerly handed over his hook and yarn, an amused smile dancing on his lips.

Kais had never in his life seen any use in the skill his mother had taught him when he was small. But suddenly, he wanted to thank her. Had she been alive, he might have written her a letter. He was concerned his skill might be rusty, but as he held the hook, it came back to him with ease. He wrapped the yarn around the tip, pulling it through the existing loop. It only took him a few stitches before his confidence was stoked, and he was crocheting a chain the length of a scarf and then back up.

Teague clapped his hands together, letting out a laugh and rocked back where he sat. "Our leader, a man of many talents, indeed!"

Kais didn't dare to look up at Satori, but he could feel her attention on him, her eyes burning into his face.

A half smile turned up his lips. "Oh yes. I have many skills; this one just never came in handy until now."

When he looked up, Sawyer's project rested in his lap, and his face was screwed up into a mask of confusion as he watched Kais. "How are you doing that, sir?"

"Don't feel bad, Sawyer." Kais handed the chain he had crocheted back to Teague. "My mother taught me when I was very young. I don't know why, except she saw into the future and knew I would need it on this night to put you all to shame."

"Excuse me."

Kais turned to Satori. Her words and expression said she was offended, but he felt no offense from her. On the contrary—his head cocked to the side, and he had to stop the smile that threatened to overtake his mouth. She was playing. Her words were in jest.

"Yes, Princess?"

"I take issue with being included in your sweeping observation." She held up her yarn; clearly she had been busy. Her scarf was long and already a few rows deep. "There is no shame in my work. Nor do I feel threatened by your talents, s ir."

He wanted to grin as his chest warmed. She was playing with him. Was he dreaming?

He dipped his head. "Forgive me, my lady. Yours is clearly the superior project, and I would never dream of pitting my meager work against your obvious skills."

She appeared to study him for a moment before she nodded once. "You're forgiven."

Teague snickered quietly.

Bram, who had been quiet, spoke up, "Had I known this would turn into a competition, I would have taught you all how to do something productive, like mending tents."

"You should have," Sawyer said, tossing his hook and yarn to the dirt at his feet. "That's something I can do."

They laughed quietly and when the sound died away, Satori spoke up again, "What is that sound?"

Kais met Teague's eyes, confused. He looked back to Satori. "What sound, Princess?"

"It's a sort of rumbling. I thought it was my ears ringing or something at first, but it hasn't gone away."

Sawyer laughed. "The river?"

She turned wide, fiery brown eyes on him. "That's the river?"

"Yes, Princess," Teague answered. "It's just on the other side of the trees."

Satori's surprised expression changed, and Kais felt the fear as soon as it rose.

"That's the crossing." It was something between a statement and a question.

Her eyes roved over the ground as she seemed to process the idea that what she was hearing was the river they would cross in the morning. Large, violent, and waiting.

Then her eyes met his, and the emotion he felt from her, if only for just a moment, threatened to send him backward to the dirt. She quickly masked it, fear taking its place once again, but it had been there.

Concern. When she had looked at him. It was concern. Not for herself. Not for his men. For him. He swallowed and then swallowed again, trying to get the lump that had appeared in his throat to move back down. But it stayed, lodged there. She cared. She didn't want to, but she did.

He latched onto that one emotion and wrapped it tightly inside himself, holding it there. He would keep it as a reminder until something came of it. Unless, of course, it was just a by-product of the bond. He pushed that thought to the side.

"Kay?" Teague nudged him, and he turned toward the other man. "Are you okay?"

"I am," he breathed out the words.

He stayed there for the rest of the evening, listening to the men joking and letting loose a bit around him. Allowing them this time to relax before the morning.

Kais had been listening to Bram tell yet another story when Teague tapped him lightly on his arm. He looked up, and Teague inclined his head toward where Satori had been seated. She was still there, but instead of sitting, she was curled into a ball on the ground, her head resting on the crook of her arm. As he watched, she pulled her knees closer to her chest and a shiver shook her.

He stood and moved to where she lay. Dirt scraped, and leaves crunched as he reseated himself on the ground beside her, his back pressed against a thin tree. She shivered again, and he reached down, carefully cradling her head and lifting it onto his lap.

Her hair was softer than he had imagined, and he had well-imagined. He had wondered what running his fingers through the golden waves would feel like. He ran a palm over her head and placed his other hand on her shoulder. Immediately, beneath his fingers, the tension dissipated from her body. Her tense limbs relaxed, and instead of curling in on herself, she stretched slightly once and relaxed into a more comfortable position.

Wonder filled him as he watched her sleep. Her eyes moved behind her lids as though she were observing something, but it wasn't distress there, simply a dream.

Kais spoke just above a whisper, "Oh, Princess, you may hate me in the morning for this, but I won't regret it."

Her comfort transferred to him, and he allowed his head to fall back against the tree, basking in the warmth.

He felt Teague's gaze on him and turned his head to meet the other man's eyes. Teague offered him a soft smile, and Kais returned his attention to the woman asleep on his lap.

He ran a hand lightly over her hair again, and the contrast between his darkly tanned skin and her light, cream skin struck him. What would his palm on her face look like? Or their fingers woven together? Or their legs side by side, his hand splayed over her stomach? Kais blinked, shaking the images away. Kezia had said she would be his, but she'd also said the future could change. And if he put his trust in the idea of having her, would he also have to believe the part where he would die? Another question struck him: what if both were true? What if she would be his, and what if he would also die? Would his death be worth having her in his arms of her own free will? To have her tell him that she loved him? He could almost convince himself that if he could only have that moment with her first, he might not mind dying.

He closed his eyes again and was asleep in moments, visions of Satori wrapped in his arms playing in his mind.

CHAPTER TWENTY-TWO

SATORI

The scent of coffee filled the space around her, and she opened her eyes to find a steaming tin mug sitting beside her. On the ground. She'd fallen asleep on the ground, and someone had thrown her cloak over her. She let out a small groan, afraid to move. What kind of soreness would she be dealing with throughout the day, thanks to how she'd slept? Pushing herself to a sitting position, she stretched her stiff muscles as she rewrapped the cloak around her shoulders.

She picked up the coffee cup, savoring the warmth that bled into her palms as she sipped the hot liquid. The men were already up, packing the bits from the night before and securing things for the trip across the river.

The river. She focused her attention on the sound of the water. The rushing sound was still there, and apprehension shot through her. If it was that loud on this side of the trees, what did it sound like—what did it *look* like—on the river's edge? She watched the men working and suddenly wondered if they would all be there at the end of the day. Would *she* be there at the end of the day?

Warmth spread through her, dulling the chill of the morning.

"Good morning, Princess."

Turning toward Kais, she found his face pinched, concern lining his features. Of course. Was it concern for her, or was it concern for his men?

"Good morning."

"How did you sleep?"

She looked down at the ground beneath her, strewn with leaves and rocks. "Actually, I slept very well." She met his eyes again. "Surprising."

"Very," he responded quietly.

Something sat behind his gaze, behind the word, but she couldn't place it.

She cleared her throat. "When do we leave?"

He swallowed thickly before he answered her. "Soon. As soon as everyone is ready."

Her heart stuttered.

Kais crouched in front of her, catching her eyes with his own. "Teague will cross first to ensure the rope is attached and sturdy."

Teague? Wasn't he Kais' right hand? Why would he go first?

Almost as though Kais knew her thoughts, he went on, "He volunteers. Every time. And every time I argue with him about it, and I lose." He swallowed again, and his gaze grew distant. "It scares me to death, and I know it makes me some kind of monster, but I would choose anyone to go over him."

It felt like a secret, like he was confiding something to her that no one else knew. Maybe not even Teague. She knew there was a different relationship between the two men. Knew from the way that Teague sometimes called him by his name when the others weren't around or when they were enjoying downtime. But she could feel Kais' emotion when he spoke those words. Teague was different to him; he was special. Without thinking, she reached out and touched him. Something jolted through her from where her fingertips met his arm. His eyes shot to the place where they touched and then to her face. When their gazes met, it seemed to break the spell, and she withdrew her arm.

Kais closed his eyes and blew out a breath. When he opened them, he continued as if nothing had passed between them, "When he has everything secure, you'll be next. I'll take you across myself and then return to see the men across."

Return? "Why wouldn't you stay on the other side?"

"I can't be safe on the other side while my men are still crossing. I'm the last one across."

Her chest tightened at his words, a reaction that surprised even herself. She nodded.

"Bram will follow you. Then it'll just be a matter of waiting while everyone else crosses with all the supplies," Kais finished.

Supplies. She thought of something she hadn't yet considered. "What about the horses?"

"We leave the hores and the tents on this side. I have men that will come and collect them to take them across in a safer place. Kais answered.

"Kay?"

She looked up and swallowed the lump in her throat at the informal way Teague addressed Kais in front of her.

Kais' eyes met hers, and she felt the fear reflected in his deep brown irises. She felt the way his heart picked up its pace. He held her gaze, and she wished she could impart to him some sort of extra strength for the day. Why did she even care?

He answered Teague, still looking at her. "Yeah?"

"Ready when you are." Teague looked at Satori, his blue eyes sparkling a bit. "Good morning, Princess. I trust you slept well."

She stood, brushing her pants off. "I did, thank you. And please, call me Satori."

Teague's brow rose slightly, and a smile spread across his face as he glanced at Kais. "Of course, Satori."

A flash of jealousy, not her own, hit her, and she looked at Kais, but in a moment the jealous feeling she thought she felt was gone, and instead, something warm sat there. Satisfaction? Happiness? She wasn't sure, only that it was warm.

Teague's voice interrupted her musings. "Ready to see the river?"

Not at all.

Satori held her breath as Luna emerged through the trees, revealing the wide banks of the river. By now, the water was so loud the men were shouting to be heard over the roaring. White water splashed and churned, charging downstream. They were crossing *this*? How?

Kais slowed his horse to come alongside her. He pointed to her left just a bit upstream, raising his voice to be heard above the din of the raging water, he said, "There's where we cross. There's a bridge and a rope."

Horror struck her at the sight of the *bridge*. It was not a bridge at all; it was a ruin seemingly fortified by several fallen trees. She looked at Kais, and even if he hadn't been able to feel what she felt, it would have been obvious she was appalled. And it looked *cold*.

He didn't try to tell her it looked worse than it was or convince her she was overreacting. His eyes held hers, and she felt the sincerity seep into her as he spoke, "I'll keep you safe, Satori. By all means in my power."

When she looked back at the bridge, Teague was already there, no coat, sleeves rolled up to his elbows. He worked, tying, wrapping, and knotting a massive coil of new rope around a large tree to which a much more worn looking rope was already tied. The old rope stretched across the river to the tree in the middle, wrapped around the trunk there and continued to stretch to the far bank. Sweat glistened on his brow and she had no idea if it was from exertion or fear. Maybe b oth.

Fear gripped her for certain, and when she looked at Kais, she found him watching Teague as well. Even though there was no sign of it on his face, the fear she was feeling was not all her own.

"What is he doing?"

"We use the rope as a guide," Kais explained. "We'll tie another rope around our waist, loop it over the guide rope, and tie it again. Then we follow the guide rope across, and if we lose our footing, we're saved by the rope around our waist."

"Like a pulley?"

Kais glanced at her for a fraction of a moment before his eyes were on Teague once more. "Yes, like a pulley. But the guide rope is old and there's no way to tell how well it'll hold up, so Teague is going to replace it with the new one as he goes across."

"How many times has he done this?"

Kais answered her again without taking his eyes from his friend. "We try not to come this way. If we have more time we always go farther downstream where there's an actual place to cross and the water is calm."

She didn't get a chance to respond because Teague's voice interrupted their conversation. "Sir!"

Sir. He was back to addressing Kais as his general.

Kais reached out, touched Satori's arm, and then moved away from her toward Teague. She could still feel the place where his touch had connected, but she wondered if he had even noticed he'd done it. And had he done it to reassure her or to soak up some sort of comfort?

Kais walked to Teague, and she watched as they had an animated conversation, gesturing to the river, the ropes, and that accursed *bridge*. No, she wouldn't think of the bridge like that. It was their lifeline, and she would revere it.

Finally, Kais held out an arm in front of him, and Teague reached out, clasping his forearm in his hand. The men pulled each other in for an embrace, slapping each other's backs. Then, just before pulling away, Kais rested his forehead against Teague's, and Satori could feel, even from a distance, the torrent of emotions inside Kais. Love, fear, admiration, terror. All of them churning inside him like a storm as he stepped back.

Then he was shouting orders.

"Princess!" He waved her toward him, and she joined them. "When he's across, you'll be next. The rope goes around your waist so you aren't swept away."

Her heart thumped and thudded, but besides that, she could feel a second pounding, like an echo, and she knew it was Kais. He had entered General mode on the outside, but inside, his heart threatened to burst from his chest. She was filled with admiration for how he could shoulder such stress and not show it.

Kais had turned away, but suddenly he ceased all movements, stilling completely. She watched from behind him as his chin lifted slightly and his shoulders rose on a deep inhale, as though he were soaking something in. He turned his head slightly, meeting her gaze for only a moment before he resumed his task.

Teague tied the pulley rope around his waist, securing it tightly and pulling again to double check that it was sure. The end of the new guide rope was draped in coils over his shoulder, allowing it to unroll easily as he made his way across the river.

Satori studied the setup. Ropes tied to trees, ropes tied to Teague, and a half-swept away bridge.

Teague gave one last massive tug on the rope overhead, and the knots at his waist, then shouted, "Going!"

Absolutely everyone froze, stopping what they were doing to watch him pull himself across the raging river.

Teague wrapped his hands around the pulley rope above him and stepped carefully onto the bridge. Satori gasped as immediately his feet were swept out from beneath him. He would have already been taken with the flow if not for the ropes.

He regained his footing quickly, taking his next steps more carefully. The water rushed around him, covering his feet and, in some places, coming to his waist. How he could see where to place his feet was beyond Satori. She found herself drifting closer to Kais, closer to where Teague struggled across the water.

Kais paid absolutely no attention to her and at times she wondered if he was even breathing as he watched his friend maneuver the questionable bridge. Finally, Teague made it to the island. Satori held her breath as this was where Teague would essentially have to untie himself briefly to remove the pulley rope from one side and move it to the other. He would also be wrapping the new guide rope around the tree.

The first thing Teague did was shake off the large coil of rope. Holding it in one hand, he tucked his foot into a root and stretched his arms around the tree, catching the coil in his other hand. He repeated this process a few times, looping the guide rope.

Finally, he tossed what was left of the coil back over his shoulder and began to work on the knots at his waist. When half the rope was untied, he held tight to the coil around his shoulder and, with his free hand, pulled the pulley rope off the guide rope on one side of the tree and tossed it over the guide rope on the other side. When it was over, he retied it at his waist and began moving again.

With only ten feet to go to the opposite shore, the old guide rope that stretched from island to shore snapped.

Teague's shout rang out over the sound of the water, and Kais dove for the rope as though he would go after him.

Without thinking, Satori leaped from where she stood to catch Kais' arm. "No! Wait!"

Thank Shala Teague had been replacing the guide rope because he still had its remaining coils securely in his grip. When Satori tore her attention from Kais and looked again, Teague was chest deep in the raging rapids, fighting to keep the foam out of his face and mouth as he clawed his way along the broken bridge.

More than once, his head disappeared under the rapids, and each time, Kais went stiff in her arms, his panic threatening to send her to her knees. He twitched in her grasp but never pulled away. A good thing because had he wanted to break free of her hold, she could have done nothing to stop him. Teague disappeared again, and Kais' hand came to her arm, where she held him. He gripped her so tightly she thought it might leave a bruise. She said nothing.

Then Teague was back up, his hands in fists around the bits of the bridge that remained. Thankfully, the closer to the shore, the more pieces of bridge survived. Then he was out. Out of the water and collapsing onto his back. His knees were drawn up, his feet planted on the ground, his arms splayed above his head, and his chest heaving, but he was out of the water. A moment later, Teague raised his hand, waving toward them before letting it flop back to the ground.

Beside Satori, Kais dropped to his knees, air blasting from his lungs. She had no choice but to go down with him as he still had a hold on her arm. She was watching Teague and didn't see Kais move, but in a moment, his arms were around her, his head buried in her neck. She thought he let out a sob, but it was only once, and the sound was drowned out by the raging waters. She brought a hand up to run it over his back, and at her touch, he seemed to come to his senses, looking at her.

"Forgive me, Princess," he said as he released her, moving slightly away.

All the warmth his body had enveloped her with went with his touch. And then fear took hold again as she realized she was next. Her heart began to pound and skip as she looked at the water. Across the river, Teague was up on his feet and tying off the new rope, pulling and tugging to ensure it was secure. But the sound of the rapids pounded in her ears, seeming to grow too loud to concentrate on anything else.

Then a hand closed gently around her forearm, and heat radiated from the contact point. She looked up to find Kais, his chocolate brown eyes intent on her, waiting for her to give him her attention.

She heaved another breath as he spoke, "I won't let you go." He emphasized each word, the hand on her arm tightening just a hair.

She took two more long breaths and nodded.

"Come on. Let's get it over with," he said as his hand slid down her arm, and he caught her fingers in his own, squeezing them gently. He pulled her toward where the ropes waited.

Kais released her to retrieve another rope. "It's about to get a bit damp, Your Highness." He flung the new rope over the top of the guide rope, pulling the ends even. He held one end up in front of her. "May I?"

It was time. She stepped closer to him, nodding.

He stood in front of her, looking into her eyes for a moment before he pulled in a heavy breath. "Arms up, please?"

She lifted her arms away from her sides, and Kais leaned in, wrapping his arms and the rope around her waist. The heat from his hands left a trail as he knotted the rope. He did the same with the other end. His breaths on her ear as his arms encircled her sent shivers from her head down her legs. When he stepped away, she was secure to the guide rope, and he began tying another around his own waist.

He turned to the men behind him. "When we get to the island, don't wait. Pull the rope back and send the next one over."

"Are you coming back across?" one of the men asked, looking at Kais.

She felt it immediately, the uncertainty, guilt even, as Kais glanced at her and then back at the men. "I'm not, I'm taking the Princess over and staying."

She did not doubt that Kais would have been the last to cross the rapids if she weren't there. She didn't know what to say. She certainly couldn't cross alone. And telling him not to worry and that he could return was putting him in danger again. She said nothing, waiting.

Kais turned to her. "Are you ready?"

She shook her head no. "Sure."

His mouth turned up in a smirk that she knew was forced. "You are a beautiful liar."

He'd said it to her before, and it gave her comfort for some reason. He held out his hand, and she took it, ignoring the spark that passed between them. He nodded once, giving her what she knew was his best reassuring look. Then he stepped onto the dilapidated bridge, and she followed. When he entered the water, she immediately felt the strength of the rapids tug at his footing, and she closed her hand tighter around his.

She stepped into the water after him. It was freezing and the force of the flow would have carried her away had Kais not had a grip on her. She reached up and wrapped her free hand around the pulley rope again and again until it hurt. Kais had already done the same. They moved slowly and carefully, her feet slipping on the slick wood submerged in the froth.

When they made it to the island, a voice called out to them. "Kay!"

She and Kais looked to see Teague waiting on the opposite bank. Kais took her hands and wrapped the second pulley rope around her arms and through her hands.

"Hold on." He didn't look up at Teague as he called, "Yeah?"

His hands worked the knots at her waist until they were free. Then he tossed the rope, which was pulled back the way they came, for the next person.

"You good?" Teague called, the words barely discernible above the din.

"Perfect!" Kais called back, still not looking at the other man as he unwound one of Satori's hands and tied that bit back around her waist.

When she was secure, he untied and retied himself, the first rope disappearing back to the men.

"Second half is worse!" Teague called. "Watch your step."

Finally, Kais looked up, giving him a nod of acknowledgment before refocusing his attention on Satori. "Ready?"

"You need to stop asking me that," she said, wrapping the rope around her wrist and taking Kais' hand with the other hand.

They stepped off the tiny island and back onto the broken logs of the bridge. Kais' grip on her hand was almost painful.

He took a step and slid, his foot going out from under him. His grip on her tightened, as well as his grip on the rope above him, as he righted himself.

"Watch there." He nodded toward where his foot caught.

She stepped and found no purchase as the rapids caught her feet, sweeping them from beneath her. The force of the water ripped her grip from Kais' hand, and she cried out as she flailed, searching for anything to latch onto, finally finding the rope that was thankfully still wrapped around her wrist.

The flow caught her body, tossing and pulling her downstream. The water was so cold it knocked all the breath from her lungs.

"Satori! Satori!" Kais screamed her name. "Hold on, hold on, I'm coming."

Fear gripped her as she squeezed the rope in her hands so tightly that they ached. Kais held tightly to the rope with one hand as he stretched toward her, but he couldn't reach her, and she didn't dare let go to catch his hand. He heaved again and caught the rope she held, and slowly, with more strength than she thought he possessed, he wrapped the taut rope around his arm, steadily pulling her in toward himself.

Satori could do nothing to help except hang on and wait, and beg Shala and Miram and whoever else would listen to let Kais reach her.

Long agonizing minutes later, his hand brushed hers, and she lunged as much as the rapids would allow until his grip closed on hers and he pulled her into himself. There, in the middle of the rapids, Kais wrapped her in his arms, pressing his cheek to her sodden hair. His warmth surrounded her like a blanket and she pressed his face into his wet shirt.

"Alright, come on. Almost there." He pulled them across the remainder of the bridge to where Teague waited, arms outstretched, to pull them in.

Teague pulled them both onto the damp shore, and immediately she was wrapped in Kais' arms, both of them soaking wet but safe on the bank.

Teague knelt beside them, an arm on each of their shoulders. "That wasn't so bad, was it?"

Kais released her, glanced at Teague with an exhausted expression, and then laughed. He raised an arm, and Teague stood, taking hold of Kais and pulling him to his feet. Satori stayed seated on the ground. The idiots could joke all they wanted; she needed time for her soul to re-enter her body. That was if it hadn't been permanently lost to the rapids.

CHAPTER TWENTY-THREE

SATORI

For the next few hours, the men came two at a time across the water, mostly without incident. Bram had come across soon after Satori, and she quickly learned that the older man was not only the tent mender but also the doctor in the group. Thankfully, up to that point, his services had only been employed for minor cuts and scrapes suffered from crossing.

A huge fire had been built just off the bank of the river, and as soon as the men emerged from the water, they crowded around the leaping flames, soaking up the warmth and drying their clothes.

Satori sat as close to the flames as she could without singeing her hair. Next to her, two men spoke of the last time they braved the crossing and how the water hadn't been nearly as high or treacherous.

Laughter sounded from Satori's other side, and she closed her eyes, soaking in the warmth.

The calm was broken moments later by the eruption of shouts from the bridge. Panic slammed into her chest, and it wasn't her own. She leaped to her feet, eyes scanning wildly for the source of the commotion. The last two men were just beginning their trek across the water. They seemed secure, except that they were screaming, waving wildly toward the opposite bank.

Satori's eyes ran the length of the guide rope, past the island, to— not to the other guide rope, because it was gone. There was no guide rope stretching from the island to the shore they had crossed to. Kais ran along the bank downstream, screaming, Teague right on his heels. More men raced after them.

She scanned the banks, looking for the cause of the commotion but finding nothing. She moved her gaze out farther into the water, and her heart slammed to a stop.

Sawyer, not a safety rope in sight, clung precariously to a boulder jutting up out of the foam. The water rushed over him in relentless blasts. How he was even still holding on, she couldn't tell.

Kais and Teague and the others had arrived on the bank, in line, where Sawyer clung desperately.

"Sawyer! Sawyer, hang on! I'm coming!" Kais was wrapping a rope around and around his waist, knotting it. He took another coil of rope and slung it over his head so it sat across his body. On the other end of the rope, Teague and the other men wrapped themselves up, digging in their heels.

Satori drew as close as she dared, not wanting to be in the way. Kais moved back upstream just a bit before diving into the waiting rapids.

Terror shone on Teague's features as he tightened his grip on the rope, his eyes darting wildly from Kais to Sawyer and back.

Kais' head disappeared under the rapids, and Satori had no idea if it was her horror or his that squeezed her chest, making breathing a chore.

Kais fought the current to get to the middle of the river even as it carried him downstream toward where Sawyer waited.

Satori's chest tightened, and she gasped for air. Who was feeling this? Was she having trouble breathing? Was it Kais' trouble breathing she was experiencing?

She watched as the current carried him directly into the rock, slamming him against it with enough force that she wondered if all his bones would make it out unscathed.

Carefully he pulled himself around the rock to the side where Sawyer clung. The water was too loud to hear anything that happened; they could only watch.

Satori had heard about people wringing their hands in distress, but she had hers clenched into a single tight fist and pressed against her mouth. She glanced at Teague, still holding the rope with the other men, still digging his heels in. His face had drained of all color as he focused his attention on Kais and Sawyer.

In the water, Kais was attempting to wrap his extra rope around Sawyer's waist, his arms, anywhere he could. When he had secured the other man, he shouted at the men on the bank, and they began heaving on the rope, reeling them in.

Fear wrapped a fist around Satori's lungs and squeezed as the men were hauled through the frothing waves. Then suddenly, a massive billowing cloud of raging water hit Kais, tearing the rope out of his hands. The only thing holding him now was the tie at his waist. He was tossed backward, the waves catching his body and flinging it into another rock that jutted from the river.

The second string of fear that had been thrumming inside Satori's chest snapped. She gasped out a breath as the thread that had been Kais disappeared. She sprang into motion, rushing toward the bank.

"Satori!" Teague shouted behind her, but his voice was drowned out by the river and her own panic.

Where had Kais' emotions gone?

Sawyer reached out and, by sheer luck, managed to latch onto Kais' belt. He let the current carry him back to Kais, where he began unwrapping his own rope and retying it to Kais.

Men on the bank shouted at Sawyer not to untie himself, to use the rope that Kais already had, but he ignored them, or maybe he couldn't even hear them. He hadn't fully unwrapped himself, but Satori could tell he wasn't as secure anymore.

Then the froth churning beside the rock turned pink, and all the air left Satori's lungs.

"Blood!" Teague screamed to the men.

Satori's own blood ran cold in her veins. Kais was bleeding.

"Pull!" Teague shouted, and, as one, the men on the shore heaved the rope, fighting against the current as they pulled Kais and Sawyer back toward the shore.

When the men were almost to the banks, another great surge of water latched onto them, pulling them back and under the surface, out of sight.

The men on the shore pulled, and suddenly they were stumbling backward as though their weight had grown significantly lighter.

"No!" Satori called, rushing farther toward the water's edge.

"Satori, don't! We can't come after you too!" Teague called.

She froze, waiting. Seconds passed, and Kais' body bobbed to the surface again as relief flooded her lungs. With another great pull, Kais was dragged onto the banks. Only Kais.

CHAPTER TWENTY-FOUR

SATORI

A mix of relief and horror flooded Satori as she rushed to his side. Teague and the others joined her. A few of the men ran downstream, hands over their eyes, searching the rapids for Sawyer, but he was gone.

Satori would be sad later; right now, she was focused on the large gash on the back of Kais' head that seemed to her to be pumping blood onto the wet grass.

"Get Bram!" Teague said as he scooped Kais off the ground with seemingly no effort and ran back toward the fire.

A few tents had been set up, and Teague yelled again for Bram, voice edged in a panic she'd never heard from him before he disappeared into one of them.

Satori froze, arms wrapped around her middle, eyes wide. Sawyer was gone, Kais was injured, and she didn't know where to go or what to do.

A breeze hit her as two more men, one of them Bram, ran past her, following Teague into the tent. Her legs no longer held her; she simply dropped to the ground where she stood and watched the tent.

Why was she even so concerned? Days ago she was sure this man would take her home, kill her father and herself, and claim the throne. Now she was fighting for air to breathe, thinking he might be mortally injured.

And Sawyer— She blinked away the thought of Sawyer. She couldn't focus on two tragedies at once.

Teague emerged from the tent, his eyes searching the camp wildly until they landed on her, mere feet away, kneeling in the dirt. In a second, he was before her, crouched down to meet her gaze.

"Satori, will you come with me?" His eyes and voice were quiet and pleading.

She nodded through the fog that clouded her head. Teague reached out, and she took his hand, allowing him to pull her to her feet. He led her to the tent where they had taken Kais. The other men who had been inside exited as she and Teague entered.

She stopped on the threshold, brought up short by the sight before her. Kais lay on the small cot, eyes closed and so pale. Bram sat at his head, holding a blood-soaked cloth to the wound with one hand, digging in a bag beside him with the other. The bed linens were wet and red. And from Kais, she felt nothing.

There was nothing. She had grown oddly accustomed to feeling the thread of whatever emotion he was experiencing, and now there was nothing—like a void sat around him.

Bram looked up as she entered. "Princess, come here."

He abandoned his search in the bag, motioning her over, urgency in his eyes and gesture.

Teague's hand pressed gently on her back, and she moved frther into the tent to Bram's side.

Bram glanced at Teague before he turned his attention to her and held it for a moment. "Princess, I could be wrong, but there's something between you and Kais, isn't there?"

She swallowed the large lump in her throat. Tears pressed from her eyes as she nodded her head. Why would denying it matter now? What would it help? Conversely, she couldn't fathom why it would help to admit it.

"I can't lie, and I can't deny what's in front of me." Bram held her gaze. "Kais, he's . . . I can't do anything."

Breath hissed from her lungs. Teague's fingers curled into her shirt where they rested on her back. It was the only reaction he showed.

"Nothing can be done?" Was this connection that she had only just found—literally only just admitted to—gone?

Bram's lips pressed together. "I'm no expert on this thing you share. In fact, I know very little. I only know what Teague has told me and what I know of the legends. No one can be an expert on something so rare. But as I have no other options and at this point, nothing can do him further harm, I'm willing, if you are, to entertain any alternate possibilities that come to mind."

She shook her head, her mind refusing to form a complete thought out of his words. "I don't know what you're saying."

Bram's eyes darted once to Teague, once to her, and then rested on Kais' still form. "Would you be willing to part with a bit of blood, Princess?"

Blood?

"I don't understand."

Bram released his hold on the rag at Kais' head, and it fell away, revealing the wound. Satori's hand flew to cover her mouth as Bram reached toward her with fingers stained red with Kais' blood.

"Your hand?"

Teague's fingers closed tighter around her clothes, revealing to her the level of his distress, before releasing her. She swallowed and stepped forward, holding out her hand. She hadn't realized she was shaking until she saw her hand extended between the two of them.

Bram took it as he reached into his bag again and drew out a small, shining knife. Gently he took her hand in his, and she held her breath as he placed the blade's edge on her palm. She winced, gasping at the cold bite of the metal as it cut into her flesh. Immediately blood welled, and she fought the desire to close her hand into a fist.

Now what? Still so gently, Bram pulled her to where Kais lay and turned her hand over, placing her bleeding palm on the wound on Kais' skull. A shudder worked through her as her wet fingers met Kais' wet hair. She closed her eyes. She didn't know what Bram thought would happen but didn't want to watch when nothing came of his desperate effort.

She felt it before she heard the ragged breath. It was a foggy presence at first, then the connection sharpened to pain, then panic, then fear. Her eyes snapped open just before she heard the intake of breath from Kais.

Behind her, Teague hit his knees, eyes wide.

"It worked." His words came on what could only be described as a gasp.

"What's happening?" she asked Bram.

The man had his hands raised, away from Kais, a grin slowly forming on his weathered face. "You did it, Princess. You saved him."

Kais was not awake, but his presence was back, the warm honey seeping over her once more, warming her chilled soul, the thing which connected them reforming in her chest. She raised her hand slightly to find the large gash closed, blood still matted Kais' hair and coated her hand, but the injury was nearly gone.

All the breath in her escaped her open mouth in a shaky exhale as she focused her attention on her hand. The cut from Bram's knife had also closed, leaving no pain behind, just a bit of tenderness.

"How?"

Teague looked up toward Bram as well, waiting for an explanation.

"I didn't know if it would work," Bram admitted. "It was the longest chance, but it was all I could do."

"What? What was it? How did it work?" she asked, still staring in wonder at Kais' head and her own hand.

"It's the bond in the blood." Bram shrugged. "I've never seen anything like it. I'd heard of it. My grandfather told a story once of a woman he knew who had been injured, and when her husband, her mate, touched her with his blood, her injury healed. I've seen it tried once, but it didn't work then. I assumed it was because there was no actual bond. They were in love, but there was no blood b ond."

"Blood bond," she repeated the words.

Before, she could have written her connection with Kais off as odd but not extraordinary. Now, staring at the blood that coated them both but with no injuries in sight, she could no longer deny it.

Teague caught her hand in his. "You saved him."

She was going to need time to process the events of the evening. "Don't tell him."

"What?" Teague turned his attention on her from where he still knelt beside Kais. "Why?"

She tossed around for words, for a reason she didn't want him to know.

"He has to take me home. I have to go back; my country is depending on me." Tears edged her words. "This will only make it harder. Teague, please?"

She knew it was asking so much of him. He and Kais shared everything.

Turmoil swirled in Teague's eyes, his head shaking ever so slightly until he finally pulled in a deep inhale. He glanced once at Kais and then met her eyes again. "Very well."

CHAPTER TWENTY-FIVE

KAIS

His head was pounding as he blinked open his eyes and groaned. Movement beside him caught his eye and he turned his head to find Teague leaning forward in his seat.

"Hey."

Slowly Kais pushed himself up to a sitting position, groaning as his muscles protested. "What happened?"

"You don't remember?" Teague's brows were drawn into a deep V. The expression was a bit disconcerting for someone as easygoing as Teague.

Kais rolled his eyes, moving his feet off the side of the cot. "If I remembered, I wouldn't ask, would I?"

A long stream of air issued from Teague's lips. "What do you remember?"

Kais took a moment to sift through the fog currently filling his head. They were crossing the river. Everyone had made it across. No. Not everyone. Sawyer. His eyes shot to Teague's waiting gaze.

"Sawyer."

Teague's eyes closed, his head lowering, and Kais knew.

"No." He shook his head, sending another stab of pain through his temples. "Please."

Even he didn't know what he was asking for. He just needed to hear that Sawyer was well and safe.

"He was taken by the current," Teague sighed. "You tried, you hit your head, but Bram... he took care of it."

That explained the headache.

"So Sawyer is . . ." He couldn't form the words to finish the question.

Teague sat in silence for a few moments before answering the unspoken question. "We tried. You tried. There was nothing we could do." He wiped a hand over his face as though brushing away the images in his mind before changing the subject. "How do you feel? Do you want me to get Bram? Get you a drink?"

"I don't need Bram. But I won't turn down a drink."

Teague nodded. "I'll be back in a minute."

Teague left and, true to his word, returned a short time later with a glass filled with a touch too much liquor. He didn't stay, and Kais was grateful. He just wanted to be alone for a few moments. *Sawyer . . .*

Kais held the drink in one hand as he ran the other back through his hair. It was odd having a piece of your memory missing. Though, maybe it was a mercy. Did he want to recall Sawyer's last moments? Sawyer. He had argued with Sawyer only days before about the dangers of the crossing. Sawyer hadn't wanted to take it. He'd said it was too dangerous. Of course, Kais knew better. Kais knew they needed to take the crossing. Kais was in charge. Kais was right. No matter who argued with him about the route, he'd made up his mind.

And Sawyer had paid the price.

Kais was alive, with only a headache to show for it, and Sawyer was gone. Not even a body to properly bury. Nothing. Simply washed away by the unforgiving current. All because Kais' decision had forced him.

Swept away by the river. Kais clenched his jaw together. Sadness and absolute fury churned inside him. His fault.

The glass in his hand shattered, shards raining down around his boots. The high-pitched yelp behind caused him to spin toward the tent flap.

Satori. How had she managed to approach him without him knowing it? He stood.

Her eyes dropped to his hand, now dripping blood from the broken bits of glass. "You're hurt." She took two steps toward him before stopping to grab the water pitcher and towel from a small table. She seated herself on the cot and nodded toward the place beside her. "Sit."

He sat slowly, concentrating on the warmth that she brought. It was a sort of comfort he couldn't explain, but at that moment, he was deeply grateful. She didn't wait or ask permission; she only reached out and took his hand in hers, sending a jolt across his skin.

"How did you get in here?"

She glanced at him, a look of concern crossing her features. "I walked in."

He huffed a breath. "That's not what I mean; how did you get in here without me knowing it?"

Her brow creased with understanding. "Oh, I don't know. Maybe you were distracted." She indicated his bloody hand in her grasp.

That was a possibility. He was so wrapped up in his own thoughts and emotions that he may have missed her presence.

"The same way you didn't know I was there the first time we met."

She gave him half a glance as her fingers moved carefully over his palm, pulling bits of glass from his bloody skin. When she was finished ridding his hand of debris, she took the pitcher and poured. The water cascading over the cut stung as the blood washed away. She took the towel and then carefully picked up one of the larger pieces of glass, cutting the fabric so she could tear it into strips. He took in her features as she concentrated on wrapping the strips around his injury. A slight V sat in her brow, her brown eyes focused intently on her task. Wisps of her blonde hair brushed her creamy cheeks. His breaths came a bit fuller as he studied her.

"Did you see what happened?"

Her fingers froze mid-wrap, and she looked up to meet his gaze. Her brown eyes were inches from his own, and he could have drowned in their depths if not for the pain he saw there.

"Satori?"

She pulled in a sudden breath, her throat worked on a swallow, and she nodded once.

Did he want to know? Would it be better to remain ignorant? He realized he'd been lost in his thoughts, staring for too long. He blinked.

"Will you tell me? Please?"

Her head tilted, and her eyes moved around the tent, apprehension pressing in on her. She opened her mouth, licked her lips, and closed it until her eyes finally met his again.

"It wasn't your fault, Kais. You tried. You tried so hard." Her eyes shone as tears pooled there.

Before he realized what he'd done, he had reached out and covered her hand, the one still holding the bandages, with his other hand.

"Please don't blame yourself."

He pulled his hand away. "It was my order that brought us here. He didn't want to come. Sawyer debated with me on the merits of the crossing instead of taking time to go farther downstream. I'm the one who made the decision, and now he's dead because of it."

"Kais, you tried," she repeated. "I saw you get in the water. You were injured as well."

Kais reached up and brushed a hand through his hair again. "Yeah, my head is killing me. Did I hit it?"

"You don't remember?" She slid back away from him. It was only slightly, but he felt her absence like he felt her presence.

"I don't." He cleared his throat. "Maybe you could tell me one day."

With a quick shake of her head, she was up and clearing away the glass from both the pile she had removed from his hand and off the ground.

"So, what now?" She asked.

"We'll spend the night here and go on in the morning. The village we're heading to isn't terribly far. We could be there by mid-day. But now . . ." He trailed off, still thinking of Sawyer. "We should hold a memorial for Sawyer."

A memorial. Kais hadn't performed any sort of memorial since . . . He shook the memory off. He'd have enough memories to wade through when they arrived at the village and he was reunited with Lena.

"Will you do it in the morning?"

Kais heaved a sigh. "Yes, and then we'll be on our way away from here."

Satori stood, gathering the items she had used to clean his injury. "I'll leave you alone. I hope your head feels better."

"Wait, why were you here? Did you need something?" He suddenly realized she had come in just as he had broken the glass, and they hadn't spoken of anything besides what had happened.

"No, I was only coming to see if you were well."

She moved to the tent flap.

His heart fluttered with her words; it felt like some kind of breakthrough. She cared.

"Thank you, Princess." Kais held up his newly bandaged hand. "And for this. I appreciate it."

She dipped her head. "You're welcome."

She exited quickly, leaving him alone.

He let his head fall back, closing his eyes, allowing his shoulders to drop. What right did he have to speak anything for Sawyer? No doubt others among his men would ask the same question. What could he even say? Maybe he should let Teague speak.

As if summoned by thought, Teague appeared at the door to the tent. "May I come in?"

Kais made a sweeping motion with his hands, beckoning Teague in. "Enter."

"You look better," Teague observed with a raised brow before they crashed together at the sight of Kais' hand. "Except for that. That's new."

Kais raised the bandaged appendage. "Clumsy."

"Uh, huh." Teague's response was full of disbelief.

"I broke a glass."

Teague moved closer, pulling a stool up beside where Kais sat. "Bandaged it yourself?"

"No." Kais turned his hand over in his lap, examining the knots in the cloth. "Satori was in here."

Teague leaned forward. "How'd she do it?"

"What?" Odd question. "She cleaned it and wrapped it. How else would she do it?"

Teague shook his head, laughing lightly at himself. "Never mind. Ignore me, it's been a long few days."

"Right," Kais agreed. "Speaking of, tell the men we'll have a memorial on the bank for Sawyer at sunrise. Then we move out. I'm ready to be away from this water."

Teague nodded. "He had—has—a sister. I heard him talking about her."

"I know." Kais let his gaze drop, scanning the ground. "We'll have to get word to her. I'll write a letter. We can dispatch it from Burnell." He paused for a few moments, both men sitting in silence. "I don't know what to say. I feel like it's my fault that he ended up in the water. I gave the order to take the crossing."

Teague leaned forward, his gaze intent on Kais. "This isn't your fault, Kais. This was our option. We didn't have time to go all the way down the river. If you would have left it up to me, I would have ordered we take the crossing. And they all saw what you did to try to save Sawyer. They all saw that. It's not like these men think you're indifferent or don't care. They know you, Kay. They're not blaming you. The only person blaming you for this is yourself. Knock it off."

Kais looked at Teague. "You're very free with your words."

A glimmer of a smirk appeared on Teague's face. "You want me to stop?"

Kais leaned forward, placing a hand on Teague's knee. "Never, my friend. Never. Now go, so I can figure out what to say."

Teague stood. "You'll do well. Remember what I said."

CHAPTER TWENTY-SIX

SATORI

The unrelenting rush of the water pounded behind them as they gathered along the bank to pay tribute to Sawyer. The sun had only just risen and the air was cold, mist from the river hanging heavily over everything. Some of the men stood still, hands clasped behind their backs or in front of them. Others rubbed their hands together, blowing into their palms and stamping their feet.

Teague, standing off to the side with Kais, rested a hand on his friend's shoulder briefly before they turned and walked toward the front of the group. The men instantly quieted.

Satori could see Kais swallow the lump in his throat, but beyond that, she felt. The emotions raging inside him were enough to rival the river. Silently she asked Shala or Miram or both or whoever would listen to help him as he spoke.

"We know we're not guaranteed a tomorrow or even a today. We just can't know what comes next or when our time will be.

"Today, we stand here, mourning our friend, taken from us too soon. He was barely out of his youth, eager to serve and to please. Eager to be a friend and a help to anyone who might need him.

"We petition Shala and Miram to take hold of our friend, Sawyer's, hand and guide him into Vesper and lavish him with all the accolades due him for a life so well lived."

The men gathered around altogether, lifted their voices in one phrase, "Let it be." The solemn sincerity of it brought tears to Satori's eyes.

Then Kais raised both his hands toward the river, and the men each reached down toward their feet, digging a handful of soil or moss or stones, whatever was available where they stood. They moved as close to the edge of the river as they could and still remain on solid ground. One at a time, they lifted their fistfuls of dirt toward the cloud-covered sky before they cast them into the water. When the men were done, Teague and Kais each took turns digging up the earth.

Tentatively, Satori stepped up to Kais. These weren't her people, and she had no desire to offend, but she wanted to participate.

"May I?"

Kais' eyes landed on her, and his surprise washed through her.

When Kais said nothing, Teague answered her. "Please, Your Highness. I think Sawyer would also have appreciated that. He seemed to like you."

A space opened inside her. She had liked Sawyer, as well. Following the other's leads, she reached down and pressed her hands into the damp, mossy ground, digging her fingers into the earth and pulling up a fistful of wet dirt.

Kais and Teague moved toward the water's edge, and Satori followed. Teague tossed his tribute, and Satori did the same. Kais seemed to weigh the earth in his hand, and Satori felt the guilt he harbored. Her chest ached. She had seen what Kais had done, what he had gone through and suffered attempting to save Sawyer.

She found herself torn, wishing he could remember but at the same time dreading the day the memories did return. There was something even deeper between herself and Kais than he knew, and when he found out, it would make parting with her even more difficult.

There were no horses for this part of the trip. They had left the horses on the river's opposite shore, having no way to get them across. They simply walked, the whole group trekking what looked to be a well-worn path toward the village.

They'd tied up their supplies in tarps and packs, secured them to ropes, and hauled them across the river. Without the supplies, the entire purpose of their trip would be null. Now the men carried the packs on their backs, having opened them and dispersed them throughout the group.

Kais had been telling the truth. It was blankets and tinned foods: supplies to help a village through the coming winter. When she looked around at all the packs, she realized there should be more. Many of the supplies Kais had traded to the thieves on the road to ensure her safety.

Her stomach grew queasy at the thought that someone might be going without during the winter because of her.

"There are plenty of blankets and supplies." Kais had come up beside her. He handed her a canteen, and she accepted it, taking a drink. "I always overpack for this trip."

She didn't question how he knew what she was dwelling on; no doubt he had felt the guilt that swirled inside her.

"I don't want to think someone might go cold because of me."

"No one will go cold because of you." Kais leaned closer, his voice quieting. "And you were worth every blanket."

She felt the heat creep into her cheeks at his sincerity, a sensation confirmed by Kais' half smile.

The look left her feeling flustered. She cleared her throat and handed the canteen back to him. "How far yet?"

He swallowed down a large gulp of water, his tanned throat bobbing with the action. Entirely unbidden, a thought pushed its way into her mind: running her fingertips down the side of his stubbled jaw... how the hairs would scrape against her fingertips...

What in Helias? She shook her head to clear the image, but not before the embarrassment at the thought poured through her. That was followed closely by fear that she had actually felt desire, and would Kais have noticed that?

She chanced a glance out of the corner of her eye. He had stopped drinking, but the canteen was still poised at his lips. No expression shown on his face.

Then, as if he had remembered something, he lowered the canteen and turned his head to face her. "About an hour, I'd say."

"Huh?" What had she even asked?

He let out a small laugh. "You asked how far yet. From here, about an hour."

"Oh." She blushed again and wanted to slap herself for letting these emotions out around him.

"Are you alright, Princess?" Amusement glinted clearly in his eyes, but he said nothing else.

"I'm fine," she huffed out, annoyed at herself.

Kais had a good sense of time. In just under an hour, they came upon a village. They passed a few huts at first, away from the more populated center, then they were crossing into a much more bustling portion.

They had barely arrived when someone off to the right, sitting outside what looked like a small storefront, called out, "Is that Teague Rhone? Are my old eyes deceiving me?"

The woman came closer to the group, her face more wrinkled than anyone Satori had ever seen. She stepped closer, eyes squinted against the sun and maybe against her age as well.

"That tall, broad-shouldered man there. It must be, I'd know that coat any-where." She pointed.

From somewhere behind her, Teague's laugh was loud and deep and full of delight. Teague moved past them toward the woman until he stood before her, scooping her carefully off her feet.

"Marta!" He set her down and kissed each of her cheeks through her laughter. "I've missed you."

She slapped him playfully on the arm. "Oh, you're a liar. You don't miss me, you miss my venison stew."

Teague pulled back, an affronted expression playing on his features. "That is nonsense, woman. And you know it is." He glanced around. "Where's Nico?"

"Oh, off, gossiping at the fountain, I'm sure." She waved a hand in the direction of the center of the village. "He'll be glad to see you, my boy."

"I am glad to see you." Teague placed another kiss on Marta's forehead, but this one was much softer and seemed much more sincere.

From the direction that Marta had waved came a series of shrill, ear-piercing shouts, and Satori turned to see a little girl, maybe eight years old, sprinting toward them as fast as her small legs would carry her. She moved so quickly that she almost flew, dust kicking up around her heels, leaving a cloud in her wake. Her arms were held above her head, and laughter danced in her eyes.

Beside Satori, Kais laughed and lowered himself to one knee. "Bug!"

The little girl's laughter didn't cease until she had launched herself into his awaiting arms. "You're here! You're here! You're here!"

"I am," Kais laughed, wrapping his arms completely around the little girl.

Satori took a moment to observe the girl. Both her hair and her skin were the same color as Kais'. Both of them looked like they lived their lives in the sunshine. Though when the girl opened her eyes, they were a deep blue instead of the chocolate brown of Kais'. And Kais loved her.

"I didn't think you were ever coming back!" the girl said into Kais' neck. "It's been ages!"

"Never coming back?" Kais pulled the girl away to meet her gaze. Her eyes shone as though filled with tears. "I would never not come back to you."

Immediately the girl's serious expression jumped into a massive grin. "Good." She looked around. "Did you bring Teague?"

"Do I ever go anywhere without Teague?" Kais gave her a playfully exasperated look.

"Adalyn." Teague's voice sounded from behind them. "Do I not get a welcome?"

The girl, Adalyn, broke free of Kais' hold to launch herself at Teague. He caught her in his arms, spinning her around twice before setting her back on her feet.

"You grew."

Adalyn rolled her eyes. "Mama says I do that all the time."

"Well, your Mama's a smart woman; she can see." Satori didn't miss the glance that Teague shared with Kais.

"Speaking of your Mama, Bug." Kais lifted his gaze to survey the group of people who were beginning to gather and greet them. "Where is she?"

Adalyn shrugged. "She was hanging laundry, so I left to play. I don't like doing laundry."

Something like resignation flitted through Satori from Kais. The feeling of someone who had to do something but wished they could avoid it. Satori took in the little girl again; her hair, her skin, even her smile was so similar to his. She was practically Kais' twin.

From nowhere, a thought struck her. Adalyn and Kais were close. Close enough to be related? Close enough for her to be his daughter? The resemblance could not be denied. And if this girl was his daughter, who was her mother? Did Kais have a wife in this village? Was that why he had been in such a hurry? He'd never mentioned a wife or a daughter, though she hadn't had a lot of conversations with him where his family might have come up.

But he'd flirted with her, hadn't he? Or, not precisely flirted, but he had pulled her aside to discuss the bond between them. Why even acknowledge it if he had a family already? Why explore it at all? No wonder he wanted to get here so quickly.

She couldn't explain the emotion that hit her chest. Betrayal? That was silly, there was nothing to betray. Sadness? Was it sadness that Shala and Miram had thrown her and Kais together, only to show her his family? Why did she even care? She wasn't staying with him, anyway. And had he mentioned them? Had he brought them up, and she just hadn't been paying attention? Had there been signs that she'd missed? Why hadn't Teague told her? But he had, hadn't he? Or he had implied it. Satori had asked, and Teague had told her that was Kais' story to tell. Had Teague been talking about Adalyn and her mother?

Satori pressed her eyes closed and shook her head, blowing out a shaking breath. She opened her eyes when she felt Kais' attention on her. He still knelt on the ground, listening to Adalyn's animated stories, but he looked up at Satori, his brows pinched.

"Alright?" He mouthed the word at her.

Satori forced a smile and nodded, moving her attention to anything but the sight of Kais and the girl who had to be his daughter.

She moved away from him, joining Teague, who seemed to have an audience around him. He turned and beckoned her toward him.

"This is my friend, Satori," he said. "She's spending some time with us as we see her safely home."

A young girl, maybe eleven or twelve, stepped shyly up to Satori. "Your hair is so beautiful."

"Thank you."

"It almost matches Teague's," another child said, eliciting a laugh from the small gathered group.

Then Teague looked up and his smile fell.

"Here we go," he muttered under his breath, and Satori turned to see what he was looking at.

A woman stood a length away, one hand on her hip, a laundry basket perched on the other, and a disapproving expression on her face. She had auburn hair wrapped in a loose bun. Satori couldn't see her eyes from this distance, but she would bet they were a deep blue.

Kais, who was still kneeling on the ground chatting with Adalyn, looked up. Recognition lit his features, and he nodded toward the woman. Adalyn stopped her animated story to look over her shoulder.

She gasped and rushed in the direction of the woman. "Mama! Mama! He's here!"

"I see that." Annoyance played on the woman's face. "I don't recall asking him to come, yet here he is."

Adalyn either ignored her mother's jab or didn't even notice. "He brought blankets, Mama. And food!"

Kais stood and brushed off his pants. "Lena."

"Kais."

Whatever it was Kais was feeling towards the woman, it certainly wasn't affection. Maybe she was his wife, but they had separated? Was that why he'd thought discussing the bond with Satori was okay?

Teague moved quickly to join them. "Hey, Lena."

Lena's expression softened only slightly as she looked at Teague. "Teague, you're still with this one?"

"Always, Lena." Teague shrugged. "You should know that."

"Oh, I do." She glanced behind them at the men still coming, greeting people they knew or just sitting on the ground for a rest. "I suppose you'll all need some space."

"Don't worry about that," Teague said. "Marta's kept a small supply of tents for us. We'll double and triple up, and it won't cause you any worries."

"No, you folks never cause me any worries."

There was definite sarcasm in the woman's reply. Satori focused on Kais. Maybe if she could figure out where his emotions stood, she would know how to react to this woman. Then Lena turned her attention to Satori.

"Who's this?"

Kais stepped once toward Satori. "She's a friend."

Lena's eyes cut to Kais. "Of yours?" She glanced at Teague. "Or yours? Or are you sharing?"

"Hey!" The word was out of Satori's mouth before she could stop it.

Who did this woman think she was to imply that Satori would even be okay with Kais and Teague *sharing* her? What in Helias was this woman's problem?

"Really?" was all Kais said.

Lena rolled her eyes and then shook her head. "I don't even care. I have laundry to get to. Addie?"

Adalyn's face had crunched with the adult's exchange. "Can I stay, Mama? Please?"

Lena blew out an exasperated-sounding breath, and with a dismissive wave of her hand, she turned and walked away.

Kais turned to Satori. "I'm sorry about that. I'm not her favorite person."

Satori was about to say, "*clearly,*" when the emotion hit her. Grief. Kais seemed to be mourning something, but Satori couldn't tell if it was his marriage, Sawyer, or something completely different.

Then it was gone, and Kais was turning to the men. He clapped his hands. "Alright. Follow Teague, grab a tent from Marta, group up, set up, and then rest up. In three hours we distribute goods. Then you can relax."

Kais turned to Satori. Hesitation edged his thoughts.

"What is it?"

"I don't know if we have enough tents, or if Marta has enough tents, for you to get one on your own."

Was he joking? "I'm sorry?"

He crossed his arms over his chest. "Don't worry, Princess. I won't make you stay with any of the men. You can stay with me and Teague."

Her stomach fell. Stay with them?

Then Kais started laughing. "I'm sorry. I can't continue. Don't worry; we'll make sure you get your own space. Even if we have to sleep four to a tent."

She breathed out her relief, but then felt guilty for inconveniencing others so that she could get her own tent.

"Don't feel bad. The men are used to sharing." Kais began walking, waving at her to follow. "Come on, let's go get you a tent."

When Kais and Satori got to Marta's, there was a line. Teague stood at the front, tossing tents to men and shouting out numbers. Satori followed Kais to Teague's side.

"Single, please."

Teague glanced up, surprised at the request. Then his eyes drifted to Satori, and he nodded. He stepped inside the small storage space and emerged with a tightly wrapped, deep green bundle.

"Smallest one we have." He held the tent out toward Satori, but Kais intercepted it, taking the bundle.

"While you're here," Teague said, and reached inside again, coming out with a bigger bundle. "Ours." He handed it to Kais as well.

Kais took the tents and looked at Satori. "Ready to build some tents?"

"I am."

Kais' eyes grew wide, almost playful. Speaking as though he was about to embark on an adventure, he said, "Follow me."

Teague had returned to handing out tents, but he called after them to Satori, "Don't let him put me on rocks or in a swamp."

Satori called back that she would do her best while Kais let out a stream of exaggerated evil laughter, the sound doing things to Satori that she fought to ignore.

She followed Kais just outside of what seemed to be the village limits. Other men were already there, erecting their tents. Kais moved a bit away from the rest of the men and stopped, looking around.

"This good?"

"This is fine. Thank you."

He let the packs fall and dropped to his knees beside them, pulling the smallest one close. He began untying the ties and unwrapping the green canvas.

"May I help?" She didn't like standing there and watching him do all the work.

He paused, turning his head and looking up at her sideways and squinting as the sun shone into his eyes. "Have you ever put up a tent before, Your Highness?"

She placed her hands on her hips. "No, but I can learn. I'm fully capable of mastering whatever I put my mind to, I assure you."

He studied her for a moment, the corner of his mouth quirking up. "I don't doubt that, Princess." He inclined his head to the ground beside him. "Please, join me."

Satori lowered herself to her knees beside him, and he handed her the still-folded canvas. "You unwrap this, and I'll build the frame."

Kais stood and began pulling poles apart and pounding them into the ground, hooking them into each other. Beside him, Satori unwound a long strap and stood to give herself more room. She pulled the folded fabric apart. When she found two corners, she took them in her hands and heaved, flapping the tent open.

This tent was even smaller than the one she had slept in before, and it occurred to her that it certainly wasn't large enough for a cot. A shiver rushed through her at the thought of sleeping on the ground. She hoped Kais had enough of those blankets.

"Okay." Kais turned toward where she stood, holding the tent and waiting. He brushed his hands together and beckoned her toward him. "Ready?"

She moved forward, pulling the canvas with her. He reached down, took the opposite end, and tossed the whole thing over the frame. Then they worked from the sides, pulling the ends down and securing them. One last piece of canvas was stretched over the ground.

"We have extra blankets for us. Then when we leave, we'll leave them here," Kais said as he stepped back to survey their work.

A thought occurred to her, and she turned to face him. "How will you go back? Back across the river?"

He turned to her. "No. Well, yes. We have to go back across the river, but we won't take the crossing back."

"You left the horses and other things on the other side of the river." It was a statement but it was also a question. How would he get his things back?

"Just as another group of our men collected our horses from the opposite shore, another group will deliver us fresh supplies at a town farther downstream," Kais explained. "When we leave here, we'll travel downstream and collect the supplies. Then we'll travel on until . . ."

His words seemed to falter, and she caught the thin line of regret before he seemed to bury it.

"Well, until we deliver you home, Princess." He took a quick breath and bent down to snatch up the second larger tent, which he began to build not far from hers.

Home. The thought of seeing her Father warmed her, but then another face pushed into her mind, and she shook her head to rid herself of the image.

Beside her, Kais, mid-way through lifting a tent pole, paused, his head snapping toward her. "Satori?"

She opened her eyes to see the concern in his gaze. "What?"

He let the tent pole drop to the ground with a thunk as he stepped in front of her. His knees bent just enough so he could look her in the eye. His voice was as serious as she had ever heard it. "What were you just thinking about?"

There was no chance she would tell this man her deepest secrets, bond or no bond. She shook her head. "What are you talking about?

He studied her for another moment before giving his head an exaggerated shake once.

"No, there was something. You were scared. It's the same as that night . . ." His voice trailed off, and his concern burrowed into her chest, making it hard to keep her breaths even.

"Satori." Something like a subtle warning edged his words, and he reached out, a featherlight touch of his fingers sweeping over her arm. "What is it that scares you like that?"

She pulled her arm away, wrapping herself tightly in her own embrace. More thoughts of Henrik pushed into her mind, and she shook her head from side to side.

"Nothing."

He pulled his hand back, not touching her again. "That's not nothing. Is there someone at home that you're afraid of? Your father?"

She snapped her attention to him. "No. No, my father does not scare me."

"Well, something does." He crossed his arms. "I won't take you back to that."

Anger flared. "What are you going to do? Hold me against my will?"

His chest deflated, exasperation seeping from him. "No. Satori, I'm just trying to tell you, you're safe here. You don't have to go back there."

"I don't?" Now the anger came more easily. "I am a Princess. My father will die, and I will inherit the throne. I have a country counting on my return. Counting on me. I do have to go back there. I can't expect you to understand, but that is the way of it."

"No." His voice quieted. "I wouldn't understand."

CHAPTER TWENTY-SEVEN

KAIS

Kais rammed the tent rod into the ground before he picked up the small mallet and brought it down on the top. The pole drove five inches into the ground.

"What did that pole do to you?" Kais turned his still annoyed expression on Teague, who threw up both arms in a gesture of surrender. "No offense meant. Seriously, though . . ."

Kais dropped the mallet with a huff before bending to grab the last pole.

Teague moved around, lifted the canvas, and shook it out. "Where's Satori?"

"She went to see if Bram needed anything." Kais worked for a few more seconds before tossing the supplies to the ground and rounding on Teague. "Something's wrong."

Teague looked up. "What do you mean?"

"With Satori."

He could feel it. Whatever it was she had been thinking of while they were talking of her home had sent a jolt of fear directly through her. And she wouldn't tell him what it was. But it was the same thing he had felt the night she'd had the nightmare.

"Something at her home scares her. but she refuses to tell me what. Refuses to even acknowledge it, even though she knows I can feel it."

"Something like they have rats in the dungeon, or something else?" Teague shook the tent in Kais' direction.

Kais took his end of the tent. "Something else. I think it's someone. But I don't think it's her father."

The two men hurled the canvas over the frame. When they had straightened it, Kais stood back, hands on hips. He was looking at the structure, but all he could see was that look on her face.

"I think it's that advisor."

Teague turned his head. "The one from the dance?"

Kais remembered the man, tall, thin, light brown hair, and a slimy air about him.

"Yes." He pulled his lip between his teeth, pushing it out before speaking. "That night, I danced with Satori and he tried to cut in. When I asked her if she would rather dance with him, she froze. She chose me over him. And I noticed it then, but I didn't realize it."

"Do you think he's threatening her?" Teague asked.

"I don't know. She said he was on the list of people her father would approve of her marrying. Some old king, a young prince, and this advisor."

Teague tossed his brows into the air. "What a selection." He paused for a moment. "Might there be another name on the list?"

Kais shot Teague a long-suffering look. "What about me would ever make her, or more importantly, her father, add me to that list?"

Now it was Teague's turn to share an exasperated look. Of course Kais knew what might get him on the list. But he didn't want to play that card, not with her. Did he want her? He did. He'd wanted her since the moment he saw her at her castle. Did he want her to choose him based on her desire and not preconceived circumstances? Yes, he did.

"Kais!"

Teague leaned around the tent toward the sound of the voice; when he looked back at Kais, his brows were up near his hairline, his mouth twisted into a grimace. "Incoming."

Kais squared his shoulders. He knew this moment had been coming; it was practically a ritual with her. That didn't stop him from hoping they could skip it just once, or at least push it off. No matter how much he thought he had gotten over the past, her presence always brought the hurt freshly to his mind. It was painful, and the constant rehash was exhausting.

From around the tent, the woman stormed. Her hair was tied at the base of her neck, but flyaways escaped everywhere as though she had put in a hard day's work. That or she had been pacing and flailing in her home, spouting about his presence. At least Bug still loved him.

Kais recognized the bundle in her hands as she approached. He shot a look at Teague, the other man having leaned back to rest against a tent pole as though settling in for the inevitable.

She stormed up to him, stopping mere feet away, and tossed the folded bundle at his feet. "Why do you come here?"

Kais looked from her to the blanket on the ground and back up. Gesturing to the blanket, he said, "That's why I came here."

"We have our own blankets."

"Lena, are you really angry with me for bringing you supplies for the winter? If you don't want to use them, don't. But that shouldn't deprive everyone else." He shifted his weight. "Adalyn shouldn't suffer because you don't want to see me."

"If Adalyn understood, she wouldn't want to see you, either." The woman's voice dripped with venom, but Kais could see the hurt behind her gaze.

He pulled in a deep breath. Her comment had done its job, stabbing at him with the truth of it. But he was so tired of apologizing to this woman. She wasn't the only one to experience loss here.

"If it makes you feel better, we won't be staying long. Just a few days for the men to relax, and then we're off. I have a stop to make before I go home."

"Yes, the Princess. I heard," Lena nearly sneered. "I figured she was a conquest, spoils of war, and all that."

A spark of anger ignited, and he curled his hand into a fist before quickly releasing it, flexing his fingers and cracking a knuckle. "She is no such thing."

A surprised expression appeared on Lena's mocking face. "Touchy, Kais. Calm down. We all know you can have anyone you want. You really should choose, already. Maybe you'll earn some respect."

"I'm fairly well respected, Lena," he quipped. "Except by you."

She shook her head dismissively. "They don't know you like I do. I don't care who you are. You'll only ever be one person to me."

"Not that it will matter, but I am sorry, Lena."

Hurt stung his lungs, and he needed to be away. She would never forgive him, but her constant hatred made it hard for him to forgive himself. Memories crowded into his head, causing a dull ache.

"Now, if you'll excuse me." With a nod toward Teague, which the other man returned, Kais stepped over the bundle at his feet and around Lena, walking away.

Before he was out of earshot, he heard Teague say, "He doesn't deserve that. In fact, he deserves quite the opposite."

"Shut up, Teague," Lena snapped back.

Then Kais was away, heading in no specific direction. He just needed quiet. He felt her before he saw her. The warmth washed over him, and he stopped walking, closing his eyes and allowing the feeling of comfort to envelope him.

He took one long slow breath in and blew it out equally as slowly. Did she know how she made him feel? How, when she was close by, his cares seemed less? His tension dissipated? When he opened his eyes, she was there, standing only yards in front of him, watching him.

He said nothing, holding her gaze for just a moment longer than might have been comfortable.

She stepped toward him. "Are you alright?"

Physically? Emotionally? Which? And was he? Physically he was well, so that's how he answered.

"I'm fine."

She took another step, her eyes darting to the ground and back up. "I . . . I didn't mean to, but I heard. Are you sure you're alright?"

She had heard the exchange with Lena. He ran the interaction back over in his mind. Had Lena insulted Satori, as well? He couldn't recall. Weariness washed over him.

"Would you mind if we sat?"

Her eyes widened. "I'm sorry, I'll leave you alone."

No, that he did not want. He held out a hand toward her, imploring, begging. "No, please. Stay? I don't mean to take advantage of you, Princess, but when you're around, my head is so much quieter."

He realized quieter wasn't necessarily the correct word. He still had the same thoughts and concerns. His problems didn't go away. It was just that they seemed more manageable—smaller, somehow. Her presence seemed to bring comfort and a sort of strength.

She smiled softly. "I'll stay."

She moved toward where a small fire burned, though no one was around. Gone to get food or interact with people in the village, he didn't care. It was a place to sit and be alone.

She sat, and he took a seat a few feet away. She reached out, warming her hands by the softly glowing embers. When she spoke, she didn't look at him.

"Your daughter is beautiful."

He whipped his head toward her and coughed, choking on his breath. *Daughter?*

"What?"

"The little girl. She's beautiful." Something like a quiet sadness flitted through her for a moment, and then it was gone. "She looks just like you."

He ignored the immediate thought that popped into his head: she thought Adalyn was beautiful *and* that she looked like him. Instead, he focused on the *daughter* comment. He bit down on his lip to keep from smiling.

"Adalyn isn't my daughter."

Satori turned her head toward him, surprise on her face. "She's not? How does she look just like you?"

Kais ignored the absolute, unmistakable relief he felt from her, swallowing down the lump it brought to his chest. He would unpack that later.

"Adalyn is my niece."

"That woman is your sister?" The surprise on Satori's face turned to absolute shock.

"No." He punctuated the word with a raise of his brows. "Adalyn's father was my brother." An ache he had grown familiar with accompanied the words.

"Oh." Satori's surprise changed quickly to a sort of confused sadness. "Was?"

He closed his mouth, letting his gaze drift to the fire and then to his feet, his brother's laughing eyes appearing in his head.

"I'm sorry," Satori was quick to apologize. "I shouldn't have asked; I don't mean to pry."

Kais looked back up, meeting her gaze, feeling her sadness and regret for his loss and her questions. "No, it's alright, really. You're not prying. I don't mind you asking."

Actually, her questions gave him a sort of hope. She sat there alone with him, and he felt no fear from her, only curiosity. She wanted to know about him. He'd unpack that later, as well.

"It was quite a few years ago. It's just that when Lena comes attacking, it's all drawn back up to the front."

Satori shook her head. "I'm sorry."

This time she wasn't referring to her questions, it was more a sympathetic apology for the way Lena came at him.

He shook his head dismissively. "I'm used to it by now."

And he was. Sort of. He was used to Lena coming to attack him; he *wasn't* used to the emotions it brought up. He didn't expect he would ever be used to that.

"My brother, Silas, was one of my men."

He let out a small laugh, remembering the friendly ribbing they gave each other the day he had become his brother's superior, circumstances that were nearly unheard of.

"We met some trouble, and he didn't make it." That was boiling it down to the very simplest explanation. But it was making a long story short, for now.

Horror flitted through Satori, and if he couldn't have felt it, he would have seen it in her eyes. "I'm so sorry."

"Thank you." He offered a small smile. "It was a long time ago, as I said. Adalyn was barely brand new; she doesn't even remember him." He paused for a moment, for a breath, and swallowed deeply. "And that's sad. But at the same time . . . Well, you said you saw how Lena is with me. She blames me. And why wouldn't she? It is on me. I, as the leader, gave the order, and he followed it. It was dangerous. He wasn't the only one that didn't make it out. I was injured myself. But what I'm saying is that Adalyn doesn't have that bitterness. She only knows me, and I love that little girl. She's adventurous and explorative and wild as a new colt. And she only sees me."

Satori was silent for a few moments. "Do you think Lena will ever forgive you?"

Kais snapped the branch he had been handling, tossing both pieces into the fire. "I don't know. It's been years now, and it's always the same. When I show up, she basically tells me she wishes I wouldn't have and lets me know I'm welcome to leave whenever I can."

Satori shook her head. "I don't have any family like that. No brothers or sisters. My lady's maid is my closest friend. And she *is* my friend. I couldn't imagine losing her. I am sorry for your loss."

She was completely sincere, and Kais soaked it in like a sponge. "Thank you, Satori."

There was silence for a short time, and then voices greeted them, mingled with the sounds of tin dishes clanging together.

"Sir, Princess." Jameson nodded toward them and sat down. "Marta has food. Better go before it's gone. Teague's going to eat it all."

"Well." Kais stood. "We can't allow that, now can we, Princess?"

He moved his hand and paused, but then decided he didn't care. He reached out, holding it out to her.

Only a beat passed before she reached out and slid her fingers, warm from the fire, into his waiting palm. Her eyes widened at the familiar shock that passed at their touch. But she didn't pull her hand away. He helped her to her feet and held her hand, daring to slide a thumb across her knuckles as she stepped around where she'd been seated. Then he loosened his grip, releasing her, and she quickly stepped in front of him, moving toward the food. He followed, running his thumb over the palm of his hand where he could still feel her touch.

CHAPTER TWENTY-EIGHT

KAIS

"What's this?" Kais held his hands out in front of him, letting mock shock flood his voice. "Aren't we here to rest? And here are my men, up far too early, exercising."

Everett, one of his long-time men, laughed. "We knew you would show up. We're just here to impress you."

"Right, and now that you're here," another man spoke up, "now that you've seen us, I guess we can go."

Kais laughed. "Yes, go. Relax."

"And what are you doing here, then?" Teague's voice came from behind him, but Kais didn't bother to turn.

Kais unsnapped the loop holding his whip, and took the strap in his hand, shaking it out a bit to loosen the coils. "I'm here to blow off some steam; what else?" He glanced over his shoulder in time to see Teague chuckle.

Kais walked toward a large tree trunk that stood on its side and then bent to examine the ground. He snatched up three large pinecones and placed them on the upended tree so they came to about chest height.

Kais backed up, looking around to be sure he wasn't running anyone over. He let the coils of the whip fall to the ground beside him. Weighing the handle in his grip, he rolled his wrist slightly.

The men in the space moved back, out of range. Kais snapped his arm once, causing the long braid of the whip to lash out and crack loudly. He did the same thing twice more, warming up in the chill air.

He focused his attention on the pinecones. One at a time, quickly and consecutively, he sent the whip flying in the direction of the trunk, and one at a time, the pinecones crashed to the ground.

Excited applause drew his attention off to his right. Adalyn stood, giggling, clapping, and bouncing on her feet.

Kais turned toward the girl, and with one hand behind his back and the other across his front, he bowed deeply.

This caused her to giggle even more. "Do it again! Do it again!"

Kais straightened and gestured with his whip. "Put them back."

Adalyn rushed to where the pinecones had fallen and, on tiptoes, reached up to replace them.

"Wait right there!" Kais called, weighing the whip in his grasp. "Put that one on your head."

The girl froze as she looked from the pinecone in her hand to where Kais stood with his whip. Then the giggling came again.

"No!" she squealed, her voice pitched excessively high.

"Why not?" Kais gave her a mock offended expression, covering his heart with his free hand. "Don't you trust me?"

She looked again between him and the pinecone in her hand, as if weighing his words. Her face scrunched up, causing the top of her nose to wrinkle. She was adorable.

"Well..." she drew the word out, making it last about four beats. "I do trust you. You're you. But I like my head."

Kais laughed. "Wise." He pointed his chin toward the log. "Go ahead, put it up there, and come back here."

Quickly the girl placed the last pinecone on the trunk and rushed back to Kais, making sure to stand far off to his side and out of range of the braided cord.

Kais snapped the whip, knocking the first pinecone off, and then again for the second.

"I have questions," Adalyn spoke up before he could snap the third one off.

"What's that?" He aimed and knocked the third pinecone down.

"She's very pretty."

Kais wanted to laugh as he turned a quizzical look on the girl. "That's not a question."

Adalyn seemed to consider for a moment. "Do you think she's very pretty?"

"Who?" Kais asked, confused for a moment.

"The girl with you." Adalyn gave him a look like she was concerned he may not be well.

Satori. He breathed in deeply. Yes, he certainly did think she was pretty. "I suppose, yes, she is pretty. Set those pinecones back up, please?"

"No, I said *very* pretty," Adalyn insisted, her voice serious, as she replaced the pinecones.

"Yes, Bug, she is *very* pretty." Kais shook out his whip. "Move back, please."

He aimed and brought the first pinecone down, then the second. He turned to Adalyn.

"Do you want to try?"

Adalyn's eyes grew wide. "Yes!"

She rushed to his side, taking the whip in her hands. He stood back and allowed her to attempt to crack it a couple of times.

"It's too big," the girl whined.

"Where's yours?" Kais asked.

He had given Adalyn a whip of her own two years prior as a gift.

Her face fell. "It's at home; my Mama won't let me use it."

Kais made a show of looking around, as though to see if anyone was listening. "Go get it."

"But Mama . . ."

"Go get it," he repeated. "Let me handle your Mama."

He was already on Lena's hate list; this wouldn't change anything.

"Okay!" It was a conspiratorial whisper shout, and he couldn't help but chuckle as the girl took off in the direction of the village proper.

"Hi," Adalyn shouted as a greeting as she raced off.

"Hello." The responding voice held laughter, and Kais turned to see Satori.

Adalyn had skidded to a stop in front of her. "I'm going to get my whip! I'm coming right back! Do you want to watch? Uncle Kais is going to show me how to use it. Maybe he'll show you, too. You're very pretty. Uncle Kais thinks you're very pretty, too. I know, he told me. Just now. He thinks—"

"Bug!" Kais shouted to get the girl moving again, especially before she said anything else. Though as he looked at Satori, he found he wasn't embarrassed with Adalyn calling him out.

"I'm going!" Adalyn shouted and took off again as Satori laughed, watching her go.

Very pretty. Kais let his eyes linger on the woman as she watched his niece run off, allowed her laugh to wash through him. Bond or no bond, the woman was beautiful, and he welcomed the effect she had on him.

CHAPTER TWENTY-NINE

SATORI

She lay on the mat, breathing in the cool air. She'd slept far better than she had expected on the ground, not to mention she hadn't froze. Though she supposed that had something to do with the proximity of Kais' tent. However, the extra warmth had disappeared some time ago, and she'd woken up. She wasn't cold, really; she still laid there, buried under the covers. That wasn't the problem. The problem was climbing out from beneath those covers and dealing with the air.

She was willing to ignore her bladder's prodding as well as her stomach's growling if only she could remain warm for a few more moments. When she could avoid it no longer, she slid out from beneath the folds of the blankets and quickly dressed, exiting her tent and finding a place to relieve herself.

She followed the voices and the scents. A group of people were gathered outside Marta's hut, but it was clear the majority of the people had already eaten and dispersed to do their own thing. When she made it to the food, she found something she'd never seen before. There were eggs, sausage, and cheese, but they were all wrapped up in a piece of dough so it could be carried and eaten as one stood or even walked. She would have to remember this when she went home. Tessa would love it.

Breakfast in hand, Satori began to walk the streets of the small village. Marta, the woman who had been responsible for feeding them and who had also stored their tents, had a small shop. She sold almost exclusively handmade items. Candles, soaps, socks and scarves, jams and pickles. If it could be made by hand, it was available in the shop.

Satori wandered the shelves, reading every single label and wishing she had some money to purchase some of the things for herself. Maybe one day she would be back.

She passed a pump house built over a stream that diverged from the river. A large barrel sat outside the door with a ladle hooked to the side. A sign said, *Drinks*. Satori paused to have a drink of the fresh cool water before she continued.

Voices from the treeline drew her attention, and she approached to find Kais and his men seeming to be practicing or training, though not seriously. They seemed to be goofing off, mostly. Kais stood in the middle with his whip, placing something on a large log. Stepping back, he sent the whip out in front of him, and it unfurled to the tree trunk, snapping one of the pinecones to the ground, leaving the other two undisturbed. It was amazing how precise he could be with such an odd weapon. He repeated the action twice more, easily flicking the last two remaining pinecones to the dirt.

Laughter and applause broke out, and Satori saw Adalyn standing off to the side, enthusiastically clapping for Kais. He motioned toward her, and she ran to replace the pinecones.

Satori stepped closer, enthralled by the precision with which he wielded the long leather strap. She'd never seen a weapon of its kind before. Adalyn rushed back to Kais' side, and he repeated his earlier actions, knocking two of the three pinecones off the log.

The little girl announced she had questions, and Satori moved in closer, hoping to also learn a bit more about the whip. But Adalyn didn't mention the whip. Instead, she started talking about how pretty someone was. Satori assumed she meant her mother, but she soon realized they were talking about *her*.

She stood there wanting to listen but also not wanting to hear. But then the conversation was over, and Adalyn was running up to her, talking faster than she could breathe. And then she was gone just as quickly, and Satori couldn't help but laugh. When she looked up, Kais was watching her. She felt her cheeks warm and hated herself for it. Why?

In an effort to get some of the attention off her blush, she pointed to the whip. "You're very good with that. I didn't expect it could be so precise."

"With enough practice." He held the whip out toward her. "Would you like to try?"

She was interested in how it worked. "Okay." Still, her feet wouldn't move.

Kais cracked a smile. "You'll have to come a little closer, Princess. At least close enough to reach the whip."

"Of course."

She nearly rolled her eyes at herself as she moved closer. The chill of the air left with Kais' proximity. That was one thing she might actually miss when she finally made it back home. He offered so much warmth physically. But when she met his eyes, she realized they held warmth, as well. Warmth entirely different from what she could feel.

Kais moved slightly to the side so she could stand where he had been. He handed her the whip and when she took it, she was surprised again at its weight. Wrapping her hand around the solid handle she realized that must be where most of the weight lay, since the rest of the weapon was basically just a rope.

She gave it a little swing, snapping her wrist.

Kais held up his hands. "Whoa, wait a minute. We don't snap our wrist; we use our whole arm. Like this." He stepped behind her, his chest extremely close to her back, and covered her hand with his.

A spark shot through her hand and up her arm, leaving goosebumps in its wake. She felt the breath that Kais blew out as he, no doubt, noticed it as well. She turned her head slightly, peeking out of the corner of her eye. He was watching her, his eyes running over the side of her face. Then he seemed to shake himself and remember what he was doing.

His rough skin coasted over the back of her hand, and her breath caught in her throat. More heat crept into her face, though she barely noticed, all her attention focused on where their skin made contact.

Kais cleared his throat. "Like this," he repeated, but his voice had grown lower and quieter. His hand closed around hers.

Shala, she couldn't think. What was she doing again? Kais lifted her hand. Right, the whip.

Slowly he bent her arm up and down. "Loosen your elbow, lock your wrist."

She did as he said, allowing her arm to become pliable in his grasp.

"Good," he purred the word into her ear and the goosebumps returned. "Now, relax. Don't do anything, let me have control right now."

Helias! Was he kidding? She closed her eyes momentarily, pushing away the inappropriate thoughts dancing around inside her head. She nodded.

Behind her, she thought he huffed a small laugh but wasn't sure. His grasp became more secure over her hand and the whip. He lifted her arm until it was pointed in front of her, then he lifted her hand, bending her elbow.

"This is what you want." He let her arm back down and then repeated the motions as he explained them. "Arm up. Bend elbow. Whip pointed up."

"Okay," she hadn't meant to whisper, but her voice just would not work.

"Okay," he repeated with a smile in his words. "When you swing, make sure the end goes all the way up in the air, pointed up and unfurled. Then bring the whip back, let it fall, and pull it back around. You want a little loop. Then when the loop hits the end of the braid, you get the crack."

He moved her arm through the motions slowly twice before releasing his hold on her hand and stepping farther to her left. "Your turn."

She was unsure at first as she brought the whip up in front of her, the way Kais had explained. She did it slowly a few times to get the rhythm, then tried for real.

"Ow!" When she brought her arm back around, the leather braid snapped her in the back.

Kais was back at her side. He reached out and straightened her wrist. "Make sure it's pointed slightly away so it doesn't hit you when it comes around."

"Now you tell me," she teased as he stepped away.

She raised the whip again, being careful to angle her arm slightly away. She started over, speeding her movements. The first time did nothing. There was no crack, but she also didn't hit herself.

The next time also produced no crack.

"Make sure you get the extension above your head," Kais said from her side.

She nodded, concentrating on the whip. She extended her arm, bent her elbow, and pulled the whip up. It stretched far above her head, falling behind her. She waited for a moment and then quickly pulled the braid back forward. A small loop formed and unfurled to the end of the whip, making a small cracking sound.

She couldn't help the excited shout that burst from her lips or the small hop she did where she stood. "I did it!"

When she turned to Kais, he was grinning at her, a full face smile that lit his eyes. And it was for her. She felt the blush and quickly returned her attention to the whip. She tried repeatedly, getting it to crack on at least half of the attempts.

"Me next! Me next!" Adalyn had returned with her child-sized whip in hand.

"Absolutely. I'm here to teach today," Kais said as he motioned Adalyn to him and proceeded to show her the same movements he had shown Satori.

Adalyn's first attempt resulted in a satisfying crack of the whip, and Kais picked the girl up and tossed her easily into the air. "I knew you could do it!"

Satori came to Adalyn's side. "Well done! It took me a couple of tries." She bent to speak conspiratorially with the girl, "He didn't toss me in the air, though. That looked like fun."

Kais stepped up beside them and placed his hands on his hips. "Well, if you'd like me to throw you in the air, you need only ask."

"Do it!" Adalyn squealed, and Kais and Satori both laughed.

"I think I might be a bit big for your uncle to be lifting me like that," Satori said.

Adalyn's face scrunched up, wrinkling her tiny nose, and she spoke ever so seriously, "Oh, no, he's very strong."

"I am very strong." Kais shrugged.

"I think I'd like to keep my feet on the ground, if you don't mind. Thank you, though."

"Very well, Princess." Kais turned toward Adalyn. "She said no, do you want to go again?"

The girl bounced on her feet. "Yes, yes, yes!"

Kais snatched her up and tossed her into the air again, catching her easily.

CHAPTER THIRTY

KAIS

She stayed for hours. She played with Adalyn, the two of them taking turns cracking their whips. He stepped in to offer help when he was needed but eventually they were both getting consistent cracks every time.

Adalyn had set up her own pinecones and was ceaselessly trying to knock them off. Occasionally she made it, occasionally she didn't; none of it was due to aim, all due to luck. She talked Satori into trying as well. The results were much the same, but the laughter was nonstop.

He spent too much time staring at Satori. He knew, so everyone else surely knew it, as well.

"Kay!"

He pulled his attention from Adalyn and Satori to look at Teague.

Teague stopped beside him, his eyes dancing between Satori and Kais, a knowing smirk on his face.

Kais rolled his eyes. "What?"

Teague raised his hands defensively. "I didn't say anything."

"Yeah. You were thinking it," Kais said, unimpressed but knowing the other man was only teasing. "What are you doing here?"

"A few of us are going to do some hunting." Teague indicated over his shoulder with a backward nod of his head. "Thought we could try replenishing some of the supplies they used on us. Interested?"

He was interested, of course; he wanted to help. But as his eyes drifted to Satori, he realized just as much he wanted to stay right where he was and observe.

Teague reached out with an elbow and knocked into Kais' arm. "Ask her to come along."

Kais swiveled his attention to Teague. "Hunting?"

"Why not?" Teague laughed. "It's not dangerous. Since you're in the *teaching* mood, you could show her how to use a bow. She'd probably be excited to learn."

Kais let his gaze wander back to Satori. Why not? She was eager to learn the whip.

"Princess?"

Teague spoke just above a whisper, "There ya go."

Kais shot him an annoyed look, and the other man laughed quietly, walking away.

Satori made her way to Kais, followed closely by Adalyn. "Yes?"

"We're about to go hunting, and I was wondering if you'd like to go along?"

Satori's brow rose as skepticism bloomed in her features, and mild excitement bubbled below the surface. "Hunting?"

"Sure." Kais shrugged, smiling because he knew she wanted to. "Have you ever been?"

"I can assure you, I have never been hunting." Her head tilted, and a small smile played on her pink lips. "But I think I might like to."

Adalyn jumped in front of Kais. "Can I come?"

Kais laughed and reached down to ruffle her hair. "I'm afraid not, Bug. You stay here and hold down the fort until we get back."

The girl's face fell, her bottom lip protruding slightly, but she didn't argue. "Fine."

"Good girl." Kais dropped into a crouch before her, tapping one finger on the hand holding the whip. "You keep practicing. We'll try to hit some pinecones again before I leave, alright?"

The frown disappeared, replaced by the kind of seriousness only a small child could muster. "I'll practice the whole time you're gone."

Kais stood back up, eyes on Satori. "Ready, Princess?"

She nodded and offered Adalyn a smile. "Good luck."

"You too," Adalyn said. "Uncle Kais is a good teacher. I bet you shoot a hog!"

The last word came out in a child's sort of growl, and Kais laughed.

"Well, we won't shoot anything if we never leave." He held out his hand for Satori to go first. "Princess?"

Satori began moving toward the tents. As they walked, she turned to him. "May I ask a question?"

He turned his head toward her, angling his chin down to meet her eyes, pausing just a moment to take in the deep brown color. "Of course."

She stared up at him through her lashes. "What's a hog?"

The laugh punched out of him before he could stop it or make her think he was laughing at her.

"Forgive me, Princess." He placed a hand over his heart. "I'm not laughing at you. It's just Adalyn. Sometimes she doesn't use proper terms. I didn't expect you wouldn't know what she spoke of."

"I know what a hog is?" He was glad to see slight amusement in her eyes and no offense at his laughter.

"You do." He caught his breath and cleared his throat. "A hog, Your Highness, is a boar."

"A boar?" she repeated. "Is that what we're hunting?"

They made it to the tent Kais shared with Teague, who was already there gathering his things.

"I don't think I've said good morning to you, Princess," Teague said as he strapped a quiver of arrows across his back, his long coat nowhere to be seen. "Good morning."

"Good morning, Teague."

"Yes," Kais spoke, answering her previous question. "Boar, deer, squirrel, fox, bear... Whatever crosses our path." He shrugged, ducking into the tent to retrieve his things.

"Turkey, pheasant, rabbit..." Teague offered.

"Bear?"

Kais remerged with his bow and arrow. "The bear isn't nearly as concerning as the boar."

"The hog?" she joked, and Teague laughed.

"Yes, the *hog*. Stay out of its way if we see one. They're mean and dangerous." Kais held his large knife out in her direction. "Take this. Don't be afraid to use it."

She reached out, wrapping her slender fingers around the large handle of his blade. Her fingers curled softly but firmly around the black stone scales. His mind began to wander and he shook his head slightly, lifting his gaze. He met Teague's eyes, and the other man stood, watching him, his eyes sparkling with amusement. Kais glared. Teague understood him far too well. The other man just shook his head, a smile pulling at his lips.

Teague held out his hand. "Give me your canteens. I'll go fill them."

Kais handed him two canteens, his own and one he'd grabbed for Satori, and Teague walked off, leaving them alone.

He turned to Satori. "I'm serious about the boar. They're vicious, steer clear."

"Noted," she said as she strapped the knife to the belt at her waist.

When Teague returned, they gathered the last bit of supplies and headed out. There were about eight of them, seven of his men and Satori, who decided to hunt.

When they had made it a significant way into the forest, Kais spoke up, "Split off, two in each group. Start here and fan out. Watch out for each other and stay alert." He smiled. "I'll give a bottle of my best whiskey to the man who gets the largest kill. Good luck."

The men began to pair off, and Kais turned to Satori. He didn't want to presume, and certainly didn't want to force her hand, but he had to work to get the words out, anyway. "You're welcome to stay with me, or you can go with Teague, if you'd like."

Teague paused at the sound of his name, turning back and waiting for her decision.

Satori appeared to grow shy as she looked between them, her cheeks taking on a pinkish tinge. Kais sucked the inside of his bottom lip between his teeth to keep from smiling at the sight. Did she know how beautiful she was?

"I'll stay with you," she said, and Kais' heart dipped into his stomach.

Teague nodded and raised a hand to wave. "Stay safe! Kill something large."

And then he was gone with his hunting partner, leaving Kais and Satori alone. She had chosen him, willingly chosen to be alone with him. He could have skipped, but he refrained.

Kais pointed his chin into the woods. "We should head this way. Get out of the path of everyone else."

Satori followed him deeper into the woods. "How far will you go before you start hunting?"

"Well, technically, we're hunting now," Kais answered. "If we see something while we're walking, we're not going to ignore it just because we're still walking. But ideally, we want to get farther away from the others so we don't mistake one of them for an animal."

"And shoot them," Satori finished.

"Correct, Princess." He smiled at her. "So, you've never been hunting, either?"

She gave him a look like he might have something wrong in his head. "Why would I ever have been hunting? We have people who hunt for us."

"But surely your father's been hunting. And he has people who hunt for him," Kais pointed out.

She huffed a breath. "I don't get out much."

"Your father doesn't believe in training women?"

She considered him for a moment. "I don't think it was so much my father as . . ."

Her voice trailed off, and he felt something odd from her. Disgust? Annoyance?

"His advisor." It wasn't a question—he assumed from Satori's reaction that was who she meant.

That guy must be a real gem. Kais wanted to ask a question but didn't want to trigger anything. Would she shut down? Or, was it possible, maybe she would open up? There was only one way to find out, though it would be an awkward hunt if she chose the former.

He focused his attention in front of him, not looking at her, not wanting to put her on the spot, any more than he had to. "Was he afraid you might learn to fight back?"

The question implied something that Kais had been suspecting for some time. The very idea of it made his blood run so hot he thought it might boil and burn him up.

Her steps faltered, and her breath caught twice. Kais hated to cause her pain, but he had to know. And there was no turning back now. *Please, Princess, talk to me,* he pleaded silently as the silence stretched.

When she spoke, her voice was thoughtful, "No doubt."

He closed his eyes at her words. There was a dull ache inside him, but he pressed on. "Have you ever fought back?"

A wave of sadness washed over her, followed by another wave of shame.

"No." Her voice cracked on the word, and his heart rent with it.

He stopped and turned toward her, touching her, barely, on the arm. "Do you want to learn how?"

She stopped and looked up at him. Her eyes shone as tears pooled there.

"Please? Please? I'll do anything." Then the tears fell, and she covered her eyes with her hands as her shoulders shook.

Kais stood helpless for a moment, not knowing what to do as her pain and shame poured into him. But then his instinct, tired of waiting on him, took over. He lifted his hand and placed it on her shoulder, sliding it slightly around her back. It was an invitation that she could either accept or reject. Much to his shock, she stepped into him, her arms met his chest along with her forehead, and he wrapped his other arm around her. He held her, silently praying to Shala that she felt the same comfort at his touch that he felt when she touched him.

He ran a hand up and down her back, speaking quietly, his chin brushing the top of her soft hair, "I'll teach you, Princess. And, if you wish, I'll kill him for you."

He smiled when he felt the tiny laugh. She stepped back and cold rushed into the space where her body had been. Had he ever missed anything so much?

"Thank you." She swiped at her eyes. "I'm not usually one to cry. I'm not sure what's wrong with me."

"Princess, this may sound silly, but if you ever need to cry, you can come to me." He hoped his words sounded sincere and not ridiculous. "Anytime."

She huffed a small laugh. "Thank you again."

Kais clapped his hands together. "Now, allow me to teach you how to bring a grown man to his knees. And not in any way he'll enjoy."

The corner of her mouth quirked up, and he couldn't help but respond with a smile of his own.

CHAPTER THIRTY-ONE

KAIS

For the next few hours, Kais showed Satori every way she could use to defend herself against another person. He allowed her to hit, punch, flip, and trip him, among other things he could think to teach her. The entire time his anger seethed against the man who made this necessary. What had this man already done to this woman? Where had his hands already been where they were unwelcome?

"Are you alright?" Satori's uncertain voice interrupted his thoughts.

He looked up, surprised at first, before he realized why she'd asked. His mouth fell open slightly. It hadn't been the way he held himself or the expression on his face. No, her knowledge was much more intimate. She knew because she could feel the rage seething inside him. Her face had gone slightly pale as she faced him.

"I'm sorry."

He let his eyes drift over her, not in a possessive or leering way, but in admiration. He met her gaze. She may not know how to fight or hunt, but she was strong. She had experienced he could only imagine what, and yet she still went on. She *still* counted the possibility that she might marry this man, this advisor, this tormentor, for her kingdom. She would do what she had to do for her country.

He admired the trait. He shared it. But while he ran from it, she faced it head-on. While he camped in the woods and traveled with a band of soldiers, she lived in the castle with someone who was a constant danger to her person, only to do her duty and what was right. He wanted to protect her. He wanted to keep her safe. He wanted to destroy that advisor, send him to Helias and let him rot there. Precious, she was precious, and how was it that not everyone could see it? It was so clear to him. She stood there in front of him, looking at him expectantly, waiting for him to tell her what was wrong, her blonde hair braided down her back, her brown eyes holding questions. She was precious.

"Kais?"

He blinked. Would he ever get used to the sound of his name on her lips? He hoped not.

"I'm sorry," he repeated his earlier words but with an entirely different meaning this time.

She laughed slightly. "You said that."

He smiled. "I know. The first time I was apologizing for the anger. I was just thinking of . . . your father's advisor."

Her smile faded immediately.

"The second apology was for staring off into space for so long," he continued. "I apologize. I was lost in thought. It happens occasionally."

"I understand. It's something I also experience." She looked around at the dirt they had trampled and torn up. "We didn't do very much hunting, did we?"

Kais shrugged. "I have faith in Teague and the others. They've probably brought down a buffalo by now."

"Or a *hog*." Satori giggled.

"Or a hog." He laughed as well at the way she said *hog*.

"Well, if we're not going to hunt . . ." her voice trailed off as though she was uncertain about her next words.

"What is it?" he encouraged.

"Maybe you could show me more with your whip?" She gave him a hopeful expression. "It's so fascinating to me. It's like a rope you can aim."

He chuckled at her enthusiasm. "Indeed. Yes, I would be happy to show you more. I think you need your own whip. You can amaze all your subjects with your skills."

She scoffed. "My father would love that."

"You're a grown woman, Satori. And a Princess." He leveled a look at her. "You will have a whip."

She laughed. "I'll need to learn to use one first."

He popped the snap that held his whip to his waist and pulled it off, letting the braid unfurl to the ground. He held the handle out toward her and she accepted it. Kais walked about 8 feet toward a large tree. He pulled out his knife and plucked at some of the bark until there was an obvious bare space about the size of his spread hand.

He made his way back to Satori and pointed at the mark. "Hit that."

Satori laughed at him, and the sound traveled the length of his spine. "I can't hit that."

He shrugged. "Why not? I can."

She shot him an incredulous look. "You've been doing this quite a bit longer than I have."

"The only difference between us is practice." He crossed his arms over his chest. "With practice, you can do what I do. So, practice." He moved out of the way of her and the whip and waited.

Tentatively she cracked the whip a few times before trying to aim at the spot on the tree. She missed by leagues every time. But that was alright. Kais wasn't lying when he said it was only practice. With enough practice she could do what he did. And she seemed to have a natural affinity, she just needed to work on her aim.

Satori let out a frustrated grunt, and Kais smiled. He approached and she shoved the whip at his chest. "You hit the mark."

He took the whip and moved a safe distance from her. Pulling his arm back, he sent the tip flying, hitting the mark directly in its center. When he looked at her, she was shaking her head.

He handed the whip back to her. "You'll get it."

She rolled her eyes, shaking her head, and then something drew her attention. She turned her head, focusing. Kais followed her line of sight but saw nothing.

Satori squinted. "What is that? Do you see it?"

"I see nothing, Princess," Kais said, squinting in the direction she was looking.

She began walking silently in the direction she had been looking, Kais following. Then she stopped.

"Shala," she breathed.

He stepped up behind her and finally saw what it was that had caught her attention. "Well, you do get to see a hog today. A very dead hog."

An enormous, dead boar lay at their feet, mostly covered by brush and leaves.

"It's so big." Satori stared, eyes wide. "How did we miss it?"

"I don't know." Kais' eyes ran the length of the animal that must have weighed the same or more than he did. "It's over here pretty far and mostly covered."

"How long do you think it's been here?"

"Can't have been here that long." He pulled in a breath. "It doesn't stink."

Suddenly a small gasp escaped Satori, and her hand shot out to Kais' arm. "I know why it doesn't stink."

Kais pulled his attention from where her hand rested on his arm to look up. "Why?'

"It's not dead."

"What?"

Alarm shot through him. Being so close to an injured animal wasn't safe; certainly not an injured boar. He scrutinized the animal more closely. Then he saw the most subtle rise and fall of its stomach. It wasn't surprising they had missed it at first. The animal wasn't dead, but it didn't look as though it had much life in it.

Satori stepped closer to the animal, and Kais held a hand out toward her. "Careful."

"I know." She said over her shoulder. "What should we do?"

It was a good question. Did they leave it? Kill it? Put it out of its misery? Kais wasn't even sure what was wrong with it. Slowly he stepped around the end of the beast, moving in a circle, examining it from all angles. When he got to its back, it was obvious what the problem was. A long seeping wound ran from the animal's right shoulder down its back, nearly to its flank. It was a mortal wound, for sure.

"It has a large cut down its back. I don't know what caused it, but it won't live."

Satori's face fell. "How sad."

Kais stepped again toward the animal's head, and his foot came down on a large branch, snapping it in half with a resounding crack. The next moments happened so quickly, and yet he seemed to watch it at a much slower speed.

The sound woke the sleeping giant, filling it with a burst of adrenaline. It leaped to its feet with a vicious, snarling growl and spun on the first person it saw: Satori.

White hot fear shot through Kais as the boar began to charge, squealing out threats. "Satori, move!"

Satori did move, but she and the boar changed directions at the same time, sending them careening into each other. The boar caught Satori in the thigh, flinging her into the air like one of Adalyn's rag dolls. She screamed, and the sound drove into Kais like he had been struck by lightning. Terror burned in him, and he didn't know if it was his or Satori's or some combination of the both of them. Satori cried out again, and the boar turned on her, intent on finishing what it started.

Kais' first instinct was to rush to Satori, but if nothing was done about the boar, they stood no chance. His legs pumped as he raced for his bow and arrows. He hit the ground, sliding to where they sat. He snatched them as he rolled back onto his knees, nocked the arrow, aimed, and fired. The arrow flew into the beast's eye, dropping it to the ground in a second.

Kais dropped the bow and ran to where Satori lay. The boar's first attack had cut into her thigh; the wound bled through the cut in her pants. But the second one, the second one was the wound she would not survive. A slice ran down her side, from just at her rib cage to her hip. The injury was wide, gushing blood, and Kais could see clear through to bone and muscle.

A sob burst from his lungs as he pressed his hands onto her wound. She cried out at his touch.

"Satori, shhhhhh." His voice came out shaking. "Just don't move. We'll get you help. We'll get you help."

This was wrong, it wasn't supposed to be her. He was the one—he was supposed to die. Not her.

She tried to swallow and choked, and a thin stream of red trickled from the side of her mouth. Her brown eyes, which had been joking only moments before, were filled with agony.

"You- you-" She tried to swallow again. "You're scared."

Everything in him hurt, and he bit back another sob. "Yes, but I'm going to get you help."

"No time. It hurts." Her voice was quieter. "Your- your knife."

"What?"

What was she saying? His knife? Did she know how bad it was? Was she asking him to kill her? To end the suffering? He couldn't. He couldn't.

"Satori-"

"Kais." Pain laced her words. "Knife. Please."

His gaze tossed around frantically, searching for the fallen blade. The knife lay among the brush and leaves. He had to move to get it. He had to let go of the pressure on her wound to get to the knife.

"Satori, I can't. I can't reach it. If I let go-"

She coughed again more violently, and a fresh gush of bright red blood pushed out between his fingers. The air left his lungs, and he had to fight to replenish it.

"Go."

He took a moment to look at her, she had grown so pale from the blood loss. Too pale. Tears filled his eyes. This wasn't how it was supposed to go. Kezia had said it would be him.

"Hold on."

Reluctantly he released the pressure, and the blood flowed. He groaned as he dove for where the knife lay.

"Hurry." There was a desperate plea in Satori's quiet voice.

"I'm coming, I'm coming."

His fingers closed around the hilt, and he scrambled back to her side, clutching the knife, terror at what she might ask him to do with the blade squeezing the air from his lungs.

Her arms rose weakly, and her fingers rested on his forearm. "Cut your hand."

"What?"

Was she hallucinating—going out of her mind? Why would he cut himself?

"Do it." Her fingers closed ever so slightly on his arm, and fear hit him that it was the most strength she could muster.

He didn't want to cut his hand, he wanted to heal her. But it was painfully clear there was no help for her. She had only moments left. He wanted to take her in his arms and hold her, but he would humor what would surely be her last request. He lifted the knife and laid it across his palm. The blade bit into his hand, blood welling immediately.

"It's done. I cut my hand."

With strength he didn't know she still possessed, she reached out.

Frustration and confusion built inside him as he allowed her to take his shaking, bleeding hand. She placed it on her wound, allowing their blood to mingle together.

"Satori, wha . . ."

"Shh, wait."

His shoulders slumped as he did as she said and waited. Then he felt it. The oddest sensation he had ever—or, he was sure, would ever—feel. The gaping gash in Satori's flesh began to pull together beneath his touch.

"What in Helias?"

A small smile drew up the corners of Satori's mouth as she closed her eyes and let her head relax. "Told you."

"What is this?" Wide-eyed, he watched, watched it happen with his own eyes; the skin of the wound drew together and closed.

"It's your blood," she said weakly, but already sounding better.

His blood? He moved his hand, letting the blood coat the length of the gash. His blood was healing her. The term *blood mates* was far more literal than he had thought. He moved his hand from her waist to the wound in her thigh and pressed his bloody palm to her leg.

Looking up, he found her watching him, life returning to her brown eyes.

He stared wide-eyed and amazed, and then joy, unmatched, unbridled joy, bubbled up and burst from his lips in shocked laughter. She met his laughter with a smile. A smile he thought he would never see again in this world. He reached up to brush hair out of her face, the action leaving a red streak. They were both already covered in blood, so he ignored it.

"How did you know?"

She pulled in a breath and looked him in the eye. "When you were hurt in the river... You were very hurt."

He had woken up with a headache. That's it.

"I wasn't injured, I hit my head."

She nodded once, slowly. "You did hit your head. Hard. It was large and bleeding. Bram made them come get me and . . . There was so much blood, it was everywhere. He'd been suspecting about the bond. He said the only thing he could think to do was call me."

Kais listened, wide-eyed and shocked.

"He asked me if I trusted him, and when I said yes, he cut my palm and placed it on your head," she continued. "It healed immediately. I'd never seen anything like it."

"How bad was it?"

"It was bad, Kais." Her fingers closed tighter on his arm. "You wouldn't have survived."

"What happened?"

The shock of how close he had come to death was nearly overwhelming.

"When you went into the water, the rapids tossed you into a rock; you hit your head so hard." She blinked as if seeing the memory. "I didn't know a head could bleed so much."

"There was no blood when I woke up. I only had a headache. Why didn't you tell me? Teague didn't even tell me."

"I made them promise they wouldn't," she said. "I'm sorry. I made them. We cleaned everything up."

"Why?"

Why would they do that? Why wouldn't they tell him how close he had come to death?

"I thought it would make it easier," her voice cracked. "I thought if you knew, it would make it harder to let me go."

She wasn't wrong there. Now that he knew the extent of the bond they shared, he had no intention of letting her go. And he would make sure she felt the same way.

He stared, his mouth slightly open, just looking at her. This woman had saved his life, and he hadn't even known it. Hadn't even been able to thank her properly. She was an angel, *his* very own guardian angel.

He didn't think he would have talked himself out of it if he had thought about it. He simply leaned down, cradling her neck in his blood-soaked hand, and pressed his lips to hers. The charge was immediate; red hot fire burned in his chest as his lips molded to hers. She must have felt it too, because she let out a small gasp, and he took the opportunity to deepen the kiss. Then she was responding, her lips moving beneath his, their tongues dancing together.

Every touch felt like magic, and he could have stayed in that place all day and all night, forever. This woman was his future. If he hadn't known it before, he did now.

"Kais! Satori!"

They pulled apart, turning toward the voice. Teague was walking past them at a distance.

Satori shifted, and Kais turned his attention to her again. "Are you okay?"

She smiled at him, her eyes once again alight. "Thanks to you, I am. I'm just trying to sit up."

"Here, let me help."

He moved to help her shift into a sitting position. The amount of blood that soaked the ground around them, not to mention their clothes, boggled his mind. He looked back at her, now seated, drenched in red.

"What?"

"I just . . ." He gestured toward their clothes. "I'm so glad I met you."

She looked at their clothes and burst into laughter.

"There you are!" Teague shouted, coming to join them. He moved closer, his vision falling on the scene before him. He froze, eyes growing round. Then he was running. "Kais!" Teague hit his knees by Kais' side, terror blazing in his eyes. "Shala and Miram! What happened? Are you okay?"

"Teague, Teague." Kais held up a hand to halt the other man's ramblings. "We're fine. We had a run-in with a boar."

The breath whooshed from Teague's lungs. "This is boar blood?"

Kais and Satori exchanged looks.

"It's my blood," Satori said.

Teague's eyes fell to the slice in Satori's shirt and the large hole torn in her pants.

"Helias," he breathed the word. "Princess, how are you alive?"

Satori glanced up at Kais and reached out to take his hand. She turned it over to show Teague the slice down his palm. The only thing that remained was a long pink mark, her blood having healed him as his healed her.

A laugh punch from Teague. "That's a handy little trick the two of you have."

"Yes it is." Kais shot Teague a pointed look. "Especially handy when you hit your head on a rock and nearly die. Much more trusty than some friends who refuse to tell you how close you were to your own mortality."

Teague had the good sense to look at least a little sheepish as he exchanged a look with Satori, she tossed her eyebrows. Kais couldn't stay angry with them. He was far too grateful that both he and Satori were still in the realm of the living to be very upset with her or Teague.

"So..." Teague shook his head slowly as he surveyed the area around them, taking in the bloody ground as well as Satori and Kais' clothes. His eyes met Satori's. "You saw a hog."

Satori gave a tired-sounding laugh. "Up close."

Teague looked again at the ground and then back between Kais and Satori. "You two ought to carry vials of each other's blood at all times."

Kais huffed an unimpressed laugh. "We'll get right on that."

Then Teague gestured toward the enormous dead animal. "Who won the whisky?"

"I did." And Kais fully intended to collect his winnings after the day he'd had.

Teague's eyes turned serious, moving between Satori and Kais. "How bad was it?"

Kais' chest tightened at the thought, his imagination taking him to what could have been a grim reality. He pressed his lips together and looked down at Satori.

She reached up and took his hand, looking at Teague. "It was very bad, but thankfully, for some reason, Shala and Miram chose to bind us together, and it's saved both our lives."

Kais scoffed, saved them? "It's put both our lives at risk."

"I don't think so," Satori said. "I would have been attacked and kidnapped on the road either way. Then again, maybe you're right. The only reason you saved me was because of the bond."

Kais was quick to respond to that one, "That's not true."

Was it though? Would he have decided to trade away so many supplies to save her if there hadn't been a connection? If he hadn't walked up to that wagon and felt her heart thundering in her chest and the terror radiating from inside like it was its own entity?

Satori offered him a knowing smile. "Even now, you're not sure."

He studied her for a moment, her brown eyes, her hair, and clothes matted with blood. "So how can you trust any emotions with regards to me? Aren't we being played by the gods?"

Her eyes dropped as though she was thinking before she returned her gaze to his. "Don't you trust the gods?"

"With the crops? The weather? Sure." He could say that because gods or no gods, there would be crops, and there would be weather, and life would go on. "With my life?" He could only give her an uncertain expression.

"If Shala and Miram can handle the crops, weather, and the state of the world, then I think they can handle two insignificant people."

"Insignificant?" Teague scoffed, reminding them of his presence. "I would wager neither of you is insignificant."

Kais shot Teague a look, speaking up before the other man said anything more, "Certainly not you, *Princess.*"

Out of the corner of his eyes, Kais saw Teague roll his eyes. It had been a long day, and he wasn't interested in delving any further into his own life story.

Bitterness permeated her. "And what good will it do me? I will return home; you will return . . ." Her eyes swept over him. "Wherever it is you came from, and that will be it."

"Do you really think that after Shala and Miram connected you, gave you a chance to meet, threw you back together, and allowed your connection to grow, you would both be able to just go your separate ways and forget this ever happened?" Tegaue's eyes moved unbelieving between the two of them.

Was he right? Kais took her in again, this woman who had been on the brink of death in his arms only a short time ago. Did the gods have bigger plans for the two of them? Could he convince her father that he was a worthy option for her hand, despite the tension between their lands? And was that what was best for him? For her? For their countries? She had asked if he trusted the gods. He had never given it much thought before, but now that his actual life was wrapped up in the answer, he realized maybe it was something he should settle on. Could he have her? Could he have her legitimately? He cleared his throat, trying to clear his thoughts as well.

"What I do know is that we should go. I've been staring at this blood for long enough. I need to wash."

"Absolutely." Satori moved to stand and swayed dramatically.

Teague and Kais reached out at the same time, each catching an arm. Her eyes grew wide for a moment.

"Blood loss," she breathed.

For the third time that day Kais didn't think, he simply acted. He slid an arm under hers and in one fluid motion swept her legs out from beneath her.

She let out a surprised sound. "I can walk."

He turned his head to the side, and her face was there—right there. Her eyes were so beautiful, her lips inches from his. "And you're a beautiful liar."

Her eyes dropped to his lips for a second, and desire washed through him. Hers. His breath stuttered for a moment as his heart missed a beat. Her eyes returned to his, and he did nothing to mask the twin emotion churning inside himself. There was no hiding from her, even as she couldn't hide her feelings from him. They were open to each other. It was the most intimate thing he had ever experienced.

CHAPTER THIRTY-TWO

SATORI

She felt like a child. The problem was that she was significantly larger than a child, and yet Kais seemed to have no issues carrying her. She allowed herself to relax into him, feeling safe, and didn't miss the slight tightening of his fingers where they held her. Safe. She felt safe in his arms. If someone had told her, even a week prior, that she would be feeling the things she was toward Kais, she would have laughed at them. Yet, here she was, nestling into his hold and drinking him in. A warmth radiated from him that had nothing to do with temperature, and she was sure it was because he knew what she was feeling at that moment.

She was feeling other, less complicated things, as well. She was desperate for a wash. Some of the blood on her clothes had begun to dry while in other places it was still soaked. She was also beginning to feel nauseous from the coppery tang that permeated the air around them.

She had been attacked by a boar! Now, in Kais' arms, having nothing else to focus on, her mind wandered back to the moment the boar had torn into her. There had been no pain at first, and then all at once it had felt like her insides were being pulled out.

If she hadn't been awake to tell Kais about the blood, she would be dead by now. Dead. Then what? Would her father pass his crown onto Henrik? Her nausea increased at the thought of her country in the hands of that man.

Kais' attention shot to her, his brows drawing together. "What is it?"

Her first instinct was to assure him it was nothing. But instead, she decided to talk to him. "I was only thinking what might have happened to Dunleigh if I had died."

"Don't think about that," Kais said. "There's no point in dwelling on what might have been when you are alive and well and perfectly capable of running your country when the time comes."

"Thanks to you."

"I wouldn't have known if you hadn't told me."

An edge of panic seemed to flit through him. No doubt he was also imagining what might have happened, even though he told her not to.

She reached up and touched his cheek, waiting a moment as the sensation of their contact passed through her. "It is a good thing we found each other."

His eyes ran over her face for a moment before he moved his head to the side and pressed his lips to hers. It was the same jolt as when they touched but magnified by 100. She had to leave this man, leave him behind and go home to who knew what. How could she do that? She broke off the kiss and met his eyes, and when she smiled at him, he returned the expression.

"When we get back, there's a stream they use for washing. I'll show you where it is so you can get cleaned up," Kais said.

"Thank you. I've never been this disgusting in my life." She sighed. "I'm making myself sick."

They had grown close enough to the village that she could hear voices and the sounds of daily life. "Put me down, please?"

Kais smiled. "I'm not struggling, Your Highness."

"I know, but look at us. People are going to ask what happened. If I'm walking on my own two feet, we can tell them this is boar blood. But if you're carrying me, they'll want to know why." She met his eyes. "It's not exactly a common occurrence."

"Maybe it is in my country," Kais countered. "You don't know."

Satori rolled her eyes at his joke as Kais set her gently on her feet, keeping an arm around her waist for support. Soon they started seeing people. Or rather, people started seeing them. Eyes grew wide with shock and horror. At least one person slammed a hand down over their mouth and turned away.

Teague drew up closer to them. "You are going to be telling this story for a month."

"Longer," Kais shot back with a huff.

As he said the words, a group of people swarmed them, everyone wanting to know what happened.

"It's boar blood," Kais said, his voice raised to be heard over the din.

Satori didn't miss the look that passed between Kais and Teague. It was pointed, and Teague nodded his head in answer. Teague would tell their story however Kais wished it. She and Kais would go down in the village history for fighting a boar, being soaked in its blood, and coming out unscathed.

After explaining at least four times, Kais finally stopped, causing her to stop beside him. "Alright, we don't need to keep repeating the tale; you can go share it now. But will someone please find us some clothes so we can get cleaned up?"

"Right away, sir," a middle-aged woman called out before quickly disappearing into the crowd.

Sir? Satori had only heard his men refer to Kais as sir. It seemed odd that a woman from the village would call him that. Maybe she was just used to hearing it from the soldiers?

They were stopped yet again, recounting their fabricated tale, when the woman reappeared, handing a bundle to Teague who nodded his thanks. Teague turned and gave it to Kais.

"Thank you. Now," Kais surveyed the crowd, "if you don't mind?"

"Not at all." Teague turned toward the group and laid a finger and thumb just inside his teeth.

The sound he emitted was ear-splitting, and Satori laughed at how quickly everyone ceased their chatter and focused on him.

"Thank you. As I'm sure you can tell, Kais and the Princess would like very much to clean up. If you could all disperse and give them a chance to do that, no doubt they can share their tale again later."

Kais laid a hand on Teague's shoulder, shooting him a grateful look before leading her away from the crowd and into the tree line. "It's right through here."

They emerged into a small area clear of foliage, the trees replaced by a small pool, a light mist floating on its surface. Water fed into it on one side in a small stream, and then drained out the other, keeping the water from growing stagnant.

Satori stepped to the edge and looked in. A small laugh escaped her at what she saw. The bottom. She could see right to the depths of the crystal clear pool. Brown, grey, and speckled rocks covered the bottom.

"It's so clear."

"And deceptively deep," Kais answered, observing the water. "In most places, it will nearly cover your shoulders. Over there," he pointed to the far side of the pool, "it will cover your head. Try to stay on this side."

She peered into the depths, fascinated. "It doesn't look that deep."

Kais' attention turned to her, and she could feel his eyes on her. "Not everything can be taken at face value. Sometimes there are far greater depths to be discovered."

She looked up, holding his gaze for a long moment until he suddenly looked away. "Well, I'll let you get to it. I'll be inside the tree line if you need me. I promise I won't look."

Satori's cheeks warmed at the thought of him watching her bathe, and beyond her own will, her breaths came slightly quicker. Then she felt it, the same sort of frenzy that was inside her, coming from him. She looked up and met his gaze, and his eyes seemed to burn into her. *Shala.* She had to pull herself together. She was here to get cleaned up.

"Thank you."

With a single nod, he turned and began to walk back toward the trees. *Helias,* she was losing her mind.

"Wait?" Her heart began to pound in her chest.

He froze mid-step, not turning, just waiting.

She swallowed down the large knot in her throat and spoke, "Will you help me? Please? First, before you go?"

She felt like an idiot. She didn't need help. Her corset tied both in the front and the back. She dressed and undressed herself every day without the need for assistance. But she wasn't ready for him to be so far away; she didn't want to be alone.

He turned and met her gaze, his eyes on fire, sending a thrill through her from the top of her head to her feet. He stepped back toward her slowly, as though he was trying not to startle her. He moved in front of her. Her eyes darted away from his, and she turned, pulling her hair over her shoulder, off her back. If Kais noticed that she could undo her own laces, he said nothing.

She could feel the pressure of his fingertips resting on her back through her corset, then his right hand traveled down to her side as he took hold of the destroyed material. The boar had sliced it over halfway down the side, as well as her flesh. The tips of his fingers feathered lightly over where the enormous gash had been, but only for a moment, and then his hands were back on her laces.

Slowly he pulled the ties apart, thread after thread sliding from their places in slow agony. He stepped closer, and she felt the heat from his body through her clothes as his breath coasted over her ear. Her corset fell open, and she moved her hands to hold it in place as he pulled the last laces free. Air hit her back through her shirt and sent goosebumps chasing up her arms.

Kais placed his hands on her hips and gently turned her toward him. She knew her cheeks were blazing, could feel her face on fire. She kept her gaze down, embarrassed for him to see her blush. His fingers found her chin and lifted it until she met his eyes. When his fingers left her chin, they held each other's gazes as his hands found the shoulder portion of her corset and pulled. He pulled until she was forced to remove her hand as the brown leather was removed. Kais held it out and dropped it beside him, still holding her gaze.

She felt so exposed, only a tattered shirt covering her. Another chill raced over her, her breasts peaking beneath her shirt. She couldn't be sure if the reaction was from the chill in the air or something else.

Then, Kais, still holding her gaze, lowered himself down until he was crouched before her, his fingers finding the laces of her boots and working them free. He looked up through his lashes.

"Put your hands on my shoulders."

His voice had taken on a husky quality, and the sounds sent stirrings straight to her core. *Helias!* He lifted her feet, one at a time, and removed her boots. The blood had even found its way inside her shoes.

Kais' hands moved to his own boots, expertly undoing the top portion of the laces and pulling them from his feet as he stood. He was so close, towering over her, her head tilted nearly impossibly far back to look him in the eyes. If either of them breathed in too deeply their bodies would surely brush against each other. Her breaths became shallower as the weight of his gaze pressed on her.

CHAPTER THIRTY-THREE

KAIS

K ais was almost appalled at the number of times in the past day—hours, really—where he had shut his mind off and just let his body, his heart, lead. This would be no exception.

As she stared up at him, her cheeks blazing and expectancy lighting her brown eyes, he pushed rational thought to the side once more. He lifted her off her feet, cradling her in his arms. A startled gasp escaped her as her arms closed around his neck, bringing her face inches from his.

Careful of his footing, he stepped toward the edge of the water and then into the gentle flow. Underground hot springs heated the water, so no matter how cold it was outside, the pool was still warm. Another surprised sound issued from her lips, her breath light on his face.

When he was deep enough, he let her go, allowing her to rest her feet on the smooth rocks at the bottom of the pool. His eyes drifted down, and air left him as he forced his gaze back up. Her loose shirt was beginning to cling to her in the warm water. This may have been a very bad idea. Her eyes met his as her hands slid around his back. He thought she would stay that way, holding on, her body pressed to his, but that was clearly not her intention.

Her fingers closed around the material of his black tunic, and she tugged, pulling the shirt from where it was tucked into his pants. When the shirt was free, he didn't wait for her, he reached for the hem and pulled it over his head, letting it fall into the water with a splash.

Her hands left his waist, and a jolt ran through him as they landed on his chest. She ran her fingers lightly across the area. He held his breath and mentally plastered his hands to his side, afraid of what he might touch if he allowed them free rein. When her fingers slid down his side, to his waist, and dipped just slightly into the band of his pants, he gave up.

He raised a hand to her shoulder where her shirt rested. As he trailed his thumb down, along her neck, and over her collarbone, he was rewarded by the sight of goosebumps pebbling on her skin. Heat rushed up his neck and then down as he let his touch drift over her shoulder and down her arm, taking the collar and sleeve of her shirt with it until it hung off her bare shoulder.

He lifted his eyes to hers again, checking in. The last thing he wanted was to cross a line. She stood with her eyes closed, her face a picture of calm. There were no signs of protest, and he felt no discomfort from her. Her heart fluttered and a mostly unfamiliar sensation pooled inside her. He'd thought he'd felt it from her once before, but this time, he was certain. Desire. He kept his attention on her face as he slid his hands back down her side and brought them up again, under her shirt, along the soft skin of her back. Her eyes opened, and she sucked in a breath at the contact of his skin on hers.

Her eyes met his, and the flutter of her heart kicked up to a much more rapid tempo, or was that his own? He wasn't even sure anymore.

Satori's hands left his chest, and she stepped away, slowly backing farther into the warm water. Confusion pressed in, her movements said she wanted to be away, but the swirl of emotions inside her told him something very different. He remained still, waiting to see what she would do.

The sun had begun to sink and the moon to rise. The full moon was only two days past. The large bright orb lit the night through the space above the pool where no trees grew.

Her hands disappeared beneath the water's surface, but her eyes remained on his. There was movement, but the waning light made it difficult to see what she was doing. That was until she drew her tattered shirt, still pink with blood, over her head and dropped it into the water beside her.

Now Kais was certain whose heart was thudding as he took in the moon's glow on Satori's wet shoulders. She disappeared beneath the surface for a moment before reemerging, head back, letting her hair wash out of her face with the flow of the water. Her tattered pants floated to the surface beside her as she pulled her braid over her shoulder and began to work the matted strands loose. Kais tore his attention away from the pants to watch her fingers move over the tangles and snarled areas. His own fingers twitched, the desire to be the one combing through her hair rising inside him.

Why couldn't they be his fingers? He stepped toward her until he was close enough to take her hands, stilling them. He lifted the braid back over her shoulder and, with the barest nudge, she turned around, giving him her back and better access to the hair.

He tugged slightly, pulling her head backward to wet the hair, and the sight of her hair in his fist and her neck bared did things to him. He closed his eyes and pulled in a deep breath, releasing it and returning to work on the tangles at the base of her skull.

When he was finished, he combed his fingers through her hair, washing away the day.

Satori turned her head to the right and spoke over her shoulder. "Thank you."

"You're welcome." He moved back around in front of her as she stared into his eyes. He reached out again and trailed a finger down her cheek, pausing at her shoulder to push the rest of her hair back behind her, allowing his thumb to trace circles over her collarbone.

"Kais." Her voice was quiet and hoarse.

"Yes?" he breathed in response.

"Will you touch me?"

His heart skidded to a dead stop in his chest and then resumed at twice the pace. He wanted nothing more than to touch her. *Helias,* he'd wanted to touch her since almost the moment he'd seen her. He wanted to touch her all night long. He took the slightest, tentative step toward her, barely daring to hope he'd heard her correctly.

"Are you sure?"

"I asked, didn't I?"

He chuckled and her returned smile was all he needed. He stepped close, aware that she was about two seconds from knowing just how much he wanted to touch her. He slid his hands onto her hips and moved until his body was almost pressed to hers. Her eyes widened slightly as her smile grew knowing, and he gave her a half shrug.

He allowed his hands to wander up the curve of her waist until his palms brushed the bottom of her breasts.

"Helias," he hissed through his teeth.

She didn't move, and he pulled his hands forward, moving them to cup the swell, allowing his thumbs to brush across the peaks. Her lips parted on an exhale.

Her heart rate increased, fluttering in his chest. He brought his eyes to her face. Her eyes were closed, a small crease sat above her nose, her mouth parted slightly. He might have asked her if she was in pain if he hadn't been able to feel the pleasure emanating from her. This time he watched her as he brushed across the place again. The crease deepened, and more breath pushed from her parted lips. He smiled, carefully rolling one of them between his thumb and finger. Satori's eyes shot open, a small breathy moan, pitched high, emerged from her as she reached out and grabbed his wrist.

He ceased his motion, concerned it was too much or she didn't like it. But his worries were soon gone when she whispered, "Do that again."

Her words sent a jolt of desire directly to his middle.

"Yes, Your Highness," he obliged, pinching once again, eliciting the same sound.

He moved his face closer, allowing his lips to skim over her jawline. He smiled against her skin as she turned her head slightly, craning her neck to the side, giving him better access. He let his mouth wander over her jawline and down her neck, moving farther down. He pulled in a breath and dipped his head under the water's surface, replacing his fingers with his mouth.

Her hands dove into his hair, tugging gently, though not to pull him away, to move him closer. Helias, he was about to burst.

Kais stood back up, pulling in a quick breath before moving his lips to Satori's. "Princess, are you okay?"

"Do you have to ask?" she breathed out, her eyes still closed.

He didn't. He could feel all the ways that she was okay. Kais reached around her back to her opposite shoulder and gently turned her until her back was flush against his chest, parts of him touching places on her that made it very difficult to concentrate on anything. He slid his palms across her chest, just under her collar bone, and up until he tilted her neck enough to provide him access. He dipped his head to the left side of her neck, nipping her gently. She didn't move when he released her chin, and he moved his hand slowly down her chest, brushing across her breasts, lower, over her navel, and lower.

She froze in his hold, and he froze as well. The last thing he wanted was to make her uncomfortable.

He felt no discomfort, but he asked anyway. "Satori, are you okay?"

Her chest rose and fell with great breaths, and she nodded her head vigorously.

He chuckled deeply in her ear, licking the outer shell. "Just checking."

His hand resumed its course until he was greeted with evidence of just how *okay* she really was.

"Satori," he breathed into her ear as he ran his thumb over that sensitive bud that he knew ached for his touch.

She moaned softly, her head falling back to rest on his chest. She turned back around, wrapping her arms around his neck.

"I need you." Her words were desperate and quick before she leaped up, wrapping her legs around his hips and bringing her mouth crashing down onto his.

He caught her with one arm, holding her securely as he raised his other hand to cup her cheek. Their eyes locked, and he brought his forehead to hers, taking in the need that burned in her gaze.

Kais had never wanted anything so much in his entire life, but he refused to go too fast or push her too far if she wasn't entirely ready.

He closed his eyes, taking in the moment, holding his breath for a beat before he let it out and whispered, "Are you sure?"

She pulled back the slightest bit, just enough that he opened his eyes and met her gaze. She was smiling.

"Please stop asking me that. I am sure."

He would not need to be told again. He moved his hand from her cheek, over her shoulder, down her waist and over the curve of her backside as he slid his fingers carefully to her core, slipping inside her.

Her arms closed tighter around him, her head dropping to his neck, and the sound she let out was the most seductive thing he'd ever heard.

A breeze kicked up around them as he spoke softly into her ear, "I've never felt anything like you, Satori."

Her breaths pushed out in soft gasps as he worked, his ministrations making him more than ready to move on.

With her arms wrapped around his neck, her body pressed to his, she lifted her head slightly, their gazes locking as he held her. He brushed his lips against her, removing his hand, pushing at his pants before grasping her waist. He lifted her slightly and then slowly lowered her back down. He clenched his jaw as he slipped inside her, not stopping until they were fit together.

Her eyes closed, her lips parted, and her head fell slightly back. He would have done the same if he hadn't wanted to drink in every single reaction from this woman. The water's surface rippled around them, but Kais barely noticed, all his attention focused on Satori.

He moved once, twice, and her fingers dug into his shoulders as she tilted her hips, and Kais nearly saw stars. *Helias.*

Buoyed by the water, they moved in unison. Kais kept one hand behind her, holding her up. With his other hand he reached between them, sliding into that spot just above where they were joined. He worked his hand between them and let his thumb slide over her. Satori's back arched, her head flying back, her mouth opening as heavy breaths issued from her in gasps.

"Satori," he breathed her name, pleased by her reaction.

Her body tensed beneath his touch, her legs tightening around him, her arms pressing her body into his until there was barely enough freedom for him to continue to move his hand between them, but he did.

Spurred on by the sounds she made and the reaction of her body, he continued, his legs beginning to shake as his own pleasure grew almost too intense to stand. Satori's head suddenly dropped to his shoulder, her face pressed into his neck, her gasps turning to short moans. He pressed her as close as he could, trying to get as deep as he could as her nails dug into his back and a guttural sort of scream tore from her lips, followed by his name. She buried her face further into his neck to muffle the sound, but he wasn't sure it had done any good. Someone might come any moment to make sure she was alright.

He picked up his tempo, not planning to be left behind. Once, twice, three more times, and his release hit him. He threw his head back, letting it wash over him, his breath punching out of his lungs.

Above them, the wind, which had been nonexistent, billowed, causing branches to bend and leaves to swirl violently.

"Look," Satori's breathless whisper drew his attention. "The water."

When he looked down at the surface of the water, it seemed to vibrate. Almost the same as it looked when the finest of rain fell, just barely enough to disturb the surface, but still it moved. And not just from their movements, all across the pool, the surface rippled, small waves covering the entire body of water.

She met his eyes, inches away from his. "Is that us?"

He looked around again. "I think it might be."

Something about the energy around them as they came together affected the air and the water. What was this force that connected them?

"Do you think it's only here or in the village too?" A sheepish look crossed her face, and he imagined she was blushing, though the lighting was too dark to tell for sure.

He chuckled. "It seems to be only around us. I don't see the trees blowing farther out."

She met his gaze again. "Wow."

A smile turned up the corner of his mouth. "Indeed."

"We should get back, maybe?"

The last thing he wanted to do at that moment was let her go. He had no desire to feel her body slide off his and leave him only one person again. "Do we have to?"

She laughed. "I think if we don't soon, they'll send a search party."

That was a thought he didn't want to entertain. "We can't have that."

Slowly he lifted her up and away from him, their eyes locked as they disentangled. She was only inches from him, their bodies nearly still touching, and still she felt miles away after the connection they had shared.

He lifted his hands to her neck, sliding to cup her jaw as he bent and kissed her one last time before leaving the place where they were alone.

They climbed out of the water, dressing in the new clothes they had brought along and gathering up the old, torn, and bloody things to take back to camp and dispose of. They walked side by side, and surprise hit him when she slid her hand into his. He was pleased to find that the spark when they touched remained in spite of them taking their relationship to the next level.

Was that what it was? Was it a relationship? Or a fling that would be over when he dropped her off at her door? In her mind, at least. He had no intention of that being the end of their partnership.

When they finally returned to their small camp in the village, the place was quiet. It had grown late, and nearly everyone had turned in. Though one person remained.

Teague stood from where he was seated beside a fire sharpening a blade, his long coat back in place. "Well, I was concerned that maybe you two got lost or attacked by another boar. But then I heard screaming and decided you were fine."

He kept a straight face though his eyes danced with mischief.

Mortification from beside him hit him as Satori turned her head and buried it in his shoulder. Kais wrapped his other arm around her, trying to stifle his laugh. "We appreciate you not coming to check."

"My pleasure," Teague replied with emphasis. "And I'm pretty sure I'm the only one who heard, if that helps."

"It does not help," Satori replied with a large breath. "Oh, I don't know why it bothers me at all, he would have told you, anyway."

Kais turned a mock offended expression on her. "I think I should be offended that you believe I would share secrets like that."

Satori tossed a hand toward the other man. "It's Teague! I'm surprised you two don't have a blood bond."

Teague laughed. "We never needed one before."

Kais chuckled. It was amusing but ultimately probably true. Though he liked to think that he would have kept it to himself if she had asked him not to say anything.

They lapsed into silence for a few moments. He didn't want to ruin the atmosphere, and he was afraid his next words might. But they needed to be said.

Kais turned to Teague. "We'll pack up in the morning."

Satori's gaze shot toward him and he felt the disappointment, which actually made him feel good. Until he realized that if he could feel her disappointment, she could feel his relief, and that probably wasn't translating correctly. *Helias.* That trick could come in handy, but could also be slightly problematic.

Finally, he turned to her. "We'll talk in a moment."

Teague spoke. "Down the mountain, we had a message waiting from Devlin when we arrived. I'm sorry, I forgot to tell you. But he said they're waiting at the meet-up point with our supplies." Teague paused and his eyes drifted to Satori for a moment.

"What is it?" Kais asked.

"He said they also have a message for you from your father."

Kais let out a quiet breath and nodded. His father was probably wondering why he hadn't heard from Kais recently since Kais was a few days behind schedule, thanks to Satori.

"Alright, I'm ready for sleep. I'll be in in a minute."

Teague nodded. "Goodnight. Princess." He dipped his head slightly in Satori's direction.

"Goodnight, Teague."

Teague turned, disappearing into the tent he shared with Kais.

Kais turned to Satori and held an arm out toward her tent in invitation. She turned, dropped the pile of torn laundry outside the flap, and stepped into the small tent. He followed.

"How long before we reach your men down the mountain?" She found a cup and filled it with water from the pitcher, taking a drink and passing it to Kais.

He took a long pull from the cup and returned it to her. "Less than a day. We'll camp with them tomorrow night. Then we'll see if there are any messages from anyone regarding you."

"Me?" She refilled the cup and drank again.

"In case your father is looking for you, they'll no doubt have news, or even direct communication, if the men that took you divulged your whereabouts to anyone."

"And then you'll take me home," she said quietly.

"Only if you want to." He *knew* what she would say, but had to leave the option there for her.

She gave him an almost sad look. "You know I have to go home. I have responsibilities beyond my desires. I can't just abandon my country."

He took her in for a moment, the thought crossing his mind about whether or not he would abandon his country for her. He wouldn't, of course, but he wanted to.

"If there was a way you and I could work things out, would you want to?"

"If only that were possible." She stepped closer and slid her arms around his waist. "We'll just have to make the most of our time until then." She stretched up on her toes, kissing him. "But I've had a very long day." He laughed at that. "I think it's time we get some sleep."

He rested his forehead on hers. "I'm going to work on our problem; you sleep well." He pulled back and kissed her forehead, leaving her alone.

Kais stepped into the tent and stopped as the flap closed behind him. Teague sat on his cot, a book in his hand, eyebrows raised in expectancy. Kais let out a puff of air, shaking his head.

Teague snapped his book closed. "You were really only supposed to show her where the pool was."

"I wanted to convince her to stay?"

Teague produced an expression of mock shock, glancing down briefly. "Someone thinks very highly of himself."

"Shut up," Kais sneered. "Don't make me pull rank."

Teague raised his hands, palms out, in front of him, though still rather insincerely. "I meant no offense, and I beg your pardon, Your Majesty."

Just the sound of the title made him want to groan. He threw his head back, gazing at the tent ceiling as he sat.

Teague continued, his expression turning a bit sympathetic, "She doesn't know about that yet, does she?"

Kais looked at his friend. "No. And I'm honestly surprised, being here in the village."

Teague chuckled. "These people are like family. I doubt they even remember you are the Prince."

"Lucky for me."

"You are going to tell her, though." It was a question phrased as a statement.

Of course he was going to tell her. "Yes."

"Look, Kay, I know you already know this, but I'm going to say it anyway . . . You need to tell her sooner rather than later. You've already waited too long."

He wanted to snap at the man, but he held his tongue because Teague was right. Helias! How had he let this go on so long?

He blew out a breath, his shoulders sagging. "Yes."

"It may work out in your favor," Teague said. "She's being urged to marry, you're eligible. Not only that, but the alliance will make your countries much stronger."

"Eligible?" Kais scoffed, running a hand across his scruff. "A letter sits on her father's desk even now petitioning him for her hand."

Teague placed his hands behind him, leaning back. "I wasn't going to bring it up."

Kais couldn't sit any longer, he stood and began pacing the small space. An easy thing since two strides covered the distance.

"For all I know, the letter from my father at camp contains news of her father's response." He barked a bitter laugh. "Which is probably a large *no* since no doubt they think I've kidnapped her." He tossed a hand in the direction of Satori's tent.

"I suppose we'll know tomorrow." Teague's eyes followed Kais as he made two more laps across the tent. "Kay, you can do nothing about any of it tonight. Why don't you sleep? It's been a long day, and another waits for us tomorrow."

Kais stopped, propping his hands on his hips, staring into nothing. "You're right." He seated himself once more on his cot. "And I'll tell her tomorrow."

CHAPTER THIRTY-FOUR

SATORI

She lay on her cot, staring at the canvas ceiling—the memory of Kais' touch playing repeatedly in her mind. The way the leaves swirled and the water danced. She laughed and then laughed some more, throwing a hand over her forehead. She stopped laughing—she was an idiot. What had she been thinking? She never should have let him touch her, never should have touched him.

Tomorrow they would meet back up with Kais' men and send a message to her father to let him know that she was well and safe and on her way home. Home. Then what? Then absolutely nothing. Nothing. She would go home to her father and her castle and marry either someone she didn't know or, worse, someone she did. Kais would go back to leading his men without a woman in tow. They would go on with their lives and never see each other again.

Something like actual pain burned inside her. What had Shala and Miram been thinking? There were no two people less suited for a blood mate bond than she and Kais. A Princess promised to another, and a soldier, the enemy of her land.

"Helias!"

For a long time she lay awake, contemplating the turn her life had taken. She must have eventually fallen asleep because, at some point, she became aware of the now familiar warm honey feeling, and then the spark of contact.

Unconcerned by his presence, she opened her eyes slowly and found Kais kneeling beside her bed, one hand gently brushing the hair away from her face.

"Good morning, Princess."

Morning. She had spent half the night dreading morning. But with Kais' rough palm in her hair, the dread seemed to lessen.

"Morning."

"It's time to pack up. I'm afraid we need your tent."

"Of course."

A yawn pushed out, and she covered her mouth as she sat up.

Kais nodded to the small table in the tent. "Marta heard about yesterday and sent you a fresh set of clothes. She assures me they will fit."

Satori looked to where Kais indicated. A white shirt, black corset, and maroon pants rested on the table. She returned her attention to Kais, still kneeling beside her cot.

"I'll be out in a minute."

He rested both hands on her knees, where she sat with her legs crossed, staring up at her.

After a few moments of silence, he smiled softly. "I'll be waiting."

The clothes from Marta fit perfectly, and Satori made her way directly to the woman to thank her. She found Marta dishing out pre-rolled breakfast pies, and instead of interrupting, Satori slid in beside the woman and began helping her distribute food.

"Thank you so much for these clothes, they fit perfectly. And they're beautiful."

"Ohhhh." The other woman waved a hand, as if dismissing Satori's thanks. "After your ordeal yesterday, you deserve them. Only the best for our Princess."

Satori's hand was halfway to a man's plate when she paused. *Our Princess?* She wasn't their Princess. She wasn't even sure exactly whose land she was in. King Lexon, she thought. She'd never met the man and only knew what she was told, mainly that he was interested in overthrowing her father. Though, after having met Kais and his men, she was beginning to question everything she'd been told. She was pulled from her thoughts when the man she had been handing the wrapped breakfast to finally reached out and took it.

"I'm sorry."

"It's alright, Your Highness."

"Alright, grab your gear!"

Satori turned toward the voice she had come to know so well. Kais, Adalyn riding atop his shoulders, grinning, and Teague beside them, were walking toward them.

"We leave in ten minutes."

The last of the men made their way through the line, and Satori began to clean up the leftover bits.

Marta's hand closed on hers as she worked. "Please, Princess, let me do that."

"Marta." Kais stopped beside the woman. "What would we do without you?"

"Starve," Marta answered, unimpressed.

Laughter danced around the group as Kais lifted Adalyn off his shoulders and turned to wrap his arms around Marta. "We appreciate you."

"Thank you, sir."

"None of that." Kais turned to Teague. "I need all the sustenance to keep this one in line."

"Indeed." Teague's voice dripped sarcasm, and Satori smiled.

She loved the relationship Kais and Teague shared.

It was Teague's turn to embrace Marta. "You know it's the other way around."

"I know, I know," she said, patting his back. Marta released Teague and turned to Satori. She tossed a thumb in the direction of Kais and Teague. "You no doubt will have to keep them both in line."

Satori laughed, her cheeks heating at Marta's implications. Ignoring it, she stepped up to the woman and hugged her. "Thank you again for the clothes. All of them."

Marta stepped back and rested a gentle palm on Satori's cheek. "I'll always have clothes for you, all you need to do is show up."

Emotion flowed through Satori. She was touched by Marta's kindness and also saddened when she thought of how she would most likely never see the woman again after today.

"Thank you."

"Alright, alright, Marta," Teague teased, stepping up beside Satori and offering her his arm, which she accepted. "Leave the Princess alone."

Marta slapped playfully at Teague as he led Satori away from the woman and toward Kais.

"Ready for another walk?" Kais asked.

"I suppose I have no choice."

She pulled in a deep breath, squaring her shoulders for the journey. Not only for the walk, but for what seemed like the first step toward her separation from Kais. How odd to her that it even mattered. It wasn't that long ago that she would have done anything she could to run away from him, and now she only wanted to run *into* him.

"I'll meet you both at the front." Kais moved around them, presumably to talk to his men.

As he passed Satori, he rested a hand on her arm. It was only for a second, but that feeling—she would miss that spark.

She held Teague's arm as they walked.

"He's had female friends, he's not a monk," Teague began. "He's thirty. I mean, it's expected that he would have some experience."

She turned her head toward him, slightly bewildered at where he was going with this line of thought.

"What I'm trying to say," he continued, obviously sensing her confusion, "is that I've seen him with other women. None of them affected him the way you do. And I don't just mean physically with the bond."

Satori sighed. "Teague, what am I supposed to do? What would you expect someone who was to inherit a throne to do? Throw it all away to be with a soldier in the woods?"

Teague looked down at her, leveling his serious blue gaze on her. "He's more than just *some soldier,* and you and I both know it. And you and I both know that if Shala and Miram planned this connection that's so very rare between the two of you, you could at least give them the benefit of the doubt that they would know what they're doing."

"But do they?" Exasperation filled her. "A Princess from one country and a soldier from another? The two countries themselves at odds? It's unthinkable, Teague. Why?"

Teague glanced over his shoulder at the same time that Satori felt the comforting warmth cover her.

He stopped and disentangled her arm from his. "Talk to him."

Teague moved his gaze behind her, where she knew Kais was standing. He nodded once and then turned to disappear into the large group of men behind them.

Kais stepped into the place Teague had vacated. "I've known Teague a long time. Truly, he is a better man than I am. But if you would allow an inferior substitute, I would be honored to escort you, Your Highness." He held his arm out with a warm smile.

Satori slid her hand through the crook of his arm, smiling. "You could never be an inferior substitute."

She let the spark of contact wash through her as she nestled closer to him, uncaring of what those who saw them might think.

After a moment of silence, Kais spoke, "What did you and Teague talk about?"

She smiled. "He told me you were not a monk."

Kais cleared his throat. "Indeed? I'll have to have a discussion with him."

She laughed quietly. "He also said he didn't think Shala and Miram would bond two people who would not work together."

She felt it when he stiffened slightly beside her. She turned to focus on him more fully. "He said to talk to you."

Kais' eyes stayed focused on their feet for several strides, his face a mask of contemplation. She could feel his indecision, as though he wasn't sure he wanted to speak, or that he did want to speak but wasn't sure how to say the words. Her stomach tightened.

"Kais?"

He looked at her at the sound of his name.

"What is it?" she asked.

He was making her nervous with his silence.

"I don't mean to make you uneasy," he said quickly. "It's just that there is something I need to tell you, and I'm not sure how to say it. Or how you will take it."

"If you don't mean to make me uneasy, this is not the way to go about it."

Kais lifted his eyes, surveying the area around them. Finally, his gaze came to rest on a large boulder off to the right of the path. "Would you mind sitting with me for a few moments?"

She looked from the rock to the men behind them. "Won't we be holding up the group?"

"No, they know where they're going. They'll just get there before us." He pulled his lip between his teeth, dipping his chin to level his gaze on her. "Please?"

Her chest tightened, unease clawing at her insides. Whatever he wanted to discuss with her was serious. She couldn't even form words, such were her nerves; she only nodded at him.

He held out his hand and led her toward the boulder. She didn't miss the look he shot at Teague or the approving nod Teague returned it with. If Teague looked like that, this couldn't be a bad conversation, could it? Unless Teague thought it was a bad idea for them to pursue any kind of relationship? But it hadn't seemed that way when he had been speaking to her earlier.

She took a seat on the rock, Kais seating himself next to her. For a few moments they watched the rest of the men pass by, most lost in their own conversations.

When her stomach had knotted to the point where she could stand it no longer, she broke the silence. "Kais, I'm sure you already know, but just in case, I'm going to tell you anyway: you're making me nervous."

She was hoping he would laugh her nerves off, or assure her there was nothing to be concerned about, but when he looked at her, she felt the same from him. He was just as nervous about this conversation as she was. And he knew what he was about to say.

She disliked the delay. "Please?"

Kais pulled in a long breath. "I'm afraid you'll view me as deceptive when I tell you this. Please understand that was not my intention. I never started out to deceive you, and my men were given no orders on what to say or what not to say. We simply continued our lives as usual, even after you arrived with us. And you can check that with any one of them. This is just how we live.

"I did wonder how we made it through the stay at the village without this coming out. But, again, this is the way we live. We don't acknowledge any special status and the people of the village know I prefer it that way."

She squinted at him, trying to understand what he was saying. Special status?

"Satori, I have a title other than the General of these men."

"I don't understand."

"You've no doubt heard of King Lexon?"

"King of Evandor? Of course."

Kais swallowed deeply. "He *is* the king of Evandor. He's also my father."

The air left her lungs. *Father?* She could have been knocked off her seat with the slightest touch, the slightest breeze. She shook her head slightly. But she knew the King's sons' names.

"I've never met the King, but I'm not ignorant, either. King Lexon has two sons, Octavian and Leopold."

"Yes," Kais answered softly. "Leopold Theron Silas and Octavian Roland Kais. My brother and myself."

Now it was Satori's turn to swallow. Octavian Roland Kais, son of King Lexon. Son of the King. Prince. A prince. Kais was a prince. The longer she sat staring, processing, the farther her mouth fell open until she felt the touch of Kais' finger, lifting her jaw back into place.

His thumb ran gently over her chin. "I'm very sorry I didn't tell you. I didn't want you to presume anything, and then I just didn't think about it. Because we don't." He gestured toward where the men had disappeared. "We don't recognize the royal titles among the men. And in the village, I've finally gotten them to stop referring to me as the Prince. I'm just Kais, and I just want to be Kais. That isn't to say that I won't take on my responsibility when the time comes, but I like to be out among the people. I want to know them, not just rule over them."

Satori's eyes found his. "You're a prince."

He pulled his lip between his teeth, slowly pushing it out. "There's more."

"More?" How could there be more? Wasn't that enough of a shock for one day?

"As you're aware, parents of royals, no matter how old, are often eager to marry their children off."

Satori's heart sank. He was engaged. Or at least spoken for. Promised to someone else. Her stomach twisted inside, and she couldn't help the soft whoosh of air that left her lips.

A small, almost sad, smile passed over Kais' lips. "It's not what you think."

"What do I think?"

Annoyance was beginning to rise in her, and she really didn't even know why. All he'd said had made sense. She didn't believe he'd been trying to deceive her. So why was she feeling this way?

"You're thinking that I've been promised to someone else?" He said the words as though they could be a question or a statement.

Of course he knew what she was thinking, what else would she be thinking after what had happened in the pool?

She shrugged helplessly. "Aren't you?"

Unexpectedly, he reached over and covered her hand with his own. "I told you, it's not what you think."

"What then?" She shook her head, trying to think of what it might be.

"After we attended your festival, I reported back to my father. He immediately decided it would be in the best interest of everyone if he wrote to your father and bargained for your hand, aligning our countries. You could make us stronger and we could help your people."

What?

"Your father wants to marry me?" The thought twisted her stomach.

Kais chuckled. "No, Satori. Not for him." He glanced down and then looked up, meeting her gaze, something burning in his eyes. "For me."

Satori's head spun. "Your father wrote to my father to propose an alliance between our two countries through a marriage between you and I?"

"An alliance and an integration, of sorts."

Something seemed to buzz in Satori's limbs as his words sunk in. She could sit still no longer. She stood and began pacing back and forth in front of the stone on which Kais still sat. He watched her silently, waiting.

"But how did I not know about this? My father presents all offers to me."

"My father's proposal likely arrived after you were already taken."

She stopped pacing, turning her gaze on him. She felt like she was in a dream, like everything she'd been told was wrong. There's no way the things he was saying could be real. Kais. Kais?

"You're a prince?"

He smiled. "Yes, I am."

"And your father is seeking my hand for you?"

His voice grew quieter. "Yes, he is."

It was a joke, it had to be. It was too easy. "Truly?"

Kais stood and came to stand before her, taking both her hands in his. "Truly, Satori. I told you Shala and Miram wouldn't do this to us only to tear us apart. They seemed to have worked it all out."

"You?"

She could have him? Have him and their bond, and her kingdom and his kingdom joined together? Have peace? Have Henrik thrown off a cliff?

Kais stepped closer until their toes touched. He released her and lifted his hands to cup her face. Dipping his head, he locked eyes with her.

"There have been things in my life that I've been uncertain of, questions that I've faced that I didn't know the answer to. I had to guess at my decisions. But sometimes, I'm handed things to which I know the answer, beyond a shadow of a doubt. You're one of those things, Satori. I've never been more certain of anything than I am of the fact that you and I were meant to be together. I was very literally made for you, and you for me. You are mine, and I am yours. If you'll have me?" His brows rose with his last words, with hope and fear, his uncertainty filling her.

He was right—nothing had ever felt so right. She nodded her head as a smile spread across her face. "Yes. Yes, of course."

A grin broke across his face like she had never seen from him before, relief pouring from him, and she responded with one of her own. Then his mouth was on hers, intense at first and then slow and full of passion, and she wanted to melt into him.

He broke off the kiss but kept his forehead pressed to hers. He looked like he was in pain, but Satori felt no pain from him.

He breathed out a deep sigh. "As much as I would like to stay here and forget about everything else, if we take up much more time, we won't make it to my men by nightfall."

She closed her eyes again and breathed him in for a moment before stepping back. "Alright then, if you insist."

His hands closed on her upper arms and squeezed gently. "Trust me, I don't want to."

When he released her he held out a hand, and she took it, lacing her fingers into his.

They walked in silence for a bit as Satori's thoughts turned over and over. Had she agreed too quickly? Was it the right decision? Was this best for their countries?

"That's a lot of indecision over there," Kais said quietly, not looking at her. "Are you having second thoughts?"

She snapped her attention to him, squeezing his hand. "No, no, I'm not. It's just . . . Is this all because of the bond? What would our relationship be like if we didn't have this thing connecting us?"

"I want to say everything would still be the same. Provided we survived." Satori chuckled at those words, something she could do, now that it was over. "But I don't know. On the other hand, why should we be concerned about that? It's clear this is meant to be, predetermined by something higher than us. Even if we wanted to argue it away and say it wasn't real." He shook his head, holding up their joined hands. "It's in the blood. I've never heard or seen anything like what's between us. There's no way to explain away the fact that our blood will heal each other. The only way to explain it is that this," he tightened his grip, "is real and meant to be."

They lapsed into silence again until she felt something like nervous hesitation from him. "What is it?"

He looked at her with a face that showed concern, his eyes dancing over her face.

"Satori…" He hesitated.

"Yes?" she prompted.

"I want to ask you something, but I don't want you to feel pressured, and I don't want you to be uncomfortable." He paused, inhaling as if bracing himself. "But I feel I need to know. Before I wanted to know, I wanted to know everything about you. I still do. But this is something I need to know."

Nerves danced low in her stomach as she anticipated his question. She couldn't be certain, but she had an idea what it was he was going to ask.

"Tell me about your father's advisor."

There it was. Even though she'd expected it, her breath still hitched, and a pit still formed in her stomach. She could feel her lip about to tremble and clamped her mouth shut tight to keep it from doing so. She hated to appear weak, and she hated to think about Henrik because he made her feel weak.

Kais stepped in front of her, placing both hands on her face again, compelling her to meet his gaze. "You don't have to worry about him anymore. You're with me now. I am yours, and you are mine. Not his. I'll kill him for you if that's what you want."

He wasn't joking or jesting. There was only seriousness in his words. If she asked, she had no doubt Kais would end Henrik. Is that what she wanted? It gave her pause when she realized she had to think about it.

Kais' voice quieted to a whisper as his thumbs ran lightly over her jaw. "Tell me."

"He—" She drew in a sharp breath and cleared her throat. Then she lifted her head and looked Kais in the eye, siphoning the courage she saw there. "He would come to my room anytime he wished. I had no knowledge or resources to stop him or fight back." She looked away. "He took what he wanted and left. Whenever he wanted. And he threatened people I loved if I were to tell anyone."

Anger flared from Kais, a white-hot thing she'd never felt from him before, though when she looked up, she found his expression hadn't changed. His eyes closed for a moment, and when he opened them again, the anger had ebbed significantly, like it was washing away. Instead, she felt . . . Her eyes widened as she lifted her head to better take in his features as the feeling flowed through her. An ache formed in her throat as she fought to hold the tears at bay. He didn't say anything at first, but she felt it.

He wrapped his arms around her and drew her to his chest. She pressed her face there, breathing him in. Basking in the warmth and in that one emotion.

He spoke into her hair. "I love you, Satori."

She hadn't known if he would say it out loud, and he was just as surprised as she was when he did. With anyone else, she would have questioned the sentiment. After all, they hadn't known each other all that long. But with him, she had an advantage. Not only did she hear him express his love, but she could feel it emanating outward from within him.

The tears she had been holding onto flowed from her in a rush she hadn't anticipated. "I love you."

And she did. She did. Once again, she was shocked at the feeling herself. His arms closed tighter, and he held her. She didn't know how long they stayed there, but it was until she stopped crying.

"Thank you for sharing with me, for trusting me," Kais said. "I know it was hard, but it was there, unspoken between us. I didn't want you to feel like you had to hide it, and I didn't want you carrying it alone anymore. You never have to carry anything alone again."

She sniffed and nodded into his chest. She did feel better, lighter, and more at ease knowing he knew. "We should go. If we keep stopping, we'll never make it ."

CHAPTER THIRTY-FIVE

KAIS

He saw them before they saw him. Two of the soldiers, seated at their post, watching the perimeter.

The one on the left looked up. Recognition flashed across his face, and he quickly reached over and slapped at the man next to him. They both jumped to their feet, backs straight.

"Sir."

The sun had begun to sink into the horizon.

"As you were. Where's Teague?"

"At your tent, sir. Waiting for you."

"Thank you."

Kais led Satori into the center of the large camp. Tents were erected in neat rows, torches and fires burning brightly around the space. As they made their way through, men jumped up to salute and then took their seats again when he and Satori passed.

"It's like you're important," Satori teased, and he chuckled.

Teague approached, arms spread wide, his coat flapping at the back of his legs as he walked. "I thought you would never make it!" When he was in front of them, he stood at attention, arms stiff at his side and dipped his head. "Sir. Princess." Then he was back to Kais' friend and not his soldier. "You have a letter from your father." Teague looked at Satori. "And one from hers."

"A letter from my father?"

Teague nodded. "Also, we've heard that there are some soldiers staying at Mooran. So far, they haven't come this way; they're just there. And we're told they've been there for some time."

Mooran was a town barely a half day's ride from where they now camped.

"And you don't know why?" Kais asked.

"No idea." Teague tossed Satori raised brows.

"Well, let me see these letters." Kais could only imagine what his father or Satori's father could have to say to him.

Teague stepped to the side and held out an arm, inviting them to go ahead.

They entered Kais' tent, the familiarity enveloping him. He'd been too long away. He'd missed having a desk. He held an arm toward a chair, inviting Satori to sit. She perched on the edge of the seat, nervous about the letter he now saw on his desk.

He unsnapped the whip at his hip and rested it on the surface of the desk as he rounded to his chair where he sat and reached for the letter from his father.

Breaking the seal, he unfolded the missive. As he expected, the ultimate point of the letter was to let him know that his betrothed had been kidnapped and he was the suspect. He glanced over the top of the letter, meeting Satori's expectant gaze.

"I kidnapped you. I have not been given permission to contend for your hand."

"Of course not. If you've kidnapped me, you should not be allowed to marry me. That makes sense."

He smiled as he put the letter down and picked up the next one. He eyed the seal and then looked at Satori, flipping it so she could see.

"My father."

"Indeed." Kais shot Teague a look as he cracked the seal and read the first few lines. "Well, now we know who the men in town are."

At his words, dread coiled inside Satori; he felt it in his chest, the sinking feeling pulling her under.

He turned his attention to her. "Satori, it's alright. We'll clear it up."

The dread did not quiet, but she still nodded at him. He reached into the drawer in front of him and pulled a pen, a piece of paper, some wax, and his seal. He scribbled a reply on the paper, folded it, and sealed it.

"Have someone run this to the town," he said, handing it to Teague. "We'll see them tomorrow."

Teague nodded as he accepted the letter and disappeared out of the tent. Kais' eyes found Satori again. Fear still painted her features and her emotions. He stood and moved around to where she sat. Taking her hands, he pulled her to her feet, and with one finger he tipped her chin up so he could look her in the ey e.

"Don't fret. We'll take care of it. And until then . . ." He dipped his head, capturing her soft lips with his. He took a moment to savor the reaction of their contact before he deepened the kiss.

He'd been waiting for this moment all day.

"Wait right there," he said with a smile as he moved to the tent flap. He opened it and stepped halfway outside. Two men stood guard. "Have someone bring some food. Leave it outside."

The man nodded. "Yes, sir."

"And Reed?"

"Sir?"

"No one comes in this tent. For any reason."

"Yes, sir."

Kais stepped back inside, arranging the heavy flaps to fall closed evenly. When he turned, Satori still stood where he'd left her, facing him. He allowed himself to take in her form. The black corset was a definite step up from the brown one. And yet, his fingers still itched to remove it.

He covered the distance between them in three strides, sliding his fingers into her hair and claiming her mouth. She moaned softly and he blew a breath out his nose at the sound.

Walking her backward, he led them to the bed. Satori didn't hesitate to sit, and then he was laying her down, lifting one knee to kneel over her on the bed, each of them half on and half off the matress.

With his left hand still cradling her head, Kais trailed his right down her jaw, along her neck, and over her chest until he located the laces of the corset. He tugged and worked the laces until it was loose enough for Satori to lean up and pull it off. He cupped her breast, running a finger over the tip the way he knew she liked. She moaned into his mouth, and he nearly came undone at that one small sound.

Her hands came up to pull his tunic from his pants, and he paused what he was doing long enough to pull his shirt over his head. Something lit in Satori's eyes, and she pushed him up, off of her, but not for long as she followed him, gaining better access.

As he sat on the bed, she knelt one knee between his legs, facing him, her mouth exploring, kissing his temple, his cheek, his jaw, his throat. *Shala.* She proceeded to kiss down his chest until her hands found his belt. He didn't wait for her to do it herself; he unlatched the clasp and, lifting slightly, pushed his pants and everything onto the floor. He sat beneath her, at her mercy, as her tongue explored everywhere, traveling down and down until she knelt before him. He let his head hang backward, propping himself up, fighting to keep himself together as she worked.

Finally, when he thought he would burst, she stopped and stepped back. He was simultaneously sad and thrilled. He didn't want to finish in her mouth, but he did want to finish inside her. He watched as she took two steps back and, holding his gaze, slowly removed her own shirt and pants, leaving her just as bare as he was.

When she stepped back to him, she placed a gentle hand on his chest, and he slid back slightly. She lifted one leg, straddling him, still keeping that eye contact. His breath left him in heavy puffs. Her lips found his and she kissed him as she lifted herself and sank onto him.

"Shala," he breathed the word.

She pulled away from his mouth just barely, just enough to speak.

"No, Satori," she corrected.

He laughed as he wrapped an arm around her back, kissing her again. When she began to move, he saw stars, like the very air around him sparkled.

Her hips moved slowly, rhythmically. Stretching his neck up, he took her mouth in his, biting down gently but firmly on her bottom lip.

Her arms rested on his shoulders as she moved, and he watched as she closed her eyes and let her head fall backward. He could feel his own release coming, but he would hold out, if only to watch the scene in front of him.

Satori's mouth was open, air leaving her lips in soft puffs. Her brow drew together into what was almost a look of pain, but he knew better. Her thighs clenched tighter around his legs, and he tightened his grip on her back just slightly, mesmerized by her beauty.

Her head fell back, and she cried out, snapping her mouth shut suddenly and biting down on her lip. Her eyes flew open as her chest heaved, and she shot a glance toward the tent flap. He smiled; it was definitely no secret what was happening in here, and he couldn't find it in himself to care at all. He stopped concentrating so much on holding back. He let himself go, and his release came in seconds, chasing after hers.

Her head rolled until her forehead came to rest on his, eyes closed in exhaustion, contentment washing through her.

"I love you," he whispered.

Her eyes remained closed, but she smiled widely. "I love you."

Shouting pulled Kais from sleep. He was reluctant to wake Satori from where she was nestled and resting so peacefully on his arm, but the shouts grew louder, and then Teague's voice joined them. As carefully as he could, Kais slid out from beside Satori and quickly pulled on his clothes. He attached his whip and stepped outside.

"What's going on?"

The shouts were still out of his line of sight, and the guard at his door gave him a shrug that said he was just as confused as Kais. Kais moved in the direction of the shouts. When he arrived at the ruckus, he found his own men, Teague included, with swords drawn. They stood facing a couple dozen men Kais didn't recognize, and one he did. Fury raged to life inside him, and he fought it down, needing a clear head.

He stepped past some men and came to Teague's side. "What's going on here?"

"Where is she?" the tall blonde man hissed.

The King's advisor sneered at Kais, looking at him as though he was something on the bottom of his horse's shoes.

Teague turned his head toward Kais, but only looked at him for a moment before returning his attention to the other men.

"They seem to think we've kidnapped the Princess. I have assured them we did not. But," he waved his free hand at the scene in front of them, "as you can see, they don't believe me."

Cautiously, Kais stepped out just in front of Teague, hands raised. "Please, surely we can resolve this without the need for violence."

The advisor spoke and his features remained calm, the only indication of his anger was the set of his clenched jaw, "I am about to become very violent if you do not produce my Princess."

Kais' hackles rose at the way he claimed possession of Satori. His eyes dropped to the man's hands for a second, and he imagined them on Satori, hurting her, touching her against her will. Fury built inside his chest, but that would not help. He pulled in a few deep breaths. When he spoke, even he was surprised at the calm in his voice.

"We have not kidnapped the Princess. If you would allow me to explain—" His words were cut off by the presence behind him, fear and determination washing off of her. He turned just as she came into view.

"Henrik?"

"Satori!" Henrik shot Teague a look. "It appears you've been lying to us."

"Not at all," Teague said, his voice even. "I said we didn't kidnap her."

"Satori, come here this instant. We're going home."

Kais stood still, his eyes shifting between Satori and Henrik. She looked frozen and he could feel the waves of fear. She met his eyes, and a sense of calm washed over him, warmth and love. Most couples had to rely on trust when they said 'I love you,' but not him and Satori. They could feel it, they knew it was real.

She lifted her chin. The fear was still there, but it had dimmed. She moved as though she would come right next to him, but at the last second, Teague's hand shot out and stopped her. *Thank Shala*, Kais thought. The last thing he wanted was for Satori to be in the middle of this. Next to Teague was close enough.

Henrik lifted his sword higher, pointing it at Teague. "Let her go."

Kais turned to look at Henrik. "She's not our prisoner. She is free to choose to leave if she wishes. However, if she wishes to stay, she's free to do that as well."

Henrik sneered. "Stay? Why would she stay?"

Kais was still facing Henrik when he felt the soft press of her palm on his arm. His attention shot to her beside him, in the middle of everything. He shot Teague a look. He would talk to him later if they made it out of this alive.

"I'm not a prisoner." Her voice shook at first, but then it became clear, and he heard in her the royal that she was. "Kais and his men saved my life and welcomed me. I owe everything to them." She slipped her hand in Kais', and Henrik's attention zeroed in on the gesture. "I will not allow you to harm them."

"Satori, I don't know what they've done to you or what's going on. But you will not be staying here. If we have to kill every one of these men to get to you, you will be going home with us." As Henrik spoke, more men appeared, stepping out from behind trees, growing their numbers. "And if we can't manage it today, we will be back with more men. However," Henrik lifted his free hand, one finger held in the air, before pointing it at Kais. "Your friend there dies to day."

One man stepped forward from the group with Henrik, holding a bow, an arrow already knocked, pointed at Kais' chest.

"No!" Fear spiked through her as she screamed. She tried to dive in front of Kais, but he caught her arm, hauling her back behind him. "No, Henrik, please!" she pleaded, her voice shaking once again.

Henrik's chin lowered as he took in Satori's hand in Kais' once more. His features finally changed. The change was subtle, but with a slight shift, his look grew menacing.

"This man," Henrik pointed his sword tip at Kais, "is your *enemy*."

"He's ten times the man you are," she sneered at him.

"Is that so?" Henrik looked between the two of them, considering. "Do you think he can keep up that shining reputation when he's dead?"

Henrik's head tilted slightly to the side, and the archer raised the bow once again.

Fear, love, bravery all poured over him as Satori wrenched herself from Kais' grip and jumped in front of the arrow, out of his reach. "No! No. Please!"

"You're bargaining?" Henrik asked her.

Kais couldn't see her face but he felt the surge of hope rise inside her. "Yes. Yes, what do you want? I'll give you anything. Just don't harm him."

Kais' stomach bottomed out. *No.*

Henrik dismounted his massive white horse and moved toward her, pushing the arrow out of the way so he could move to stand directly in front of her. Raising his hand, he touched her face and ran a finger down her cheek, her neck, sliding it over the top of her corset.

"Anything?"

Disgust and shame crashed through Kais. Hers.

Kais could stand this no longer. "Satori, don't do this. This isn't worth it."

She turned her head to look at him. Pain pooled deep in her brown eyes. "You're worth anything. I love you." And then she turned back to Henrik. "What do you want? What will you take to spare him?"

He bent toward her, voice low. "I will take so much. Including you, as my wife."

Kais' heart plummeted. He would rather die. What good would it do him to live in a world where he knew Satori suffered at the hands of this man?

"Satori, no," he begged.

She ignored him, speaking through clenched teeth, "You'll spare his life? Your word?"

"My word," he nearly sneered the words at her.

She lifted her chin and turned to meet Kais' gaze. "I'm so sorry." She faced Henrik again. "Fine. Yes, you can have me if that's what you want. But you will spare him and his men."

Henrik studied her for a moment before holding out an arm. She slid her hand through the crook, the fear practically dripping off her. Henrik kept his eyes on Satori as he spoke to his men, "Fall back; we have what we came for."

All of Henrik's men lowered their weapons, backing carefully away from the rest of Kais' men. Henrik turned his back and began walking away, Satori's arm in his like a vise.

Agony cracked Kais' heart into pieces. Bile churned in his stomach, and he thought he might vomit as the distance between them grew. At one point, Satori tried to turn but Henrik did something that nearly caused her to yelp.

Kais was about to lunge toward them when Teague caught his arm.

"Live to fight another day," he whispered.

He certainly would. He would not give her up so easily. Henrik's men mounted their horses, Henrik hauling Satori up to sit in front of him. He laced an arm around her middle and placed a kiss on her cheek. She did her best to turn away, but seated on a horse, there wasn't anywhere for her to go. Kais' breath heaved out of him.

Henrik turned his horse, as did each of his men. Each but one.

As Kais watched, the men began to gallop away and then Henrik called, "Kill him!" before kicking his horse into a gallop, Satori's screams tearing through the forest.

There was no time to react before the archer sent the first arrow through the air with a whoosh and a thud. Searing pain ripped through Kais' shoulder and then again through his chest as three arrows, one after the other, lodged inside him.

Shouts erupted around him as his men gave chase. Then he was in Teague's arms, being lowered to the ground, the clouds above him swimming and fading.

"Kay? Kay? Kais!" His friend's voice held more panic than Kais had ever heard from the man before. "Kais!"

The world spun around him, and the air seemed to grow cold. "Satori…"

"Help me! Help me get him to his tent. Someone go get Bram!" Teague was shouting.

Others were shouting.

Then everything seemed to quiet, and the only thing he could hear were Kezia's words, words he had somehow forgotten about as Satori lay in his arms.

"She will rest in your arms and be safe. You will die."

CHAPTER THIRTY-SIX

SATORI

Her chest burned. Her breaths came in short, shallow intakes that were not satisfactory. Her eyes and throat ached. Her head spun.

"Really, Satori," Henrik's voice dripped with disgust. "You're making a scene."

"Go to Helias, you bastard," she choked out the words.

Henrik's hand came up, caressing her cheek with the back of his knuckles. "Is that any way to speak to your husband?"

The very idea tore a sob from her throat and she jerked her head away. Kais was dead. He'd been shot through with arrows. Her blood could heal him, but she was too far away to tell them. Bram was a good doctor, but she knew what kinds of wounds arrows inflicted. She thought of Kais' father. She'd never met him, but she knew from what Kais had told her that he'd already lost one son. It seemed like a cruel thing for Shala and Miram to take both of his children.

It seemed like a cruel thing for Shala and Miram to give her Kais and then take him away, as well. It seemed like a very cruel thing to leave Henrik in his place.

Her shoulders shook as she tried to rein in her sobs.

"Your father will be so pleased to see you." Henrik's cheek rested against her hair as he spoke. "He's been so distraught. Really, I've feared for his health."

His words snagged something inside her. His health? "Is my father unwell?"

"Fret not, my Princess, I make sure your father has a nightly tonic. It calms him and keeps him from becoming too distraught regarding your absence or the state of the country. He tends to leave much of the decision-making up to me. And I'm sure when you return home and stop making such a fuss about a barbarian in the woods, he'll be much better. Of course, should you continue fighting me, his health could decline swiftly."

Her breath caught at his words and the threat they held. *Nightly tonic.* Henrik was poisoning her father. She shouldn't be surprised, it was absolutely something he would do. She also wouldn't put it past him to outright kill her father if she didn't see her bargain through. The hand Henrik had around her middle slid to her thigh, and she fought the bile that rose in her throat. She had truly thought she was done with this man.

The large doors burst open, and Tessa raced down the stairs toward them. "Satori! Satori!"

Tears began to flow again. Satori hadn't realized how much she'd missed Tessa.

Henrik pulled the horse to a stop and dismounted. Reaching up, he took hold of Satori's waist and lifted her down. She squirmed under his touch as his fingers dug in a little too hard. But then Tessa was flying at her, and they caught each other in an embrace, both crying freely.

After traveling with Henrik, camping with him for days, being at the mercy of his constant presence, Tessa's arms felt like a refuge. If only for a short time.

"Are you okay? Are you alright? I was so afraid I would never see you again!" the words poured from Tessa. "When Henrik told us what happened, we feared the worst." Her arms closed around Satori tighter.

"I'm well," Satori cried. Physically well, anyway. "I wasn't harmed, I'm well."

"Tessa, take the Princess to her rooms and get her cleaned up. And you," Henrik turned toward another servant, "have the kitchen prepare a meal. We'll eat in an hour."

Satori turned toward him, still clutching Tessa. "No, I want to see my father."

"Of course," Tessa agreed.

"No." Henrik's tone was sharp and final.

Satori shot a glare at him. "You have no right to tell me no. I will see my father now, before I do anything else."

Henrik stepped closer, and Satori's stomach quivered, but she kept the glare on her face.

"Princess, your father is resting. He will be just as glad to see you at dinner as he would be now."

Why would Henrik keep her from her father? No doubt it was based on control alone. "How dare you keep me from him."

Henrik closed the remaining space between them, snatching her upper arm in his fist and dipping his head slightly to speak quietly in her ear, "I realize you think you're in charge here, but we both know I'm the one with the power." Henrik stepped back and took her hand, forcing it through the crook of his arm. "Allow me to show you to your room, Princess."

Satori shot Tessa a look. She had never told Tessa what had happened with Henrik, and the look of shock on the other girl's face made that obvious.

"I-I'll take the Princess to her room to get her ready."

Henrik turned his head to look at Tessa. "Go and make sure the kitchen knows to have dinner ready in an hour."

A sick feeling grew in the pit of Satori's stomach as Tessa's gaze jumped between her and Henrik. "Sir, I believe you already sent someone to do—"

Henrik cut her off with a barked, "Go!"

Tessa jumped, eyes growing wide, shooting Satori an apologetic look before rushing off.

Henrik began moving, all but dragging Satori along with him, through the entryway and up the large center staircase, branching off to the left and heading up another flight, leading her to her room. He turned the handle, pushed open the door, and shoved her inside. She tripped into the room, nearly falling onto the plush carpet.

He strode toward her, latching onto both of her arms painfully. "You will never disobey me in public again. Or you will regret it." He released her, stepping back once and smoothing his hands over his tunic. "I suggest you accustom yourself to the idea of a long and happy life with me. Quiet and acquiescing to my plans and," he ran a finger from her temple to her neck, "wishes. It will be significantly less uncomfortable for you this way."

She swallowed the lump in her throat, hating how it sounded in her ears. She suspected Henrik noticed because his mouth ticked up at the corner.

There was a quick knock on the door, and it flew open, revealing Tessa, panting heavily. She looked at Henrik, voice shaking. "Dinner will be ready in an hour, your Grace." She entered the room swiftly, moving past him toward Satori. "I'll get your bath ready now."

"Thank you, Tessa."

Tessa moved swiftly to the bathing chamber to start the bath.

Satori looked at Henrik. "You're free to go now."

The smug look remained on Henrik's face as he sauntered to a chair in Satori's sitting area and lowered himself into it. "This is my room now."

Satori's stomach dropped.

"You're not my husband yet," she snapped.

"Technicalities matter little to me, my dear." He leaned back, resting both arms on the sides of the chair. "Whether now or next week, you're my wife in practice, at the very least. And I do intend to practice."

Next week? Satori's breath caught at the prospect of being wed to Henrik within the week. So soon. Though, why prolong the inevitable? Her lip shook, tears threatening to overtake her again. Life with Henrik and without Kais was nearly unbearable to consider. The chasm in her chest, once filled by Kais, seemed to yawn open wider at the prospect.

A throat cleared behind her and she turned to find Tessa eyeing Henrik nervously.

"Do you need something?" Henrik asked smoothly.

Tessa gave a quick shake of her head. "No, apologies. Princess, your bath is ready."

Satori closed her eyes, trying to shake off the thoughts in her head and the ache in her heart. "Thank you, Tessa."

With a last look at Henrik, seated smugly in her room, she entered the bathing chamber. When Tessa entered behind her and shut the door, Satori hissed, "Lock it."

"Already done," Tessa assured her. She moved to help Satori out of her clothes, keeping her voice low. "Satori, what's going on?"

Ignoring her question, Satori posed one of her own, "Tessa, is my father unwell?"

Tessa paused her work for a moment and shrugged slightly. "He hasn't been entirely himself, but we all assumed it was because you were missing and no one knew what had happened. When we got word that those brutes had kidnaped you—"

Satori turned to take Tessa's hand, it hurt to know people thought of Kais and Teague and the men that way. "I wasn't kidnapped. Well, I was, but not by who you think. I was kidnapped in the woods with Henrik. But then Kais and his men, from the ball, rescued me. Tessa, he traded winter supplies to those criminals for me. They kept me safe. They were kind. Tessa, I—"

She couldn't continue. Her throat ached; she couldn't talk about Kais just then, the chasm inside her ached too much.

"They were kind to you?"

"So kind. So much more than kind."

She'd met the other half of her soul with those *brutes*. And then he was ripped away, and she was left with the monster in the next room. She brought her hands to her face as a sob punched out of her unbidden.

Tessa's hands came down softly on her arms. "I'm so sorry you've been through so much. Here." Tessa gently turned Satori toward the waiting tub, "a bath will help you feel better."

Satori finished undressing and climbed into the steaming water, sinking down to her neck, wishing it could wash away the pain in her heart.

She closed her eyes as Tessa dipped a pitcher in the water and poured it over Satori's hair. Immersed in the warmth, she could almost imagine the evening she had spent with Kais in the pool in the woods. Could almost feel his hands running over her skin. The image was quickly replaced by the sound of Henrik's order and Kais' men screaming.

There was no knock or warning as the door opened, and Henrik stepped into the bathing chamber.

Both Satori and Tessa jumped, Satori, trying in vain to cover herself, was thankful that the water at least was deep.

"Leave." He stood in the doorway, his tunic sleeves rolled past his elbows.

Tessa jumped to her feet, the half-filled pitcher clattering to the floor. "How did you get in?"

She shot Satori a fearful look, and Satori actually felt bad for her. She knew the girl didn't want to leave her. She also knew Henrik would give her no choice.

"I have a key." He stepped to where the pitcher had fallen and retrieved it. "I can take over from here."

"Your Grace, I don't believe this is-"

Henrik turned the full force of his attention on Tessa, and she shrunk under the weight of it. "If you continue to question me when I tell you to do something, you will find yourself permanently in the stables."

Tessa's face fell as she again looked at Satori.

Exhaustion pressed on Satori. She was tired physically, tired mentally, tired emotionally. She didn't have it in her to fight Henrik or reassure Tessa. She simply looked at the other woman.

"Go, Tessa. Just go."

Henrik stood, turning the pitcher over and over in his hands, waiting. Finally, tears brimming in her eyes, Tessa fled the room.

Henrik said nothing as he knelt behind her, dipping the pitcher and pouring it over her hair once more before setting it down. Then his hands landed softly on her shoulders, and she shuddered, her stomach rolling as they slid over her and below the surface of the water. The contact was gone just as quickly as it had been there as he picked up the shampoo bottle and dumped some on his hands. He worked the soap into her hair, his long fingers kneading her scalp. Normally she loved having someone wash or fix her hair, but every touch of Henrik's fingers caused her muscles to grow tauter.

"You're so tense, my dear," Henrik said, moving his hands to her shoulders. "Relax."

She ignored him, praying that he would finish his task quickly. He dipped the pitcher in the water and rinsed the suds from her hair.

He stood and strode to where her robe hung, lifting it from the peg and turning back to where she still sat. He held the robe out, waiting.

"I wish we had more time together, but it is almost time to eat." He gave the robe a slight shake. "Come now, Satori, let's not keep your father waiting."

The promise of seeing her father was the only thing that could drag her out of that tub and into Henrik's waiting arms. But while she shook on the inside, she would not give him the satisfaction of seeing it. As confidently as she could, she stood. She held his gaze, chin high, before he broke off their stare to allow his eyes to crawl slowly over her soaking form.

She needed to wash again. "May I have my robe, please?"

Slowly, Henrik's eyes came back to meet hers. "If only we had more time."

He stepped forward, and she slid her arms into the sleeves as he draped the robe over her shoulders. He moved to the door, holding it open for her.

Tessa stood nervously beside Satori's bed, hands clasped so tightly in front of her that her knuckles were white. Her voice shook when she spoke, "I laid out a dress for you, Your Highness."

On the bedpost hung a silk and tulle dress with full skirts and a built-in corset, all the color of a cerulean blue lake. It was beautiful.

"Thank you, Tessa."

Henrik moved and seated himself again on the chair he had vacated earlier, and hatred burned in Satori's chest as he leaned back, unabashedly watching her.

"Satori . . ." Tessa whispered.

"It's fine, Tessa." Satori tried to keep the shake out of her voice. "Will you please help me dress?"

With another glance at Henrik, Tessa retrieved the dress and began helping Satori out of the robe and into her clothes. Henrik never took his eyes off of her. Tessa tried to remain in his line of sight, but she was smaller than Satori, and her petite frame only blocked so much.

Satori did her best to ignore Henrik's leering gaze, a task that was much easier said than done. After dressing she worked her hair into a braid, not willing to waste anymore time. When she was finally finished, she turned toward him. "If it's alright with you, I'd like to see my father now."

Henrik stood, covering the space between them in two strides of his long legs. He stopped in front of her, running a finger down her jaw. "I appreciate that you've acknowledged the fact that it is indeed my authority that allows you to do anything."

She pulled her head away, doing nothing to hide the hatred that simmered in her gaze.

Henrik laughed deep in his throat. "I'll enjoy breaking that."

"You can try," she countered.

Then his fingers were wrapped roughly around her jaw as he squeezed, pulling her face closer to his. "My dear Satori, as evidenced by my presence in your chambers and our upcoming union, I never fail when I set out to accomplish something."

He released her, and she refrained from rubbing her sore jaw, not wanting to give him the satisfaction. Henrik took a step back and offered his arm to Satori. She ignored it, stepping past him toward the door. But in a moment, he had blocked her way, once again offering his arm, one brow quirked up.

She had to pick her battles. Defying him in everything for the rest of their lives would grow tedious quickly. So, instead of fighting on this trivial point, she reached up and slid her hand through the crook of his elbow.

His brow relaxed, and his head tilted. "Was that so hard?"

Satori ignored him as Tessa pulled the door open, and they exited the room.

CHAPTER THIRTY-SEVEN

SATORI

Satori held her breath as the door to the small dining room, which she and her father enjoyed sharing, was pulled open. Across the room, one wall was actually a set of large windowed doors that looked out over the gardens. In front of the doors, gazing out, her father sat, one leg crossed over the other, an elbow perched on the arm of his chair, his chin resting on his knuckles.

"It looks as though it may snow tonight, Henrik." Her father's voice sounded disjointed, as though he spoke because it was expected, but his words held no conviction. "Must tell the servants to bring in extra wood for the fires."

Satori moved to rush to him, but Henrik's hold on her arm tightened, keeping her firmly by his side.

"Please?" She was not above begging at that moment.

Henrik gave her a sideways look before he spoke, "Your Majesty, I've found something we had thought lost."

"What's that?" her father asked the question before slowly turning his head. When his eyes met Satori's, his hands fell to his lap, his gaze going wide with shock. "Satori." Her name was but a breath on his lips.

"Father."

She didn't wait for Henrik to release her. She gave a firm tug, jerking her arm from his grasp. She rushed to her father, hitting her knees before his chair. Her head rested on his lap as he leaned down, closing his arms around her.

"Satori, my sweet, darling girl." His hands ran over her back and hair as though he didn't quite believe she was there. "I didn't think I'd ever see you again."

She stayed there, holding him, letting him hold her.

"Oh, Henrik, my girl is back," her father's words were muffled where his face was buried in her hair.

"Indeed." Henrik's smooth voice sounded from directly behind her. "And the news is even better than that. She's agreed to be my wife. We will all be family as we were meant to be."

Satori ignored the turn of her stomach.

"Satori, Satori, this is truly a wonderful day."

The smile in her father's voice made her chest ache. He was so relieved to have her back, and she was happy to be reunited with him, as well. But how her father could think that marriage to Henrik was for the best, she had no idea. She couldn't comprehend a life of being subjected to that man. How long would she last before she felt she had no choice but to do something drastic? Helias, she missed Kais.

"Let's eat, let's eat." Her father patted her excitedly on the back. "I feel my appetite returned for the first time in weeks."

Satori ate very little at dinner and contributed almost nothing to the conversation as it was monopolized by Henrik and her father, making plans for her future. Her stomach rolled as she listened to them, as her father agreed with every suggestion and plan Henrik put forth. Despair pressed in on her like the walls of a cage, visions of life with Henrik playing in her mind. All the while the idea of Kais was standing by, his image like a ghost in the corner of the room. Hollowness filled her, the nothingness there almost a thing itself.

Her chest and throat ached with the tears she held back. Finally, she could bear it no longer. She stood.

Henrik's hand closed around her wrist. "My darling, where are you off to? You've hardly touched your meal."

She pulled her arm away, trying to dislodge it from his grasp, but his grip tightened, keeping her in place. She forced a pleasant sound into her voice for her father's benefit.

"I apologize. I'm just very tired, it's been a long day." The sounds of Kais' men shouting echoed in her head, and she fought to keep her voice even. "I'm just going to go to bed."

With a swift jerk of her arm, she dislodged herself from Henrik's grasp. With a look, daring him to manhandle her in front of her father, she moved away from him to embrace the King. "Good night, father. It's so good to see you."

"I'm so relieved to have you home, my sweet girl," her father said. "Rest well, I'll see you in the morning."

She exited the room, feeling Henrik's gaze on her the entire time. She had no doubt she would pay for that bit of defiance. But at that point, defiance was all she had.

She entered her room to find Tessa waiting. The other girl rushed to her as soon as the door closed behind her.

"Satori, Satori, I'm so sorry."

Tears poured down Tessa's face as Satori reached out and pulled her into an embrace. "Don't cry, Tessa. We can only go on from here."

"He made us move his things." A look of panic lit Tessa's face as she spoke. "Everything. He's moved everything in here."

Nothing about that surprised Satori. Another stab of pain hit her that it was Henrik and not Kais. Kais was supposed to be the one to share her bed and her life. The sob she'd been holding in for hours finally broke free as her knees crumbled beneath her, and she landed in a heap on the plush carpet.

She allowed herself a few moments to grieve, but the threat of Henrik's return loomed heavy like a cloud about to burst. She had to compose herself. But as she sat there on the floor, remembering Kais so clearly she could nearly feel his arms around her, she had a thought. It was probably ridiculous and certainly pointless, and no doubt it would cause her more pain, but still, she had to make the request. She pulled in a breath, composing herself as she grabbed Tessa by the upper arms.

"Tessa, I need you to do something for me."

Tessa's eyes went wide. "Anything, Satori. Anything. What is it?"

"It's going to sound ridiculous. I need you to go to the market and buy something for me. But you can't let anyone know what you're doing. No one can know." Tessa's head nodded vigorously. "I need you to find me a whip."

"A what?" Tessa's brow knit with confusion.

"Go to the tanner and tell him you need a whip. Six feet, eight feet. I don't care." She didn't know why she wanted the whip or what she would do with it. She would certainly have to hide it. Henrik could never know about it. "Pay whatever it costs."

"Of course," Tessa said, drying her own tears.

Satori pulled in a fortifying breath, letting it out slowly. She stood, brushing a hand over her skirts. Her timing was perfect as the door behind her opened, and Henrik stepped into the room.

He leveled his gaze on her, glancing once at Tessa. "Get out."

Then, his attention was back on Satori.

Satori turned to her friend, forcing the best smile she could manage. "Good night, Tessa."

"Satori?"

Henrik's attention snapped fully to Tessa. "Do you have trouble hearing, insolent girl? I said *leave*."

Tessa jumped at his tone, and with an apologetic look and a quick curtsey, she was out the door.

Still not taking his eyes from Satori, Henrik stepped back toward the door and threw the bolt.

"You left early and missed the entire conversation." He stalked toward her. "He's delighted to have you home and ecstatic to see us wed. In fact, we've set a date."

Satori held her breath, waiting.

Henrik prowled toward her until he was directly before her. He raised a hand and brushed a finger along her jaw, letting it trail down to the low neckline of her dress. "You will be mine before the eyes of Shala, Miram, and all the Kingdom in two days. Your father agreed we should not put it off."

Two days? The air left her as though he had punched her in the stomach, and Henrik smiled at the reaction.

"Until then..." He moved his hands to the laces at the front of her dress, twisting his fingers into them and giving a sharp tug, causing her to stumble into him. "You'll still be mine, but only before the eyes of Shala and Miram."

She pressed her mouth into a line, and as her stomach churned, a lump formed in her throat. She hated to cry in front of him. She'd always hated it because he liked it. He enjoyed the thrill of power it gave him when she felt weak. But it was all just too much. Kais gone, her future a nightmare of marriage to this man.

CHAPTER THIRTY-EIGHT

SATORI

The next day was a whirlwind as servants were in and out of her room with questions and concerns about the wedding. Many of them complained under their breath about the short time they had to throw it all together.

Henrik stayed close, seated beside her, answering the questions she didn't, which were most of them. She could sense the tension rising in him as he waited for her to answer every time a question was posed and ultimately answered himself, as she had neither opinion nor care regarding the whole horror show.

Finally, when a team of servants sat with them, and one of them asked her what type of flowers she wanted and she still didn't answer, Henrik seemed to have enough. He stood so swiftly that he knocked into the small table in front of them, sending flower samples tumbling to the floor.

"Please." The word came out in a barked, impatient tone, and he took a breath before he continued, "Please, give the Princess and I a moment, if you will."

Servants scrambled to right the mess before swiftly exiting the room. Satori knew what was coming—some sort of comment on her attitude. But she really couldn't find it in herself to care.

When the door closed, Henrik's head turned toward her, a sneer and a glare on his features. He rounded on her, planting his hands on the arms of her chair, his body caging her in, his face in hers. When he spoke, his words were hissed and sharp, and she flinched as spittle hit her.

"It is time to stop acting like a child and accept your future. This wedding will happen with or without your input. But these people are trying to make it a pleasant experience for you, so your opinions would be helpful."

She met his eyes. "Pleasant experience? Nothing about this will ever be pleasant for me. And I will do my best to make it as unpleasant for you as I possibly can."

His mouth pressed into a thin line as his eyes narrowed. His attention shifted to something beside her, but only for a moment because in the next second, his hand was flying at her face, connecting with her cheek, a crack resounding through the room.

She brought her hand to her stinging face, eyes wide. Henrik had done many things to her over the years, but he had never struck her. A fresh wave of her new reality hit her, and in that moment, she decided she would not just sit back and take it. If this man thought that she would roll over and submit, he was about to get a very rude awakening.

She knew she would pay dearly for what she was about to do. She wasn't so naive as to think that he would back down when she started standing up to him. Not Henrik. He would become worse, but she couldn't be the victim any longer. She curled her fingers slightly into her cheek, her short nails scraping at the tender skin. She set her jaw, and before Henrik could react, she lashed out, bringing her clawed hand across his face.

The look of shock on his face was rewarding even as his hands moved from the chair to clamp around her arms. "How dar—"

A knock on the door interrupted him, and Satori silently thanked whichever servant it was. He would surely retaliate, but she let out a shaking breath, relieved it would not be this moment. Another insistent knock caused Henrik to stand and straighten his clothes.

"Later," he sneered before he turned and shouted toward the door, "Yes?"

The door opened, and Tessa practically fell into the room, the servants with flowers behind her. She took in the scene, and Satori didn't miss the look of alarm on her face before Tessa schooled her features back into indifference. She stopped, dipped into a curtsey, and straightened, turning to address Henrik.

"The King has requested you meet him in his office at once."

Henrik shot Tessa a hateful look before repeating his warning from earlier at Satori, "Later."

She suppressed the chill that ran through her as Henrik stalked from the room.

When he was gone, Tessa spoke to the other servants, "Please feel free to take a break. You can meet back here in an hour. Thank you."

"Of course, miss." They bowed to Satori and disappeared out the door.

Tessa locked the door behind them before she rushed to Satori's side, pulling the bag she had slung across her chest over her head and dropping it to the floor as she wrapped Satori in a hug. "When I got here, the servants were whispering that they could hear the two of you fighting."

"He hit me, so I scratched him."

Tessa pulled back to look Satori in the eye. Her expression was one of horror and pride. "Satori, he'll—"

Satori placed a hand on Tessa's arm. "Don't worry about that. What did my father want?"

Confusion crossed Tessa's face. "What?"

"You told Henrik that my father wanted to see him."

"Oh." Tessa's head rolled to the side as her eyes found the ceiling. "I may have made that up."

Satori let out a breath with a slight shake of her head. They were playing a dangerous game with Henrik.

Tessa met Satori's gaze, seeming to read her thoughts. "I know. But I had to get him out."

Satori took Tessa's hands in hers, touched by her friend's willingness to put herself in harm's way. "Thank you."

Tessa shook off Satori's thanks, her eyes lighting up as a smile spread across her lips. "Come sit, I have something for you."

They moved to the small sofa, sitting side by side as Tessa pulled her bag around in front of her. She handed it to Satori with a proud smile.

Satori took the bag, hoping she knew what it contained. She opened the flap. Inside, coiled in a loop, braided and shining black, was a new whip. She breathed deeply, inhaling the leather scent as her heart clenched. The memory of Kais was so strong she could almost see him beside her, examining the weapon.

"Tessa," Satori breathed the other girl's name, awe filling her voice. "Thank you so much."

"I hoped it was what you wanted. I've never seen one before."

"This is perfect." She pulled the whip from the bag, letting her fingers drift over the braid. "Absolutely perfect."

"What does it do?" Tessa reached out, running a hand over the handle. "I mean, what do you do with it?"

Satori looked up into Tessa's eyes, suddenly feeling a bit foolish. What could she do with this? Nothing. Why had she even asked Tessa to get it? She had put Tessa in danger, and for what? She let her gaze drop again to the whip in her lap, imagining Kais there, running his hands over the leather and then over her.

"I don't know."

"You don't know what to do with it?" There was shock in Tessa's words.

When Satori spoke, it was so quiet she barely heard the words herself, "Kais had one, he showed me how to make it crack. I—" Her voice broke.

Tessa slipped an arm around Satori's shoulders. "I'm so sorry." A moment of silence hung between them before Tessa spoke again, "Kais was the one from the ball? Did you and he really . . .? I mean, there was talk among the servants that you had fallen for him."

One painful sound, half laugh, half sob, punched out of Satori. "Yes. I never believed in fate. I thought I would live my life, marry, and rule the Kingdom when my father was gone." She turned her head toward Tessa, though she didn't look at her. "Have you heard of blood mates?"

"My mother told stories of Shala and Miram and their blood bond. Myths. Tales to entertain children," Tessa answered and, after a pause, looked more closely at Satori. "Satori, you're not saying that . . .?"

Satori swallowed, her blood seeming to roar in her ears. "It's real. It's all true. I never believed it, but . . ."

The memory of Kais' head broken open and gushing blood over the pillow hit her. Her imagination quickly replaced that image with one of what Kais must have looked like shot through with arrows. She'd saved him only to lose him in the end, anyway. She dropped her face into her hands as another round of tears began.

"They're true. My blood, it healed him. Healed him, Tessa." Even now, after seeing it happen twice, she was in awe. "It healed him, and he was mine, and I knew it. I knew he was mine. I was for him, and we were for each other. And, Tessa!" She looked up, wide-eyed, the image of Tessa blurred by her tears. "He was a prince! His father had written to my father to ask for my hand. Before we even knew any of this. It was all real, and it was perfect." Tears ran again. "And Henrik killed him, and now I'm marrying a monster. I would be better off dead."

"Satori! Don't talk like that," Tessa scolded, pulling her closer into her embrace.

Satori said nothing else, but Tessa had to know she was right. Surely, she saw that marriage to Henrik was not the better choice. And if she was dead, she could be with Kais. How was he gone from the world? Tears fell down her face as her throat seemed to close up. Her fist closed again around the whip. If this was all she had left to remember him, she had to hide it. If Henrik found it... She stood, pulling free from Tessa's hold and moving around her bed, the whip clutched tightly in her hand. She lifted the heavy mattress as much as she could and pushed the whip underneath, right beneath where her head would rest. She couldn't risk placing it under her pillow. No doubt Henrik would be sharing her bed from now until . . . well, until one of them was dead.

Satori turned back to Tessa. "You have to go. You can't be here when he gets back. He'll be angry."

Tessa stood. "Satori, I can't leave you here with him. What will he do?"

Satori gave Tessa a sad smile, grateful for her friend's concern. She had done a good job of hiding Henrik's visits from everyone.

"Nothing that hasn't been happening for years. Please, you have to go."

Tessa's face contorted into a mask of horror at the word *years.* "Satori. Years?"

"Since I was of age," Satori answered. "The night of my birthday, he came to my room, and he's been present ever since."

"Satori." The despair lacing Tessa's voice was nearly tangible. "How did I never know? How did you hide this?" Tessa's face turned to disgust. "I liked him. The things I said about him... Oh, Satori, I'm so sorry." She reached out and took Satori's hand, squeezing her fingers so hard it brought pain.

Satori eased herself from Tessa's grip. "He's very good at being charming, and I didn't want anyone to know. I felt . . . I just didn't want anyone to know. I suppose now, because of the wedding, he doesn't have to hide anymore."

The thought of Henrik pawing at her even in public now made her want to be sick. There would be no relief. No end to her fighting.

That's when it happened. She recognized the moment she shut down, but the disconnect was so strong that she didn't care, like turning off a tap. This was her life, this was the way it would be. There was no way out.

"Tessa, you need to go."

"Satori, I'm afraid—"

"Tessa," Satori cut her off. No words would help. Fear would do no good. "Just go. I'll see you in the morning."

"But do you need me to run you a bath?" Tessa asked.

"No, I can do that myself." She forced a smile onto her indifferent face, hollowness taking root in her chest as she moved toward the other girl, backing her to the door. "Thank you, Tessa. Goodnight."

Tessa reached behind her and opened the door, concern clouding her features. "Alright." She gave Satori one last overall look before stepping out the door. "Goodnight."

Satori closed the door, not bothering to latch it. It would do no good, anyway. She moved to the bathing chamber, turning the tap. Scalding water poured into the tub. She removed her clothes and slipped into the tub, barely noticing the heat of the water, even as the steam rose from the surface. She dipped her head back, wetting her hair, and then she sat, eyes closed, soaking in the heat.

She didn't notice when the water grew cold, didn't notice anything around her until he spoke.

"Surely the water is cold and no longer comfortable."

She didn't even startle at the sound, at his presence—she had expected him. She opened her eyes. He stood in the doorway, leaning against it with one shoulder, arms folded over his chest, legs crossed at the ankles. He wore no shirt.

"Satori."

"What?" she asked.

His eyes widened just slightly at her question. "The water. Cold?"

She lifted her head and took in the water, her golden curls floating on the surface. "I suppose it is."

She stood, the water cascading off her like a fall.

Henrik's head raised slightly, his eyes narrowing a fraction before he moved. Stepping across the room, he retrieved her robe. He reached her just as she stepped out of the water and wrapped it around her shoulders, his fingers brushing against her collarbone. She barely registered his touch.

She took the edges of the robe, pulling them around herself as she exited the bathing chamber, stopping beside the bed. Henrik approached behind her. He pulled her wet hair from inside her robe and let it rest on her back, running his fingers through the dripping strands. When he spoke his voice was quiet, as though he cared or wanted her to *think* he cared.

"Satori, I don't want to be your enemy. We're to be wed. To be one. United."

United. Could they be united? Not likely. But she said nothing. Didn't speak as he swept her hair to the side and leaned in to kiss her neck.

"I don't want to fight with you," his soft words vibrated against her skin even as she stared across the room at the large blue and gold tapestry that hung on the wall.

Henrik's other hand came around her waist, his finger slipping into the folds of the robe, brushing the sensitive skin of her stomach. He kissed along her jaw, up to her ear.

"We don't have to be enemies. I could give you everything."

Then, both his hands were on the shoulders of the robe, pulling it from her body. Cool air touched her skin, but she had already retreated into her own mind, blue and gold blurring into bare brown trees and flowing water, Kais' voice in her ear, his lips on hers.

CHAPTER THIRTY-NINE

SATORI

When Satori woke the following day, she was alone. She couldn't tell how late it was as the drapes still hung heavily over the windows. It must have been very early for Tessa not to have been in yet.

Satori stood and pulled her robe from where it hung on the post of her bed. Sliding her arms into the sleeves, she tied it as she moved to the large window that led to her balcony. She took hold of the heavy drapes and threw them open. Blinding light poured into the room, causing her to squint.

It was later than she'd thought. Where was Tessa? It was unlike her—actually, unheard of—for her not to wake Satori. Was she ill?

The door to her bedroom opened, drawing her attention. Two female servants entered, arms laden with items. One of them held a full white dress draped across her arms. Satori's stomach turned at the sight as reality hit her. It was her wedding day. *White*. A bitter laugh punched out of her. She had no right to wear white to her marriage to Henrik, of all people.

Both servants stopped and dipped into a curtsey. "Good morning, Your Highness."

They swept into the room and laid out items across every surface. There were things for her hair, a curling rod, an armload of tiny fresh flowers, lotions and perfumes, the dress, underclothes...all items one might need for a wedding.

Satori stepped closer, watching, arms folded across her chest. "Excuse me, where's Tessa?"

Both servants froze, stealing a glance at one another. A sinking hole opened in Satori's stomach.

"What is it? What's happened? Where is she?" Her gaze jumped between the two, staring at her wide-eyed.

"Your Highness, we're only here to prepare you for the ceremony. I'm sure—"

"Stop!" Satori bit out. "I'm not preparing for any ceremony until you tell me where Tessa is."

The door crashed open as Henrik strode into the room, his long legs carrying him quickly to her. He stopped in front of her, his harsh gaze boring into hers. "Tessa lied to me. She defied me. Actions have consequences."

Satori began to shake, a coldness flowing through her limbs, stealing her breath. Her voice trembled when she spoke, "What did you do?"

He stepped closer, his body brushing hers as he latched onto her upper arms, pinning her with his cold blue stare. "What was deserved."

Satori's legs gave out, but she didn't fall as Henrik held her fast in his grip.

"What did you do? What did you do?" With each question, she fought him harder, but the only purpose it served was to cause him to tighten his grip until pain lanced through her arms.

He pulled her up, stooping slightly to meet her gaze. "She, and you, will learn that defying me is a poor choice." He set her back on her feet. "You'll see her at the wedding. Now, get ready."

At the wedding? With difficulty, Satori swallowed. Tessa would be at the ceremony? Henrik hadn't killed her. She turned her head away from him, and her attention fell on the two servants who had come to help her prepare. They stood seemingly petrified, eyes wide, mouths slack.

Satori inhaled deeply, pulling herself together for their sake. Henrik released his hold on her, and she fought the urge to rub at the sore places on her arms—refused to give him that. She glared up at him, and he responded with a ghost of a smirk.

"By the end of today, you will be mine. I am so looking forward to the wedding night."

She raised a hand to hit him, but he caught her wrist easily in his large grip. "I wouldn't, Princess. Remember the consequences. It may not be you who suffers." He released her once again and turned to the servants. "Get her ready."

"Yes, sir," they mumbled in unison as Henrik swept from the room. Cautiously they approached Satori. "Are you alright, Your Highness?"

"Hardly." She turned to face them fully. "Where's Tessa?"

Again, they exchanged a glance.

"Tell me."

"She was taken from her room down to the prison," the dark-haired servant girl—Satori thought her name was Maci—shrugged. "We haven't seen her since."

The other servant spoke up, "I heard he was going to have an example made of her at the ceremony."

Despair spread through Satori, her hands beginning to shake as she dropped into a seat by a small table. "This is my fault."

Maci and the other girl moved to her side, dropping to their knees. "It's not your fault, Your Highness. I don't think any of us realized what he was really like."

"He always seemed so charming."

"Zari," Maci chided the other girl.

"What?" Zari asked. "He did."

"No, you're right," Satori said. "He is. And horrible. So, you must help me get ready. Or he'll punish you."

"You can't marry him," Zari whispered, as though someone might overhear.

"Zari," Maci snapped again.

"Maci," Zari snapped back. "She can't marry him. You saw him. You heard what he's doing to Tessa."

"Thank you, Zari." Satori placed a hand on the girl's arm. "I appreciate your concern. But I do have to marry him. He'll take it out on all of you. If he has me, he'll have a place to focus his attention."

They stared, mouths open, clearly appalled at her reasoning. Satori twisted in her seat. "You can start with my hair."

There was silence for a beat before they both began to move, gathering their things and getting to work on her hair.

Hours later, Satori stood in front of the full length mirror in her room. Her hair had been curled and pinned in an elaborate crown-like style with small white flowers placed all over her head. It was loose, and tendrils of hair fell around her face. It was beautiful. She was wasting it on Henrik.

Her dress was white, with layers of tulle and lace and a bodice that barely covered her breasts. No doubt Henrik had chosen this dress himself. Her shoulders and upper arms were also completely uncovered, the sleeves attached just slightly under her arms and were sheer, draping lightly just above her elbow, falling nearly to the floor with a slit for her arms.

She sat and waited, shoving all her thoughts and feelings deep inside her, unwilling to let anyone, especially Henrik, see her weak. Eventually, there was another knock at her door.

"Come in."

She didn't bother to ask who it was. It didn't matter, she was no longer her own person, anyway.

The heavy door pushed open, and her father appeared. A grin spread across his face as he stepped into the room.

"Satori, you look beautiful."

She attempted to force a smile for his benefit, but her face would not cooperate. "Thank you, Father."

His grin fell, and his eyes dipped to the floor. "I know this isn't what you wanted, but I really do think this will be a good match. Henrik is intelligent and will make a good king consort as you rule. He has much wisdom to offer. And I think he does care for you."

Satori bit down on the inside of her lip. How could her father be so blind to Henrik? Most likely because she had done a good job of shielding him. At first, Henrik had made threats to keep her quiet, but eventually, she just didn't want anyone to know what was happening. She didn't want to think about it any more than she had to.

Her Father approached her, taking her hands in his. "Oh, Satori, it will be good. It will be."

A thought struck her, and she suddenly had to know, even though she knew it could very well break her. "Father, after I was taken, did you receive a marriage proposal for me from King Lexon of Evandor?"

Her father looked confused at her question at first. "I did. It seemed like a decent match. That is, until Henrik told us that it was the prince of that land who had kidnapped you."

His words repeated in her head, sinking in. "Henrik told you that the Prince, Kais, had kidnapped me?"

"Of course he told us," her father replied. "We were all so shocked. The nerve of the man, especially after his father had requested an alliance. It would have been good for our countries. Why he would take you and leave Henrik for dead . . . It made no sense."

As her father spoke, Satori's head shook. "No. It wasn't the Prince. It was bush thieves. Nothing more. The Prince saved me. Henrik . . ."

As she spoke, the true meaning of the words became clear. *Henrik*. Henrik had set the entire thing up. Henrik had her kidnapped. She knew he didn't truly care about her, but to put her in that kind of danger…Of course, he could then present himself as both the victim and the hero when he swooped in to save her. Had he intended for Kais to be involved at all? Or was it just so that Henrik could blame it on him?

"Henrik lied. He set it up. He—"

Her words were cut short as the door to her chambers flew open, and Henrik entered.

"Ah, my Princess. And my King." He offered a sweeping bow to her father before stepping up to her and taking her hand. "You are lovely, it will be a pleasure to call you mine." He placed a kiss on the back of her hand.

She tried to free her hand, but he held her fast in his grip. "You are a liar."

Henrik made a show of looking affronted by her accusation. "I beg your pardon?"

"It was you." Satori fought to keep the emotion from her voice. Why she should be surprised, she didn't know. It was exactly something he would do. "You hired those men. You had me kidnapped, and you blamed it on Kais."

Her father's eyes grew wide. "Satori."

"Are you mad, woman?" Henrik questioned, releasing her hand. "I was injured in that incident as well, if you will recall."

"That only makes you more mad," Satori snapped. "That you would have yourself injured just to blame another for my kidnapping."

She stepped toward him as fury bubbled inside her. Reaching out with both hands, she shoved into his chest, sending him staggering back a step, eyes wide.

"Do you know what they threatened to do to me? What they would have done if *Kais* hadn't saved me? You are a monster!"

Henrik's mouth pressed into a line, his eyes hardening slightly. He turned to her father. "Your Majesty, this is but a misunderstanding. And I'm sure you have better things to do. Like preparing for the ceremony. Please do go dress. I assure you that the Princess and I will speak and clear this all up. I had the servants fix you some tea."

To her horror, her father nodded his head. "Of course, I do need to dress, and this seems like a private matter."

Private matter?

"My dear, I'll see you soon." His eyes moved between Henrik and Satori. "Don't quarrel on the day of your marriage."

Satori watched in disbelief as her father slipped from the room. She turned her glare on Henrik, who was still watching the door. A muscle in his jaw ticked.

"Your father is such a kind and understanding soul." He turned to look at her, gaze threatening. "It would be a shame if something happened to him so close to your wedding."

She stared, rage burning through her. It wasn't the first time she'd heard him threaten her father. She didn't doubt that he would follow through with his threats. Of course he would, he'd already had her kidnapped. But her father had agreed so easily...

"How do you make him do that? Why does he do whatever you say?"

Henrik studied her face, and his mouth twitched up at the edge. "I make wonderful tea. I'll be sure to let you taste it one day."

Tea? Henrik could control her father simply through tea? As she considered this, a memory surfaced. Mending tents with Bram. He'd spoken of Helian Currents that would make the person who eats them susceptible to suggestion. Compulsion berries, he'd said.

She held Henrik's gaze for a moment before breaking the connection, her attention dropping to the floor. This man was a menace and needed to be dealt with. And she would do it. She would marry him if that was what she had to do, and then she would kill him herself. With her own hands, if need be. She would rid the world of this beast.

Henrik stepped closer to her, apparently mistaking her stance as acquiescence. Submission. His palm cupped her face, bringing her gaze to his once more. She did her best to force a look of sad resignation.

"That's better. Now, let us be wed and put this all behind us. People are waiting."

Her stomach turned as she dropped her gaze and gave a slight nod.

She wanted to cry. She wanted to scream. She did neither. If she was going to make it through the ceremony, she would need to rein in her emotions. At the very least, for her father's sake. They stood in front of the large wooden double doors that led to where the ceremony would be held.

Her heart thudded against her ribcage as she thought about what awaited her on the other side. She just had to get through this. Just this, and then she could take care of the man once and for all.

"I hope you and Henrik cleared everything up," her father said, patting her hand where it rested in the crook of his elbow. "I hate to see you at odds. You'll need to be united for the country and your own happiness."

She looked at him and forced a smile. At least he would be safe from Henrik's vileness.

Trumpets sounded from the opposite side of the door and Satori jumped, startled at the sudden noise. Her father chuckled softly at her reaction.

The doors began to open, and Satori held her breath. The rows of chairs had been spaced far apart to give the appearance of many guests. The small crowd stood as the doors opened. The room wasn't filled, but with the short notice of the wedding, she hadn't expected even this many people to be in attendance. The aisle stretched out in front of them, a white cloth covered the stone floor leading to the altar. There, Henrik stood beside the High Rector, waiting. He had foregone his usual light colors, choosing instead to wear black. Black pants, a black shirt with gold buttons, and a long robe covered in intricate gold threading. He watched as she stood frozen at the doors.

"Come, darling," her father whispered, encouraging her to move as he attempted to do so himself.

She released the breath she had been holding and drew in another quick one before allowing her father to lead her up the long aisle.

The walk was both too long and terrifyingly swift. She looked anywhere but at Henrik, even though she could feel his attention on her. Mostly she searched for Tessa. Henrik had said she would be there, but so far Satori hadn't seen her. Though, it was difficult for her to see anything past the number of people standing in honor of her.

She refrained from rolling her eyes at the looks on their faces. Smiles, tears, joy—their Princess was finally marrying. Had they not noticed the wedding was announced only days prior? Did they not think there was something odd about that? What about the fact she was marrying her father's advisor and not a prince from a neighboring kingdom? The thought brought Kais to her mind. It should be him. It could have been him, her prince. Tears pricked her eyes. Shala and Miram were cruel.

They reached the end of the aisle, and her father stopped, turning to her and lifting the veil from her face. He kissed her once on each cheek, and she dipped into a deep curtsey before the King. Then her father placed her hand in Henrik's, and her skin crawled with the touch of his warm fingers.

The king moved to his place in the front row, and Henrik took her hand and slipped it into the crook of his elbow. Pulling her along with him, he moved to stand before the High Rector.

Henrik tilted his head toward her. "You are lovely, my dear."

She ignored him, facing the High Rector.

Henrik's voice dropped in volume even as his arm closed tighter on her hand and he pulled her closer to his side. "Do not make a fool of me, Satori. Tessa wouldn't want you to."

Her resolve snapped as she whipped her attention to him, her eyes meeting his. He held her gaze for only a moment before moving it up and behind where Satori stood. She followed it, turning her head to glance behind her.

The sight that greeted her knocked the air from her lungs and weakened her knees.

Tessa was there, dressed in a simple white shift, the garment not quite covering her knees and certainly not fit to be worn in public. But she neither stood nor sat. Instead she hung, arms stretched far over her head, suspended from a beam. The rope was just long enough to allow her bare toes to brush the ground. A length of purple cloth wrapped around her face, gagging her. Tessa's eyes met Satori's, and she wanted to scream.

Satori had only enough time to take in the sight before Henrik's fingers were on her jaw, turning her attention back to him. Her breath heaved out of her in great gulps as she fought to control them.

He spoke quietly, his eyes on hers, "Calm down, Princess. It would be a shame if you made a scene and Tessa was forced to suffer further. After the ceremony, she will be dealt with, and then we can put this all behind us."

Dealt with? She gulped, her voice shaking. "What do you mean?"

"She must be punished for what she's done." Henrik's eyes glanced toward Tessa, and Satori thought she saw a smirk. The beast. He looked back at her. "Fear not, she will live."

She wanted to be relieved, but cold fear washed over her at the thought of what Henrik might put Tessa through first.

The High Rector, clearing his throat, brought Satori's attention back to the present. "If you will both respond when I ask the question."

"Of course, apologies." Henrik straightened his shoulders, still not loosening his grip on Satori's hand. "Please, continue."

"Do you, Henrik, promise to love and respect this woman, to protect her with your life and honor her authority as Princess of the realm?"

Henrik tensed beside her at the words "honor her authority." As if the man would honor, respect, or love her. He certainly wouldn't protect her. That much was certain in the way he already treated her and that he'd sold her to kidnappers.

"Of course I do." His words were soft, dripping with sweetness.

Satori wanted to be sick.

"Do you, Your Highness, promise to love and respect this man, and give him the honor due his position as your advisor?"

Not even remotely. Did she dare lie before the High Rector and before Shala and Miram? To Helias with Shala and Miram. They had given her Kais and then taken him away. She no longer cared what they thought of her.

"Of course."

She felt Henrik's attention on her, but she ignored him. She needed this to be over. So she could end it once and for all. They were nearly there.

The High Rector raised his hand, drawing an arc over the top of their heads. "I proclaim this man and this woman bound together in this present life, in the presence of Shala and—"

The High Rector's words were cut off as alarm bells began pealing outside the castle. Every head in the building turned toward the doors where shouts could be heard. Soldiers shouting orders and warning cries.

Henrik's hand closed around Satori's upper arm, squeezing like a vise. She yelped at the pain as he began to drag her away. Soon, the warning cries turned to full-out battle sounds. Metal on metal clashed, and people cried out in pain. In seconds, pounding could be heard on the doors.

"Protect the Princess! Protect the King!" Henrik shouted as he pulled Satori roughly from the room.

Satori could see guards ushering her father from the room as the people who had gathered for the ceremony attempted to disperse, running from the room to find hiding places. Satori's gaze flashed to Tessa, whose terrified eyes watched the doors as she pulled desperately at her bonds only to swing slightly on her toes.

CHAPTER FORTY

SATORI

"Wait!" Satori dug in her heels, trying to stop Henrik. "Tessa!"

Henrik ignored her pleas, dragging her through a doorway and hauling her as quickly as he could up the stairs.

"Where are we going?" Satori cried using her other hand to try to break the vise-like grip Henrik had on her. "Henrik! We have to get to the safe room!"

Henrik didn't break his stride as he pulled her along to her room. "Don't worry, Princess, I'll be sure to keep you safe."

"Who is that? Who's here? Did you set up an attack on the castle?"

He'd already had her kidnapped once. Why not have the whole castle attacked?

He pushed open her door and shoved her into the room, slamming the door closed behind him. He locked the door and placed the heavy wooden beam across it to bar it as well. Satori backed away. If Henrik had ordered the attack, he wouldn't have to be so concerned.

He spun around to face her. "No, Princess, I did not order this attack." He stalked toward her. "This is undoubtedly your little band of rebel friends from the forest, here to take their revenge since I killed their leader." Henrik shouted the word *killed* and she jumped, backing away farther.

She looked toward the door, the sounds of battle were barely distinguishable in her room with the door bolted. Was it really Teague and his men? She glanced to where Henrik still stalked in her direction, almost directly in front of her, and then to the door behind him. If she could make it out of the room and down the stairs to them... But what if it wasn't Teague? What if whoever was there was there to take over the castle? To take advantage of the distraction of the wedding and kill the King and herself? She tossed another glance at Henrik. Would it matter? Would it be so different being their prisoner or his? Maybe they would kill her and get it over with.

She flung herself toward the door. Did she really have a chance? Probably not, but she would try. She lunged and was brought up short by an arm around her waist. He caught her, lifting her from her feet and twirling her back around. He strode to the bed and threw her down, the force causing her to bounce across the mattress.

"Allow me to share something with you, Princess," Henrik snarled over her. "I have no intention of allowing this day to pass or anyone to get their hands on you before this marriage is consummated."

She scrambled backward toward the head of the bed, but it was no use. Henrik pounced, jumping onto her, his legs straddling her hips. She beat at him, but he caught her hands in his grip, pinning them to the pillow above her head. He moved her wrists together, clamping them down with one hand as his other found the skirts of her dress and began pulling at them, freeing them from beneath his legs.

Her heart thumped wildly, and a wave of anger so fierce it seemed to heat her blood washed through her. She was done. Done being a victim of this man. Done allowing other people to dictate her life.

Henrik had managed to tear her skirts, exposing her bare legs. She was barely aware of his hand sliding up her thigh as she drew in a breath, allowing resolve and the red-hot anger to fill her. With all the energy she could muster, she began thrashing, screaming with the force of her effort. As Henrik grunted and shouted curses at her, she twisted her upper body left and right, pulling at where his hand held hers.

And then, for one moment, she was free. She used all the strength she could rally to fling herself over the edge of the bed. Undeterred, Henrik gave in, allowing her to turn only to push her along, climbing on top of her from behind.

At that moment, she didn't care. Nothing else mattered—nothing except the cool braided leather curled in her fist. Tears sprang from her eyes as relief flooded through her. Quickly, she pulled herself together. Henrik had his pants undone, and she could feel his flesh pressed against hers.

She gave a final prayer to Shala and Miram, who she wasn't sure were even on her side, but if they were, she needed all the help she could get. She tightened her grip on the handle of the whip and brought it in an arc around the back of her head.

Henrik let out a loud, pained grunt as the stiff leather connected with his head, knocking him to the side. It was enough for Satori to roll beneath him, and enough distraction for her to wrap the long end of the rope around Henrik's neck and pull.

Henrik's eyes bulged in shock and pain as she flung another length around his head and pulled. His hands released her, his fingers going to the leather around his neck as he grasped and clawed. But it was no use, she pulled so tight he couldn't get any hold of it. Satori leaned back and planted one foot in the middle of his chest, pushing there as she wrapped the ends of the whip around her fingers and heaved backward.

She barely registered the pain in her hands as she let the hot anger pour from her. Henrik's face had turned purple, his eyes bulging, his expression pure shock, and then his eyes closed, and his body went limp. Still she pulled and pulled, unwilling to release him too early, or to allow him to breathe again.

She strained and heaved, squeezing her eyes shut as she sobbed. The sobs shook her shoulders and pained her throat, but she held on. This man would never touch her again. Never hurt her friends. Never harm her father. He would pay for killing the man she loved.

Distantly, she became aware of a pounding, thick wood meeting thick wood. She pried her eyes open even as the door across the room buckled, a hinge tearing from the wall, followed by another. The door crashed in as a man, clad in black, sword drawn, rushed through the opening.

She was hallucinating. She had gone mad from the anger, the fight, the life she had taken. She'd lost her mind.

He was rushing to her side, slowing only as he approached her. He tossed his sword to the floor. Bringing his hands up in front of him, he stepped toward her again. His chest heaved in and out with his breaths.

Satori couldn't speak. Her eyes wide, her mouth open in shock as he approached and sat softly on the edge of the bed.

CHAPTER-FORTY-ONE

KAIS

She was disheveled, her hair pulling from where it had been piled on her head, tiny flower petals crunched in the chaos. Her dress was torn, hiked up over her thighs, and her hands were wrapped around the ends of a whip, her fingers purple. The middle of the whip was coiled around that advisor's neck, and it was clear she had not needed anyone to rescue her.

Pride mixed with horror bloomed inside him as he carefully sat on the edge of the bed. Her eyes stared at him wide and surprised, and he wondered if she was even seeing him or if the shock had been too much for her.

Slowly, he reached out, curling his hand around hers and unwrapping the whip from her fingers, the air sparking with that familiar sensation as their skin brushed. She seemed to register the touch, finally blinking.

He reached for her other hand, unwinding the leather braid. Kais moved closer, shoving the body of the purple-faced man, sending it off the edge of the bed. He took her fingers in his own, massaging them lightly, urging the blood to flow again.

When she spoke, her voice was a whisper, pitched high with disbelief. "Kais?"

His heart tightened at the sound of his name on her lips. "Princess."

She lifted one hand and brushed it across the short scruff of his beard. "Are you real?"

He covered the hand with his own, bringing his other palm to her cheek. "I'm real, Princess."

There was no warning as she dropped her hand and lunged for him, nearly crawling into his lap. Her arms encircled him, and her fingers dug so tightly into his back that it hurt. He welcomed the pain as he pulled her close, pressing her into his chest and burying his face in her neck. She sobbed into his shirt, and he held her, waiting for her to release all the emotion that coiled inside her.

He could feel it as she cried, like a rope pulled taut, slowly slackening. He moved his face to her hair, inhaling her scent, allowing his own heart to slow and breathing to return to normal; to relax at the feel of her in his arms, at the warmth her presence brought.

He'd woken in his tent, cold, filled with terror, knowing she'd been taken by a monster and thinking he was dead. He'd been up and on his way in moments, ignoring the protests of his men, telling him to take it easy. He wasn't going to waste any time getting to Satori.

He could only guess what she'd been through by the sight that had greeted him when he had entered the room, but he could feel the trauma wound inside her. He wanted to hold her until it was gone, until all she felt was his love.

"How?" The word was muffled in his shirt, but he heard her. He knew what she meant.

How was he there?

He couldn't stop the slight chuckle. "You know how. You left your blood for me."

He'd been shot through with arrows. At first, there had been no feeling, then blinding pain, and then nothing. The last thing he remembered was watching that vile man ride away with Satori in his arms as she screamed.

He'd been told that when his men had taken him back to his tent, he was too far gone for any treatment.

Teague had been distraught and angry. He was the most level-headed person Kais had ever known. Something that could send Teague over the edge left no doubt that hope was truly gone. He'd cleared the surface of Kais' desk with a swipe of his arm, sending everything flying. One item landed at Bram's feet. A vial of blood.

The men had stared at the item in a daze before Teague pulled himself together and snatched it from the ground, knowing immediately what it was.

They found the note later. "*Just in case. Thank Teague for the idea.*" Satori had left him a small vial of her blood.

He had been on the very brink of death; as far as anyone knew, he was dead, and she had saved him. Again. The words of Kezia's prophecy filtered through his mind, and he nearly laughed. He had died, and he had been brought back by this woman in his arms.

He held her tighter.

"Satori, I love you," he breathed the words, feeling them deep inside. "My soul loves you. If you'll have me, I never intend to be parted from you again."

She slid farther into him, pressing herself as close as she could. "Forever and ever."

CHAPTER FORTY-TWO

SATORI

Her hands rested on the rough stone balcony rail as she closed her eyes and turned her face toward the bright sunshine. In the three months that had passed, the air had grown much warmer, and the soft spring breeze blew through her hair, causing her light dressing gown to billow around her. Far above, flying on each parapet and along the wall, were a hundred small dark cyan and ivory pennants. It felt like a wedding day. She smiled.

"Satori. Satori?"

"I'm out here."

Tessa swept through the sheer flowing curtains out onto the balcony. "What are you doing? You're supposed to be getting ready for your wedding!"

Satori closed her eyes again, throwing her head back and letting the breeze wash over her. She was getting married today. To a prince, to the man she loved more than anything. To her blood mate. She grinned. Shala and Miram had not forsaken her, and she would spend the rest of her days thanking them.

Of course, Kais had essentially invaded her country. Thankfully, she was the Princess and held a rather large amount of sway with the King. Everything was cleared up and after many inquiries as to whether or not she was sure she truly wanted him, Kais was given permission to marry her.

Tessa's hands came down on her shoulders. "Alright, swoony, that's enough of that. Time to get ready."

Tessa guided Satori back into the room to a seat in front of a large mirror. Satori's eyes met her friend's in the reflection.

"You look really happy." Tessa smiled.

"I've never been so happy, Tess."

Satori couldn't keep the smile from her face. She bit her lip to try and tamp down her grin, but it was useless. She truly had never been happier.

For the next few hours Satori sat through skin and hair treatments until her face glowed and her hair shone. Tessa had worked Satori's hair into a full loose braid that began on one side of her head and curved around to fall over the opposite shoulder. An ornament of thin braided leather was worked through it all. It was perfect.

Her gown was fit for a queen. She couldn't stop looking at herself in the mirror. It didn't have layers and layers of tulle; it was a simple satin gown covered with a layer of chiffon. Lace trimmed the bottom, and patches of it dotted the skirt before weaving intricately through the bodice. The neckline created a deep, but not too deep, V, and the sleeves were sheer and fitted to just above her elbow. All of it was a gorgeous ivory.

"Wait until he sees you." Tessa smiled at Satori's reflection.

"What about you?" Satori turned to take in the other girl's plain dress. "You need to get ready! Stop worrying about me. I assure you I will be fine. Go."

"Okay." Tessa threw her arms around Satori, careful not to crush anything. "I'll be there, waiting for you. And not like last time."

"Good."

In an hour, Satori once again stood outside the large double doors to the room where she would be married. But this time the sunshine and a soft breeze filtered through the open windows, and the love of her life stood on the opposite side of the door, just a short walk away.

Hordes of people had turned up for the marriage of the Princess of Dunleigh to the Prince of Evandor. People who showed up because they wanted to and not because someone paid them.

Satori's father stepped up beside her, and when she looked at him she found his brow knotted in concern.

"What is it?"

Her father reached out and took both of her hands in his. "Satori, is this what you want? Is this the man you want? Because if you are not certain that this is your wish, I will walk in there and send them all away. By Shala. The last time we were here— Satori, I'm so sorry. Even through what he was doing to me, I should have known, I should have seen."

Satori placed her hands on her father's arms, looking him in the eye. "You are forgiven. I've told you that. You were his victim as well, and he had so many people fooled. But this time—" She glanced at the door beside her, the only barrier between her and Kais, and a grin spread across her face. If she wasn't careful, her cheeks would become sore. "I promise, by Shala and Miram, this is what I want, and Kais is who I want. And he could never be anything like H enrik."

"You're happy?" The look on her father's face was still skeptical.

"Ecstatic, Father."

She leaned up and kissed his cheek even as the trumpets began to play and excited butterflies danced in her chest. She faced the doors, schooling her movements so she wasn't bouncing on her toes when they opened.

CHAPTER FORTY-THREE

KAIS

The doors opened, and every person and thing in the room faded to nothing. There was only her. The sunlight filtering through the door behind her lit her golden hair, causing it to shine like a halo around her head. Never in his life, in his wildest imaginings, had he expected to find what he had with this woman. It was as if his own life's blood flowed in her veins, and he supposed, in a way, it did.

Satori and her father began the walk down the aisle toward where he stood, and he simultaneously wanted to rush to her and to crumble to his knees as the warmth of her presence enveloped him.

"Are you doing okay?" Teague's whispered words revealed his smile without even having to see him.

"I've never been better."

She held his gaze as she made her way toward him. He grinned at her, wanting to tell her to hurry up.

A loud squeal from the second row drew nearly everyone's attention. Adalyn stood, bouncing up and down, silently clapping her hands together. Satori shot the little girl a grin and a wink, and Kais' heart did another flip. She was perfect. What had he done to deserve this gift from Shala and Miram?

And then, after an age, she was there, standing in front of him. Her father took both of her hands in his and kissed them. When he released her, Satori dipped into a low curtsey, and then her father moved to his seat. She turned to where Kais' own father stood and offered him a deep curtsey as well. Finally, she turned to Kais.

Kais' heart thundered as he stepped down and offered his arm to Satori. She slipped her hand into the crook of his elbow, placing her other hand gently on his chest, smiling as his heart raced beneath her palm.

She spoke so only he could hear, "Calm down."

He took in her hair, braided through with leather, her warm chocolate eyes, and her soft pink lips as he placed a hand over where hers rested.

"I couldn't even if I wanted to. Have you ever had a dream come true?"

Her gaze became more intense, as though she was peering into his soul. "Yes."

A quiet cough brought their attention to the High Rector. He looked at Satori, meeting her gaze with intensity.

"Are you ready, Your Highness?"

His brow rose, and Kais appreciated the man checking in. Clearly, he had no wish to repeat the previous disastrous ceremony. Kais respected that he would make certain this was Satori's choice.

Even though he was already sure of what she would say, he still held his breath as she answered.

"With all my heart."

Air puffed out through his lips, and she shot him a teasing smile.

Kais barely registered the vows or the questions or the guests, his sole focus on the woman before him. There were certainly points in his life where he expected he would never marry. There had never been anyone who he thought he could spend a lifetime with, even with pressure from his father. But after he'd met Satori, he knew if he couldn't have her, he would have no one.

With the prophecy from Kezia he expected only heartache. And yet, here they were. There had, of course, been heartache, but it had led them here, and he had no complaints.

A quick prod to his back had Kais snapping out of his head and back to the present. Satori was grinning again.

Teague's voice in his ear made it clear why. "Kiss her, sir, before someone else does."

"Don't you want to kiss me?" Satori teased as Tessa giggled behind her.

As if that were a possibility. He took her words as a challenge, giving her a slow shake of his head and a wide grin. Stepping into her space, he slid one arm behind her back, the other into her hair, savoring each place where they made contact. He brought his mouth down to hers, and she opened to him as he worked his lips over hers, and everyone else faded away. He decided then to kiss her like this every single day he had the opportunity.

A soft rumble of something like awe went through the crowd, and Kais and Satori looked up to find that a gentle breeze blew through the entire room, swirling flags, hair, and dresses.

"Is that us?"

He grinned down at her and pulled her close. "I think so."

He kissed her once again, not caring how many people watched.

EPILOGUE

In the five months since Kais and Satori had been married, the change in the land was already remarkable.

Once Henrik was gone and Satori's father was free from his drug-induced suggestions, the change was nearly immediate. The King had been appalled at the state of the land and had immediately begun to remedy it. They'd had people delivering stores and supplies all over the land for months.

Covington had never really been affected since it was so close to the castle, though the influx of travelers had dwindled. But now, the streets bustled. It was as if the town was refreshed. Tourists poured in, wishing to see the roses in bloom.

The Rose Ball was scheduled for four days hence, and from the looks of it, it would be a large celebration. It was by invitation only this year, and many people from Kais' land had been invited, as well.

Satori couldn't help but stop and take it all in. They had worked hard, and it was rewarding to see the results.

Kais turned to her. "Why are you so happy?"

She met his dark eyes—she could drown in them—and smiled. She had been blessed by Shala and Miram, and she would never take this man for granted.

"I have many reasons to be happy."

Kais reached a hand toward her, and she slid hers into his warm grip, savoring the shock of contact that always passed between them.

"You've done well, my Princess. The people are thriving. You and your father have turned your country around."

She took his other hand. "I couldn't have done any of this without you."

She suppressed a shudder when she thought of where she might be today if she hadn't met Kais. Married to Henrik, her position ignored, with her country slipping further and further into decay. Would he have killed her father by now? Made himself King? Would he have killed her by now?

"Hey." Kais' brow creased, no doubt sensing the change of emotions inside her. He released her hand and placed his palm on her face, brushing her cheek lightly before tilting her chin up. "Wherever you just went, come back to me. You are safe, your country is thriving, your father is well, and I love you more than life itself. The past is over and done and will never be again. Only good things from now on."

She held his gaze for a moment, once again wondering how she had deserved this man.

"I love you," she whispered.

His response was to lean down and place a soft kiss on her lips.

"My Prince and Princess!"

Kais' mouth grew into a wide grin as they broke off the kiss. They turned to find Kezia, gold eyeliner accenting her dark eyes, a deep purple scarf wrapped neatly around a mass of curls.

Satori had met Kezia at their wedding and, of course, heard the tale of the ominous prophecy she'd given to Kais so many months prior. She liked Kezia, but she had to admit the ability to see the future was disconcerting.

Kais' arm slipped around her back, and he pulled her to him in a reassuring gesture. With his other arm, he reached out and took Kezia's hand, placing a kiss on the back of her palm.

"Good day to you, Kezia."

Kezia gave him an exaggerated quizzical sort of look, complete with a dramatic head tilt. She lifted one arm toward him and stopped, glancing at Satori.

"With your permission, Princess?" With her thick accent, the syllables rolled off her tongue.

A giggle burst out of Satori, and she grinned. "Be my guest."

It was easy not to feel threatened by other women when she knew precisely Kais's feelings towards her.

Kezia needed nothing more as she wrapped her hand around the back of Kais' head and pulled his face towards hers, kissing him.

"You taste different," Kezia said, her eyes brightening as she glanced at Satori. "Like you are happy."

Kais' hand closed tighter around Satori's waist, his fingers pressing into her side. "I have never been happier."

"I told you, futures can be changed."

"I take issue with that. I did indeed die, and I didn't enjoy it." He gave Satori a sidelong glance. "Maybe we shouldn't invite her."

"It's not her fault." Satori smiled.

"Indeed it is not. I merely share the messages," Kezia replied. "It's up to you what you do with them."

"In that case, Kezia," Satori began, "we would love for you to be one of our personal guests at the Rose Ball. We would also like to offer you a permanent position as advisor to the crown and a place at the castle."

When Kezia said nothing, Kais spoke up, "For a seer, you look a bit taken by surprise."

"I do not see everything." Kezia's face softened as she looked at Satori. "I have known Kais for a very long time, and I respect and honor him. And if the gods have seen fit to place you both together, I shall honor and serve you as I would him. I would be honored to serve in your court." Kezia dipped into a low curtsy with her last words.

"We would be honored to have you. And to have you join us at the ball."

Kezia took both Kais' and Satori's hands in hers. "My Prince and Princess." Then she paused, her eyes taking on a faraway look. But the look only lasted a moment before she seemed to return to them. "Princess, allow my first act of advice to encourage you not to drink too much at the ball." Kezia smiled and directed a pointed look toward Satori's abdomen.

Confusion hit Kais, and then his hands tensed on her again as shock rolled through him, quickly followed by a reserved joy.

He looked down at her, lips parted, eyes wide. "Satori?"

A slow grin spread across Satori's face. "I was going to tell you."

"When?"

She answered the question she knew he was asking, "In the Spring."

Kais released her waist, instead wrapping his arms fully around her and pressing a kiss to her lips that left her breathless, Kezia's presence forgotten in his joy.

He pulled back, running a thumb along her cheek, his eyes running over her face.

Love poured through Satori. Her love for Kais, his love for her. Their mutual love for the life they had created.

"You will make the most wonderful father, and I can't wait to watch."

A tear slipped down her cheek as Kais recaptured her lips with his.

THE END

Did you enjoy Blood and Fate?

If you enjoyed this book, please consider leaving a review on Amazon and Goodreads and anywhere else you can think of!

As an indie author, word of mouth is vital. I would be forever grateful. Thank you!

Also, if you would like to keep up with my shenanigans, please feel free to subscribe to my newsletter or find me around the web:

Newsletter: www.antoniakane.com/newsletter
Instagram: www.instagram.com/antoniakaneauthor
Website: www.antoniakane.com

Acknowledgments

I am so excited to finally have Kais and Satori's story out in the world! And I am so excited that you decided to give it a shot! Thank you so much! I'm more grateful than you could know to every reader who's ever picked up one of my books.

Thank you to my biggest fan, my sounding board, my alpha reader, my beta reader, my ARC reader, my marketing assistant, my encouragement, and my friend, Shae. You don't know what you mean to me, and I'm so blessed to have met you!

Thank you to my editors, Savanna and Hanah! This story wouldn't be where it is today without your notes and encouragement. I've learned so much from you guys. But I still haven't learned how to properly use a comma, so thank you for fixing those for me!

Thank you to my cover artist, Lexie, at Selkkie Designs! This book is gorgeous! I get compliments all the time, and I'm always sure to tell them you're awesome!

Thank you to my beta readers, Donna Wall, Ruby Gay, Rebekah Hemmens, Jane Taylor, Mary K., and Kim Gerstenschlager! The notes that you provided were extremely helpful! I appreciate you taking the time to read my little rough draft.

Thanks to my street team and everyone who's ever shared my work on social media or with a friend! You don't understand how much this helps!

Thanks to my family for sharing me with my word processor. Special thanks to my oldest son, who listened quietly while I talked about this story, even though I'm pretty sure he wasn't all that interested. Always, thanks for providing me with names for characters and locations, whether you knew it or not. I love you bunches and oodles, always and forever!

Thanks and praise to God for saving me and creating me with a mind full of stories. Without His strength, I would be a mess.

Thank you to everyone who had a hand in helping to create, polish, promote, and encourage this story! You all rock! On to the next!

About the Author

Antonia began writing fan fiction at a very early age and has never looked back.

She loves writing fiction, escaping into new words, and getting to know new characters. Writing is a form of therapy for Antonia, and she thrives on it, even when it's difficult.

Along with writing, she's an avid reader and is always on the hunt for her next book boyfriend. Of which she has a finely curated collection.

When she's not writing or reading, she's Mom to three boys and two dogs. She's also active in her church. For obvious reasons, coffee is her best friend.

Antonia and her family live happily nestled in the center of Oklahoma.

Blood and Fate
Spotify Playlist

Other books by Antonia Kane

Persuasion of Deceit

Persuasion of Destiny

Blood and Fate